SUWANNEE
DIVIDE

BY GENE JONES

ISBN: 1477451978
V2 December 2012
ISBN 13: 9781477451977
LCCN: 2012918188 CreateSpace, North Charleston SC

Every kingdom in which civil war has raged suffers desolation; and every city or house in which there is internal strife will be brought low.

MATTHEW 12:25

1860

I never knew a man who wished himself to be a slave. Consider if you know any good thing that no man desires for himself.

~ABRAHAM LINCOLN

NORTHWEST FLORIDA FROM GADSDEN TO DUVAL COUNTY, 1857

(Courtesy Florida State Archives)

CHAPTER ONE

WHITE OAK PLANTATION
South Carolina

As Mingo pounded a hoe into the soggy dirt, rain flowed from his straw hat and down his bare back. The chilly water didn't cool his body nor his anger from being forced to work in a deluge. Once again, the masters had violated the unwritten rules. The veins in his neck and arms bulged as he smashed one muddy clod after another. Sweat broke out on his forehead despite the nip in the air.

Like most slaves, he usually expended just enough energy to do his work, but being forced out in the rain irritated him too much to plod along at his usual sluggish pace. He pounded the ground so hard that he couldn't pull the hoe free without tugging on it. As it broke loose, he glanced up and saw Phillip, the overseer, riding his gray mare on the dirt road bordering the field. The white man's appearance surprised him because the boss man rarely checked on the bondsmen as long as Ned, the black slave driver, kept them on schedule to complete their tasks.

All the slaves stopped working as Phillip reined his horse to look them over. He focused on the lanky, young man holding a long hoe, cupped his hands and hollered, "Mingo, git over here."

Mingo had never been called from the fields. He shivered, dropped his hoe and gathered his sopping shirt from a cotton plant. As he jogged toward Phillip, he could see a smug smile on the white man's face which made him angrier. Phillip yelled out as he wheeled his horse, "Follow me to the smitty shed."

Running to keep up with the horse, Mingo worried, *Sure nuff, de white devil has a filthy task waitin' for me now.* At a small building, Phillip dismounted, hitched his horse, and ducked under the low doorframe followed by his panting charge. Inside, Pompey, a gray-haired, stooped mulatto stood at the forge pumping air with a hand bellows towards the red-hot coals. Although the old craftsman often had taught the young man to forge iron at odd hours, he ignored him.

Before Mingo could say hello, the overseer announced, "Master Myers is sendin' you to Charleston for a year to apprentice to Nigger Ellison so you can learn a trade."

The young man's eyes widened. Everybody in the whole state knew about Ellison, a freedman who owned numerous slaves and rented them out to build and repair cotton gins. The wealthy man also operated the best machine shop in South Carolina. As his apprentice, Mingo could learn a trade. Then, with a skill he could earn money to buy his freedom.

Mingo knew that Ol' Man Myers doled out a small share to Pompey when he produced more ironwork than his quota. Once, the smitty had flashed a shiny gold dollar, a treasure field slaves rarely saw. With his money, he bought the latest fashions and owned a linen suit, several wool Stetson hats, and soft leather shoes while the other slaves wore homespun clothes, straw or hand-made palm frond hats, and hard leather brogans. The blacksmith had earned more than enough money over the years to buy his freedom, but never had. He squandered everything he earned although he dressed much better than any black person in the entire county; most white folks too for that matter.

Phillip said, "Mingo, you've got to be shackled for the trip to Charleston."

"Why, Mas'r Phillip?"

"You're a good boy, but peckerwoods see you on the road without chains, they'll git after me."

"Yassuh."

Pompey slipped manacles around Mingo's wrists and then his ankles while averting his eyes from his friend's. He clanked the cuffs closed and then padlocked them. After he snapped the last one shut, he abruptly stood up. Turning away, he picked up his heaviest hammer, adjusted a red-hot, steel bar over the anvil and pounded it with all his strength.

Mingo had no desire to run away. He'd been born in a log hut at the White Oak plantation seventeen years ago. He still lived in the same shack with two sisters and his parents. None of them had ever been off the place. His father was the best field hand and knew all the 'tasks' as well as Ned. As far as Mingo knew, his family lived as well as the other chattel, and he expected to stay with them in the quarters until he could earn his freedom.

Until the last year or so, the slaves at White Oak plantation worked a tolerable schedule under a well-defined accommodation between the bondsmen and their owner. Everybody understood the tasks to be accomplished each day such as hoeing an acre in growing season or seeding fifty rows during planting time. When the slaves finished their jobs, they could tend their own gardens, fish, weave baskets, or engage in other personal pursuits.

Myers viewed himself as a progressive slave owner. As long as his plantation stayed profitable, he allowed his chattel to work the farm at an untroubled pace. In the past, he had not pushed them to the utmost, and his minions followed his lead. If the blacks completed their tasks, they were left alone under Ned's supervision.

For years White Oak had operated under this accommodation until the cotton market collapsed in The Great Crash of 1857-1858. After that, low prices combined with decreased harvests from the exhausted soil forced Myers to take harsh measures. Unless production improved, he threatened Phillip with dismissal. Terrified of losing his job, the overseer added to the tasks which forced Ned to work the slaves harder and faster.

When they resisted, Myers ordered beatings. The cruel punishments gave Mingo nightmares and instilled fear. The memory of one in particular convinced him never to run away.

Six months earlier, a boyhood friend ran off after being ordered to muck stables in addition to his normal tasks. When Ned reported the escape to Phillip, he grunted, saddled his horse and rode away. That afternoon, he returned with nigger chasers armed with shotguns and accompanied by Cuban bloodhounds. They barged past the boy's wailing mother into the shanty where he lived and held his bedding to the dogs' snouts. Once the vicious animals had his scent, they ran howling out the door. Pompey mumbled, "Boy'll be tree'd for long."

The next morning, the ruffians returned on their horses. They pulled the youngster by a rope around his neck that forced him to run to avoid being dragged. He foamed at the mouth and gasped for breath.

Myers locked the dirty, bloodied captive in an abandoned chicken pen until the next Sunday afternoon. After church service, Phillip ordered several field hands to drag him from the wire enclosure to a timber with an iron ring set ten feet above the ground. The overseer forced a rope under the youngster's shackled hands and then men hoisted him by the wrists off the ground where he, caked in white dust from chicken droppings, hung like a zombie.

Myers ordered five lashes as punishment. Phillip tore off the remnants of the escapee's pants and handed a short quirt to Ned. He hesitated, gnashed his teeth, then snapped the cow-whip across the lad's bared buttocks. Blood flowed from the gash. The slave driver bit his lip when he hit the boy for the second time. More blood. The third lick flayed skin. Bodily fluids gushed down the youth's skinny legs. Again the whip cracked. The recoil splattered slimy liquid in the torturer's face. When he popped the whip for the last time, the victim fainted. The taskmaster handed the lash to the overseer and lurched away. Field hands dragged the captive back to the pen where he stayed chained until his wounds had healed enough that he could be sold.

Phillip rattled the shackles to check the locks which startled Mingo from his thoughts. The overseer looked outside to check that the rain had stopped and said, "Let's go, Mingo. The stockman's supposed to have Sally hitched to the cart so I can drive you to Charleston."

The day heated up fast. A hot sun scorched the men in the open wagon and soon dried the road. Sweat moistened their straw hats and trickled into their eyes. Dust swirled up from the horse's hooves and from under the wheels, sticking on their wet bodies. In early afternoon, Phillip said, "I'm stoppin'. Sally's tuckered out in this heat."

"Yassuh."

Shortly, Phillip pulled into a grassy, bottomland clearing beside a blackwater creek. As he looped the reins around the brake handle, he jumped down from the wagon. Walking to the stream, he crouched on his knees at the bank splashing the cool water on his face before drinking from his cupped hands.

Mingo rolled his legs from the wagon bed in order to ease himself to the ground. Unaccustomed to the shackles, he shuffled to the water's edge, rinsed his face and neck, took a long drink, and slowly rising, tottered away from the creek into the shade under a tall pine. He lay down on the ground speculating about his future as he watched the dark water ripple by.

Sally stood motionless except to snap her tail at the horseflies buzzing around her flanks. Phillip unhitched her and led her to the creek. After she drank, the overseer hobbled the mare and returned to the wagon. Reaching into a tin pail under the seat, he pulled out a loaf of bread and wedge of hard cheese. After tearing hunks from the loaf and cutting the cheese into cubes with his pocket knife, he sat gobbling the food. After eating all he wanted, he threw the remainder on the ground by Mingo.

Phillip then rustled around in a box under the wagon seat until he pulled out a chain with a padlock. He ran the chain through his captive's shackles, around the pine tree and snapped the shackle shut. After double checking the locks and then making sure the mare was secure as well, he spread a tarpaulin in the shade cast by the wagon, curled up and went to sleep.

Rattling chains and voices awoke Phillip and aroused Mingo from his thoughts of being treated like a cur. Ten slaves with shackles around their necks shambled into the clearing. They all wore ragged homespun clothing. Most were barefooted. Some didn't even have a hat. Mingo's threadbare cotton trousers and shirt, worn-out brogans, and handwoven hat made him look well-dressed compared to them.

A white man with a big pistol hanging from his belt drove a wagon behind the slaves. He jerked his horse to a stop and said to Phillip, "Mind if I camp here with these moaks for the night?"

"It's a free country."

"Name's John Bradley. I'm a nigger trader takin' these here boys to the Charleston Slave Auction."

"Phillip Knight, I'm headin' to Charleston too. Where'd ya get 'em?"

"Buy 'em on spec. In this economy, plantations here 'bouts need cash. I've got a circuit. Buy 'em, sell 'em at auction. Whata 'bout you?"

"I'm the overseer at White Oak up the road."

As the slave trader jumped from his wagon, he noticed Mingo. "What you got here?"

Without waiting for answer, Bradley strode to Mingo, grabbed him by the jaw and snarled, "Open your mouth."

Unused to such treatment, Mingo jerked away. Bradley clamped his right arm around his neck in a headlock. "Open up, boy, or I'm goin' knock a knot on your head."

"There ain't no need to git rough with him. Mingo, show the man your teeth."

As the young man opened his mouth, the white man pressed hard at his jaw hinge with his thumb and forefinger. Bradley grunted, "Wider. Yes, sir, you got a fine nigga here. I'll give you $750 cash."

"No can do. Ol' Man Myers told me to sell him at auction."

Mingo's knees buckled. He squalled, "No, Mas'r Phillip. You told me I was goin' be apprenticed to Mr. Ellison."

Phillip laughed, "You're dumber than I thought. The ol' man is puttin' you in his pocket."

The other blacks howled with laughter then taunted the captive.

"You're sure nuff stupid."

"Look at de apprentice, chained like a dog."

Mingo slumped against the pine tree.

At twilight, John Bradley lit a campfire to which he added wood until it flared several feet. Then he covered the flames with Spanish moss which smothered the fire causing it to smolder with heavy, gray smoke that drove away all but the most persistent mosquitoes. Bradley's slaves huddled around the fire to avoid them. Far from the smoke, Mingo kept moving, swatting and slapping to fight off the buzzing insects.

Bradley pulled a croker sack from a big box in the wagon bed and poured black-eyed peas into a soot-blackened kettle to which he added a slab of salt pork. Then he filled the pot with water from the creek and settled it over a hot spot on the fire. He ordered his slaves to move to a swamp maple tree. After he shackled his chattel to it, he walked to his wagon where he retrieved a pint bottle filled with a clear liquid.

"Want a snort?"

"What ya got?"

"Best head buster in the entire state. From Walnut Hill near Columbia."

Phillip held out his blue enameled coffee cup. Bradley filled it half full. As the peas simmered, the two white men drank moonshine. After a while, Bradley stood up to check the pot. He took one step and almost stumbled into the fire, so he plopped back down.

"Why don't you put your boy to good use servin' supper? Everythin's in the box."

Phillip unlocked Mingo from the pine tree and told him to fetch plates and spoons from Bradley's box in the wagon. Mingo shuffled to it, found the implements, dished up two plates and then hobbled toward the slaves who all had their eyes on him.

"Hold it!" Bradley slurred, "Don't you know to serve whites first?"

He altered course to hand the plates to the white men. After serving everybody else, Mingo tried to eat but slowly put his plate down while the others scraped every morsel.

Although bleary-eyed and garbling his words, Bradley noticed when his slaves finished eating. Without standing, he ordered Mingo to gather up all the dishes and scrub them in the creek. As soon as he finished, Phillip ordered him back to his spot and locked him to the pine tree again.

Far from the smoke, the mosquitoes attacked Mingo, but they were not the reason he couldn't sleep. Fear and uncertainty had replaced his jubilation. Now, he imagined a stranger buying him and taking him to the new cotton land being developed in the Deep South which made his head throb and stomach ache. Hope to buy his freedom had vanished, and he feared that he had seen his family for the last time.

Before first light, Bradley arose and punched up the fire to make coffee. Once it boiled, he unlocked his slaves from the maple tree so they could straggle into the bushes up the road away from the camp. Twisting from the others as much as the chains allowed, some pissed while others squatted. Then they scuffled to the creek to drink the tea-colored water.

When Phillip unlocked Mingo from the pine tree, the young man circled behind a palmetto patch. Then he splashed into the stream to wash. Wading back toward the bank, his leg irons tangled on a root that tripped him face down in the water. The current pushed him under as he thrashed and twisted to break free in order to thrust his head up for air.

Some slaves saw him and howled with laughter. Suddenly, a huge, muscled man leapt toward him with such power that he yanked down several men, tugging them all toward Mingo.

"Help him!" he yelled as he strained to reach the water. When the other slaves realized the big man's intention, they scrambled to make slack in the chains so he could wade into the creek to reach the drowning youth. Grabbing him under the arms, he tugged with all his strength to break the snag. When it broke, he jerked the lad's head out of the water.

After several coughs, Mingo caught his breath and gasped, "Thank the Good Lord you grabbed me. Lest you did, I was a goner, sure nuff. I hope I can repay you someday."

The rescuer put his arm around him. "Just remember dat we have to look out for one another. Dat's payment enough."

From his wagon, Bradley yelled, "What's the ruckus? Get your asses over here right now or I'm goin' tan some hide" as a crack from his bullwhip reverberated through the camp like a shotgun blast.

As the slaves scrambled toward Bradley, Mingo took several deep breaths then followed them until he reached Phillip who sat waiting for him in the cart.

"Climb aboard, Mingo. See you in Charleston tomorrow, Bradley?"

"I doubt it. These damn lazybones walk so slow there ain't no tellin' when I'll get there."

Unlike the ride the day before, Mingo didn't appreciate the lush, green woods in full summer leaf as the wagon rolled along. Now the forest was a lifeless blur without texture or color. He no longer noticed the subtle yellows and reds of the sumac, Virginia creeper and swamp maples that were turning early. Towering, gray, cumulous clouds billowing up from the heat added to his foreboding.

Late in the morning, Phillip stopped in front of a board and batten, ramshackle general store. When he walked inside the gloom, he spotted a skinny, full bearded man standing behind a case.

"Smells like fresh bread."

"The old lady baked this morning," and in a quieter tone, "I have a new run of shine too."

A fly walked atop a giant glass jar in which pickled eggs floated in a murky liquid. It flew up, circled, and then settled on a cheese wheel. Phillip waved it off, took a whiff of the cheese and said, "I'll take a loaf of bread, a quarter pound of cheese and a pickled egg."

While reaching for the bread, the storekeeper commented, "Your coon must be a bad one to keep him chained."

"Naw, just takin' him to auction. Can't risk him runnin' off."

"Lotta people on the way to auction with slaves. Reckon it's the tough times."

"No joke. Plantations here 'bouts have more darkies than they can use though there's big demand for them in the new cotton land opening up in Mississippi, Louisiana, and Florida. Cotton's played out in South Carolina; the soil's burned up. Boss man plans to put several in his pocket this year."

The storekeeper sliced a cheese wedge with a razor-sharp knife. "Business is bad. Damn Yankee banks have us by the balls and Congress keeps tariffs too dern high. If Lincoln's elected, it'll get worse."

"Yeah, the tariffs prop up New England industry at our expense, but I reckon things will turn around. Most likely, Douglas will whip Lincoln although, truth be told, I can't figure out what the hell Douglas stands for. What does he mean that we ought to follow the decisions of the Supreme Court? Does he want slavery protected in the territories or not? Douglas better start talkin' straight or he could lose."

"If he does, South Carolina will secede."

"How could we? Our economy is tied to the North."

"Friend, we ought to be a free country without Northern bankers and politicians steppin' on our rights. Yankees can't stop us from declarin' independence. If they intend to keep us in the Union by force, I say, bring 'em on. One Southern boy can lick ten Yankee city slickers."

As he weighed the cheese the storekeeper muttered, "Damn it, I cut off too much. You can have it."

"Well, then. Let's add a pint."

As Phillip walked through the door onto the porch, the storekeeper hollered, "Ya'll come back, ya hear?"

CHAPTER TWO

CHARLESTON
South Carolina

At twilight, the horse clopped along on Charleston's cobblestones streets until Phillip reined him by a large archway with an iron gate. Above the arch, between two gilded iron stars, a red lettered sign on the smooth plastered wall read Chalmers Street Slave Mart.

Mingo eased from the wagon and followed Phillip into the building. Across a long room, a diminutive mulatto dressed in expensive, well-tailored clothes met them. Startled by the man's appearance, Phillip managed to say, "I want to sell this here boy at auction."

The black man eased behind a desk illuminated by a whale oil lamp. Putting on spectacles, he opened an account book and picked up a pen. He looked up at Phillip and said, "What you gawkin' at? I'm a free man and a clerk here. Who are you?"

"Phillip Knight. I'm the overseer at White Oak Plantation. This slave belongs to Mr. Myers."

"What's the boy's name?"

"Mingo."

"Age?"

"'Seventeen"

"Health?"

"Excellent"

"Brands?"

"Mr. Myers don't brand his darkies."

The small man glanced up.

"Skills?"

"Field nigger and ironwork."

"Attitude?"

"Hard worker, trainable. Takes orders well."

The clerk eyed Mingo from head to foot and said, "He ought to bring top dollar. Give me the keys to his shackles. We'll return them to you after the sale."

The clerk scratched out a receipt and handed it to Phillip. "Hold on to this. No receipt, no money."

The clerk ordered the lad to follow him. Mingo shuffled behind till they came to a rusty barred door where a potbellied white man with a pistol and blackjack hanging on his belt stood guard. He unlocked the door and opened it just wide enough for the young man to squeeze by.

Inside the dim room, Mingo discerned dark bodies huddled against the walls and sprawled across bundles scattered around the floor. The room stank as bad as the outhouses at White Oak. He stepped back.

The guard pulled his blackjack and slapped it against his leg, "Behave yourself. Git in there and take your chains off."

As he stepped inside the stinking room, the iron door clattered shut behind him. He felt lightheaded and reached for a wall to steady himself. The jailor reached through the bars and handed a key ring to

Mingo who sat down on the floor and fiddled with the locks around his ankles, but his hands were shaking too much to engage the key in the worn padlock.

A prisoner said, "Give me the keys." As the man inserted the key he continued, "They'll treat you OK in here if you don't cause no trouble." The first padlock popped open and he turned his attention to the next one without a pause in the conversation. "You hungry? There's a little cornbread in dat bucket over der. Der's water in de pail next to it." After the last padlock snapped open, the man rolled the chains into a bundle and handed them through the bars to the guard.

Mingo rubbed his chaffed ankles and then walked to the bucket. When he tilted it to look inside, flies buzzed up around his face. He swatted at one and then scraped up crumbled cornbread with his fingers. It tasted stale and gritty. A dried gourd, cut to make a dipper, hung by a string on a nail above the water pail. He filled the ladle and after a long drink, returned to the door and slouched against the wall next to the prisoner who had helped him. He counted thirty prisoners sharing the room which was quiet except for a baby whimpering in a corner.

Mingo asked, "What's goin' happen?"

"We're goin' to be sold day after tomorrow. Mas'r is puttin' me in his pocket to settle his debts. When buyers come to look us over, pick out one who don't seem mean and talk him into buyin' ya."

Mingo slumped farther down the wall.

The next day after sunset, a commotion outside the door roused the slaves. Above the rattle of chains, Mingo recognized Bradley's hateful voice. "Move it. Git in dat barracoon right now." A whip cracked.

The iron door swung open and the coffle from the campground shuffled into the room. As the last slave passed through the door, Bradley shoved him hard. The man tumbled to the floor which snapped the chains tight and jerked several men down in a heap.

The burly man who had saved Mingo at the creek untangled the men and pulled them to their feet. As before, the guard passed keys through the door and ordered a man to unlock the ten slaves. Once they were unlocked, they became agitated and asserted their personal space long denied them while locked together. Some yelled at their fellow prisoners. Two pushed one another. A lanky man screamed and beat his fists against a wall. Someone hollered at him to shut up. Moving fast, the brawny man pushed the angry men apart then grabbed the berserk man and penned him in a bear hug. The wild-eyed slave struggled to free himself until he realized that it was impossible. His captor barked, "Everybody shut up!"

The room quieted instantly. Then he whispered, "Calm down. Der's nothin' we can do now," and added in a louder voice, "Somebody bring dis man water."

Mingo scrambled to the water pail. Grabbing the gourd off its nail, he filled it and hurried to the skinny man to hold the dipper to his lips. After the slave took a drink, the muscular man eased his hold and allowed his captive to slump against the wall. The room stayed quiet as everyone gawked at the powerful man who had brought calm to the barracoon. He said, "Is there any food?"

"No," Mingo replied.

"When will we be fed?"

"Tomorrow morning."

People shifted about and some stretched out on the bare floor in effort to get as comfortable as possible for the long night ahead. Nobody slept well and everybody was awake by the time diffused sunlight shone through the smudged clerestory windows. As the detainees stirred, they stood up and made their way to an oversized bucket behind a blanket suspended on a rope across a corner. They soon filled it to overflowing.

Before full light, a white guard came to door. "Time to eat, but before I feed you, somebody has to empty the slop bucket. If nobody volunteers, you ain't gettin' fed."

Nobody moved till the muscular man stood up.

The guard lifted a pair of leg irons from a peg and handed them to him through the bars.

"Put these on."

The brawny man closed the shackles above his ankles and then the guard handed him two padlocks which he snapped shut. Hobbled by the chains, he waddled behind the blanket to fetch the slop bucket, but almost changed his mind when he noticed the filthy container had no bails. He held his breath, bent down and lifted the slimy bucket as far from his body as he could and carried it towards the doorway.

"You nigs stand back," the guard yelled.

As the husky man waddled close, the big bellied guard opened the door to let him pass, slamming it shut behind him.

The jailer gasped from the stench, "Damn, ya'll are rotten."

"Where do I takes dis?"

"There's a cesspool behind the barracoon. Dump it there."

After returning to the room, the powerful man unlocked himself and passed the shackles and keys back to the guard who hung them on a peg and walked away. The skinny man rocked back and forth while howling unintelligibly. People jostled one another in the crowded room. A baby bawled. One person threatened to kick another's ass and slammed him against the wall causing those nearby to scatter. The only person in the room strong enough to stop the fight stepped between the combatants just as the jailer returned carrying a tin tub. He yelled, "Ya'll ain't gittin' nothin' lest you calm down."

The room quieted and nobody moved except for the skinny man who continued to rock back and forth. The guard ignored his madness and said to the burly man, "You, I'll give you the food if you keep order."

"Ya'll hear de man. I'll pass de portions out so dat everybody gits a fair share."

With that, the guard passed the pail filled with red beans and rice along with plates and spoons through a hatch in the door.

"Mas'r, de water is 'bout gone."

"Bring me the bucket."

As Mingo hurried to fetch it, several men pushed forward toward the big man. Keeping the tub behind him he hollered, "Ya'll stay put. Everybody will get a share."

Squatting down, he dished dollops on two plates and said to Mingo, "Here, take dis to de woman with de baby and de old lady against de back wall."

After dishing out several portions, he reduced them so that there would be enough for everybody. When only a few spoonfuls remained, he asked, "Who ain't been fed?" Mingo pointed at the man rocking back and forth and said, "Me and him, dat's all."

"Here's a plate for you."

Dishing out the last serving, the muscular man carried it to the madman. Crouching, he held out the plate and told him to eat. The skinny man ignored him. The big man set the dish on the floor and then walked back to his place by the door where he picked up the bucket to scrape out the leavings. After a bite, he asked Mingo his name and where he was from.

Mingo told him and asked, "Who're you?"

"Name's Brutus. I was born up yonder in Maryland near Washington on a plantation called Clean Drinkin'. 'Bout your age I was sold and brought down here to Carolina. I worked like a dawg as a field hand for a few years till de overseer put me to work in de mill. 'Fore long I was runnin' it. After Mas'r cut all de good timber on de place, he shut down de operation and sold me to dat vicious devil who brought me here."

"What ya reckon will happen to us?"

"All I knows, we goin' be sold. People say hands are needed to work new cotton land, but I'm goin' to run away."

"I wouldn't do dat. Once a boy ran off from de home place, white men chased him down wid dogs. 'Bout killed him."

"I know the risks, but runaways don't always git caught. Some make it to de North and sometimes all de way to Canada."

"Patters or nigger chasers will hunt you down."

"Not always. Some white folks might help. I read 'bout it."

"Say what?"

"Mingo, I tricked folks. See here, when I was a little fellow up yonder at Clean Drinkin' my Mama mostly raised de young'uns, white and black. We all played together. De white boys showed me McGuffey's readers and dey taught me a little bit. After a while I could read pretty good. When I got to Carolina, Mas'r Dixon, the owner, ordered a brand new, shiny engine straight from England. It came with instructions and pictures dat showed how to set it up. The boss man couldn't puzzle it out, so I studied dat pamphlet till I got dat engine runnin'."

"You can't read. See dem words on dat flour sack yonder. What dey say?"

Brutus read aloud, "50 pounds, Rock ground red wheat flour, Smucker Mills, Goshen, Indiana."

"Sure nuff, you can read, but how you goin' git help from white folks?"

"Gotta find de underground railroad."

"What ya talkin' 'bout, underground railroad?"

"Folks called abolitionists want us free. Dey will help us. You ever hear 'bout John Brown?"

"No."

"He was a white preacher who said slavery ain't Christian, dat slave owners are devils and dat God will curse America for its sins. From where I sit, I sure nuff believe he's right." Brutus chuckled. "Anyhow, he gathered some white folks together to 'mancipate us. At a town called Harper's Ferry in Virginia where de gov'ment makes army rifles, Brown planned to steal guns so we could fight for our freedom. Soldiers caught him 'fore he got 'em."

"Where'd ya hear such foolishness?"

"I heard de boss man and Mas'r talkin'. I read a newspaper story too. At de old place, dey sometimes got newspapers and magazines. Most de time, dey burned dem so we couldn't see 'em, but now and again de house servant sneaked one for me."

"Will you teach me to read?"

"Yes, but you got to be careful. Some white folks catch you readin', dey'll whip ya."

With that, Brutus pointed to the flour sack. "See dem letters? I'm goin' teach you the alphabet. You know numbers?"

"I can count, but I can't read numbers."

"We'll start slow," but he stopped talking when he saw white buyers on the balcony above the barracoon watching them. One was in his mid-thirties. He had a ruddy face, a paunch, and greasy hair. He wore a rumbled linen suit and a Panama hat with a red feather in the band. The other was about the same age, well-proportioned, and sported a goatee. He wore heavy cotton trousers and a flannel shirt. They appeared to be matching the prisoners to the descriptions in a catalogue.

The entries for Mingo and Brutus read:

#31 Mingo: male, 17, healthy, field worker, some blacksmithing, docile.

#35 Brutus: male, about 25, healthy, tall, muscular, mechanic.

The slaves could hear conversational snippets, laughter, and crude comments from the buyers on the balcony.

"Look at the size of that buck against the wall."

"That old hag ain't worth nothin'."

"That one o'er yonder with the baby looks sick. You reckon she has consumption?"

"Nobody will buy that old man."

"Stay away from the crazy one."

"I'd sure like to get my hands on that wench's ass."

Mingo concentrated to hear what was being said about him and Brutus.

He heard the sloppy one in the suit say, "The darker ones are docile and more valuable. They ain't tainted with white blood which makes them feisty. Look at those two ebony ones sitting by the door. They'll make good workers. The older one is a muscular rascal, but I'd bet you the wiry one can outwork him."

"The brawny one is too stocky. Bucks like that tire out too fast and eat too much. You'd have to supplement his rations."

"Let him raise his own food in a garden. Daddy's slaves have gardens, but I wouldn't buy him for a field hand. I'd make him a driver."

"I don't want field workers anyhow. I'm lookin' for sawyers and mechanics for a lumber and turpentine operation down in Florida. Let's go down for a closer look."

Shortly, the door to the barracoon opened and the two white men flanked by burly, armed guards stepped inside. "Stand up," the man in work clothes gestured toward Brutus and Mingo.

Mingo stood up. Brutus held back. "You too. Ya'll together?"

Neither slave answered. "I asked you a question - ya'll together?"

"What you mean, Mas'r?" Brutus answered.

"You belong to the same owner?"

"No, Mas'r."

What were you two talkin' 'bout just now?"

"Just passin' time, Mas'r. Ain't nothin' much to talk 'bouts in here."

"What's your name?"

"Brutus, Mas'r."

"In the catalogue it says you're a mechanic."

"I worked de sawmill at Clean Drinkin'."

"Doin' what?"

"Sawed logs into timbers," Brutus looked at the floor and scratched his forehead.

"What kinda saw did you use?"

"What you mean, Mas'r?"

"How big was the saw blade?"

"Um, I reckon several feet round, Mas'r."

"Oh? What turned the blade?"

"A steam engine, Mas'r."

"Did you run it?"

"Nosuh, Mas'r, de boss man looked after de engine."

"Did you help him?"

"Not much, Mas'r."

The man turned to Mingo, "What's your name?"

Mingo mumbled his name.

"Speak up, nigger!"

"Mingo, Mas'r."

"Umm, the catalogue says you're a blacksmith."

"I helped de smitty now and den, dat's all."

"Doin' what?"

"Put de charcoal on de fire, pumped de bellows."

"Take off your shirt." When Mingo stood bare-chested, the man squeezed Mingo's right bicep then his left. "Hold out your hands, palms up."

The white man looked at them and then mumbled, "Un huh."

The two buyers worked their way around the barracoon asking questions and making notes in their catalogues. The ruddy faced man took more interest in the women squeezing their breasts and buttocks. When women turned away, he jerked them around and ordered them look him in the eye. Several women sniffled in humiliation.

Brutus whispered to Mingo. "I can't stand much more. I'm goin' kill dat bastard if he keeps it up."

After the two buyers examined every slave in which they had an interest, they returned to the balcony to compare notes. The man with the goatee said, "Those two by the door ain't as stupid as they act. They play dumb to keep the bidding down in hopes they can buy their freedom cheaper. I'll bet you anything that that big buck against the wall knows how to operate a steam sawmill himself. I know damn well that one beside him can blacksmith. They've smart. Neither one will work out as field hands."

All afternoon buyers peered over the balcony and several more came into the cell to examine the stock. As the light from the clerestory windows dimmed, the buyers left and a mournful murmur recommenced in the barracoon until the guard opened the door and pushed an adolescent girl into the room. She was tall with a complexion that the whites called high yellow. Her fine white, polished cotton dress accented her skin color. She whimpered and rubbed her swollen left cheek.

A sweaty, fat woman said, "What's the matter, honey chile? Come o'er here by me."

The girl wailed.

"Calm down. Come on now. You can tell me all about it."

Between sobs she related her story. "Me and Mama been house servants for a rich family or our whole lives. Some say Mama's de best cook in Charleston and I'm her helper. Lately, Mas'r took to givin' me presents, tellin' me how pretty I am and pettin' on me. Mama warned me to stay away from him, but I couldn't all de time."

The girl bawled. The fat woman patted her arm, "It's OK. You'll feel better if you tell Auntie what happened."

"Dis afternoon, my mistress was bathin' upstairs while I was downstairs preparin' her afternoon tea dress when Mas'r came into de room. He shut de door real easy and then tried to kiss me, so I yelled and scratched him in de face. He slapped me hard. 'Bout den Missis burst through de door screamin' like a banshee. She smashed a lamp against de wall den told him to sell me or she was goin' back home to her family in Boston."

She sniffed, then continued, "Mas'r ordered de head servant to bring me here."

"You poor chile," said the fat women as she patted the girl's arm.

"Me and Mama fell on our knees beggin' him not to sell us. Mas'r said I was a she-devil always temptin' him. The Missis carried on so, he wouldn't listen to us."

The woman hugged the girl while repeating, "Shhh, you'll be OK. You'll be OK. Calm down."

Everybody in the barracoon eavesdropped, but nobody interfered until Mingo edged over beside the young woman. She ignored him. After a while, she stopped sniffling and wiped her nose with the sleeve of her dress. He whispered that he knew how she felt. She didn't even lift her head as he told her how he was tricked by Phillip and brought to Charleston.

When he finished, she looked into his eyes. Mingo took a deep breath and asked her name. She looked away, then mumbled, "Molly."

As the evening wore on, the young people chatted in low undertones. Well after dark, the fat lady curled up on the floor and fell asleep. One by one all the other slaves nodded off. Brutus kept his eyes open the longest. As he dozed off, he could still hear Molly and Mingo whispering.

A mockingbird's song woke Brutus before first light. When he opened his eyes to scan the barracoon, he saw the pretty girl's head resting on Mingo's shoulder and her hand intertwined with his.

CHAPTER THREE

CHARLESTON
South Carolina

On auction day, Brutus dumped the honey bucket and then dished out beans and rice again. As the slaves ate, they listened to the commotion from the adjoining auction room as it filled with buyers and onlookers. Just after midday, the iron door opened and the clerk came into the barracoon with a black helper while three, burly, white men stood guard outside the door.

"Listen up!" the clerk yelled. "We're goin' take you out to de block. My helper here is goin' lead you. After you pass through dis door, follow him to de platform out yonder in de center of de room. Walk right up de steps to de middle and stop. I'll be right der. You listen to me. Don't you do nothin' lest I tell you. Folks will be yellin' and carryin' on. Don't pay dat no mind."

The slaves edged away from him as if trying to hide.

"If you act up, we'll hog-tie you. Don't even think 'bout runnin'. De gate to de buildin' is locked. You can't go nowhere. If you git ornery, we'll whip you. Understand?"

The clerk pointed at a strong, swarthy, young man about twenty years old. "We'll start wid you. Take off your shirt and follow me."

The slave handed his shirt to a friend and followed the two men from the barracoon to the platform. When the shirtless slave reached the steps, the clerk yelled out his number to the auctioneer, who nodded as he pattered and paced around the platform, joking, praising the lot, and speaking to buyers.

"Best lookin' bunch this year. Strong workers, house servants and fine women! We gonna start with field hands. Here is the first one, number nine in your catalogue."

On the platform, the young slave looked wide-eyed at the white men jabbering and pointing at him. Like a jester, the clerk's helper skipped around him clapping and pointing at his features with exaggerated gestures. The crowd whistled and yelled in anticipation of the fun to come.

The auctioneer hawked the stock, "This one is an excellent specimen in a first-class lot. Check his strong arms and back, jet black, perfect field hand."

Although he knew the price was low, the auctioneer started the bidding at 700 dollars to build excitement. "Do I hear 700?" Hands all around the platform went up and heads nodded. "750. Do I hear 750?" Buyers shouted out bids. The auctioneer heard 800 from somewhere near the back wall.

"I see ya'll are so eager I ain't messin' around. 900. Do I hear 900?" Hands waved. "1000. Do I hear 1000?"

"One thousand," someone boomed.

"Yessiree, this here is a mighty fine nig. 1,000. Do I hear 1,100 dollars?"

Usually the auctioneer wouldn't jump the bidding in hundred dollar increments, but the crowd's enthusiasm encouraged him. Buyers gestured at the auctioneer.

"1100, I see 1100 dollars. "1,200, 1,200 dollars there," the auctioneer chanted.

At 1,300 dollars the bidding slowed and only two, well-dressed men directly across the platform from each other kept bidding. "1350, 1350 dollars going once, going twice."

"1400."

Before the auctioneer could respond, the man across the way yelled 1,450. The helper ran over to the other bidder who had bid 1400 encouraging him to go higher. The crowd laughed. The clerk ordered the young slave to turn around.

The man signaled "no" with a flat palm and grumbled, "Ah, let him have him." The auctioneer counted, "Going once, going twice, sold: 1,450 dollars to the man with the cigar."

A clerk at a table by the wall jotted down the buyer's name and the bid beside the slave's number. In the lull as the helper took the young slave back to the barracoon, the auctioneer kept chattering and joking. The buyers paid him little attention as they talked among themselves or studied their catalogues and notes. Others drank whiskey.

One after the other, shirtless slaves walked to the platform. As the auctioneer had promised, most were in excellent condition, young and muscular, but not all. After several young men sold for more than 1300 dollars, the helper brought out an arthritic man with short, gray hair and beard who wore a house servant's uniform. The auctioneer did his best to encourage bidding. He described the man's household experience while the stoop-shouldered lackey stood on the platform with his head down.

The crowd showed no interest. The auctioneer started the bidding at 300 dollars. He lowered the price 50 dollars and still had no bidders. The crowd got restless. Someone yelled, "Git him outta here."

The auctioneer lowered the price another 50 dollars.

Another buyer yelled, "Quit wastin' our time with a worthless coon."

"All right, 100 dollars" said the auctioneer. "An experienced house servant is worth 100 dollars. Somebody's got a 100 dollars bill for this nig."

The crowd reacted with catcalls and insults. "Move on. Git that shit outa here."

The auctioneer ducked a wad of paper someone hurled at him.

"No sale," the auctioneer said as he motioned for the helper to take the slave away.

"Bring up the best stock," the auctioneer yelled to the helper in order to stir up the crowd again.

The auctioneer cracked a joke with a punch line calling Lincoln a monkey-man. Buyers laughed, slapped one another on the back and punched each other on the shoulders.

In the barracoon, the helper pointed at Mingo. "Get your shirt off. Follow me."

Mingo slipped his shirt over his head, handed it to Brutus, and followed the helper into the auction room. When he reached the steps, someone poked him in the arm. He side stepped to avoid falling.

"Hurry up," the helper growled.

Mingo had never seen so many white folks in one place except at barbeques held at White Oak. In his worst dreams, he had never imagined a rowdy, snarling bunch like the men crowded around the platform. He made out a comment through the confusion, "Now, this buck is worth biddin' for."

The helper ordered him to turn around. He did so in a daze. As he rotated, he saw the man with the goatee watching him and heard him bid 1000 dollars.

'Lord, don't let him buy me.'

Somebody yelled 1100 from somewhere behind him and then 1200 on the side of the platform. The auctioneer sensed the crowd's eagerness. "1200 dollars, I've got 1200, who'll give me 1250 dollars?"

"1250. 1250 I've got 1250 dollars, 1250 dollars going once."

"1275." Mingo recognized the voice.

"Going once, Going twice, 1275 dollars. The auctioneer pointed to the man with the goatee. "Sold!"

The helper tugged Mingo by the arm. He stumbled down the steps.

Next, Brutus followed the helper to the platform. The auctioneer heard praise drift through the crowd and he amplified it. "What a buck, the strongest of the lot. A mechanic. You could use him as your slave driver."

Before the auctioneer could name a price, several 1100 dollar bids rang out.

"Let's hear 1200, I see 1200 dollars." A well-dressed man bid 1250.

"1250, 1250 dollars. This one's worth more than 1250 dollars. 1250 dollars going once."

A man who looked woozy bid 1300.

"I've got 1300 dollars bid and well worth it too. 1300 dollars going once. You're goin' regret not buying this buck. 1300 dollars going twice. This is the bargain of the day."

"1400 dollars," the man with the goatee yelled.

"That's more like it, 1400 and still a bargain. Do I hear 1450?"

The jump bid foreclosed other bidders and the auctioneer knew it, but he kept trying. "1450. Do I hear 1425? Still a mighty good deal, 1400 going once, 1400 dollars going twice, sold for 1400 dollars."

Periodically, the clerk interspersed women and children for sale. Women didn't bring prices as high as the men, and children brought even less. If the clerk thought he could get more by separating the children from their mothers, he did so unless the owner restricted him. Most didn't.

Sometimes, owners gained more per child by selling children by lot because they could be trained to work as a group as several tykes could do almost as much work as an adult. Also, children cost less to maintain and they could be sold for a capital gain when they got older. As a rule of thumb, prices started at $100 for a baby and increased each year until age fifteen, or so, when a large, healthy child might bring an adult price.

The last slaves sold were three boys and two girls tied together with rope around their necks. They were about six years old and were sold as a lot for 3500 dollars.

After the auctioneer banged his gavel to complete the sale, he made an announcement, "That's all from the catalogue today, but we have surprise merchandise; a special treat. She came in too late to list, but I promise you're going to like what you see. We've saved the best for last."

Men walking away stopped. Others who had been too conservative to compete with the frenzied bidding stayed with hopes to salvage the day with a good buy. The auctioneer sensed the crowd's anticipation and grinned. Bids had jumped all afternoon without much encouragement. Out-of-town buyers had pushed up prices, but "gift flasks" for special buyers had lubricated the bidding too. The auctioneer knew he'd earned a healthy bonus as he sensed a record day.

In the barracoon matters weren't progressing as well. The mulatto girl refused to go out with the helper. As he struggled to pull her from the dank room, he ripped the sleeve on her dress which incensed her. She jerked free from his grasp, scratched him across the face and tried to kick him in the balls. He turned at the last instant then caught her foot with his left hand. As he pulled back his right hand to slap her, Mingo grabbed his arm and twisted it behind his back forcing the helper to drop the girl's foot.

Burly white guards, one as big and muscular as Brutus, stepped into the barracoon. One yelled, "Back against the wall," as the other slapped a quirt hard against the iron door. Slaves scurried away from whip, but Molly stood her ground and glared at the guards as Mingo kept his grasp on to the helper's arm. Brutus raised his hands, crouching in a fighting stance which made the guards pause.

"Don't try nothin' stupid or we'll whip you."

Brutus felt confident that he could overpower the two guards in the barracoon, but he also understood that he couldn't save the girl or escape. He put his hand on Mingo's shoulder and said, "Let him go. There'll be another day."

As Mingo loosened his grip, the helper grabbed the girl, spun her around, and penned her arms behind her. She stomped his foot. He yelled "Grab her feet!" A guard managed to catch one foot, but she kept kicking at his face with the other until he seized it. She squirmed and twisted as the men forced her through the door.

In frustration, Mingo smacked his hand against the stone wall while Brutus clinched and unclenched his fists.

A few men in the crowd heard the ruckus in the barracoon, but most were focused on the auctioneer. "Yessiree, we got a beautiful young thing for you now; a high yeller girl called Molly." Whoops rose from the crowd. "She's a spitfire too. Looky here!"

The buyers watched as the helper and the guard manhandled her onto the platform where they dropped her to the floor. Men hollered louder. Hats sailed across the room. The auctioneer encouraged the uproar, "Whattaya think bout this filly?"

Hoots, whistles and crass comments rang out. Molly pushed up to her hands and knees. Although crying and scared, she glared at the men surrounding her. An arm snaked out to grab her leg, which a guard kicked away. A chant started, "Stand her up, stand her up."

The auctioneer knew he was in luck to have such a beauty to sell to the high rolling, drunken bidders.

The guard jerked Molly to her feet. She twisted to kick him, but with less vigor. As he pinned her elbows behind her back, helplessness overwhelmed her. The auctioneer didn't hesitate. 800 dollars do I hear 8--. 900 boomed out from several directions. Again, somebody bid 1000 before the auctioneer could repeat the bid. 'Craziness,' thought the auctioneer. Already the price exceeded the highest paid for a woman all day and the bidding hadn't started in earnest. 1100 boomed from near the wall.

From a corner a rake yelled, "Show us her tittys."

The auctioneer hollered. I've got 1100 dollars, 1100 dollars. This spunky filly is worth more than that."

Molly trembled in fear. A 1200 dollar bid rolled across the room. "1200 dollars, I have 1200 dollars.

"Show us her tits, show her tits," several rapscallions along the back wall chanted in unison. The helper urged them on. Cupping his hands over her breasts he yelled "These?"

"1200 dollars going once.

The ugly man with the red feather in his hat yelled, "1250."

"1250, I got 1250, 1250 going once."

More buyers took up the chant, "Show us her tits! Show us her tits." The auctioneer couldn't make out the bids over the commotion. He thought he heard 1300 above the din although he couldn't identify the bidder among the unruly crowd. The chant increased in intensity and the auctioneer knew he risked a no sale if rowdies stirred up more tumult. He needed to end the bidding to avoid confusion and protests.

"1300 dollars, I've got 1300 dollars," the auctioneer yelled.

1400, a man hollered somewhere back in the crowd.

"1400 dollars, 1400 dollars going once," the auctioneer hurried. The entire crowd from the lowest rogue to the most cultured planter now chanted: "Show us her tits." Almost beyond control, men shoved and elbowed to get closer to the platform. At that moment, the helper grabbed Molly's dress with both hands and ripped it down to her waist. Molly squirmed harder to free herself from the guard. The helper pointed and the crowd whooped approval. To his shock the auctioneer heard 1500 dollars from a bidder he knew well.

"1500 dollars going once."

The auctioneer didn't hesitate, "1500 going twice. 1500 dollars, sold. Sold to Mr. Silas West," as the auctioneer pointed at the man in the Panama hat with a red feather in the band.

"Get her off the platform," the clerk yelled to the helper although a guard was already pulling Molly toward the barracoon as she fought to pull up her tattered dress.

The auctioneer heard a young rake declare as he stumbled away from the platform, "Best nigger auction ever."

CHAPTER FOUR

CHARLESTON

South Carolina

Silas awoke late the next morning with a pounding headache and nausea. All he could remember from the auction was a raucous party atmosphere and that he had bought a beautiful, young woman. Beyond that, he couldn't remember any details, not even his bid. He prayed that he hadn't been too carried away by whiskey and excitement.

His servant brought coffee. Once it cooled a bit, Silas gulped it. Although he managed to keep the dark liquid down, it didn't clear his foggy head. He wanted to lie around all day, but he knew he had to move fast to negate the sale. He had to clean up, dress and face the clerk. Silas yelled for his servant to set out a fresh suit.

The slave brought him a fine cotton shirt and a linen suit ironed to perfection. He tucked the shirt around his pudgy belly and then tied a purple ribbon bow tie under the high collar. As he slipped on his Panama hat, he mulled over rationalizations to renege on his purchase. *The sale's invalid. The bids and auctioneer couldn't be heard over the fracas.*

He fortified himself by slipping a flask into his back pocket and a tiny, pearl handled, one-shot percussion pistol under his belt. After striding to the slave mart, he bucked himself up with a swig at the entrance. His resolution failed as he stepped inside to find the white owner of the slave mart, the auctioneer and the black clerk huddled around a desk while a grizzled black man swept the floor with a push broom. Silas had hoped to talk to clerk alone. He turned to slip out before being seen, but the owner called out, "Mr. West, congratulations. You bought the best of the lot. Nobody had the balls to compete with you."

Silas puffed up when the auctioneer added, "I didn't doubt for a second you'd outbid that stranger."

"We can't let out of town speculators best us, can we?" Silas quipped while yearning to know how much he'd overpaid.

"Yes, sir, you bought a fine filly," a guard said. "I'll fetch her right now."

As the guard walked toward the barracoon, the clerk commented, "I can't believe you bought that beauty for only $1500."

Silas suppressed a gasp to learn that he'd paid so much for a bitch that would make him the laughing stock of Charleston, and worse, might cause his Daddy to cut his stipend.

A guard lead Molly to the table by her arm. "Mr. West, I suggest you tie her." The manhandling the day before had left Molly's face mottled and bruised. Although still sore and terrified, her bearing conveyed disdain for her tormentors. As she held her torn dress tightly against her chest with her free hand, her beauty and spitfire disposition reminded Silas why he had bought her.

The clerk presented Silas a receipt to sign.

Silas scratched his name. Reaching into his pants pocket, he pulled out a wad of cash. He counted fifteen one hundred dollar bills and handed them to the clerk who smiled.

The guard repeated his warning. "Mr. West, she kicked the crap out of my partner. Let me tie her."

"I can handle her."

When Silas grabbed her arm, Molly jerked free. She ran for the street as fast as she could while clutching her dress. The guard chased her down and dragged her back to Silas. The clerk grabbed cords hanging on a peg and tied her wrists together and then secured her ankles with just enough slack to walk.

"Follow me, bitch," Silas ordered as he grabbed the cord tied to Molly's wrists to lead her like a pony. His head throbbed even more than before.

As soon as Silas was out of hearing, the guard said, "Droopy drawers got hisself a handful now." The men laughed as the clerk divided the $1500.

To stay out of sight, Silas took a circuitous route down an ally and then through the Unitarian Church cemetery while pondering how to mollify his father.

Once on the street, he met several people, but no one he recognized. As he turned the corner toward his Daddy's townhouse by the river, the sidewalks, porches, and balconies appeared empty. Yet, his timing was bad for the second time that day. Just yards from home, his biddy neighbor stepped outside with her servant who held a black umbrella over her head to protect her from the sun. "Beautiful day isn't it, Mr.West?" she chirped.

"Yes, ma'am," Silas mumbled while looking away so the crone wouldn't stop to gab. As he walked on, he heard "Tsk, tsk."

Silas climbed onto his porch, opened the door and barked at Molly, "Get inside." As she passed through the door, Silas shoved her down. From the floor, she looked up to see an older house servant hurrying down the stairs.

Silas said, "Don't say a thing. Put her in the back bedroom across from yours."

The manservant had seen Silas drunk and unruly many times, but had never known him to bring home a half-naked slave girl. The servant said, "Leave her to me, Mas'r West. Come with me, young lady," as he bent over to help her up.

Silas watched Molly hobble after the servant then opened a cabinet and grabbed a bottle. He poured a slug of whiskey into a tumbler and gulped it down. He slammed the glass on a mahogany corner table, tromped down the hallway and yelled at his servant standing outside the bedroom door, "Go away!" The slave made one last effort to divert him, "Mas'r, is there anything you need from me?"

"Get outa here!"

As the servant scrambled to leave, Silas rushed into the bedroom, kicked the door shut and pushed Molly down on the bed.

Molly clutched her dress with all her strength. With his right hand Silas grabbed her by the hair and with his left yanked her dress. She tried to roll away. "I'll teach you to embarrass me, bitch." She strained to kick him, but the cord tied around her ankles made that impossible. He slapped her and fumbled to unbutton his trousers. She bit his ear. He jerked his head back that ripped his ear lobe from her teeth. He felt blood flow down his jaw. Enraged, he cracked his captive in the nose with his elbow.

Dazed from the blow, Molly knew she didn't have the strength to fight off the sweaty man although she continued to squirm. Feeling hard metal against her body, she realized that it must be a pistol. She grabbed it and twisted the barrel against Silas's belly, cocked the hammer with her thumb, and pulled the trigger.

She heard a pop and a scream, "You bitch!"

He punched her behind the ear and she almost lost consciousness, yet she felt the man lift himself to clutch his belly where blood soaked his expensive shirt. He bellowed, "I'm goin' to kill you!"

As Silas lunged for her, Molly rolled toward the nightstand, grabbed a brass candelabrum and smashed it against his head. He collapsed, moaned and grabbed the bed in an effort to pull himself up. She cracked him on the head again as hard as she could. He crumbled to the floor as the servant jerked open the door.

"Help me! Help me!" Molly pleaded.

The manservant gasped, turned and ran down the hall. In a few seconds, he returned with a butcher knife.

"Lord have mercy, chile," he yawped as he sliced through the cords around Molly's ankles and wrists. He pulled her into the hall and slammed the bedroom door. "I'll be right back."

Feeling faint, Molly wiped her bloody face with the hem of her dress. The servant raced up carrying a shirt, pants with matching jacket and cap, shoes and socks.

He turned his back as Molly stepped out from the remnants of her dress, jerked on the pants, buttoned the shirt and pulled on the shoes and socks.

"You gotta hide."

"Where?

"Go to the Unitarian Cemetery till dark. Then slip behind the Slave Mart to de iron steps. De caretaker lives in a room over the barracoon. Ask him for help. I hear he hides runaways and helps dem escape to de North. Hurry!

Molly grabbed the jacket and cap as she dashed out the back door into a small summer garden gone to seed. A brick wall bordered by azalea bushes and covered with dark-green ivy encircled the yard. An arched portal opened to an alley. She stopped at the wrought iron gate. Gasping for breath, she knew she couldn't sneak all the way to the cemetery without being seen, so she decided to walk as if she were a servant on an errand.

Slipping into the jacket and tugging the cap down on her forehead, Molly unlatched the catch and glanced around. Not seeing anyone, she stepped into the shadow along the wall and closed the gate.

CHAPTER FIVE

CHARLESTON
South Carolina

After the guards delivered Molly to Silas, Mingo heard someone dragging irons toward the barracoon. The steel door opened and the man with the goatee and a guard stepped inside followed by a wizened black man lugging knotted shackles. The turnkey slammed the door shut. The gray-headed black man dropped the manacles on the floor and began to untangle the knotted cross chains from a long, center one.

The guard snarled, "Listen up. Mr. Holland here wants his moaks in a coffle. If he bought you, line up right here."

Those slaves Holland had purchased, some carrying bundles, shuffled toward the guard. Their new master pointed at a slave standing against the far wall and said, "You too, you're mine!"

The slave stood still with his head down. The white man walked to him, balled his fist and punched his new chattel hard in the stomach. "When I say move, you best jump." The man doubled over then lurched toward the line.

When the doddering slave had the shackles unraveled and spread apart, the guard instructed each acquisition to stand beside a cross chain. Mingo and Brutus stepped to the front. The aged black man put a collar around Mingo's neck, closed it and padlocked it. He secured Brutus next to Mingo and continued down the line until Holland's twelve new purchases were bound together, six on each side of the center chain.

Holland then ordered all the slaves to toss their possessions into a pile. When they did, he picked up a ragged jacket. He untied the sleeves and shook out the contents. Tattered clothing, along with a tin pot and plate clattered to the floor. He slid his hand over a seam and reached in his pants pocket for a pocketknife. He cut the cloth and shook out a silver spoon. Holding the ornate utensil high, he said, "Where'd you steal this?" He slipped it into his pants pocket. Then he rummaged through all the bundles. Inside a thin wool jacket, he found a silver dollar which he also pocketed.

When he finished he said, "Listen up. Ya'll didn't come cheap and I expect my money's worth. I'm takin' you to Florida where me and my partner are setting up a turpentine distillery and sawmill. Don't test me by gettin' uppity 'cause I'll whip the hide off ya in a heartbeat." He paused as he looked over his purchase then continued, "We'll travel mostly by train. Any funny business along the way and ya'll be miserable sons-a-bitches. Behave yourselves and we'll get along just fine."

He pointed at the elderly slave who brought in the chains, "Follow him to the train station while I square up with the clerk." The turnkey opened the barracoon door. The downcast slaves jangled outside into a sunny day.

As the chained men shambled through Charleston's streets, most people didn't pay them any mind although a few gawked at the brawny slaves in the front. Near the station, two white boys picked up rocks and threw them at the easy targets. One rock missed; the other winged Brutus on the arm. He lifted his eyes. The slaves kept shuffling forward.

A storekeeper yelled at the boys as they picked out rocks for their second salvo. "Don't be throwin' rocks at a man's niggers." The boys dropped their ammunition and sprinted down a side alley.

By the time the group arrived at the railroad depot, the sun had burned away all morning coolness. Even the muggy breeze off the bay felt oppressive. Their guide stopped them in the shade of a big live oak and told them to wait.

Walking to a rusty pitcher pump bolted to a horse trough, he centered a wooden bucket under the spout and pumped the handle. After filling the pail, he lifted a gourd dipper that was hanging from a nail and slipped it into the container. Then, with a grunt, he grabbed the bail with both hands and hauled the cool water to the waiting slaves. "Drink up. Might be your last chance for a while. If ya need to piss, go behind de buildin'."

CHAPTER SIX

CHARLESTON

South Carolina

Retracing the route that Silas West had used to pull her to his father's townhouse, Molly walked fast as if she carried a special delivery. Nobody paid her any mind.

As she hurried along all she could think about was the hideous retribution she faced if captured. She knew that nigger chasers and patrols doubled their efforts to apprehend fugitives in order to collect the inevitable reward. They were bound to search the houses of friends and family. Worse, some people might betray her in for money; she had nowhere to turn.

The first hours carried the biggest risk. Alone on the streets, she had no plan and every person she met presented a threat. She wanted to run straight to the stranger's door above the barracoon but dared not during daylight. She needed a hiding place until dark.

When she reached the cemetery gate, she trembled with fear, but walked fast down the narrow sidewalk until she spied a hiding place. Where the sidewalk turned, thick azaleas bushes taller than her head surrounded an oak tree, a perfect refuge. All she had to do was slip behind the outer branches without being seen.

To scout the hideout, she walked past the azaleas to the stone church. The only people around were a young woman pushing a per-ambulator on the sidewalk and, down the block, a black workman mixing mortar in a wooden trough and singing a chantey. The woman ignored her. The laborer seemed engrossed. As she doubled back, she scrutinized the windows and porches overlooking the cemetery for anyone who might spot her. She didn't see anybody. All she heard was the workman's song in the distance and a mockingbird's warble.

By the azaleas, she bent over as if picking up something while reexamining her surroundings. Seeing no threat, she eased between branches and crawled on her hands and knees to the oak tree.

Molly felt safe for the first time since she left Silas West's town-house. Few people ventured into the cemetery and unless someone pulled back the boughs, no one could see her.

A yellow jacket flew by her face. Following it with her eyes, she noticed that it landed nearby at an oak root that trailed across the ground. The insect crawled into a hole as others flew out. Molly lifted her body weight with her arms and scooched farther away from the nest.

Gray Spanish moss hanging from the trees waved in the breeze, but only stronger puffs blew through the thick azaleas. The yellow jackets became more active as if her presence irritated them. She edged farther away from the nest. She heard thunder rumbling in the distance and noticed through the leaves that the sky had clouded over.

Before long, she heard footsteps and a small chain rattling. As she strained to see through the branches, she heard a dog whine and then bark. A few seconds later, it poked its nose under the azaleas. The dog growled.

"Dadblame it, girl. Get away from there," a man grumbled as he yanked a leash clipped to a harness on a small, brown and white splotched terrier.

Molly breathed easier to see that the dog wasn't a mastiff or bloodhound used by patrols. Still, she cringed as the dog barked louder and jumped against its chain toward her. She shuddered when she heard the owner say, "You're actin' crazy. Is there a 'possum in there? Let's have a look."

In a frenzy, the dog squeezed under the azaleas branches that brushed the ground. "What ya got, girl?"

As the man bent back the branches, yellow jackets spewed from the nest and attacked. Howling, the dog jerked hard on its leash to run away. Its owner slapped at the buzzing insects and ran from the cemetery with his pet. Soon the swarm settled down. Most defenders returned to the nest, but others, as if posted as guards, stayed on the branches and leaves. Molly vowed not to move.

Several yellow jackets flew into a gap between the buttons on her shirt. Feeling the tickle as they crawled across her skin, she eased her hand over them to smash the insects with as little movement as possible. She crushed some in her grip, but two stung her before she could kill them. Gritting her teeth, she stayed still.

Suddenly, lightning flashed and thunder clapped with a deafening roar. Rain poured down, and the yellow jackets retreated into their hole. The big live oak and azalea bushes broke the downpour so Molly stayed dry for a few seconds until the moisture seeped through the foliage above her. Soon, water covered the ground and dripped from every leaf and twig. She pulled her cap tighter and turned her collar up. Still, the deluge soaked her.

She pulled her knees to her chest and hugged them. After a while, the storm eased, but a chilling wind whirled through the cemetery that blew dead fronds from the sabal palms, Spanish moss and twigs from the oaks. Although she tried to warm herself by wiggling her toes and tensing her muscles, she shivered. Her fingers felt numb.

As sunset approached, the sprinkle slacked to a drizzle and the wind died. She took off her cap and socks to wring as much water from them as she could. The overcast thinned and orange sunlight brightened the sky in the west beneath the cloud cover. The rain stopped. Mist rose from the streets. The yellow jackets stirred for their last flights before nightfall. Molly felt warmer and waited.

When sunlight faded and oil lamps flickered from the windows in the houses adjacent to the cemetery, she stood up against the live oak. Brushing leaves, twigs, and mud off her clothes as best she could, she eased away from her hiding place and crept down the streets. Staying in the shadows, she circled behind the slave mart to the stairs. Making sure no one was watching, she tiptoed up to the landing and pressed against the door to stay as inconspicuous as possible. She rapped. No response. She rapped harder. Someone asked, "Who's der?"

"My name's Molly. Please help me."

A small, gray headed black man cracked open the door, peered into the dark and asked again, "Who's der?"

"I'm Molly. I've run away. Someone told me you could help me."

The wizened man held the door half open and said, "Quick, git inside."

She squeezed by him as he scanned the area before shutting and bolting the door. Then he stepped to the room's sole window to pull a ragged, paisley cloth across it.

"Who sent you?"

"I don't know his name."

Then before the man could interrupt, she blurted out the whole, horrible day.

As Molly finished the story, she pleaded, "Please help me. If you don't, what can I do?"

"I recognize you from de auction when dem whites was actin' like fools," the man said as he gathered up a thin bedspread. "Git undressed and put dis blanket 'round you."

Molly hesitated.

"I ain't goin' hurt you. You came to me for help. Maybe I can help, maybe I can't, but you've got to change out of dem soakin' wet clothes or you'll catch de croup. I'll go outside."

He unbolted the door, stepped out to the landing and closed the door behind him. Molly pulled off her wet clothes and rubbed the bedspread through her hair and wiped the moisture from her body. When she felt dry, she wrapped the blanket around herself which made her feel snug.

The old man came back into the room and latched the door.

"Will you hide me?"

"If anybody saw you come here, we'll both be hung."

"I'm sorry, but I didn't have no place else to go. I'm sure nobody saw me."

"I understand you didn't have a choice, chile. I'll just have to figure out somethin'. First, let's feed you some vittles. In dat box you'll find bread and jelly. Set it out while I go for water."

He grabbed a bucket, opened the door and hustled out. Not much longer than it took for him to climb down the stairs, she heard someone shout, "Halt!" She pressed her ear against the door.

"What you doin' out after dark, blackie? Where's your pass?"

"I plum forgot to fetch water during de day, Mas'r. I live right here."

A second patrolman interjected, "I know this old codger. He works at the barracoon. He's harmless; we ain't got time to be foolin' around with him when a runaway's on the loose. Let's go."

"Yeah, I reckon you're right. Nigger, you're lucky that my partner knows you or I'd have your ass whipped. Now get! Don't let me catch you out after dark again without a pass, you hear?"

"Yes, Mas'r."

After the old man came back upstairs and secured the door, he sat on the bed chuckling. "How can you laugh? Weren't you scared?"

"Course I was, but I done pulled one on dem white boys. They're lookin' for a runaway and you're right under der noses. If dey came up here and found you --- I hate to think about it. We was lucky. I should have seen dem before I went out. Can't afford no more mistakes like dat." He pulled back a threadbare rag rug, bent down and put his finger in a knothole to pull up a board that revealed a space big enough for Molly to squirm into.

"If somebody comes, hide here. It'll be dark and cramped, but you'll have to stay until I lets you out. Can you do dat?"

The cubby looked smaller than a coffin and Molly doubted that she could stand the tiny hideout for long without panicking.

"Can you stay hidden or not?"

Molly murmured, "I don't have a choice."

CHAPTER SEVEN

TALLAHASSEE AND BRONSON

Florida

The railroads through Georgia did not connect to those in Florida, so Holland had no easy way to transport his slaves to their new home. After studying a map, he decided to take the train to Thomasville, Georgia, then walk with the slaves to the railroad station in Tallahassee where he could board an eastbound train to Baldwin. From there, he could transfer to a southbound train to Bronson where he expected to meet his partner, Laurens Wall.

After detraining at Thomasville, the slaves plodded down a sandy road toward Tallahassee. After walking a few miles in the sultry air, sweat soaked everybody. Holland wanted to hurry the slaves but had to tolerate their lethargic pace. What could he do if he ordered them to walk faster and they ignored him? He could lash one as a warning to the others, but beating a slave hard enough to make an example could cause an injury in addition to making the others resentful and angry. Then, sooner or later, they'd malinger, sabotage equipment, or hurt stock. He hoped to cajole his new purchases to do his bidding without using the whip.

He noted that the mansions on the road to Tallahassee were well-maintained, and surrounded by productive acreage. Almost all the cotton had been harvested, but on a few estates pickers still dragged canvas bags along the rows plucking the bolls from dried and shriveled plants. In one field, Holland counted fifty blacks bent to the grueling work.

About twelve miles down the road from Thomasville under the canopy of huge live oaks, he called a halt by a sluggish creek. The slaves waded up to their knees in the water where they plopped down to cool off. He waded upstream from them to drink the musky water and fill his canteen. As he held the container under the water, he noted that the western sky had an orange cast. Although the daylight was fading fast, he wanted to proceed, yet he knew that would upset his slaves. Accustomed to the "can see, to can't see" schedule from daylight to dark, they'd soon expect to stop for the day, so he decided to stay for the night under the oaks where he could padlock them to a low limb.

Holland reached into his carpetbag for his sheath knife and two summer sausages. He sliced a sliver off one and popped it in his mouth. As he gnawed at it, he cut the meat into thin slices and laid them out on an oak limb while the slaves crouched on their haunches watching.

After he gave each slave a morsel, he built a small fire. Near it, on a smooth place where the ground was covered with fallen leaves, he kicked a few sticks aside and threw down a rough sewn, cotton quilt. He lay down with his head on his carpetbag and soon fell asleep.

Chained together and locked to the tree limb, the slaves couldn't sleep. Some argued that they should break the limb to free themselves. One man made the case that since they outnumbered their tormentor twelve to one, they could overpower him, take his keys, unlock themselves and then hide with the blacks on nearby plantations.

The images of his friend's whipping at White Oak, scared Mingo to the depth of his soul, but his anger and frustration at being chained up and mistreated outweighed his fear. He spoke out for a breakaway. "The devil who bought us is a thief, and we ain't bein' fed a full ration. Let's take our chances now."

Brutus said, "Where we gonna go? Niggers 'round here don't know us. How we gonna eat? If we run off, white folks will set dogs and patters on us. It's stupid to run away here in de middle of nowhere with no help. I want freedom as much as any of you, but we can't make a break 'til the time is right."

The comment reminded Mingo about the vicious hounds that trailed down his friend. "Brutus is right. Let's wait."

Mosquitoes buzzed and bit everybody all night. Nobody slept. At first light, Holland set out with the coffle toward Tallahassee.

By late afternoon, they reached the town's outskirts where small farms lined the road instead of the big plantations like those closer to Thomasville. Traffic picked up on the road and several groups of horsemen, many with weapons, passed by heading toward town. Holland waved down a rider and asked why so many horsemen were on the road.

"Governor Perry has ordered mobilization. If Lincoln's elected, Florida's goin' to secede, which may mean war. I'm volunteerin' for the cavalry."

"Looks like you got a fine pony for that. Wish I had one to ride to Tallahassee."

"You ain't got but a few more miles."

Compared to Charleston, Tallahassee looked small and seedy. Holland figured the population couldn't be more than a few thousand people, and a third or more appeared to be slaves. By far, shacks outnumbered grand homes, and only a few commercial structures radiated away from the largest building, the capitol. Atop a high hill, it looked so magnificent compared to the rest of the town that Holland assumed the Federal government must have funded its construction.

Although it looked poor, the town bustled with business activity. Warehouses lined the streets near the depot where slaves unloaded cotton bales and lumber from wagons onto the platform or directly into rail cars. By the loading dock, a locomotive with several cars coupled to it gathered steam for the run to the port at St. Marks.

Holland knew the skimpy sausage slices he had served his slaves the night before weren't sufficient nourishment. He needed to find rations for them. After settling the coffle under a shade tree near the depot, he backtracked uphill toward the capitol to a restaurant he had spotted earlier. Like most other buildings, it was a run-down, unpainted, wooden structure, but the smell of pork roasting over hickory logs had made him hungry when he had passed it.

Inside, he found workmen sitting at wooden tables gnawing ribs or stuffing themselves with pulled pork. At a long counter, he ordered a meat platter with cornbread. As the cook piled vittles on a tin plate, Holland asked, "Can you fix slapjacks for twelve nigras?"

"How much you want?"

He pointed at peck baskets stacked against the back wall. "Fill one of those. Toss in a little pork."

Clutching his plate, he found an empty seat at a long table and sat down. As he ate, he watched the grease-splattered cook grab a cloth bag filled with cornmeal from under the counter and shake the contents into a big pot. Then the man walked out a back door and returned with a tin filled with hog drippings that had collected under a rack of ribs roasting on a spit. After he poured the grease into the pot, he threw in a handful of shredded pork. After mixing the concoction to a pasty consistency, he plopped dollops on the griddle, fried them until brown, and then stacked them in a basket.

After Holland delivered the slapjacks to the slaves, he locked them in a warehouse. He rented a room in a boarding house for himself. When he came to fetch them in the morning, several were hunched over, groaning from stomach aches.

Eager to get them loaded for the trip to Bronson, Holland ignored the sick slaves and ordered the group to walk to the depot platform. Worn out and ill, the slaves stood immobilized.

"Move!" he hollered.

The healthy men prodded the others, and they all stumbled toward the platform although they stopped several times as men vomited. Fuming, Holland managed to have them loaded on a cattle car just before the engine chugged east.

At the Baldwin depot, as he unloaded his slaves to transfer them onto another train headed south, they looked so downcast, exhausted and sick that he almost felt empathy for them. He fretted that he had scrimped too much on food and transportation in an effort to compensate for the high prices that he had paid for them.

To his surprise the south bound train reached Bronson on time. As the train slowed beside the platform, he jumped onto it when he saw his associate. Wall was a stocky man with a ruddy complexion and short red beard who looked cleaner and neater than the other backwoodsmen waiting for the train. Although dressed in workman's clothing, he sported fancy alligator boots and an expensive high crowned straw hat instead of a slouch hat like the others wore. "Good to see you, partner. The coffle's two cars back." As the train crept forward, Wall asked, "How'd it go?"

"So, so. Several nigs are sick. I paid more for them than we figured."

"I've had a time here too. I couldn't lease the longleaf timber land we wanted in the sand hills. A Yankee timber company with ties to Senator Levy's railroad bought it although the damn real estate agent had promised to hold it for me. The timber on the land I leased near Chunky Pond ain't as good, mixed longleaf and slash pine, but I had to move fast and paid too much. I figured that unless I tied up property, we'd have slaves sitting on their asses while we looked for land. In the long run, we may be better off. Our leasehold's close to the railroad so we won't have to haul so far.

The train clanged to a full stop. Wall surveyed his new slaves sprawled on the car floor. "They don't look so good, but they'll do better once we're in camp. You moaks climb up on that wagon over yonder."

Some slaves needed help to stand. A fevered one behind Brutus collapsed. Brutus picked him up and carried him to the cart.

CHAPTER EIGHT

CHUNKY POND CAMP
Florida

In the late afternoon, the wagon arrived at a rise overlooking a large pond where Wall had erected a camp. Nestled under gigantic live oaks, three frame tents faced two smaller ones a hundred feet away. Between the shelters, a large tarpaulin suspended ten feet above the ground with an air vent at the apex formed a pyramid over a fire ring constructed from limestone rocks.

Beside the fire pit, Wall had built a long, wooden dining table with attached benches. On one end, he had made shelves where various cast iron pans, pots, Dutch ovens, tin plates and cups rested. A wooden bucket hung underneath the storage compartments.

Nearby, Wall had cobbled together a lean-to that used an ancient live oak trunk as a pilaster. Under the shelter, he had stacked barrels and crates containing rations and supplies. Near the pond, a green tarpaulin covered a steam engine and a small, portable sawmill. A hundred yards to one side, an ox and a horse grazed in a small corral built around a copse of trees.

Holland and Wall marched their coffle to the fire ring. Before unlocking them from their shackles, they fastened a three-foot chain attached to a solid iron ball to each slave's right ankle.

When Wall unlocked the fevered slave from the others, the sick man bent over in obvious pain. Holland told Brutus, "Tote him to one of those three tents over yonder and put him on a cot. Then get back over here."

Brutus picked up the man and started to walk, but the iron ball made him stop with each step in order to drag the heavy weight along the ground. After settling the sick man on a cot, Brutus pulled a brown wool blanket over him and re-joined the slaves standing around the fire ring.

Wall said, "Listen up. We put a ball and chain on you 'cause we don't know you. Once we see you can behave yourselves, we'll take 'em off. Don't even think about runnin'. A slave catcher lives right up the road with Cuban bloodhounds rarin' to chase niggers. The sheriff's office is in Bronson. Now then, who can cook?"

No one said anything. Wall pointed to the skinniest slave. "You're the cook. Stay here with Mr. Holland. The rest of you, follow me."

Dragging the iron balls, the slaves could not walk as fast as Wall. Several times, he waited and watched the slaves bend over to adjust the clasps to lessen the abrasions on their skin. At a pile of tools spread across the ground, Wall stopped. When the slaves gathered around, he said, "We're goin' to be loggin' this forest. We'll haul the logs to the sawmill where we'll saw 'em into timbers and lumber."

Wall handed each man an axe, and then every other man, a two person, cross cut saw that had wooden handles at each end of a ten-foot steel blade. He stepped up to a large pine and motioned for a man holding a saw to join him. Using the tool, he showed the slave how to work as a team to cut down the tree with long, smooth strokes. In a few minutes, the big pine fell to ground with such force that large limbs shattered and broke. "Once you get her down, you have to trim all the limbs. Here's the easiest way."

Wall picked up an axe. "Start at the base and lop the limbs flush against the trunk. Once the limbs are off, whack off the top where it's about ten inches in diameter." He made a circle with his hands and held them up for the slaves to see.

Next, he ordered each slave in turn to chop limbs in order to see how each man handled an axe. All of them did well except one man who hacked at a limb without cutting through it. Wall said, "You better do better than that or you won't earn your supper." The slave flailed with more effort, but with no more success. Wall watched the man a while longer and said, "You're no peckerwood, that's for sure. What can you do?"

The slave looked at the ground. "Look after animals, Mas'r."

"OK, then, you are the stockman and log cart driver, but you better not be foolin' with me or you'll find yourself on short rations."

Wall divided the slaves into teams, and worked with them until dusk when a metallic clang echoed through the trees as the new cook banged a steel rod against a rusty disc hanging from an oak limb.

For the first time since leaving South Carolina, the slaves ate a decent meal. The new cook dished out shredded pork and stew made from potatoes, carrots, turnips and onions along with fresh cornbread. Holland told the cook to keep serving until everybody had all they wanted. Most finished the first plate and asked for more, but others were still too sick to eat much.

Brutus took a plate to the sick slave where he found him writhing on the cot. The tent stank and Brutus noticed that a putrid, bloody-brown liquid stained the slaves' pants and blanket. The slave burned with fever. Suddenly, he vomited blood.

Brutus yelled for help.

Holland and Wall trotted up. The slaves hurried over as best they could. Holland took one look and said, "Jesus Christ, he must have the dysentery. Any of you know how to doctor him?"

The new stockman said, "Mas'r, I knows a little."

"Get busy then!"

While the slave treated the sick man, Holland and Wall went to their tent to discuss their finances. When they added all the costs together for the lease, steam engine, tools, equipment, supplies for the camp, and slaves, the sum staggered them.

Holland said, "We're way over budget. We'll need more money to keep the camp runnin'."

Wall agreed, "For now, let's forget the turpentine business. We can't even afford the collecting cups much less a still. Let's concentrate on lumber. I have a contract already."

All night long, the skinny slave attempted to force the sick man to drink a concoction made by boiling plants that grew in the woods around the camp. For the most part, he comforted the patient with little hope to save him. Before dawn the man died.

Wall swore under his breath when he heard the news. "A dead nigger already and we ain't sawed the first log."

After daylight, a thunderstorm pummeled the camp with heavy rain and winds that came in tropical waves that threatened to rip away the tents and tarps. The slaves didn't accomplish anything that day except to dig a grave and bury the dead man. After two slaves finished mounding the dirt, everybody stood at the graveside in the bluster while Wall recited a Bible verse and then added, "He's gone to Jesus. Let's get out of the damn rain."

1861

He that is the author of a war lets loose the whole contagion of hell and opens a vein that bleeds a nation to death.

~Thomas Paine

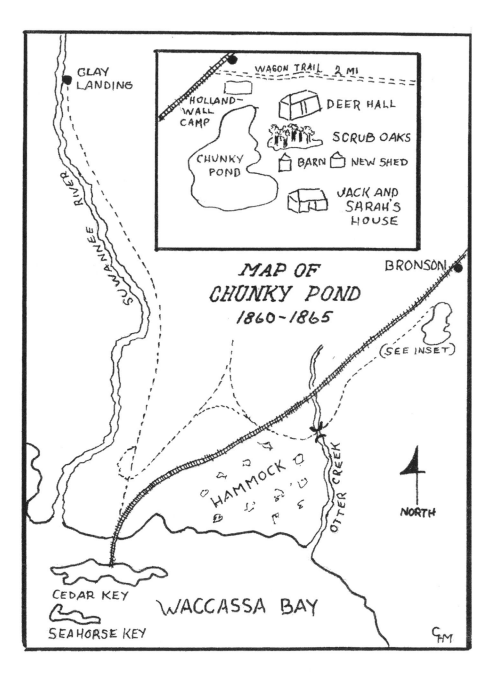

Inset labels:
CLAY LANDING
WAGON TRAIL 2 MI
HOLLAND-WALL CAMP
DEER HALL
SCRUB OAKS
CHUNKY POND
BARN
NEW SHED
JACK AND SARAH'S HOUSE

Main map labels:
SUWANNEE RIVER
MAP OF CHUNKY POND 1860~1865
BRONSON
(SEE INSET)
HAMMOCK
OTTER CREEK
NORTH
CEDAR KEY
WACCASSA BAY
SEAHORSE KEY

GᴴM

DEER HALL AT CHUNKY POND, FLORIDA

CHAPTER NINE

DEER HALL
Florida

On its east boundary, Holland and Wall's lumber camp abutted Loring Bell's homestead, Deer Hall. Although born and raised in New England, Bell came south after college in Boston to work as a buyer's agent for his family's cotton business. He stayed after falling in love and marrying Blanche Lucas, a scion of a wealthy South Carolina family.

In time, he came to believe the potential existed to make a fortune raising the commodity instead of trading it. He decided to develop a cotton plantation in the remote and wild Suwannee Valley in Florida where land was cheap and nearer to Blanche's family compared to the new cotton land farther west in Mississippi, Louisiana, and Texas. With his savings and a loan from his uncle, he built a home, slave quarters, and a barn. Using hired slave gangs, he cleared the timberland for cultivation. By 1860, when Wall leased the adjoining property, Bell already had turned his rough forest land into productive fields which provided a reasonable living and the promise of future prosperity.

Loring and Blanche loved Deer Hall and their independent lifestyle. The first crops had been profitable enough to pay down the debt to his uncle faster than agreed and Loring extended his fields. Everything looked promising except for the political uncertainty surrounding the secession issue which troubled the Bell family even deep in the Florida backwoods.

Shortly after sundown on a blustery evening in January 1861, Blanche ordered the children to bed, despite their pleadings to be allowed to sit with their father in front of the fire. She almost relented, but Loring sent them each to bed with a quick, good night kiss. Blanche tucked Little Buddy into bed while her big brother, Billy, climbed into the top bunk. After reciting their prayers, both soon fell asleep. Returning to the main room, Blanche sighed to see her frowning husband staring into the flames.

She knew why he was preoccupied. Now, for the first time in their marriage, she had to face the fact that she had an implacable disagreement with her husband about secession. They both kept themselves informed by subscribing to the *Floridian & Journal* newspaper published in Tallahassee and to *Harper's Weekly* magazine. Their differing viewpoints were reinforced by the two publications. Although published in New York City, *Harper's Weekly* took a moderate editorial position on slavery while opposing secession. The *Floridian* supported slavery as an unqualified property right and called for secession to maintain the status quo. Every week or so, when they picked up their mail in Bronson, both eagerly read every article about the controversy which they discussed in detail.

The slavery issue had enflamed the nation in 1857 when the Supreme Court in the *Dred Scott* decision ruled that slaves could not be taken from their owners without due process of law and that free states had to return fugitive slaves to their masters.

The decision incensed abolitionists who viewed slavery as evil and contrary to the Gospels. They called for authorities to ignore the Supreme Court's decision as mere *obiter dicta* and for a constitutional amendment to overturn it in any event.

The abolitionists infuriated slave owners. They believed the ultimate objective was to expropriate their wealth by outlawing slavery. That the abolitionists justified their position on religious grounds compounded their anger. In their view, the Bible condoned slavery in both the Old and New Testament.

The 1860 election brought the issue to a head when the political parties took irreconcilable positions. The abolitionist-controlled Republican Party adopted a platform plank that slavery should be outlawed in the territories. Slavery proponents viewed the Republican crusade as a cunning strategy to increase the number of free states so that, in time, a Constitutional Amendment abolishing slavery could be adopted.

The Democratic Party couldn't agree on how to best oppose the abolitionists. Southern Democrats argued that to secure slavery, slave states had the legal right to secede from the Union because they voluntarily came into the Union as sovereign states. Northern Democrats argued slavery could be maintained within the existing national framework and that, in any event, secession was illegal. They argued that ultimate sovereignty under the Constitution devolved to the Federal Government, not to individual states, and that states gave up absolute sovereignty when they joined the Union. They pointed out that the Constitution not only established federal law as the supreme law of the land, it also gave the federal government responsibility for defense, foreign affairs, and interstate commerce. Democratic President James Buchanan agreed.

As for the November, 1860 presidential election, Blanche had feared the Republican candidate, Abraham Lincoln. She viewed him as an abolitionist and a threat to the South because he said slavery was evil. She had sided with the Southern Democrats and supported its nominee for president, John Breckenridge, an unwavering slavery proponent.

Loring had taken a more nuanced view. He didn't believe Lincoln was an abolitionist or that he had any antagonism toward the South although he agreed with Blanche that radicals had too much influence in the Republican Party. However, he couldn't support Stephen Douglas, the Northern Democratic nominee, because Douglas had never clarified, to Loring's satisfaction, his position on expanding slavery in the territories. The candidate popular with Southerners, John Breckenridge, was too rigid for his taste, so he had settled on the Constitutional Union Party candidate, John Bell, who, by coincidence, had Loring's last name.

Blanche and Loring's opposing views were not unique. The entire country was polarized. The electorate trounced the Constitutional Union Party candidate but was so divided that Abraham Lincoln had won in the Electoral College with only forty percent of the popular vote.

Lincoln's election terrified Blanche. She feared that the abolitionist-controlled Republican Party would eventually outlaw slavery everywhere in the Union. In that event, she foresaw black people gaining voting rights and eventually taking power in those places where they outnumbered whites such as South Carolina and some counties in Middle Florida.

Loring pointed out that slave states controlled enough congressional votes to stop the abolitionist movement, and he believed that Lincoln would abide by his oath of office to enforce the laws permitting slavery.

Blanche's view reflected popular will in Florida. Less than a month after Lincoln's election on November 6, 1860, the state legislature passed an act calling for a Secession Convention. Loring was so committed to the Union that he ran for election as a delegate as a slave-owning Unionist, a stand that cost him friends. Like most Unionists, he lost in a landslide. Compounding the sting, Blanche pointed out that had women been able to vote and run for office, she could have won as the victors were mostly staunch, secessionist Democrats from the planter class known as Fire-Eaters.

Blanche acknowledged that the North might go to war to preserve the Union although the prospect didn't scare her in the least. "Everybody knows the South can defeat the North. We raise honorable fighting men; the North raises laborers."

Loring worried that an unconditional vote to secede almost certainly meant war. He reminded her that his relatives in Boston, who were not radical abolitionists by any means, believed that states had no right to secede and wanted the Union preserved even if they had to fight. He pointed out that the South faced stiff odds to win a war. "Let's assume that Southerners are better fighters. What can we fight with? The North has twice the population, more industry, more railroads and more food production. We have a vulnerable, agricultural, export economy based on one crop, cotton. Sure, our men will put up a battle royal, but in the end greater resources and numerical superiority will carry the day."

Blanche parried, "The North's economic superiority is irrelevant. England will help us."

"Why should England take sides in an American fight?"

"England needs cotton. Even if they don't ally with us, they have to do business. We can buy weapons from them."

Loring laughed in frustration, paused, and spoke with quiet intensity. "Bottom line, I don't want war. I don't want to fight my own kin. My Uncle Hollis, who loaned us the money to buy Deer Hall, serves in the Massachusetts militia."

"Our way of life is under attack, and I, for one, don't intend to be intimidated by the Yankees or your kin," she snapped. Each stared at the other, realizing a line had been crossed.

Loring cleared his throat and offered, "We haven't been to Tallahassee in ages and the Secession Convention convenes day after tomorrow. Let's go and see what happens."

Blanche nodded. "Yes, let's. Sarah can watch the children and Jake can tend the place for a few days."

Loring added another log on the fire. "It's cold tonight. I hope the orange trees Jake and I set out last spring don't get nipped. I'm glad we banked the trunks with dirt."

A wind gust puffed down the chimney that made the embers in the fireplace glow redder. Blanche pulled the quilt that she had hand crocheted tighter around her legs. Loring said, "I'll ride the mule, so you can ride my mare. On the way I want to stop by our new neighbors for a chat. Jake says he saw a couple of blacks around our chicken pen, but they ran off before he could collar them. We didn't have that problem till our new neighbors brought their slaves down. Besides that, I need to buy some lumber from them and see if they'll rent hands to help build a new storehouse."

The next morning at dawn, Loring and Jake walked across a frost-blanketed pasture to check the young orange trees. When they reached them, Loring said, "I don't think the temperature dropped enough to do much damage."

"Me neither. Killin' cold doesn't come with so much frost. The water in de trough only had a sliver of ice."

Jake pulled a leaf from a young tree and bent it in two. "Look here, Mas'r. De leaves ain't frozen; some goin' curl up, turn brown and fall off, but the twigs ain't hurt."

"We were lucky. When you saw those blacks the other day, Jake, did you see them stealing chickens?"

"No, but dey must be takin' 'em 'cause we're still losin' fowl. No varmints have been in de pen, and we've shot all de chicken hawks 'round here."

"That's my thinking too. Listen, can you look after the place for a few days? Blanche and I want to go to Tallahassee."

"Dat ain't no problem."

Chapter Ten

Chunky Pond Camp
Florida

After checking the cold-damaged citrus trees, Jake saddled his master's pride chestnut mare, Ginger, for Blanche to ride and then saddled Mike, a seventeen hands tall, gray mule for Loring because the ornery animal was unpredictable. For days he'd be gentle and easy to handle and then for no apparent reason, he'd kick, bite, or try to crush someone against a fence.

The mule was so dangerous that only Loring or Jake dared handle him. Loring knew he ought to sell the hinny, but he kept him because he could outwork any two horses and could pull a plow for as long as anyone could walk behind him. Also, he only needed a little corn in the evening along with good pasture overnight to be ready for work the next morning.

Ginger was spirited and strong, but gentle. She responded to the slightest nudge as if she knew her rider's intention. She lived to please, and Loring had no doubt he could ride her until she dropped if the need arose.

Blanche and Loring reached the lumber camp before the frost glistening on the grass evaporated. As they rode up, a dog ran toward them barking until a cook warming himself by the fire hushed the animal and yelled, "Company."

Holland and Wall popped out from one of the tents. Holland said, "Welcome, neighbors. It's about time you came over for a visit. We ain't seen you since I first arrived. How 'bout some coffee?"

"Thank you kindly, but we have to hurry. We're on the way to Bronson to catch the cars to Tallahassee for the Secession Convention. Thought we'd stop by on the way to say hello and ask about buying lumber and renting two slaves."

Holland replied, "We might be able to sell you lumber depending on how things go. We have a contract to supply a schooner load of heart pine boards and, quite frankly, we're pushed. One slave has died, and several more are sickly, so progress is slow. Right now, we need all our hands. By the end of the month we might be able to work somethin' out. We'd rather do business with a neighbor than Yankee agents anyhow, but we have to fulfill our contract."

"Fair enough. We'll get together at the end of the month. Oh, by the way. Some blacks were over to my place and some chickens went missing."

Wall stepped forward. "You accusin' my boys?"

"No, but we saw some blacks around the chicken pen. We're missing a few hens. I thought you'd want to know."

"Our moaks have orders not to leave our land. If I catch one off the place, I'll whup him good. It weren't none of ours."

The cook gawked at Wall because some days before, he had fried several pullets which the entire camp had enjoyed. Wall noticed the cook's expression and snapped at him, "What you lookin' at, boy? Don't be pokin' your nose where it don't belong."

Wall lowered his voice and said to Loring, "You catch any of our niggers 'round your place, let me know. I'll take care of it."

"I'm sure you will. Well then, we're off to Tallahassee."

As Loring and Blanche turned to leave, Holland said, "Hey, stop back by on the way home and let us know what happened at the Convention. I hope we declare independence. The South needs a second American Revolution."

Loring responded, "I'm hoping the convention will vote for a contingent secession so that Florida can stay in the Union, with our rights guaranteed."

Wall said, "You sound like a Yankee sympathizer. We ought to run our own affairs."

Loring's face reddened. "Are you questioning my loyalty?"

"No offense intended, but you're a Northerner, ain't ya?"

"I'll let you know what happens in Tallahassee. We have to head out or we'll miss the cars."

Loring nudged Mike in the flank. The mule jerked his head sideways, nipped at his boot and reared. Loring smacked him between the ears with his fist. Then, like nothing had happened, Mike turned and followed after Ginger.

"Better watch that mule. He's shifty," Wall said.

CHAPTER ELEVEN

TALLAHASSEE
Florida

After stabling Ginger and Mike in Bronson, the Bells caught the cars but didn't arrive in Tallahassee until late afternoon because, as usual, the trains ran late. At Baldwin, where they had to transfer, they had waited more than two hours for the wood-burner from Jacksonville.

When they arrived in Tallahassee near dark, people jammed the capitol. Crowds packed the foyer and the hallways. The balconies overlooking the house chamber were standing room only. Any chance to squeeze into them looked unlikely. They almost gave up until Loring saw a gap. They pressed in against the wall where they could hear an animated speaker even if they couldn't see him.

"The United States Constitution guarantees the right of property in slaves. In Florida, as in the entire South, slavery is the underpinning of our prosperity and culture. The uncompromising, fanatical abolitionists seek to terminate every right arising from property in slaves. Florida, as a member of a Union controlled by a party of the fanatics, is doomed. We are forced to secede from that Union in order to secure the safety, security and rights of our people.

"Plain and simple, the Yankees and abolitionists seek to take our property and destroy our way of life. We will never apologize for being slave owners. The Bible teaches us that God approves of slavery. Abolition perverts God's will. The ancient Hebrews owned slaves and Jesus never said that slavery was a sin. As the Bible tells us, Noah cursed Canaan. 'Cursed be Canaan: a servant of servants shall he be unto his brethren.' Shall we question God's infallible word? No, we shall not question our Heavenly Father. Abolitionists can't alter the Lord's plan anymore than they can make the sun rise in the West."

Like a preacher, the speaker exhorted the crowd with animated gesticulations. "Southern society is built upon Divine Law. Do our Northern enemies forget that we bring the blessings of Christianity to our slaves? Without us, they'd still be heathens casting bones and practicing voodoo witchcraft. How many plantation owners have sacrificed their personal treasure to build churches and provide preachers for their slaves?

"Science confirms Nigras are an inferior race. Medical studies show their pulmonary and nervous systems are different from whites, and anybody can see darkies are more like monkeys than Caucasians. They can't learn anything except the most fundamental, simple things and then only by patient repetition. We have a duty to take care of our slaves. What will become of them if we don't?

"If our slaves are free, they'll be exploited like wage labor in the North. Our slaves are better off working in the open air on our plantations than the workers toiling in dank Northern mills. Common sense mandates that we take the best care of our chattel. In the South, you'll never find hungry, homeless people living in slum streets like you see in the Yankee cities.

"We provide our slaves with food, housing, medical care and life time employment. Wage earners don't have those benefits. If a laborer is injured, he's on his own, but we don't cast aside our property.

"Freeing the slaves will lead to a failed society. All great civilizations like the Greeks' and the Romans' had slaves. In the North, production is dependent on wage labor which leads to socialism or unionism. Civilization can't survive under their influence. Inequality has to be built into the framework of any great society, and we choose slavery. If you tear that away, our civilization will collapse. Southern culture and gentility will degenerate to Godless collectivism if we don't stand up for our rights and God's law. Free the slaves? We'll end up with an anarchical failed society. I say no; a plain and simple N-O.

"Because of slavery our Southern culture flourishes. It is characterized by generosity, virtue, duty, and courage. Should the vulgar Yankees persist with their imperious project to force the South into submission, they will learn the depth of our resolve. We will not be intimidated by Northern threats! We shall stand firm! We shall fight to defend our way of life! The time has come to stand up for our independence and our right to secede from the Union. We entered the Union voluntarily. We can leave voluntarily. I stand before this body without reservation in full support of the Secession Ordinance. I beseech the patriotic, loyal Floridians duly elected to this convention to do likewise. God bless Florida."

Applause erupted as everybody stood up. Loring and few others didn't clap. He couldn't fathom the enthusiasm for a course of action with the potential for devastating results based on such flimsy arguments. As a Christian, Loring felt the Biblical points mentioned by the speaker deserved consideration, but he wondered why the argument he considered central for maintaining slavery was not mentioned - that slave labor generated the export earnings and capital for the entire country.

Blanche clapped in unison with the crowd. The chairman half-heartedly banged his gavel for order. The crowd paid no attention to him. A chant started: "Secede! Secede! Secede!" After several minutes, the chairman banged his gavel with authority to quiet the assembly in order to complete the business of the day. "Order! Order!" he yelled.

"Order in the chamber!" The people slowly complied as the chairman kept banging the gavel.

When the crowd hushed, he continued, "Without objection, I call for a vote on the issue before the convention. Mr. Clerk, please read the Ordinance as passed from committee."

The clerk stepped to the well of the house and read:

> We, the people of the State of Florida, in convention assembled, do solemnly ordain, publish, and declare, that the State of Florida hereby withdraws herself from the confederacy of States existing under the name of the United States: and that all political connection between her and the Government of said States ought to be, and the same is hereby, totally annulled, and said Union of States dissolved: and the State of Florida is hereby declared a sovereign and independent nation; and that all ordinances heretofore adopted, in so far as they create or recognize said Union, are rescinded; and all laws or parts of laws in force in this state, in so far as they recognize or assent to said Union, be, and they are hereby, repealed.

The chairman said, "The Ordinance is before the Convention. The Ordinance has been moved, seconded and debated. Mr. Clerk, please call the roll."

The clerk commenced in a sonorous voice. With every aye vote, the delegates and audience clapped and cheered forcing the chairman to bang his gavel for order again and again. The roll call continued with only aye votes until it reached a delegate from Jacksonville. He voted nay in a subdued voice. The audience booed and hissed. One man yelled "Traitor." The chairman banged his gavel.

When the clerk finished the vote, the chairman said, "Please publish the votes on The Florida Ordinance of Secession."

"Mr. Chairman, I'm pleased to announce…." A celebration started.

People jumped up and down, hugged, and slapped each other on the back. Some shouted, "We're free! We're free!" The clerk yelled above the din, "The vote is 62 ayes.

The crowd's racket nearly drowned out "7 nays." The lopsided vote stunned Loring. The huge margin meant that only a few delegates from the Jacksonville and the Pensacola area had summoned the fortitude to vote against the state's rich planters. Although he had expected the ordinance to pass, he had hoped for a close vote. The result made him sorrowful. He was not alone. Nearby, he recognized General Call, who had commanded Florida's militia in the Second Seminole War; tears ran down the old warrior's cheeks.

Pandemonium built and spilled from the building to merge with the crowd gathered around the capitol. In front, an artillery unit rammed a blank charge into a Napoleon field piece. The captain yelled, "Fire." The cannon boomed as fireworks lit the evening sky and men discharged pistols into the air. A chant started: "Independence! Independence! God bless Florida."

The crowd swept up the Bells. Blanche joined the chant. Loring whooped several times, but he felt ill at ease and heartsick. His wife smiled at him and drew him close for a kiss. Now that Florida was free of the Union, she felt flush and could foresee unlimited prospects for her family. She hadn't felt happier since her wedding day.

Bits of burnt paper and ash from the fireworks floated on the breeze. The air smelled of black powder and smoke from heart pine torches. A band played patriotic music on the capitol steps while boys marched like soldiers with sticks on their shoulders. Pretty girls kissed men in uniform and invited them to dinners and parties. Flasks emptied. No Fourth of July celebration had ever been as jubilant as Florida's Independence Day from the United States.

FLORIDA SECESSION FLAG. FLORIDA WAS THE THIRD STATE TO SECEDE.

(Courtesy Florida State Archives)

CHAPTER TWELVE

DEER HALL
Florida

The day after Blanche and Loring left for Tallahassee, Jake got up as usual before sunrise. After a breakfast of bacon and eggs and a left over biscuit from supper the night before, he gathered his tools from the barn to head for the new field. Shortly after sunrise, he had already grubbed long enough with a heavy hoe to work up a sweat. As the day brightened, he stopped to rest and look over the ten acre field that Loring hoped to have ready to plant in cotton by early March.

Loring wanted to switch to short staple cotton because long staple had not thrived at Deer Hall for some unknown reason. Apparently, his soil lacked some nutrient or was too wet. The problem baffled him because good cotton land stretched only a few miles north and east from Chunky Pond, but Loring could never make a bumper crop. Although long staple ginned easier, he intended to experiment with short staple to determine if he could grow a bigger yield. A new gin at Gainesville that could process it made the diversification feasible.

Jake wanted the Bells to be successful. After all, Sarah had grown up with Blanche in South Carolina and without Loring's help he could have never married Sarah. The Bells had brought Jake's entire family to Florida with them. Both families had worked together to build Deer Hall Plantation from scratch, so Jake felt committed to the place too.

Yet, he had mixed feelings about expanding cotton production. The status quo suited him. He worried that if the Bells earned more, they'd likely buy additional slaves to expand the crops which he doubted would benefit him.

Jake and Loring sometimes talked about the project while working side by side. Loring pointed out that Jake wouldn't have to work so hard if they had more slaves because he'd make Jake the overseer. Jake didn't argue, but he didn't care to take on that responsibility.

Jake mulled over his circumstances as he chopped a gnarly palmetto root. *I was scairt when Mas'r Loring won me 'cause he could have been de whippin' type. Un-uh, he never threatened to beat us. And we ain't on rations like most darkies. Here we live in a fine house with glass windows dat's dry and warm with mosquito bars for our beds just like the Bells. I shows Mas'r Loring how to do things and he listens too. His daddy was a factor so he knows de cotton business, but Mas'r Loring didn't know nothin' 'bout plantin' till I showed him. We hunts together and he lets me use a shotgun. It ain't goin' be no better with more slaves 'round here.*

Wrapped up in his thoughts, Jake dragged slash into piles with the intention to burn it late in the day when the breeze died down. Near noon Sarah, his wife, walked to the field with fresh biscuits and ribs. Four children, black and white, followed along with her playing tag. The dogs jumped a rabbit and the youngsters ran after them yelling and laughing.

The rabbit dodged back and forth over the field as the hounds closed the gap. Just before they caught him, the cottontail reached the bushes along the field's edge. He scurried under them and down a gopher hole. Sarah warned, "You chil'luns git back from der. Likely as not, a big rattler's in dem palmettos."

As the children ran back across the field toward the barn, Sarah said, "What you thinkin' 'bout, Honey?"

"Mas'r Loring's plans for de place and what it'll mean for us."

"Don't worry. Missis Blanche says we goin' be looked after no matter what."

The hounds scratched at the entrance to the gopher hole until they noticed Jake pull a rib from under a cloth. They lost interest in the hunt to watch him eat. As soon as he gnawed the meat off the bone, he tossed it toward the dogs. They growled and nipped at one another until one ran off with it.

Jake smiled at Sarah. "Mighty good ribs. I better git back to gatherin' up dis slash."

The afternoon sun and hard work warmed Jake so much that he stripped down to his undershirt. Still he sweated. As the sun dipped behind the trees bordering the field, the air chilled and the wind died as he had expected. After gathering dried palmetto fronds and chopping sap-filled lighter wood from a pine stump, he forced the kindling under a slash pile and held a flame to the dry fronds. They flashed and burned hot, igniting the wood. In no time, fire enveloped the stacked brush.

He repeated the process until all the piles were aflame and then threw limbs on them and poked up the fires. Thick smoke settled over the field as he admired his work. "Mas'r Loring goin' be happy. Dis field's ready for stump pullin' and plowin', but Ol' Mike ain't goin' like it."

Walking back toward his house he felt tired but pleased. The hounds coursed back and forth about a hundred yards ahead. Suddenly, they lit out toward the barn, barking in an agitated, protective manner that made Jake suspect a varmint was raiding the chicken pen.

He yelled for Sarah to bring him his shotgun and ran after the hounds. When he saw human footprints in the sand, Jake stopped short. He knew he had to deal with more than a critter.

As Sarah caught up to him and handed him his weapon, he said, "I wish Mas'r Loring was here. He left me to look after de place and now somebody is stealin' our chickens."

He ran faster. The dogs' bark changed pitch as they gained on the thieves. Soon, he heard the hounds snarling and he knew they'd treed. Before long, he found the hounds jumping against a big live oak. Six feet up the tree, two black men stood on a limb.

Jake yelled, "Ranger, Sammie, git back! Hey. What you boys doin' round here thievin' chickens?"

"We ain't stole nothin'."

"What you mean? I saw your footprints inside de pen."

"What you doin' with dat shotgun? Crackers goin' stretch your neck if dey catch you wid dat."

"Dat's my worry. Where you from?"

"De lumber camp down the trail over yonder."

Ranger trotted up with a hen in his mouth and dropped it at Jake's feet. Without taking his eyes off the men in the tree, he stooped down. He picked up the dead bird with his left hand while covering the men with his shotgun in his right. Then, holding the chicken by the feet, he shook it toward the men. "You ain't stealin' huh? You reckon dis here one fell from a tree? How many more did you throw in de bushes?"

Caught red-handed, the men changed their tune. "We don't get much meat at de camp. We didn't figure we was stealin' from a nigga."

"What's de difference? You're still stealin'. I ought to walk you up to Mas'r right now for a good whippin'."

"Please don't do dat. We won't come round here no more."

"If you promise never to return, I'll let you go."

"We promise. We're comin' down. Don't sic de hounds on us."

"Ranger, Sammie, stay back."

With their eyes on the dogs, both men climbed down from the tree limb and backed away.

"Now ya'll get out of here. If I catch you again, I'm takin' you straight to Mas'r Lorin'."

The sun had set and the moon hadn't yet risen as Loring and Blanche rode their mounts with tight reins down the lane toward home on their return from Tallahassee. Eager to reach the barn, both steeds wanted to run, but the darkness made the dirt track too hazardous to let them. Near the house, the hounds heard the animals and raced toward them barking until Loring whistled.

Hearing the shrill signal, everybody poured from both houses. As soon as Loring and Blanche dismounted, Billy and Little Buddy gave their mother a quick hug then all four children crowded around Loring, yelling and laughing in anticipation of the treats that he always brought back to them after trips to town. The girls jumped up and down, tugging at his shirttail. The older boys stood close by waiting. "You children calm down. Why are you hangin' on me? Doggone it, we were so busy, I plum forgot to buy you anything."

"No, Daddy, I know you didn't forget. What's that in your pocket?" Little Buddy said giggling.

"Mas'r Lorin', I sees somethin'. What is it?" chimed in Annie, Jake's little girl.

"Were you children good while we were in Tallahassee?"

"Yes, yes," the girls yelled.

"Did you mind Auntie Sarah?"

"Yes, yes."

"OK, since you behaved, hold out your hands and close your eyes. No, you're not getting anything until Little Buddy stops peeking."

Annie jabbed her friend with an elbow who grimaced to prove her eyes were shut tight.

"That's better. Here you are." Loring placed a candy nugget in each child's palm. Sarah said, "Mas'r, you spoilin' de chil'uns."

Loring untied a large box lashed behind his saddle and handed it to Blanche who took it and walked inside.

Sarah said, "What's dat, Missis Blanche?"

"I've wanted better light for the longest time and finally convinced Loring to buy kerosene lamps."

After helping unwrap the paper from around the cut-glass reservoirs with brass wick holders, Sarah exclaimed, "Dey sure is pretty,"

"They burn with a much better light than candles too."

Loring walked inside with a gallon can and a small tin funnel. "Let's see what you think when I get it lit."

Loring unscrewed the wick holder from the reservoir, filled it with kerosene and twisted the brass in place. After he lit the lamp, he slid the globe into its brackets. The flame burned brightly, but emitted black smoke that smudged the glass. "Can't have that," Loring said as he rolled the wick down with a tiny wheel until the flame burned clean.

"Look," said Loring as he admired the yellow glare. "You can read from this light."

"De lamps are beautiful, Mas'r Loring."

"I'm glad you like them, Sarah, because one is for you and Jake. You two work hard on this place and deserve to have light too. Just be careful with it. The man who sold them said that the kerosene could catch fire and explode if you let the flame burn down the wick."

"Thank you, Mas'r. We'll be careful."

As soon as Jake unsaddled the stock and turned them out to pasture, he walked to the house where Sarah showed off the new lamp. Loring instructed him how to use it then asked, "How'd it go while we were in Tallahassee, Jake?"

"Pretty good. I burned de slash in de new field so all we have to do is pull stumps and plow. We had a little excitement. Ranger and Sammie treed two boys from de lumber camp who I caught stealin' chickens. I warned dem never to come back to Deer Hall."

"Are you sure they were stealing?"

Jake related how Ranger brought up the dead hen.

Loring laughed. "Bet they changed their tune when you showed them the evidence."

"Yes, sir, but dey scared me too. Dey told me I could be hung for havin' a shotgun."

"Don't pay those thieves any mind, Jake. I won't let anybody bother you here at Deer Hall."

"Yes, sir, Mas'r. What was decided in Tallahassee?"

"The convention voted for secession. Now, Florida's an independent nation."

"Does dat mean war?" Sarah asked.

"It's hard to say, but I suspect President Lincoln won't let us go without a fight."

Blanche said, "Don't ya'll worry. He'll bluster, but once we form a Confederation with the other states that seceded, he'll not invade the South."

"Honey, I certainly admire your bravado and pray you're right. Nevertheless, the governor is worried enough to mobilize the militia and I intend to sign up or people will think I'm a Yankee sympathizer."

"We can't make it without you here, Mas'r,"

"Jake, you'll have to help run the place if I have to go off to the army."

Jake furrowed his brow. "I suppose we can git by if you ain't gone long."

CHAPTER THIRTEEN

CHARLESTON
South Carolina

Cooped up in the tiny room for weeks on end, Molly's life settled into a monotonous routine. Every day, she yearned for more company and conversation than the old man could provide. Her skin turned sallow and her body felt stiff. Boredom made her feel edgy and compounded her fear.

The old man did everything he could to help her occupy the time. When he learned she could read a bit, he brought home the book, *Narrative of the Life of Frederick Douglas* and an occasional newspaper.

She endeavored to remain stoic, but when leaves fell from the trees as the days shortened, her resolve faltered. Molly's expectation that the old man could arrange her escape from Charleston waned with each passing day.

In late December, she learned from the old man that South Carolina had seceded from the Union. She didn't understand all the ramifications except that escape would be more difficult because slave patrols had become more frequent and aggressive. After Christmas, the Union troops quartered near Charleston at Fort Moultrie abandoned their post and moved to Fort Sumter in Charleston Harbor. Militia occupied the town and Rebel soldiers patrolled the streets.

Her rescuer reassured her as best he could and promised everyday that sooner or later he'd find a way for her to escape, but nothing in the news gave her hope. He reported in early January that southern states were seizing Federal military installations all across the South. Georgia secured Fort Pulaski. Alabama occupied a federal arsenal. Florida appropriated the Apalachicola arsenal and Fort Marion at St. Augustine. War loomed. On January 9, 1861, Mississippi seceded followed the next day by Florida, then Georgia and three other southern states. By March 1861, seven states had seceded and organized themselves into the provisional Confederate States of America.

Winter dragged by. In early April, Molly had lost hope until her protector presented her with an improbable plan. "I found an Englishman dat makes loans to planters. He might help ya."

Molly asked, "An Englishman?"

"All de people I worked with before are either too scar't to help or are bein' watched. Believe me, I've tried. White folks are terrified we'll rebel. De police hound us more than ever. It's hard to slip around anymore. De reward on your head compounds de danger. Leaflets with your picture are still tacked up all over town. All de ships are searched before dey clear port. Just de other day, de militia caught two runaways who had stowed away on a schooner. Captains won't help us now. I had to find someone new."

"How can de Englishman help?"

"He's goin' to Florida and he'll take you with him."

"Florida? Are you crazy? We got to go north fer freedom."

The old timer looked at Molly with tired eyes. "Shush, chile, somebody goin' hear you. Please, listen to de plan. You ain't got to go if you don't want to."

"Sorry."

"Goin' to Florida has advantages. People ain't likely to suspect you're a runaway if you're headin' south. Abolitionists who live along de way will help. If de Englishman can get you to a port on de Gulf, you can hide till you can catch a ship to Cuba or de Bahamas. From there, you can go to Boston or New York."

"Sounds like a lot of "ifs.""

"Honey chile, I know dat. I wasn't goin' tell you 'bout it till I knew for certain de factor would help. I'm givin' you hope, dat's all."

"Uncle," Molly had started to call the old man uncle many weeks before, "I'm glad you told me. We don't have any other plan. I can't stand hidin' much longer. If de Englishman will help me, I'll go."

The next morning, Molly awoke to a sunlight-dappled room after her protector had departed. For the first time in many days she felt optimistic. It pained her too much to consider that the Englishman might be unwilling to help.

The day crept by. All she cared to do was lie on her back watching the light and shadows move slowly across the room as she focused on escape and the hoped for rescue. Throughout the day, she heard wails from the barracoon, but the screams barely registered in her consciousness. She read nothing all day.

By nightfall, when her rescuer should have returned, she fretted more than ever. She heard the slaves scrambling for food in the barracoon and a woman screaming more than usual, which scared her. Sweat dampened her body. Her mind raced. Perhaps the police captured the old timer when he tried to contact the Englishman. Perhaps a patrol was on the way to her hideout. She imagined worse and worse scenarios as she shivered in terror. Perhaps the Englishman decided not to help or to turn her in for the reward. The darkness became suffocating. A ruckus from the barracoon became unbearable. She thought she heard a patrol stopping on the street by the stairs. She bolted upright and froze.

She didn't move until she recognized the footsteps coming up the stairs. As she heard the old timer's worn key turn in the rusty padlock, she relaxed and began to cry.

Once inside, after he struck a match to light a candle, he noticed Molly's tears. "What's the matter, honey chile? Shush, everything's OK."

"Uncle, you're so late. I was scared. I thought a patrol caught you. A woman in the barracoon has been screamin' like she's being tortured."

"I couldn't help bein' late. Dat woman had a baby so de boss sent me for de doctor. I had to wait for him at his office till near dark. When we started back over here, an army patrol stopped us. Sergeant asked to see my papers which I didn't have wid me. He got nasty and threatened to arrest us both. De doctor got mad and tell him he needed to hurry 'cause he had to deliver a baby, but de soldier said he had to talk to his lieutenant. When de officer came, he finally let us go. After dat, I had to help de doctor. I'm sorry, chile."

"What about the Englishman?"

"I shouldn't have told ya nothin'. My partner never saw him. Maybe he left Charleston already."

Molly sobbed. The old timer hugged her. "Shh, shh, they goin' hear us in de barracoon," the old man cooed. "I'm sorry I got your hopes up. I was wrong to do dat without havin' a plan."

He continued in a whisper, "Honey chile, we ain't givin' up. Dis ole nigger is goin' slip you away from Charleston. Be brave. Don't you do nothin' foolish. If we ain't figured some way to slip you out in a few weeks, we'll go together. I'm fed up here. It's bad enough to be harassed by police all de time, but now I got to worry 'bout de army too. Some folks say Charleston goin' be attacked by Yankees 'for long anyhow."

"Uncle, you are so good to me. I'll do my best, but I can't stand being cooped up much longer."

The next day passed by more easily because Molly dozed all day which assuaged her fear. To her relief, the old man got home before dark, so she never slipped into the downward spiral like the day before.

Her protector beamed when he came into the room. "Praise de Lord, chile. Deliverance is at hand. My friend found de Englishman. He's leavin' Charleston in de mornin' and he'll take you."

Molly threw her arms around his neck.

"Uncle, I love you. Thank you, thank you. Come with me. We'll both leave together."

"No, it's better if I don't. It's riskier for two people. Besides, our man's only expectin' one person. You go, honey chile. I'll slip away soon enough."

Molly lifted the old man off the floor.

"Settle down now, we need to discuss de plan. But 'fore we talk about it; I've got a surprise."

The old man unwrapped newspaper from around a small bundle that held two prime pork chops. No supper ever tasted better.

The plan hinged on slipping into a carriage before sunrise and then the Englishman driving through town at dawn when curfew lifted. The riskiest part was sneaking through the streets in the dark while avoiding checkpoints and roving patrols, but from all the detail in his descriptions, Molly could tell that her protector knew all the back alleys and shortcuts. By the time he finished explaining everything, the pork chops were gnawed to the bone.

When she finally went to bed, Molly couldn't sleep. Sometime before dawn she dozed off, but couldn't have slept long when she felt the old man shaking her foot. She sat up with a start, and almost cried out. He covered her mouth with his palm and reminded her in a whisper to be quiet. After splashing water on her face, she grabbed a small bundle of clothes and huddled behind her protector while he cracked the door ajar. He listened for anything unusual for a long time, then opened the door wider and scanned the streets. He ushered her out and closed the door behind him without locking it.

Standing on the stair landing, Molly felt cool night air against her face and she saw a thin crescent moon. She felt energized. Although they tiptoed down the stairway, their footsteps sounded like drumbeats to her. Once on the street, the old man took her hand and hustled her into the deep shadows. Alert to any movement or unusual noise, he hurried through the dark alleys. A dog barked near the harbor.

They circled the checkpoints. At corners, the old guide peeked around to check for patrols before proceeding. After several blocks, they squeezed along buildings to a carriage parked just beyond a livery entrance as the sky brightened in the east. He helped Molly climb into it and told her to crouch down between two crates. After he spread a blanket over her and the boxes, she heard him walk away across the cobblestone street. The only light she could see was a dim glimmer between the carriage floorboards.

In a minute, she felt jostling as someone climbed up to the front seat. "Git up." The carriage lurched forward and swayed around a corner. The blanket muffled the sound, but from a distance she heard shouts, "Halt! Who goes there?" "Stop or I'll shoot!" followed by several shots in quick succession.

The carriage proceeded on.

CHAPTER FOURTEEN

Georgia

The Englishman trotted the carriage through Charleston just fast enough not to draw attention. He headed west toward Augusta instead of the shortest route via Savanna where slave catchers were more likely to be on the lookout. He planned to leave the carriage in Augusta where he could catch the cars to Atlanta. From there, he could make his way south by rail and carriage to Tallahassee. He breathed easier as he reached Charleston's outskirts where he pushed the horses faster.

To his chagrin, he didn't have reliable intelligence about checkpoints between Charleston and Augusta and he worried about army patrols. He told Molly to stay under the blanket until he could find a safe resting place.

"Keep going. I'm used to tight quarters."

An hour outside town, they arrived at a long, wooded straightaway without traffic, buildings or people. The tree canopy shaded the road that only allowed dim light to filter through the spring growth. He pulled the carriage into an open space beside the road where he stopped. He set the brake, tied the reins and jumped to the ground.

"You can get out now. Nobody will see us here."

"Thank you. Thank you for helpin' me," Molly said as she pushed the blanket aside. The Englishman took her hand. As he helped her climb down from the carriage, he saw his charge for the first time. Although disheveled and dressed in messenger's clothes, the tall, young woman looked strikingly handsome with smooth skin, fine features, and intelligent eyes. He had not anticipated helping such a beauty and thought, *Anybody who's ever seen her won't forget her.*

"Where are we headed?"

"To Augusta, from there Atlanta then to Florida's West Coast. We haven't been properly introduced. I'm Charles Waldock on business from England. You can call me Chad. I'm told you're Molly."

"Pleased to meet you, Mr. Waldock."

Chad could hardly take his eyes off her. She noticed his gaze and stepped back. The thought crossed her mind that perhaps she had been betrayed and delivered to yet another white devil.

"Don't be afraid. I didn't expect to be helping such a beautiful, young woman, that's all."

She relaxed a bit. "I'm sorry. I don't know who I can trust."

"We have to trust one another. We're both in the same leaky boat. You'll be traveling as my slave. Still, it'll be difficult not to draw attention, but the plebeians can snigger all they want if they leave us alone."

"Mr. Waldock, what does plebeian and snigger mean?"

He chuckled and said, "Plebeians, I guess you could say - white trash. You know about them, I'm sure."

"Yes, sir, I sure 'nuff do."

"Snigger means to make fun, to laugh at somebody behind their back."

"Mr. Waldock, you have to talk to me plain. I ain't got much learnin'."

Chad opened a basket loaded with hard-boiled eggs, bread and oranges and then handed Molly a canteen filled with water. As they ate, he sketched out the trip to Augusta to catch the cars.

At first, she said very little although after a while she relaxed enough to talk about her life in Charleston. With fitful words she related how her master ordered her sold. Without interruption, she described the dreadful barracoon and auction. When she stopped talking, Chad sensed she had more to say. "Go ahead; you can tell me everything, you're safe with me." With quavering lips, she blurted out that she had shot Silas West.

The information startled him. Now, he realized that he was risking his life. As an Englishman he could expect leniency and perhaps only a short jail time for helping an escaped slave. Aiding a slave who shot her owner raised the stakes. If captured by ruffians, he could be hung or tarred and feathered before the authorities could react if they even bothered.

Approaching hoof beats, already too close for Molly to hide, startled the travelers. Chad muttered under his breath, "Stand still and don't say a thing."

A rider in a gray uniform reined his horse beside the carriage. As his gaze settled on Molly he said, "Good morning, sir. There's a cavalry company behind me. Stay parked here till we pass."

"Yes, sir, of course. You must be on the way to Charleston to throw the Yankees out of Fort Sumter."

"You bet. Blue Bellies are threatening to re-supply. We intend to prevent that."

"I'm sure we'll whip them in short order."

"Thank you, sir. The rear guard will give you the all clear."

As the rider wheeled his horse, Chad said, "Get in the carriage and slide under the blanket. We have to be more careful. That rider could have been with a slave patrol or could have recognized you."

Chad climbed up on the front seat and held the reins as the company guidon arrived. He sat tall in the saddle clutching a lance with a red pennant fluttering below the blade. Behind him, riders dressed in gray uniforms trimmed in gold trotted by in a column of twos. Each one wore a saber and a red-plumed Stetson hat with a blue cockade on the crown. Chad counted forty pair and thought, *Some planter spent a pretty penny outfitting this dandy bunch.*

Not far behind the last pair, the rear guard rode up. As he passed the carriage, he waved and yelled, "You may proceed, sir."

Chad gave a half salute and jiggled the reins to rouse the horses.

His plan called for rest stops along the Underground Railroad where associates could provide safe haven. Most were at isolated farms except for one house only a block from the courthouse square in a small, Georgia farm town where Chad drove straight into the carriage house.

Molly found it hard to believe that in the heart of the South, white people were helping her escape. For the first time in her life, she realized that not all white Southerners supported slavery and some were willing to risk their lives opposing it.

She suspected her rescuer had helped other slaves because he knew where to stop and who to trust. At a break to water the horses on the third day from Charleston, she asked, "Mr. Waldock, how do you know where to stop? Have you helped other runaways?"

"It's best that you don't know details, but I'll tell you this much. Did you see that beautiful quilt hanging out to air when we stopped in town?"

"Yes, I saw one hanging on the clothes line."

"If that signal hadn't been there, I'd have kept moving."

"Why are white people helping me?"

"Some people believe with all their hearts that slavery is evil. They hate it so much that they're willing to help although it's against the law and dangerous. If they get caught, they'll be jailed if they're lucky – worse if they aren't."

"I know it's dangerous for dem. I heard my master say many times dat if he ever caught a nigger lover, he'd dress his hide worse than a black man."

"Molly, you know as well as anybody that slave owners can be mean and violent. Always stay on guard and never say anything about the people who help you."

"Don't worry. De nastiest devil couldn't beat nothin' outa me."

Seeing the resolve in her eyes, Chad didn't doubt her in the least. He turned away to catch his breath with the realization that he was attracted to the beautiful, strong-willed woman.

Except in the towns or villages, they met few people on the roads the farther they traveled from Charleston. Mostly, they rode through thick forests interspersed by cleared acreage around mansions flanked by outbuildings and slave quarters. As the carriage rolled by the fields, they watched slaves plow the reddish soil with mules while other black men, women and children followed behind them leveling the furrows with heavy hoes and rakes.

At the last stop before Augusta, the lady of the house suggested Molly throw away her messenger's outfit. She took Molly to a back bedroom, where she pulled several dresses from a chest of drawers. She picked out an old one that was too large for Molly with a yoke neck, long sleeves and loose waist. Scruffy brogans and a bonnet topped off the disguise.

When Molly returned to the front room dressed in the outfit, she spun around for everybody to see. Chad laughed at the costume. He already missed the tight fitting messenger's getup, but acknowledged that the ill-fitting disguise made her look like a servant for a cheap owner.

The closer they came to Augusta, the more Chad fretted about catching the cars without being noticed. After cautioning Molly several times to keep quiet and to act like his slave, she sighed and said, "Mr. Waldock, it'll be easy since I've been a slave all my life. I'll be more natural than you."

The next day, Chad walked straight to the depot with his servant girl following two steps behind toting his heavy carpetbag which she grasped with both hands. It held Chad's clothes, spare shoes, writing materials, and several books. Two full canteens were stuffed beside the clothes and a loaf of bread poked from the top.

A minute before departure, Chad walked to the cashier window, purchased two tickets to Atlanta and then hurried to the conductor who stood on the platform by the cars. Chad handed the passes to the trainman who glanced at him and his servant while tearing the heavy paper in half. Handing the stubs to Chad, he said, "Welcome aboard, sir. Seat yourself."

As he entered from the rear of the car, Chad scanned the wooden benches but didn't see any empty seats. He walked through the car and stepped across the narrow gangway to the next one. It was almost full, but the front bench was unoccupied except for a lady sitting by the aisle. He made for the seats with Molly at his heels. Chad said, "Excuse us," to the lady and directed his servant to the window seat.

As they sat down, the conductor hollered, "All aboard." The train lurched as the iron pins connecting the cars screeched against their gudgeons. Chad sighed.

"Excuse me, excuse me," a short, portly gentleman said as he squeezed in front of the woman on the aisle. He wore a brown, bee-hive style hat and expensive silk cravat that Chad had noticed when he walked through the first car. As the man pushed into the vacant seat, Chad sniffed a stale cigar odor.

"Howdy do. I'm travelin' to Atlanta on business. I'm goin' to the First State Bank to arrange a bigger line of credit. My company manu-factures brass buttons. With war comin' on, business is boomin' and I need capital. Mighty fine day, ain't it? Where you headed?"

Wondering why the blowhard had changed cars to sit by him, Chad made a curt reply, "Atlanta."

"Atlanta, huh? What's your name?

"Charles Waldock."

"Charles Waldock, do I detect an English accent?"

The man leaned forward to look at Molly who gazed out the window.

"Who's that?"

"My servant."

"You own her? Haven't the English abolished slavery?

The other passengers couldn't help but overhear the nosy blab-bermouth. Chad looked the man in the eye. "I'm English and, yes, my country abolished slavery several years ago. That doesn't affect me, as I live and work here. Slavery is legal in this country, and I own several. This one travels with me on business."

"She does? And what's your occupation if I might be so presump-tuous to ask?"

Chad wanted to tell the man to mind his own business, but he hoped to finesse his way through the interrogation without drawing more attention. "I'm a cotton broker representing an English syndicate."

"A broker? Why are you travelin' with a slave girl?"

Chad wanted to punch the man. Molly winced.

"She provides personal services for me, washes, irons, cooks. My factotum."

The man laughed, "Personal services, huh? I'll bet she's talented too."

Chad feared everybody in the first five rows heard the comment. He had to end the conversation. Seething, he bent down to his carpetbag, grabbed a book, pulled it out and pretended to read as the train rumbled toward Atlanta. The man tried to initiate conversation again, but Chad ignored him by keeping his eyes fixated on the book.

After several stops, Molly whispered in Chad's ear. A few minutes later, she stood up and squeezed down the bench toward the aisle. She walked through the car, across the gangway, and through the last car where a sliding doorway with a translucent glass window opened onto a platform. At the back right quadrant, Molly knocked on the door to a tiny cubicle. She stepped inside when no one answered.

The fat man waited for several minutes after Molly squeezed by him, then stood up and headed through the car. The coincidence made Chad so uncomfortable that he followed.

When Molly tried to exit the room, a pudgy arm blocked her way. She tried to duck under, but the man grabbed her and then yanked her bonnet down to her shoulders so abruptly that the ties cut into her neck. Losing her balance on the swaying platform, she had to grab the rail with both hands to keep from falling.

When he reached the last car, Chad couldn't see through the soot-smudged glass window. He hurried to the door and snatched it open to find the fat man struggling to force Molly's face upward.

Quickly shutting the door behind him, Chad snarled, "What the hell do you think you're doing?"

"The question, my friend, is what are you doing? I thought I recognized your so-called factotum when she walked by. Now, I'm positive. I've seen the wanted posters. You're aiding and abetting an escaped slave."

As Chad struggled to formulate an explanation, the man wrapped his arm under Molly's neck to gain more leverage to pry her from the rail. In panic, Chad slammed his fist at the base of the man's skull. Stunned from the blow, he fell to the floor and jounced across the platform. At the last moment he saved himself by grabbing a safety chain with one hand.

As the train rolled downhill at full steam over rough track that caused the cars to bounce and sway, the man slipped farther under the rail. In a desperate effort to keep from tumbling off the train, he wrapped a leg over the gudgeon. The car bucked, breaking his grip on the handrail. For an instant, his leg held him, then he fell. His body bounced on the cross ties until it came to rest between the tracks.

The train sped on. Molly looked away from the crumpled body on the railroad bed. Chad retched.

CHAPTER FIFTEEN

CEDAR KEYS
Florida

When the train reached the next stop in Atlanta, Chad and Molly hurried to leave the station. Chad hailed a carriage and had the driver drop them a mile from an abolitionist's safe house. They walked to the residence where the lady of the house whisked them inside.

The next day, Chad noticed a small article in *Atlanta Southern Confederacy* that reported that workers had found a dead businessman on the railroad tracks near Stone Mountain. Every day thereafter, Chad read that paper and also the *Daily Intelligencer* without finding another word about the accident. Nevertheless, he feared leaving the safe house. He stayed several weeks before he asked his guardian angels to drive him and Molly to a train station south of Atlanta.

While Molly and Chad hid in Atlanta, the conflict between North and South festered. Although seven states had seceded, Virginia, the most populous state in the South, held back and without it the South had little chance to win a full-scale war.

Both the Confederate and the United States Governments had well-defined goals: the North, union: the South, independence. Both wanted to avoid hostilities although the leaders in the North and

South understood military force was inevitable without a major concession by one side. Like boxers in the first round, each probed for weaknesses without going for a knockout. A few inconclusive skirmishes caused both sides to underestimate their opponent's strength. Each expected a quick and easy victory; neither envisioned a long and exhausting bout.

President Lincoln was so confident that he requested only 75,000 volunteers for ninety days to reinforce the Army's 16,000 officers and men. The Southern States mobilized volunteer militias and the Confederate government organized an army in February 1861 with 82,000 volunteers serving under 313 officers, most of whom had resigned from the U.S. Army.

The Union General-in-Chief Winfield Scott believed that the South could be squeezed into submission without a major military confrontation by severing Southern trade, the South's lifeblood. He proposed the "Anaconda Plan" to squeeze the Confederacy into submission by blockading its ports and controlling the Mississippi River.

War fever energized a somnolent Southern culture. Men from every occupation flocked to volunteer with the militia, particularly the cavalry, in which they could ride, shoot and parade with military pomp. Rich, ambitious men organized and financed units. Otherwise fainthearted men believed themselves transformed into intrepid warriors. Everybody glorified soldiers and gray uniforms were omnipresent.

Southern womenfolk encouraged the martial spirit. Ladies held their heads higher when their sons and husbands joined the militia. Matrons organized balls and soirees for the soldiers, and women's auxiliaries sewed uniforms, tents, and flags for the regiments. Girls aspired to marry officers.

Few in the South spoke out against rampant militarism. Newspapers encouraged it with jingoistic calls to support the war effort. Preachers joined the chorus. Sunday sermons called for loyalty, patriotism and service to the homeland with absolute certainty that God sided with the South.

The war created opportunities for social advancement in a stratified society. Unlike most other military organizations in history, Southern armies elected their own officers under the rank of brigadier general. Hardscrabble men who worked backwoods farms without hope for anything better now had the opportunity to be officers. For the first time ever, aristocratic and working class ladies intermingled in the auxiliaries.

When Chad reached Thomasville, he hired a carriage to Tallahassee where he found the public buildings and many private homes draped with bunting and flying the "Bonnie Blue Flag." On a field near the capitol, he watched a cavalry company at drill as horsemen rode at full gallop firing pistols and shotguns at targets nailed to trees. The men romped as if competing at a fair while whooping and hollering like exuberant teenagers at play, not soldiers at drill. Chad admired their excellent horsemanship, marksmanship and enthusiasm, but noticed that some riders shared weapons causing him to wonder how the company could be an effective fighting force without sufficient armament.

From Tallahassee the fugitives took cars east to Baldwin and then southwest to Cedar Key on the new railroad line that had been completed within the last year. Chad expected to find a bustling port. Instead, he found a sleepy village with buildings scattered around an island connected to the mainland by a railroad trestle. The tracks ended at small wharf beside several warehouses. In the harbor, a few smacks lay at anchor. Beached rowboats lined the shore in little pods. The community looked deserted except for soldiers patrolling the streets.

Chad waited with Molly on the train until the other passengers cleared the platform. After a squad of soldiers marched past the depot, the two travelers stepped off the train and walked toward a large masonry building a few blocks down the street with a sign painted across the front that read, "Parsons' General Store." As before, Molly trudged several steps behind toting the heavy carpet bag. When they arrived at the establishment, she waited outside while Chad stepped through the door to ask the owner about ships scheduled to sail.

The proprietor explained, "Gulf Coastal Schooners sail from Cedar Key, but the captains only leave when they have cargo. You never know when that will be. We expected the railroad to bring more trade, but with all the uncertainty about war, business is slow."

"You mean I'm stuck here?"

"No, you just have to be patient and ask around until you find a captain planning to sail."

"Then I'll need a place to stay for me and my slave."

CHAPTER SIXTEEN

CHUNKY POND CAMP
Florida

Jake and Loring worked with Mike from daylight to dark pulling and burning stumps. One crisp morning, Loring said, "Let's go ahead and start plowing around the stumps we haven't pulled. While you get started, I'm going to talk to the neighbors about renting some men. Jake, are you certain the thieves stealing our chickens were from their camp?"

"They told me dey was."

Later that morning when Loring walked Ginger into the lumber camp, it appeared deserted except for the cook who ignored the visitor until Loring asked him the whereabouts of his owners.

He pointed toward a wagon track that wound through the pine scrub. "Dey went down yonder."

Nudging Ginger with a knee, Loring rode the mare down the track. After a mile, he spotted an empty wagon by a bayhead where two black men were working on a wheel. As one man held it across a stump, the other beat the iron rim with a heavy blacksmith hammer.

They glanced in Loring's direction but neither acknowledged his presence when he reined Ginger by them. "Where are your masters?"

The big, muscular man pounded the iron rim with several more blows.

Raising his voice Loring asked again, "Where are your masters?"

The man lifted the heavy ball peen hammer and pointed. Riding Ginger in the direction the slave indicated, Loring rounded a fetter brush thicket to find a slave tied around a skinny pine sapling. He wore no shirt and bled from welts across his back.

Holland and Wall sat on a log by the dirt track looking at the man strapped to the tree. A four-foot bull whip dangled from Wall's hand. Fifty feet away, several other slaves stood watching.

The two white men stood up. Holland said, "Hello, neighbor. What brings you over here?"

Loring gestured toward the man tied to the tree and said, "What's the problem?"

Wall said, "Had to whip him. We told him time and time again not to overload the log cart, but he kept on and broke a wheel. Now the whole damn operation is slowed down 'cause this boy won't listen. Bet he don't do it again."

Loring restrained himself from commenting. After all, it wasn't his business how his neighbors treated their slaves. "Two of your men stole some chickens from my place while I was in Tallahassee."

Wall said, "Not likely. We keep an eye on our nigras. They ain't got the time to wander off. What makes you think they was ours?"

"My slave, Jake, caught them."

Wall slapped his rolled up whip across his palm.

"Your boy is mistaken. He ate those chickens himself and made up a story to cover his black ass."

Loring flushed. He had the urge to smash Wall's smug face for insulting Jake, but held back. He judged the scoundrel for a coward and felt confident he could whip him in a fair fight although he couldn't count on that. If he pressed Wall, he expected both men to pounce.

"If I catch your men on my place, I'll report it to the sheriff."

Wall laughed. "He won't pay a Yankee sympathizer no mind."

Loring burned. He had no doubt that Wall was correct. Like almost everybody in the Suwannee Valley, the authorities were secessionists with a grudge against Union men. He had to deal with Wall himself. Ginger sensed his vexation and stamped a forefoot.

"You better keep your slaves off my place."

"Git off our land."

Holland never said anything although Loring noticed him slide his hand over his pistol grip.

As he turned Ginger, Loring couldn't resist the last word, "If you boys had taught your slave to count the logs, he wouldn't have overloaded the cart."

In few days, the slave Wall had whipped became feverish and weak. The open sores on his back where the whip had peeled back the hide oozed yellow pus. Several times a day, the cook cleaned the sores with onion juice. After the wash, he applied a poultice made from poke root, black walnut, and willow bark.

Frustrated that the slave didn't respond to the treatments, Wall tried to speed the healing process by pouring witch hazel or turpentine on the sores. His astringents didn't work any better than the homemade salve.

The other slaves' reaction to the whipping frustrated Wall. He had beat the man as an example to make them work better, but he had achieved the opposite. They moved slower and accomplished less which motivated Wall to be more brutal.

He came into the sick man's tent one morning and popped him on the leg with his whip. "Git up, boy." The slave looked at Wall with jaundiced eyes as he struggled from his cot to avoid the lash. As he staggered from the tent, Wall said, "A day's work will make you feel better."

When Wall noticed the other bondsmen watching from a distance, he yelled at them to move out and popped his whip for emphasis.

The victim stumbled along as Wall followed behind smacking his thigh with the whip. The delirious man couldn't keep up with the others. When they stopped to wait for him, Wall snapped his whip and yelled in fury, "No more dawdlin'. Move!" They all scattered except the ailing man who cowered near Wall.

Wall jerked an axe from a stump. He handed it to the scared slave and pointed at a felled tree. "Trim those limbs." The man tottered to it and began chopping with feeble strokes. "Lift the axe higher," Wall snarled.

The slave raised the axe over his head, dropped it, and collapsed.

Wall hollered, "Help this weakling back to his tent."

The plan to force the sick slave to work had backfired. Now another person had to be pulled off the crew to help him. In disgust, the white man plopped down on a log.

All day, the slaves straggled. Terrorizing them had failed, but Wall didn't know any other way to make them work. He sat for a long time and then spent the rest of the day walking around aimlessly while smacking his whip against his leg. His captives ignored him as they muttered among themselves.

"Dey works us too hard for nothin'."

"We ain't gittin' a fair ration. All dey feed us is 'possum, coon and such mess. No wonder we're sick - we're hungry half de time."

"Dey ain't put one speck a cloth on us since dey bought us. We near freezin' to death livin' in tents without enough blankets."

"We make shoes by wrapping canvas scraps stuffed wid moss round our feet. We ain't supposed to be treated like dis."

"Dat's right. On de plantation in Carolina, I got a full ration, clothes, and new brogans every year."

"Wall is a thief. If he hits me with dat whip, I'm goin' snatch it and beat his Cracker ass so bad he'll never whip another nigger."

"You better be careful. He catch you talkin' like dat, he'll kill ya."

When Mingo and Brutus saw the sick slave being carried back to his tent, Brutus said, "Dey lied when dey told us we'd be treated fair at dis camp. Dey can't run dis sawmill without us. Engine's goin' break today."

Mingo had never seen Brutus so upset. At last, he felt the time had come to convince him to escape. "Let's run. If we don't, sooner or later we'll get sick or dey'll beat us to death. One man is dead already and another is dyin'. Half is sickly with croup. Let's go now."

"We can't without knowin' where we're goin'!"

"You keep usin' de same excuse, but I ain't waitin' much longer whether you come or not."

Holland returned to camp in midafternoon with one coot. When he dropped the dead bird on the table, he noticed that the cook fire had burned out. He walked to the sawmill and asked Mingo and Brutus where the cook had gone.

They kept pushing a log through the saw blade.

"Where's the cook?" He yelled.

"Don't know," Brutus muttered without looking up.

Holland looked around, uncertain what to do. Then from one of the tents, he heard a moan, so he walked over to check on it. When he lifted the flap, he saw the cook washing the sick slave's back with a syrupy concoction. "What you doin'?"

"I'm doctorin' dis man; he's burnin' up wid fever."

"We ain't got time for that, you need to be fixin' supper. I see you let the fire burn out again. Did you cut more fire wood like a told ya?"

"Chopped some and built up de fire too, but reckon it went out."

"Get your ass over there and punch up that fire. I bagged a coot you can fix for supper. Don't just cut out the breasts either. Pluck it and put the whole carcass in a stew. Unless you shape up, I'm puttin' you to work for Mister Wall."

The saw stopped.

When Holland walked over to find out why, Brutus said, "Look here, Mas'r. Drive belt done ripped and needs sewin'. Don't make no difference no how. We're caught up. No logs came in today."

"Get that belt fixed and don't let the steam down. Logs should be on the way." Holland walked to his tent and thudded down on his cot. He took out his pipe, pressed tobacco in the bowl and lit it. He sat puffing and thinking. *This lumber business ain't workin' out. I'm stuck in these woods with nobody to talk to but Wall, and he's surlier by the day. It's time for a heart to heart.*

That evening after the supper when the slaves had turned in for the night, the partners conferred by the smoldering fire.

Holland said, "We're behind schedule and haven't cut enough lumber to fill half the order. Our cash is almost gone. We ain't goin' make our contract. The drive belt on the saw tore apart today and it ain't easy to stitch together. We need a new one."

"A ripped drive belt ain't the half of it. We're not cutting trees fast enough. I don't know how to make our damn slackers work. Some are always malingering. This morning, I forced the sick one up; what a fiasco. Later, another one said he strained his back and walked around bent over. I popped him with the whip, but that didn't help. The log cart looks like it's about to collapse again. The left wheel ain't round no more where your boys patched it together. If it breaks, I suppose we can drag the logs, but that will be slower. You're right. We're goin' default on our contract."

"What should we do?"

"Ain't got no choice. I'm goin' to Cedar Key and talk to the lumber agent. I'm goin' to explain that we need more time and an advance."

"If he won't modify it, we're busted. Truth be told, I'm discouraged anyhow. Our boys ain't adaptin' to the lumber business. Except for those two runnin' the saw, they're all 'bout worthless. I'll bet none of them ever did nothin' but chop cotton. I've showed the damned cook the same thing a hundred times."

"The sawyers ain't worth a tinker's damn either, and I have to watch the stockman like a hawk."

"Yup, we've got a sorry lot. Maybe we should sell them and start over. Problem is, their value has dropped since secession. All the talk about a Yankee invasion makes matters worse. When I bought supplies in Bronson last week, people weren't talkin' 'bout nothin' else. Things need to calm down 'fore we sell anybody."

"You're right. And we have to get them well. Another one's 'bout to die. There's no way we could git our investment out of this stock. We're so far under water we can't see light."

Holland said, "We've got bigger worries too. Why in the world did Florida join up with the Confederacy so fast? I figured that we'd secede and the politicians could figure out a way to guarantee slavery and get us back in the Union. People are so bullheaded now, that's impossible. The damn fire-eating secessionists won't compromise and the Yankees think we're traitors. The economy's shot. Nobody will take drafts on shaky Florida banks and who has confidence in the

Confederate Government? Independence ain't workin' out like we expected."

"That's for sure. I've never seen politicians throw anything together as fast as the Provisional Confederate Government. Florida no more than declares independence from the Union and we're already tied up with a new government headed by Jeff Davis. Hotheads have chased off the Yankees. It wouldn't surprise me atal if our buyer ain't been run out of town. Even if he's still here, we'll have a tough time shippin' lumber through the navy blockade."

Holland stared at the ground. "What a mess. I favored secession, but I never figured it'd work against us like this. We're broke. Maybe we should rent some slaves to our neighbor to raise cash."

Wall jumped up. "I ain't rentin' my hands to that Yankee sympathizer. I'd rather starve."

After stomping around a bit, Wall sat back down. "I got a better idea. Nobody in Suwannee Valley knows that we have a lien on our niggers. When I go to Cedar Key to talk to the Yankee lumber buyer, I'll stop by the bank and see if I can't mortgage them for cash."

"That's fraud."

"You got a better idea?"

"Maybe I'll volunteer for the army and have some fun while collectin' a pay check to boot."

"You'd leave me out here in these woods with these nincompoops? I don't think so, partner."

Chapter Seventeen

Chunky Pond

Florida

Wall left for Bronson on horseback before dawn to catch the train. Not bothering to eat the crude camp fare for breakfast, he saved his appetite to treat himself at a boarding house in town. The wait was worth it. He gorged on eggs, ham, and biscuits smothered with redeye gravy that he washed down with strong coffee. Still irritated about his partner's threat to enlist in the army, he didn't feel guilty in the least.

He didn't enjoy the conversation as much as the food. Although almost everybody felt confident that the South could whip the North, people now realized that winning the war might not be easy.

A farmer complained, "Governor Perry messed up big time by allowing the Yankees to occupy Fort Pickens in Pensacola. Senator Levy warned everybody at the Secession Convention that we needed to take it right away because its guns control the harbor and the navy yard. Perry sat on his hands even though only caretakers were at the fort. Now that Yankee troops have moved there from the Barrancas Barracks, we can't take it without a fight."

A storekeeper chimed in, "That's right. If Perry had been aggressive like the militia captains at Fernandina, Tampa, and St. Augustine, we could have grabbed Fort Pickens easy. Yankees don't want to fight. President Buchanan never issued orders to defend Union installations with force. When we demanded the arsenal at Marianna, the Yankees surrendered. They ain't fired a shot yet."

As she put more biscuits on the table, the proprietress said, "We're already divided among ourselves. According to the Tallahassee paper, Key West people formed a militia so that Yankee troops could hold Fort Taylor. Every one of those traitors ought to be lined up and shot."

The farmer said, "Hon, no doubt about it. We need to clamp down hard. Perry hemmed and hawed, and now the Gulf Coast is bracketed by two Federal Forts. Fort Taylor controls Key West, our biggest and wealthiest town. Fort Pickens dominates Pensacola Bay which has the best navy yard in the whole South. Anybody with half a brain knows that these forts are strategic. If we can't force the Yankees from them, the whole West Coast ain't safe."

Wall's breakfast didn't taste good any longer. He pushed back his chair and said, "Ma'am, gentlemen, excuse me. Pleasure, I have to catch the cars to Cedar Key. I've got business down there with a lumber broker."

As he stood up, the farmer asked, "You doin' business with a Yankee company?"

"What's it to ya?"

"Nothin', but I heard a rumor that all the Yankees left Cedar Key."

Wall felt anxious the entire trip as the train rumbled south. When it chugged across the trestle onto the island, he noticed the town appeared sleepier than he'd ever seen it. Nobody waited at the station.

When the cars clanged to a stop, he jumped to the platform and hurried straight to the general store where Parsons astonished him with news. "We're at war!"

"What do you mean?"

"Haven't you heard? Lincoln ordered Fort Pickens at Pensacola and Fort Sumter at Charleston reinforced. He broke the truce. South Carolina troops shelled Fort Sumter early this morning."

"Good Lord, nobody said anything at Bronson when I caught the cars."

"Probably didn't know. Cedar Key station received a telegram while you were on the train."

"How do you think it'll play out?"

"Hard to say. I expect people to come to their senses before things get out of hand. There should be a political solution short of total war."

"I hope so. In any event, do you know where I can find the buyer for Davison Lumber out of Boston?"

"You're out of luck. As far as I know, all the Northern agents left town. Right after Florida seceded, some Crackers roughed up a few. There were fistfights and worse. A week ago, a local peckerwood slashed one who had the nerve to brag how the North was stronger than the South. Some ol' boys threatened to shoot them on sight. A schooner left yesterday for Key West. I believe the last Yankees were aboard."

The conversation disgusted Wall. He excused himself and hot-footed it to the boarding house where agents sometimes roomed. The owner's comments frustrated him even more.

"I threw all the Yankee bastards out. I was sick and tired of hearin' them carry on about how advanced the North is compared to us."

"You know where they went?"

"Don't know and don't give a damn. Left town I'm sure. If not, they're stupider than I think. The sheriff told the Yankees he couldn't protect them."

Wall gave up the search. The time had come to visit the bank near the municipal wharf. At the barred teller's cage, he asked to speak to the president. The clerk pointed at a well-dressed man reading a newspaper in a wood-paneled office. As Wall approached him, the banker put down his paper, stepped around his desk and extended his hand.

After introductions and discussion about the Fort Sumter bombardment, Wall said, "Me and my partner have leased yellow pine timberland up at Chunky Pond near Bronson where we operate a steam-powered sawmill. We have half a carload of lumber ready to ship."

The comment piqued the banker's interest because the bank's biggest loans were to cotton and lumber men.

"We have eleven good slaves working for us. Two are excellent mechanics who operate the mill. We've trained the others as sawyers, skidders, and drivers. Everything's goin' well."

"You have contracts for your lumber?"

"With a Boston firm. The company's agent was staying here in Cedar Key. I've searched for him high and low. Can't find him anywhere."

"You aren't going to either. All the Yankee agents have skeddadled, but I'm surprised he didn't send a message to you. Most of them shipped everything they could get their hands on before things heated up."

"We're due a payment, but ain't no tellin' when we might get it now."

"The bank's hurting too. War talk has brought business to a standstill. What can I do for you?"

"This political mess shouldn't last long. Once the Confederacy gets up and runnin', Yankee buyers will be back. They need lumber.

Fact is, we need it here too. I hear Senator Levy plans to build a spur to connect the Florida Atlantic Railroad to the Savannah Albany line in Georgia and another one to Tampa. He'll need timbers for cross-ties. We can supply them but need a loan to maintain our camp."

"How much money you want to borrow?"

"Oh, enough to operate for a year. To be on the safe side, say $2,000."

"What can you put up as collateral?"

"The lumber we've cut and our slaves."

"We usually don't take mortgages on bondsmen except as cross collateral with land loans. You own any land?"

"No, like I said, we lease the land."

Wall knew he couldn't lie about owning land because a title search would confirm ownership.

The banker said, "Our board just might consider a lien on your lumber if you'll mortgage your slaves too. You have clear title to them?

"We bought the slaves in Virginia from a broker. We have the bill of sale. Will that do?"

Wall knew he could forge the paperwork and that the banker had no practical way to verify ownership or liens on the slaves.

"Yes, that ought to do. With the slaves and timber as collateral, the bank could consider a small, short-term loan; say six months to establish a relationship. I'll have to see your camp first. When is that practical?"

"How about next week?"

"Next Wednesday then. I'll catch the cars if you'll pick me up at the depot in Bronson."

"I'll be waiting when the train pulls in."

When Wall returned to the lumber camp, he found slaves huddled around a tent from which a strange chant emanated. "What are they up to now?"

"They're droning some kind of African Voodoo. We're about to lose another one."

"This ain't good. The banker's comin' to inspect our operation next week so this place has to be ship shape. What have you done for the sick nig?"

"Nothin'. He needs a doctor and we can't afford one."

"You try to treat him yourself?"

"No, they know more about doctorin' their own than I do. We don't have any medicine anyway."

Wall kicked over a stool and walked to the tent where the slaves were gathered around the sick man's cot. Several stepped aside to allow him access.

Wall grimaced and said, "What's that awful stench?"

A slave crouching by the cot said, "Mas'r, his sores. We put medicine on them, but they ain't no better."

A greasy substance smeared across the man's back glistened and pus oozed from open gashes. Wall placed his palm on the slave's cheek. He felt fever.

"Can't you do more?"

"Doin' all we can, Mas'r. We're prayin' hard."

"You look after him. The rest of you, git out."

Wall returned to the campfire and said to Holland, "We're snake bit. There's no way the banker will give us a loan if this place isn't shaped up and our slaves vigorous."

"We should feed them better. We're down to scrapin's even after we put them on half rations. The cook's cut all the nearby swamp cabbage. The game's shot out."

Over the next week, the partners did everything they could to make the camp appear prosperous in preparation for the banker's arrival. So much maintenance had been neglected that Wall had no choice but to stop timbering in order to patch tents, mend clothing and clean the camp. He ordered Mingo and Brutus to wash everybody's bedding and clothing in a brand-new cast iron wash pot. He had placed it upside down on its rim when he had first set up the camp. Nobody had used it since. Rust from the humid air covered it from top to bottom.

Mingo and Brutus put the kettle to proper use. After filling it with water, they threw in shaved yucca root and lighter wood chips and then lit a hardwood fire under the pot. When the mixture came to a roiling boil, they pushed clothes into it and stirred them with a cypress paddle. After several minutes in the steaming water, they used a pole to lift out the sodden garments and to dump them into a trough for a rinse. After pulling them out from the cool water and twisting them to wring out the moisture, they hung everything to dry on ropes tied between trees.

Wall ordered a slave to fill in the old, slit-trench toilet, to dig a deeper one and to bury all human waste that the slaves had deposited in bushes around the camp. As soon as the slave completed the new ditch, Wall gathered everybody around it. He explained that they had to use it and cover their waste with dirt. He reinforced his serious intention by threatening to whip anyone who didn't.

Camp food improved. Every morning and evening, Holland hunted with grim determination. Most days he bagged a few squirrels, quail, doves, or ducks. On several trips, he killed several whooping cranes. Once he shot a large sow. Wall salted the pig's hindquarter and hung it to cure in a makeshift smokehouse. Wall re-tacked the tops on the empty food barrels and stacked the remaining rations atop them to make the camp appear well-stocked with staples. The camp's general shabbiness couldn't be disguised, but the effort to perk it up helped. At least, it looked organized and productive.

Dressed in his clean clothes that smelled a bit like pine oil, Wall met the banker at the depot as the Florida Railroad Company's powerful new locomotive, *The Governor Broome*, pulled into the station. Four drive wheels behind four bogie wheels propelled the long, heavy engine. In front, like all locomotives used in the backwoods, an iron cowcatcher bolted to the frame projected over the tracks. Dense, black, pine smoke poured from its balloon smokestack, which had smudged the headlamp on the short run from Cedar Key to Bronson.

Wall guessed the big engine could pull more cars than the Florida Railroad Company owned. Such an impressive locomotive conveyed confidence that Senator Levy, as well as the other investors in the Florida Railroad Company, had faith in Middle Florida's economic potential. As if to underline that fact, the engineer blew the whistle more than regulations required. The blasts echoed across the flatwoods, swamps and hammocks as if to announce that modernity had arrived in the Suwannee Valley.

When the banker stepped onto the platform, Wall said, "I've never seen a bigger engine."

"Neither have I. My bank tried to finance it, but Senator Levy negotiated a deal in New York that our little bank couldn't match although I'll bet the Yankee financiers are having second thoughts now that we've declared independence."

When the bank president mounted the horse Wall brought for him as well as any cow hunter, the lumberman commented, "I was worried you couldn't ride."

"What Cracker can't ride? I grew up near Payne's Prairie and I've hunted scrub cattle since I was a boy. Stuck in the bank, I miss the roundups and cattle drives."

From the previous conversation the banker knew what to expect at the camp, but to his surprise the sawmill operation looked more productive than others. He was particularly impressed with the big steam engine that whirled a four foot diameter saw through the biggest logs Brutus and Mingo guided into it.

As they walked away from the saw's whine, the banker said to Wall, "I've never seen slaves operate a sawmill by themselves. At the other camps, the white owners run the machinery."

"It took me a long time to teach them, but it was worth it. Me and my partner can supervise the sawyers and look after the camp without worryin' about the mill. Not many men can handle and cut logs like those two."

"I'm impressed. Let's see your timber."

They stopped first where the crews were working. Wall introduced the banker to his partner and then the three whites watched as the skinny slaves in tattered clothing sawed and trimmed trees. After a few minutes, Wall moved on to show the banker the entire leasehold.

They rode through first-growth longleaf pines that stood spar straight without any limbs for the first twenty or thirty feet. In the high branches, the needles trembled with a low-pitched whoosh when the wind stirred them. Where the well-spaced trees didn't shade the ground completely, wax myrtle, fetterbush, gallberry and saw palmettos competed for sunlight. After a half hour, the banker said, "You've got adequate timber."

"Sure 'nuff. We could cut for several years before we exhaust the trees, plus we have an option on adjoining property. We have the timber, but I suppose our contract with the Yankee company is not worth a plug nickel now."

"You're right. The war has killed the economy. I'm still hopeful we can convince the North to let us maintain our independence without more fighting. Both sides will be better off if Lincoln will let us go in peace. If he won't, it'll cost them more than us. We can trade cotton to England for everything we need. If Yankees can't get it from us, they won't be able to raise capital to finance their army."

Wall had already heard enough speculation about war and was eager to get to specifics about the loan. "What do you think of our operation?"

"It's well-organized. I'm particularly impressed with your sawmill. Your timber is not as good as that on the Withlacoochee sand hills, but that acreage is not as close to the railroad until a line is completed to Tampa. Here you have a short haul to the tracks which is a big advantage."

"Then you'll make us a loan?"

"I'm comfortable with your operation; I'd like to."

"Good, what terms?"

"To cut to the chase, the bank can't loan you money right now."

"Why not?"

"The war. Too many people have withdrawn money from the bank. When the Yankees left Cedar Key, they took their capital with them. Most customers bought bonds or cashed out to outfit troops.

After you visited me in Cedar Key, our biggest depositor withdrew everything. I suspect he's buying gold. I'm sorry to say, the bank doesn't have the funds to lend right now."

Under his breath, Wall cursed the war, Yankees and Rebels. Enraged that the banker led him on about a loan, his hand grasped the whip hanging from his saddle. Just before he raised it, he had second thoughts and spurred his horse to separate himself from the banker.

That evening when Wall returned to camp leading the horse he'd let the banker use, he didn't have the stockman cool the animals down or currycomb them. He did the chores himself. When he finished, he walked to the campfire, took a bottle from his pocket and passed it to Holland who tipped it up for a pull then handed it back. Both men sat in dejected silence until Wall took another long drag and muttered, "We ain't getting no loan."

"I figured that when you rode off. What didn't the banker like?"

"He liked our operation just fine. The damn bank ain't got the money."

"How come?"

"People have withdrawn too much on account of the war."

Wall drained the bottle and smashed it against the andirons. "Independence ain't off to much of a start."

Holland walked away.

The partners managed to keep the camp operating although by midsummer they were desperate for supplies. In a last-ditch effort, Holland loaded a cart with tack, tools and gear to sell or trade in Bronson. While there, he heard about a great Southern victory at Bull Run Creek near Manassas, Virginia. At the cafe, he bought a newspaper with several articles about the battle.

They reported that the Northern Command had become impatient with skirmishes and decided to capture Richmond, the Confederate capital, before August 1861 when the enlistments for the Federal volunteers expired. The Union, under General McDowell, committed 35,000 troops to attack the principal Confederate army of 20,000 troops under CSA General Beauregard that blocked the route between Washington D.C. and Richmond. On July 16, the Union army sauntered south with full confidence the smaller army could be overwhelmed.

General Beauregard prepared to meet the advance with a textbook strategy modeled on Napoleon's Austerlitz battle plan. He spread his army along Bull Run Creek where he planned to stall the Yankee army at its center, then flank it.

On July 18, Federal advance units brushed against the Rebel line. After a brief firefight, they scurried back to join their main army. The Southerners assumed the attack was simply another feint like all the previous ones. The repulse raised their confidence. Some believed they had already won.

The skirmish was no feint; it had simply taken time for General McDowell to position his inexperienced troops. On July 21, 1861, the armies met in force. Confederate command and control broke down, and inexperienced soldiers didn't understand, or couldn't execute, orders. The brigades attacking the Yankee left flank were repulsed and the Rebels' own flank gave ground. Northern units crossed the creek to attack the Confederate line in a mirror image of Beauregard's plan. Instead of destroying the enemy's flank, the Southern line fell back as McDowell's infantry advanced behind effective cannon fire against hard fighting Rebels.

As the Southern line began to collapse, General Joseph E. Johnston arrived by rail from the Shenandoah Valley with 9,000 fresh troops. The reinforced Rebel lines rallied, forcing the Federal army to retreat.

The Yankee withdrawal soon turned to a rout. Civilians had come from Washington to picnic and to watch the Rebel defeat from the hills overlooking the battlefield. When they realized the Yankee troops had turned in retreat, they made a beeline for Washington. Their buggies and carriages clogged the roads that entangled the army as shells fell among the tumult. Panic ensued. Yankee soldiers by the thousands dropped their weapons to flee an expected Rebel counter-attack. McDowell's well-equipped army disintegrated.

Holland hurried back to camp to report everything about the victory and the Southern jubilation it evoked. His partner listened without saying anything while he swigged from a bottle. When Holland finished, Wall said, "So, the bigwigs have concluded from this battle that the Yankees can't fight and the war's all but won?"

"President Davis says we won a mighty victory by sendin' the Yankee army scurryin' back to Washington. He says Lincoln will think twice before invadin' again."

"Let's hear more details."

Holland related the battle's events almost down to company maneuvers and explained how Brigadier General T. J. Jackson had rallied his men to stand firm on Henry House Hill which earned him the appellation "Stonewall." It was a clear-cut victory. "Yankees didn't fight worth a damn and lost at least 2,900 men while we only lost 2,000."

"Tell me again about Johnston's troops arrivin' by railroad."

Holland added all the particulars that he remembered about troops coming by rail. Wall paid close attention then asked if Holland had the newspaper with the articles about the battle.

"Sure I do, I wanted a souvenir."

"Show me the part about the reinforcement by railroad ."

Wall read the paragraphs about Johnston arriving at the battle-field, handed the newspaper back to Holland and took a long drag from his bottle.

"Reporters, politicians, generals. Idiots; this war ain't nowhere close to over. Look what actually happened. Forget the blather and bullshit about a great victory. We damn near lost. Our troops were retreatin' when Johnston showed up. If he had arrived half an hour later, the Stars and Stripes would be flyin' over Richmond. Besides that, we can't afford to lose 2,000 men. We don't have manpower like the Yankees. Losin' 2,000 men hurts us a lot more than 2,900 hurts them. Beauregard should have counter-attacked and destroyed the Yankee army when he had them on the run. All McDowell has to do is re-supply."

"What are you talkin' about?"

"Lincoln ain't goin' quit. Yankees have more manpower, and they're better equipped than our armies. Already they're movin' across the Ohio River in the West. What have we got to stop them? We were damn lucky at Bull Run and dumb luck won't hold in every battle."

Wall's realistic appraisal deflated Holland's spirits.

After a long pause, Wall asked, "Did you get any supplies?"

"Some. I traded tack for a sack of corn meal which will hold us for a while. We've got to sell some lumber."

"That ain't likely and matters have gone from bad to worse here. That damned sick slave ain't no better and he won't die, so somebody has to mind him. I'm ready to quit feedin' him. The nigras are sulky. I popped one this morning and he reared up real uppity. We're losin' control out here in these godforsaken woods. They know that we ain't treatin' them right. We have to remind them who's who or we're goin' have a rebellion on our hands."

Wall rocked back on his canvas chair and said, "I hate to eat crow, but maybe we ought to consider rentin' some."

Holland repressed a grin and before his partner could reconsider said, "I'll ride over to Bell's place tomorrow and work somethin' out."

He walked to his tent and left Wall staring into embers. As Holland dozed off, he heard Wall's whiskey bottle shatter against the andirons.

BATTERY LINCOLN, FORT PICKENS, SANTA ROSA ISLAND,
FLORIDA

(Courtesy Florida State Archives)

CHAPTER EIGHTEEN

DEER HALL

Florida

Holland awoke and dressed before dawn, saddled his stallion and headed for the Bell Plantation. As he walked his horse along the dark trail, mist hugged the scrubby palmettos. After the summer constellation, Scorpio, faded away in a golden radiance spread across the horizon, he mulled over his situation. *Wall's getting' crankier by the day. Sooner or later he's goin' throw one of his bottles at me and we'll tangle.*

Without warning, his horse shied causing him to grab the saddle horn to keep his balance. "Whoa," he said, and reined. From his saddle he could see above the brush along the trail. To his right, a towhee jostled a dead palmetto frond and a bobwhite called in the distance. He didn't see or hear anything unusual and couldn't figure out what spooked his animal. He kicked it with his boot heels. The stallion whinnied, refusing to move.

Before he could force the horse forward, he saw why it had shied. Twenty feet in front of it, two huge rattlesnakes slithered forward with their heads lifted high above the ground. He estimated the snakes were at least seven feet long, as fat as his thigh, with heads bigger than his fist. Inexplicably, the horse didn't intimidate the rattlers. Holland wondered, *Why are they behaving so strange? Mating behavior?*

He pulled his short, double-barreled shotgun from its saddle scabbard. As he lifted it to his shoulder, he cocked the hammers and aimed at the head of the closest snake. He squeezed the front trigger. Buckshot tore apart the snake's head. The second snake coiled. The horse bucked causing the snake to slither into the brush by the trail that camouflaged it. Its frenzied rattle sounded as if it came from all directions. The stallion jumped again forcing Holland to jerk the reins with his left hand and to press his thighs hard against the saddle to keep from being thrown.

As the horse settled, he spotted the snake in a loose, defensive coil. Holding the reins tightly with his left hand, he pointed the shotgun like a pistol toward the rattler and pulled the rear trigger. With a rifle or revolver, he'd have missed, but scattered buckshot ripped the reptile apart. Holland patted his horse, reloaded his weapon and forced new percussion cups on the nipples.

Spooked by the rattlers, he inspected the ground before dismounting. He suspected the snakes were traveling as a pair, but he didn't want to chance stepping on another one. He walked to the first one, put his boot behind the mangled head and cut it off with his hunting knife. Lifting the carcass with both hands, he talked to his horse to keep it calm and then walked beside it draping the dead reptile behind the saddle where it hung twitching.

Despite the cool morning, sweat dampened Holland's shirt. As he rode toward Bell's place, he stayed alert for more rattlers. As he neared his neighbor's farm, two hounds yelped and then tore toward his horse. He reined and yelled out a hello. The watchdogs stopped running, but continued to bark and growl. Loring and Jake rushed onto to the porch yelling at them to hush. One dog turned, but the other ignored the commands. Loring jumped off the porch and ran toward him. "Get to the house." The hound slinked under the porch.

Loring shook his head and said, "Sorry about that. What's up, Mr. Holland?"

Then he noticed the snake. "My Lord, that's a huge rattler."

"I'd say. Spooked my horse. There were two, but I splattered the other one."

Holland rambled on about killing the two snakes and how he'd never seen any crawling with their head so high off the ground. "Ya'll need to watch out with big ones like this moving around."

Loring said, "Jake, show it to the children and warn them to be careful. After they've seen it, feed it to the hogs. Come on inside. How about some coffee?"

The two men entered the dim cabin lit by sunlight that filtered through lace curtains and a kerosene lamp that burned on a table in the corner. "What brings you over here?" Loring said as he offered a homemade wooden chair with a cowhide seat to Holland.

"When you said you wanted to rent some slaves, my partner treated you pretty rough. He's hotheaded. Anyhow, I've persuaded him to do business with you. We have lumber cut and ready to deliver, but our Yankee agent left the state. We need cash."

Loring said, "I can't sell my cotton now that our politicians won't let us export it. In my opinion, we ought to be selling the English as much cotton as they'll buy so we can equip our armies and build a navy. Lincoln doesn't need a blockade. For all practical purposes our Confederate Congress has done it for him."

Holland concurred, "We haven't gained a thing either."

"That's right. England is less likely to help us if we hurt her economy. Anyhow, I'll store my cotton till the government says I can sell it. I need hands to build a storehouse and mill. Jake and I can't do the heavy work by ourselves. I'd like to rent those two who run your sawmill. No disrespect intended, but your others don't look too productive."

"Those two are the only ones who can run the mill, but what's the difference? We can't sell the lumber they cut anyhow."

Blanche came into the room and handed each man a plain, porcelain coffee cup. She wanted to challenge Loring's comment about the blockade. She had no doubt that the Confederate leadership knew more about relations with England than Loring although she held her tongue with company present.

While the two men drank their coffee, they worked out a satisfactory deal to rent the slaves and to buy lumber in exchange for vegetables and cash. When they agreed on terms, Holland added that he needed Wall's OK.

Loring said, "If he doesn't want to do the deal, forget it. I don't see eye to eye with your partner."

When he returned to the lumber camp, Holland found Wall fiddling with the steam engine. The smoke from Wall's pipe didn't mask the stale odor of sweat and whiskey. When Holland explained that their neighbor only wanted to rent Brutus and Mingo, Wall took a slug from his bottle, stared at his partner and said, "No way."

Holland pointed out that he didn't see any viable alternative. Wall took another drink. The veins bulged on his neck and his faced flushed redder than normal. "OK, I'll go along with your scheme, but once we're on our feet, I'll never do business with that Yankee sympathizer again."

That evening at supper, Holland explained to Brutus and Mingo that they were being rented to Mr. Bell at the neighboring farm. The slaves glanced at one another, shrugged and kept eating. After all, they had no say in the matter. Like the ox that pulled the wagon, they had no choice but to go or suffer the consequences.

Still, Brutus and Mingo expected the worst. They knew that owners, in their own best interest, generally treated their slaves better than renters in order to protect their capital. After all, well-fed, healthy slaves held their value better than malnourished or abused hands. Lessees didn't have to concern themselves with the long term, so they often overworked and mistreated their hired chattel.

On the other hand, Brutus and Mingo yearned to get away from the camp. Every day except Sunday they sawed logs on the sun-up to sundown schedule. Nothing broke the monotony. Even on Sundays they had to clean or repair something. Isolated in the backwoods, they couldn't slip away to a village or nearby plantation to meet a woman or drink shine. A stint at the Bell farm might give them the chance.

That night in their tent, they discussed their situation.

Brutus said, "Can't be worse at Bell's than here in dis stinkin' camp."

Mingo replied, "Maybe we'll find out 'bout de area and people who'll help us escape. If we don't git away soon, I'm bound to have a run-in with Wall."

The next morning, after they loaded a cart with lumber to deliver to the Bell place, Holland climbed atop the pile and snapped his whip to stir the ox hitched in the shafts. The emaciated animal strained to pull the loaded wagon a few feet, then stopped as the cart wheels sank into the sand. To get it moving, the slaves pushed it as the driver yelled and snapped his bullwhip between the ox's ears. The wagon lurched, and then rolled forward as long as the driver cracked the whip now and then.

Brutus and Mingo sauntered behind picking and eating huckleberries that grew in sunny spots beside the palmetto patches. The tiny berries had little flavor, but they at least helped fill their empty stomachs.

As they neared the Bell farm, the cracking whip alerted the hounds and they ran to intercept it. When Brutus and Mingo heard the yelps, they sprinted toward the cart. Mingo ran faster and taunted Brutus, "You better hurry or dem dogs goin' catch you." Holland reined the ox. Mingo scrambled up and then grabbed Brutus' arm, jerking him atop the lumber just before a dog sank his teeth into his leg.

Brutus laughed, "Didn't know I could run so fast."

Loring and Jake ran up screaming at the dogs. They ignored the men until Loring grabbed a stick, smacked it hard against his leg and shouted, "Get back! Down boys!"

When the hounds groveled, Loring said to Holland. "Sorry. The rascals took off before we could stop them."

"No harm done, but they put the fear of God in my nigras. I never knew they could move so fast."

Loring said, "Ya'll climb on down and I'll get these dogs used to you."

"You sure dey won't jump us, Mas'r?" said Brutus.

"Nah, not while I have this stick. Come on down."

Neither black man moved until Jake encouraged them. Then they eased down from the wagon with their eyes fixated on the husky beasts. The two hounds growled.

Jake grabbed one by the scruff of the neck and held him tight. Loring cowed the other one with his cudgel.

"Walk over here slow. Put your hand toward 'em. Show you ain't goin' hurt 'em."

With trepidation, Mingo and Brutus walked toward the animal while Jake talked to him. In a minute, the dog wagged his tail and then sniffed Mingo's and Brutus' palms in turn. Then he licked Brutus' hand. The other nuzzled up so the men could pet both of them. "Dey're OK once dey know you," Jake said.

"That settles that," said Loring. "Now let's get to work. We'll stack the lumber in that clearing behind those scrub oaks."

After unloading the cart, Loring directed Holland to the barn to pick up his comestibles. As soon as the men loaded several bags of peas and penders into the cart, Loring pointed to the house garden and said, "You can dig your yams over yonder."

Loring and Jake had staked out the location for the storehouse the day before and now finished digging the post holes while the others dug yams. After the tubers were loaded on the cart, Holland told the slaves to behave themselves, cracked his bull whip and headed home.

As soon as Holland drove off, Loring asked, "You men had breakfast?"

"No, Mas'r."

"We'll start work on the storehouse after we eat."

Blanche and Sarah fed everybody on the dogtrot between the main house and cookhouse where a breeze funneling between the buildings kept the area cool. The women brought out plates filled with bacon, fried eggs, a big bowl of grits and a pine straw basket that held a loaf of wheat bread along with butter and jam on the side. They set out fresh milk and coffee in gray, earthenware pitchers. Brutus and Mingo couldn't remember when they'd eaten a better breakfast.

Brutus mixed the eggs, grits, and bacon all together and savored the taste. In no time, he scraped his plate clean then swigged his coffee. When he set down his cup, he said, "Mas'r Loring, we sure 'preciates de eats. We ain't never seen scrumptious vittles like dis over yonder at de camp."

Loring said. "While you're here, you'll get all the food you want. You men could use fattening."

"Yes, sir, we needs dat, sure nuff."

Loring explained to Mingo and Brutus that in addition to building the storehouse he wanted to buy a steam-powered mill like one he saw advertised in the *Newnansville Florida Dispatch*. Then he showed them the ad with the picture of a grist mill driven by a steam engine. "If I order one of these, can you help set it up?"

Brutus looked at Mingo and smiled. "Sure we can, Mas'r. We set up de engine at de lumber camp."

"I figured as much. Let's get to work."

Loring and Jake had pre-cut and notched lighter pine logs for the corners, so they were ready to set. After the men placed the posts and tamped dirt around them, Brutus lifted one end of the cross beams into position while Mingo and Jake pushed up the other. When the timbers slipped into place, Loring augured holes through them with a brace and bit, tapped bolts through the holes and snugged them tight with hex nuts. The work progressed quickly.

By midafternoon, all the cross beams were bolted in place. "Let's take a break," Loring said.

When the men sprawled in the shade under the nearby scrub oaks, the children lugged over water and leftovers from the morning meal.

Loring said, "You're better workers than I expected."

Brutus said, "After such a good breakfast, the work was easy."

The men rested for half an hour before Loring roused them. By late afternoon, the men had several rafters framed. Pleased with the progress, Loring called a halt. "That's it for today. We've accomplished much more than I expected. If we can keep up this pace, we'll have this building dried-in in no time. Ya'll go with Jake. You're staying at his place. Sarah will make you supper."

As the two men walked with Jake toward his house, they flooded him with questions:

"Why ain't we workin' till dark?

"How comes Mas'r Loring treats you so good?"

"Don't you have a daily ration?"

"Do you eat at his house every day?"

Jake said, "Hold on, I'll answer your questions after supper. Wash up at the barn. There's a bucket and soap by the pitcher pump."

When the men saw Jake's house, they were surprised that it looked so much like the Bells' and not at all like the usual shacks in the slave quarters on most plantations.

Like the Bells, Jake's family ate on the dogtrot in good weather where Sarah set out an excellent supper: fried chicken, yams, black-eyed peas, white flour biscuits with butter along with sweet lemonade to drink.

Mingo and Brutus sipped, then gulped down their whole glass before Sarah had a chance to ask if it needed more sugar. Neither man had ever tasted the refreshing drink before. The entire family watched in amazement as they wolfed down helping after helping. When everybody finished, Jake said, "You chil'luns help Mama clean up."

Mingo said, "Miss Sarah, thank you for de fine supper. Never had vittles dis good 'cept for Christmas dinner at White Oak Plantation back in Carolina."

The men moved to the porch on the west side where Jake pulled up a cypress rocker. Brutus and Mingo sat in a wooden swing suspended by chains from a joist. As the sun dropped below the tree line, an orange-red glow reflected across Chunky Pond. In twos and threes, yellow-crowned night herons flew into the pines by the pond to roost, squawking "quark, quark" as they settled into the high limbs. All the while, frogs croaked a raucous chorus, and a screech owl chirred in a nearby scrub oak.

"You boys want a smoke? I make my own pipes and have good tobacco from Quincy."

Both men took a pipe.

As soon as the men lit their tobacco, Brutus commenced questioning Jake again. He told them to be patient and wait till the children were in bed. As the men sat smoking, Jake concentrated on the racket made by the frogs hidden among the pickerel weed and lily pads. Now and again, a bullfrog's throaty voice boomed over the din. Jake said, "Dem ole bullfrogs are thick. We ought to gig a mess."

Inside the house, Sarah scurried around preparing the children for bed. After a while, they quieted down and Sarah called out, "Jake, say good night to the children."

When Jake returned to the porch, he sat in his rocker and took several puffs on his pipe then said, "Here's de story. Miss Blanche's daddy owned Sarah's mama who was the house servant for de family, so Miss Blanche and Sarah grew up together. When dey was young women, both der mamas caught yellow fever and died. Soon after dat,

Mas'r Loring courted Miss Blanche and married her on her sixteenth birthday. Her daddy gave Sarah to her for a wedding present. I lived at the next plantation and had my eye on Sarah for de longest time. I saw her at de church every Sunday and I visited her at de quarters where she lived. I wanted to marry her, but my Mas'r wouldn't let me."

Brutus said, "How'd you git around dat?"

"When we found out dat Mas'r Loring was going to move down to Florida to start a new plantation, Sarah begged Miss Blanche to have him buy me so I could go too. I don't know de whole story, but Mas'r Loring won me in a horse race."

"A horse race?" Brutus said.

"Dat's right. Believe me; Mas'r Loring can ride with de best of 'em. After he won me, I married Sarah and we came down here to dis place. We've made some fair cotton crops. De place supports both families. We live in good houses and have plenty to eat. Dat's all dey is to it."

Brutus said, "Ain't never seen our people treated so well."

"Well, we've been through a lot with de Bells. Missis Blanche helped birth our babies. Sarah helped birth hers. Me and Mas'r Loring work side by side every day." Mingo said, "How come you have a shotgun?"

"You need one in des woods. Bear, panthers and scrub cattle are all over de place. Snakes too. You heard about dem rattlers dat your boss man killed, didn't you? Big one like dat bites you, ain't got nothin' to do but die. When we moved down here, Mas'r Loring worried wild Indians might still be here 'bouts. We never seen none. I suppose whites already run 'em off 'fore we came. Neighbor told me de last Indian attack here 'bouts was in '47."

"Will you teach us to shoot?" Mingo asked.

"Why?"

"You said yourself dat you need a gun in des woods."

"Git ya Mas'rs to look after you. Dey have guns."

"Dat's de problem. Dey got de guns and we don't."

"What ya mean?"

"We're sick and tired of dem devils workin' us to death."

"Be careful what you say. You can't get away with nothin' 'round des parts. If you do somethin' stupid, Crackers will string you up."

Brutus said, "So far, me and Mingo ain't been sick and Wall ain't beat us, but if he tries it, I'll wring his neck."

Mingo said, "I ain't goin' be a slave my whole life. I want to work for myself."

"You better think 'bout dat mighty hard. A free nigra was scratchin' out a livin' down by Otter Creek. De sheriff come and made him leave 'cause it's agin' de law for a freedman to live in Florida. Don't know what happened wid him. Cracker got his farm is all I knows."

Mingo said, "A black man ain't ever got it easy, slave or free. Teach us to shoot."

Jake repacked his pipe; relit it and rocked for a long time. "Did you ever notice de racket dem frogs make? Dey are so loud you can't hear yourself think. Den dey all quit croakin' just like dat." He snapped his fingers. "See you boys in the mornin'."

CHAPTER NINETEEN

DEER HALL

Florida

Chad failed to find a captain willing to sail or even talk about plans to leave Cedar Key due to the effectiveness of the U.S. Navy's Gulf Blockading Squadron. It not only closed Key West, the busiest port, to Rebel shipping, it controlled the Florida Straits and the entrance to the Gulf of Mexico. By holding Fort Taylor at Key West and Fort Jefferson on the Dry Tortugas in Federal hands, the Union Navy could maintain ships on station between Florida and Cuba. As a result, captains were reluctant to risk running the blockade unless they could earn huge profits.

As he waited for a ship, Chad decided to put his time to good use by identifying prospects for loans. He broached his plan with Mr. Parsons, who encouraged him inasmuch as the undercapitalized state banks could not provide the credit needed for the Big Bend economy to grow. A London syndicate willing to advance credit to local farmers and merchants could make up the difference, so the store owner gladly listed and ranked potential customers. He placed Loring Bell near the top.

Parsons sketched a map of the Big Bend that showed a road along an arc from Clay Landing on the Suwannee River, east to Archer, past Wacahotee and then south to Ocala. "Your best prospects will be above this road. For some reason, cotton grows better up there where the land transitions to rolling hills timbered with yellow pine. There ain't many roads worth the name, but you'll find wagon trails. Follow them and you'll come to a farm or camp. It's still wild country. Ya gotta be careful."

Chad nodded then watched as the storekeeper drew X's to mark the settlements.

Parsons continued, "Loring Bell's farm is by Chunky Pond. He's reliable. Everybody in the county knows him because he ran for the secession convention as a Union man. Some folks hold that against him, but I don't. Next to Bell's place, fellows named Holland and Wall operate a sawmill with a slave gang. Wall bought a steam engine through me when he first set up his camp, but I ain't done business with him since."

After discussing several more prospects, Parsons suggested that Chad should carry a pistol. "Criminals and runaways hide out in the backwoods. Sheriff runs most of them down, but with so many men in the militia, he has a hard time rounding up a posse. Without one, it's almost impossible to track outlaws, especially if they make it into the swamps across the Suwannee or hide out in Gulf Hammock."

Chad said, "Which one do you recommend?"

"I've got two models in stock: English Adams revolvers and Colt revolvers. I like the Adams. It's lighter, double action and its .36 caliber cartridges are common. The other choice is a Colt 44. It's heavier and the barrel is too long for my taste, but it has more stopping power. The Adams has enough for me."

Chad handled both the Colt and the Adams and agreed with Parsons' preference although the Adams only had a five shot cylinder. He bought one and a box of ammunition.

Molly begged to go along on the business trip. In Cedar Key, she had stayed inside in order not to attract attention which reminded her of being cooped up in Charleston. Chad reluctantly agreed to take her. They rode the train to Bronson. As he rented two horses at a stable, he overheard a snide comment about his slave girl that made him hurry to leave town. They rode south along the railroad tracks looking for the wagon trail to the Bell plantation that Parsons had described.

When Chad found one that he believed led to Bell's farm, he followed it until he came to a house surrounded by a picket fence that enclosed a yard raked to bare sand. As the horses walked up to the gate, geese gabbled as they ran under the house. Chad reined his horse and yelled. "Hello, anybody home?"

A tall, white woman stepped out on the porch. Although she wore a plain, gingham dress like most farm women in the area, hers was clean and tidy. She wore her blond hair pulled up in a bun that she held in place with a turtle shell comb. She carried herself in a relaxed, confident manner. A black woman about the same age and dressed the same way except for a bandana wrapped around her hair followed the white woman onto the porch. Chad tipped his hat while Molly lagged behind.

"How can I help you?" the white woman asked with a pleasant smile.

Chad identified himself and explained his mission.

"You need to speak to my husband, Loring. He's working on a building over yonder beyond those scrub oaks."

Chad thanked the lady then turned his horse where she had pointed. The women on the porch eyed the pretty black girl who had reined her horse well behind the white man. When he turned his horse, she hesitated then followed after him.

The men working on the storehouse had stopped nailing and pounding froes to split cedar shingles when they heard the commotion made by the geese. As they listened to determine what spooked the fowl, they heard a man's muffled voice waft through the scrub oaks. The hounds, which had been distracted by digging under a gnarled palmetto root for a gopher, barked and bounded toward the sound. Loring yelled at them to no effect then sprinted after them with Jake.

When Loring cleared the scrub oaks, he saw Ranger jump at the forelegs of Chad's horse. The horse bucked as Chad waved his pistol over his head. Loring shooed the dogs away and said, "You weren't going to shot my dogs, were you?"

"No, just scare them. Sorry to cause trouble. Name's Chad Waldock. Mr. Parsons in Cedar Key gave me your name. I'd like to talk business with you; I'm a cotton factor."

"No need to apologize. Dogs need to be trained. Every time a stranger rides up, they go nuts."

Molly stopped her horse about fifty feet from the men. When Loring held his glance on her, Chad sputtered, "She's my slave."

Loring didn't comment although the thought crossed his mind that miscegenation laws could never keep the races apart with such beautiful mulatto women around.

Curious to know what the stranger had in mind, Loring said, "Let my man take care of your horses. Come on up to the house." As Chad dismounted, Jake took the reins and called to Molly, "Follow me to the barn. We'll give the horses some water and then you can meet my friends."

Mingo and Brutus couldn't take their eyes off the young lady. Mingo said, "Hey, isn't dat de gal who was in de barracoon wid us in Charleston?"

"You're crazy. How could she get down here?

Mingo shaded his eyes from the sun for a better look. "Brutus, you de crazy man. I'm certain."

The dinner bell pealed and Brutus grinned, "We're 'bout to find out."

Mingo climbed down from the roof and ran toward Molly. When he came close, she recognized him. "My God, I can't believe my eyes!" she exclaimed. Mingo grabbed her in a bear hug.

She pushed him away. "What are you doin'?"

"What do you mean? I'm happy to see you."

Molly shushed him. "Now ain't de time and place. How'd you end up here?"

Mingo didn't have a chance to answer before Jake said, "You two know each other?"

Unable to restrain himself, Mingo said, "Yassuh, we sure do. We was together in de barracoon in Carolina when we was auctioned."

Molly glared at him.

He babbled on, "Dis here's Molly. I never expected to see her again. White men treated her real bad at de auction. A drunken dandy bought her."

"Dat's enough!" Molly said.

Jake tried to let the matter rest. "Come on, let's eat."

Mingo grabbed Molly's hand. "I'm so glad to see you. Whatta ya doin' here?"

She jerked her hand away. "Dat drunk who bought me sold me for a profit before he even took me to his house. My new owner had to come to Florida for business and he brought me along."

"Yeah, I knows why too."

"Mingo, don't say dat. He's a good man."

"How come you're travelin' with him out here?"

"Please don't ask questions. Trust me."

As Molly approached the house, two barefooted girls ran to her and tugged at her dress, "What's your name?"

She smiled and said, "Molly, what's yours?"

"Annie and this is Little Buddy. Are you staying with us?"

Sarah sent the children scampering.

After a glass of lemonade, Loring offered to show the factor around his farm. As they walked up to Jake's place, the similarity between the two houses startled Chad. Everywhere else around the Big Bend, slave shacks were ramshackle, one room structures with dirt floors. Usually, the owners constructed them from the cheapest materials like logs, or rough timbers, which were warped and cracked. Most often, they only had a smoky fireplace for cooking and heat. Many had thatched palm frond roofs. Far from the typical hovel, Loring's slave house had board siding, glass windows, flooring, a stove, cedar shake roof, and a big porch just like the main house.

Chad liked the looks of the entire farm. The tools and equipment were well-maintained, the stock well-tended. As Chad inspected the place, the men discussed cotton production and future plans. Loring said, "I've done well with my crop every year. My slave Jake knows everything about raising cotton. I'm constructing a new storehouse to hold my harvest until the government repeals the embargo. If they don't lift the restrictions, it's going to be hard to get by for another year without income. I can make it if no unexpected expenses pop up, but if I can't sell next year's crop, finances will be tight."

"I'm impressed with Deer Hall. My syndicate can do business with you as soon as your government lifts the ban. In my opinion, the embargo is a mistake. Withholding cotton from the market will not pressure England to ally with the Confederacy. In fact, it'll be an irritant. Anyway, English mill owners anticipated that secession might disrupt supply. They stockpiled thousands of bales which was one reason prices ran up last year. Supplies are so high that we're actually selling cotton to New England mills."

Loring said, "I'm not surprised." He checked himself before criticizing the shortsighted Confederate government. He didn't want to make any comment that could be interpreted as unpatriotic or disloyal to Florida, or the Confederacy. For all he knew, Chad could be a Secesh supporter and the firebrands no longer tolerated dissent.

He changed the subject. "I have another project that your group could finance. We don't have a decent mill close by. Farmers around here have to haul corn miles to have it ground. If I had a mill, I'd have a hedge for the years the cotton crop fails or the price is down."

After the men discussed the pros and cons, Chad explained that he couldn't make any specific commitments for a loan until the political situation stabilized.

On the way back to the house through an overgrown, fallow field, Loring led Chad around the head high, pale green dog fennels. The weeds had invaded the damp areas near the pond and he wanted to avoid the itchy chaff that fell from the plants when a person brushed against them. As they reached higher, drier areas marked by patches of brown broom grass, a cottontail burst from under a blackberry bramble running in zigzags for the safety of a slash pile. "If I had my shotgun, we might have rabbit purlieu for supper," Loring said as he watched the speeding rabbit.

Chad said, "We'd go hungry if I did the shooting."

"Jake would have dropped him already."

Realizing his faux pas, Loring stopped.

The men walked in silence for a while then Loring said, "I don't mean to be presumptuous, but it's not a good idea for you to travel in these woods with your bondsmaid."

"I know, but I couldn't find a decent place for her to stay in Cedar Key."

"The men will tolerate it, but the ladies will pitch a fit. Having that beautiful, young woman along gives the appearance that she's more than your helper and reminds them that their husbands are tempted by slave girls all the time. They won't let their men do business with you if she's along."

"I know it looks tawdry, but it's not. She's not a fancy maid. I had to bring her."

Both men stopped to watch the aerial acrobatics of two eagles as they dove for a fishhawk that held a wiggling perch in its talons. One raptor swooped at the osprey, causing it to drop its catch. The other snatched the fish in midair before it had fallen fifty feet. Both shrieked in victory.

As the birds flew away, Chad stooped down to pull sandspurs off his pants. After he flicked the last one to the ground, he said, "Maybe you could help me. Do you think your wife would let her stay here while I call on the other planters on my list? I'll pay you for the trouble, and my slave is an excellent house servant."

Loring picked up a drawknife someone had left on a sawhorse.

"I need to remind the men to put up the tools. They'll rust when they're left out in the night air. I'll talk to Blanche and see if she can stay with Jake and Sarah. Maybe we could work something out so you could stay too. We need every dollar we can get these days. Anyway, it'd be more convenient for you to stay with us. You'd be closer to the other farms from here than in Cedar Key. Let's see what Blanche says."

CHAPTER TWENTY

DEER HALL

Florida

From her experience helping her mama cook, Molly taught Blanche and Sarah new recipes and how to use different spices. In a short time after she arrived, no other farm in the Florida backwoods had meals as tasty as those at Deer Hall.

She hid her sadness at being torn away from her family by maintaining a lighthearted façade. She helped cheerfully with the chores and played with the girls and taught them new skills like sewing and knitting. She gathered wildflowers and taught the women and girls how to arrange the blooms in pretty displays that brightened the bare cypress wood porches and rooms at both houses. The women and children loved having Molly with them.

One day, Blanche noticed Molly struggling to sound out words in the Bible and asked her how she had learned to read. After the young lady explained that she had picked up a few words from white children in Charleston, Blanche decided to help her although the law prohibited it.

As soon as the storehouse was finished, Loring mobilized everybody to harvest the cotton crop. The grueling work lasted all day.

The cotton bolls jabbed, cut and tore the pickers' hands so by the time the last rows were picked near dark, everybody's hands were sore from nicks and scratches.

The hard labor had proceeded faster than Loring anticipated. He speculated that everybody had worked so well due to Jake and Sarah's example and Molly's positive attitude, or perhaps, the fact that everybody, black and white, worked side by side. He knew that if he had a few more hands who applied themselves as well, he'd have the most productive farm in the Suwannee Valley.

Relieved to have the harvest complete in less time than expected, Loring made an announcement, "I want to thank ya'll for working so hard. Take tomorrow off and do whatever you want. The next day we'll have a feast before Mingo and Brutus return to the lumber camp. Jake, let's go hunting in the morning?"

Mingo and Brutus reacted with astonishment. Mingo said, "Mas'r Loring, no owner ever treated us so good."

"You deserve it. You men have worked hard since you been here."

The next morning after breakfast, Molly and Mingo walked up the hill from Chunky Pond among towering longleaf pines. On the ground under the big trees, wiregrass tufts poked through the needles that blanketed the forest floor. The air smelled fresh with a hint of turpentine. Mingo eased his hand into hers "Molly, "I never thought I'd see you again when they dragged you from dat barracoon. It's a good thing Brutus held me back or those louts would have hurt me."

"I'm glad he did."

"Molly, I'll kill Waldock before I let him haul you off again."

"Don't say such a thing. Chad ain't a bad man."

"What ya mean? He's a white devil, ain't he?"

Molly jerked her hand free. "He ain't like de others."

"Course he is. He treats you sweet, but he owns you, don't he? Sooner or later, he'll take advantage."

She knew telling him the truth betrayed Chad's trust, yet she had felt she didn't have a choice. Tears rolled down her cheeks which confused Mingo. He wrapped his arms around her.

"Mingo, you've got it all wrong."

He jerked his hand back as if to slap her. "You callin' me a fool?"

Molly pushed him away and jumped back. "Listen here, Mister Man. You hit me and dat'll be de last time. I ain't puttin' up wid dat from no man, white or black. If you'll listen, I'll tell you everythin'."

Mingo had never known a woman to behave like this. He had half a mind to smack her just to show her who was boss but he didn't dare test her resolve. His shoulders slumped, "I'll listen."

"Do you promise not to repeat anythin' I tell you?"

"I promise,"

"I mean it, mister. If you break your promise, you'll put me in danger."

Mingo wondered what she meant. "I cross my heart and swear to God."

Molly grabbed his hands and looked into his eyes.

"I've escaped and Chad is helpin' me. He's a fine man who's riskin' his life for me."

Too astonished to respond, Mingo simply stared at her as she told him about her escape and the trip to Florida.

When she finished, he said, "We have to tell Brutus."

"No, de more dat know, the harder it'll be."

He squeezed her hands. "Molly, we'll make it to freedom together. You've come dis far. No one will tear us apart again and I'm bringin' my friend Brutus too."

She sobbed and threw her arms around him.

After supper, Mingo asked Brutus to take a walk with him and Molly. Brutus said, "No, ya'll go ahead. You two don't want me hangin' around."

"Come on. We need to talk to you about somethin' important."

"You lovebirds want me to be de best man at your weddin'?"

"Quit cuttin' de fool, Brutus."

Brutus shrugged and followed them toward Chunky Pond through the picked over cotton field. Near the water where the ground squished under their feet, Mingo pointed at an almost invisible, spearhead shape that slid through the duckweed fifteen feet from the shore. At first Molly couldn't make it out until she realized the jiggles outlined a huge gator head gliding toward a purple gallinule standing on a lily pad pecking for insects. The bird froze. The reptile exploded from the water. Gigantic jaws opened and slammed shut. The duckweed swirled, then settled to stillness.

Shaken, Molly hugged Mingo and said, "Did you see de size of dat thing? It could swaller you. Let's stay away from de water."

They walked to an ancient live oak that had been uprooted by a storm. All that remained was the gigantic trunk and its biggest limbs which were bleached bone gray and charred in splotches where wildfire had scorched the wood.

"Let's climb up so we can see de pond better," Mingo suggested.

"Can gators climb trees?" Molly asked.

Mingo laughed, "Course not. Dat ol' gator put a scare in ya, didn't he?"

They climbed up ten feet, settled in crooks formed by the massive limbs and watched reflections glimmer off the water.

Brutus said, "How come ya'll brought me out here?"

"We need your help. Molly ran away from dat devil who bought her in Charleston. Chad Waldock is helpin' her."

"Lord, have mercy. You're pullin' my leg."

Molly told Brutus everything about her escape except for the shooting and the businessman falling off the train. When she finished, Mingo insisted that they all run away together.

Brutus said, "I'll go wid ya, but we can't just take off. Will Mas'r Chad help us? He's in awful deep already. We could ask him to buy us, but I doubt Wall will sell. We don't know where to go."

Mingo said, "Damn it, Brutus, you always throwin' up road blocks. We can't wait."

Later that evening after the children were tucked in bed, as Molly and Sarah stood at a table on the dogtrot washing and drying dishes, Molly asked, "You ever hear 'bout slaves escapin'?"

"Sometimes Missis Blanche tells me 'bout some poor nigger de dogs run down."

"Are dey all caught?"

"Reckon so, but Missis Blanche mentioned onct dat some runaways made it into de swamps across de Suwannee River. Dey was never heard from again. I suppose gators et 'em."

"Where is de Suwannee?"

"Why you askin' so many questions?

"I'm curious, dat's all."

Sarah stopped wiping plates and looked at Molly. "Is dat Mingo talkin' you into somethin' stupid?"

"No, he ain't. Slaves sometimes escaped in Carolina."

"I heard some slaves ran away 'fore we moved here. Dey joined up with a band of Seminole Indians who lived back in de swamps across de river, but white folks chased dem off durin' de last Indian War. I guess a few might still live down in de Everglades where de whites don't go, but dat's a long way from here."

Early the next morning, Jake bagged a running doe after Loring missed it. The two men field dressed the carcass and lugged it to Deer Hall on Mike. After skinning and quartering the deer, they cut the backstrap into strips and brought them to Sarah. Once she had sliced the meat into cubes and placed them in a huge Dutch oven along with onions, collards, carrots, new potatoes, turnips, salt, pepper, and white flour, she stirred the ingredients well and put the iron pot on the stove to simmer.

Jake killed a suckling pig with his ax. He scalded and cleaned it and then wrapped the piglet in green banana flag leaves. In the meantime, Loring dug a pit a few feet deep and built a roaring hickory fire in it. After it burned down to coals, he scooped out a depression where he placed the bundle Jake had prepared. He raked embers over it and shoveled sand on top.

Late that afternoon, as Loring uncovered the piglet and pulled it from the coals, he heard a shrill whistle that Chad used to identify himself to the hounds as he rode up the lane. When the children heard it, they dropped everything and ran to meet him hoping that he had brought them treats. As the girls jumped up and down begging for candy, they noticed a big, damp, burlap bundle lashed behind his saddle.

"What's in the bag, Mas'r Chad?"

"Before we get into that, I brought something for you," he said as he tossed rock candy to the youngsters who walked beside him as he rode his horse towards the fire pit. As Chad dismounted he announced, "I brought oysters for the dinner."

"Jake, punch up the fire," Loring said.

When the fire burned down to coals, Jake placed a rusty iron disc over them and piled oysters on it. When the mollusks cracked open, Jake forced a hunting knife with a broken tip into the slit to pry off the top. As he flipped it away, he passed someone the bottom shell with the roasted oyster still in its juice. Everybody devoured the salty morsels and savored the smoky taste except Annie and Little Buddy who agreed they were too slimy to be eaten.

After the oyster appetizers, Sarah served the venison stew and shredded pork seasoned with Molly's pepper sauce. Everyone ate too much and became lethargic, Sarah revived them with coffee and the children begged Jake to play his guitar. When darkness fell, he strummed tunes and they all sang along to his chords and clapped time to the energetic music. After he played for an hour, Blanche ended the party and hustled the children to bed.

As the adults cleaned up, Molly tarried near Chad. When they were alone she said, "Have you found a captain in Cedar Key?"

"No, I'm ready to give up. The U.S. Navy has locked down the coast. Captains are afraid to run the blockade. If they're captured, their boats are confiscated or burned. I hoped we could sail with Captain Robison, but he went to Havana some time ago. Mr. Parsons heard he slipped back to Florida and is holed up in a creek near Tarpon Springs, but nobody knows for sure. At any rate, I don't know how to contact him."

"Can't we go to Key West?"

"No, captains won't sail there. If they do, they have to swear allegiance to the Union or have their boat confiscated. Believe me, I'm trying to figure out something."

"I know it, but now we have a problem. Mingo and Brutus know about us. I'm sorry; I shouldn't have told anybody, but…" Molly sniffled.

Chad felt faint. "We're already in enough danger. Now, it's worse. I know you're under tremendous stress, but please don't tell anybody else. If you do, we'll be found out for sure. I'm doing everything I can."

He comforted her with a quick hug.

Between sniffles she replied, "I know you are, but Mingo and Brutus are determined to escape with me. Will you help them too?"

Chad sighed and bit his lip. After a long pause, he said, "I'll go to Cedar Key tomorrow and do everything I can to hunt down a captain who'll run the blockade. For God's sake, make the others understand they need to keep quiet."

CHAPTER TWENTY-ONE

CHUNKY POND CAMP
Florida

The dreaded day for Mingo and Brutus to return to the lumber camp dawned blustery as a cold front pushed into the Big Bend from the northwest. By late morning, steady rain supplanted drizzle and the temperature plummeted. To escape the storm, the hounds stayed under the house where they scratched depressions in the sand and curled up in tight balls. When people needed to use the privy or to do chores, they dashed from the house and back into the warmth as fast as possible.

In late afternoon, Holland arrived at Deer Hall with his collar turned up and his slouch hat pulled so low he could hardly see. His efforts to stay dry had failed. Rain soaked his mackinaw and dungarees, and water dripped into his scruffy Wellington boots. His dirty and sweat-stained jacket, now saturated, stank as bad as the hounds curled up in the dirt under the house.

The stiff breeze and rain masked Holland's approach, so the dogs never barked until his horse, with its head down against the gusts, approached the front gate. Once the hounds sensed the animal, they ran from under the porch with a greater ruckus than usual as if to redeem their carelessness. Loring ran out onto the stoop expecting trouble, but when he saw Holland slumped over in the saddle to ward off the rain, Loring hollered at the watchdogs to shut up. His shouts, but mostly the downpour and wind, convinced them they'd done enough, so they scurried back to their sandy depressions.

"Come inside out of the rain," Loring yelled.

Holland dismounted, tied the reins with a slip knot around a lighter wood gate post and then sprinted for the porch. Snatching his Stetson off his head by the brim, he beat it against his leg to shake off the water. Loring said, "Hang your hat and coat on one of those pegs by the door. You better warm up before you catch pneumonia. Take off your boots and set them by the fire to dry."

Holland tugged off his Wellingtons, shook out some water from them, then placed them by the stove. He wasn't wearing socks. As he edged his backside to the warm fire, he said to Loring, "You have any trouble with my boys?"

"No, they were excellent workers. We finished the storehouse sooner than I expected, so I used them to pick my cotton. If you ever want to sell them, let me know."

"Don't count on it. They're the only ones with brains enough to run the sawmill."

As Blanche walked in from the back room, she noticed wisps of steam rising from Holland's shoulders. She held out a hand knitted afghan to him. "Here. How about some coffee and a bite to eat?"

"Thank you, Ma'am. Coffee would be terrific. Don't put yourself out fixin' nothin' for me."

"No bother atal. Riding over here in this weather must have made you hungry."

Holland looked so skinny that Blanche wondered about the food at the lumber camp. She sent Billy to fetch eggs from the chicken coop.

He returned with three eggs that she fried with a slab of salt pork and fist-sized patties made from congealed grits left over from breakfast. When she brought him the plate, he blurted, "Thank you Ma'am."

After Holland gobbled the food, Loring said, "Your men are at Jake's. You ready to fetch them?"

While Holland pulled on his boots, Loring retrieved a wool jacket from a peg by the door. After Loring buttoned his coat, they stepped out to the stoop and noticed that the rain had eased to a drizzle. Low, gray clouds scudded from the northwest although blue sky showed in a few scattered patches. The air felt colder. "We'll have a hard freeze tonight," said Loring.

"This whippin' wind makes it feel thata way already," Holland said as he wiggled into his sopped mackinaw and soggy riding gloves. He untied his horse and led him by the bridle as the two men walked to Jake's house. After Holland cinched his animal to a post, they climbed the steps, crossed the porch and knocked on the door. While being careful to close the door behind him before the wind caught it, Jake stepped out. He hugged himself from the chill.

"Jake, Mr. Holland has come for his men."

"Yassuh, I'll gather dem up."

To escape the wind, Loring and Holland ducked around the corner and stomped their feet to keep warm while they waited. In a minute, Holland's two slaves stepped outside. Mingo wore Jake's wool shirt, but Brutus only wore a thin, cotton one.

Loring stripped off his jacket. "Brutus, take this. It won't fit you, but you can throw it around your shoulders. When this cold snap breaks, I'll send Billy to fetch it."

Brutus looked at the ground and muttered, "Thank you, Mas'r Loring,"

As Holland mounted his horse he grunted, "You're spoilin' my boys,"

Once in the saddle, he pulled the draw string on his hat snug and turned toward Loring touching his hat's brim. Loring nodded and watched him ride away with the two black men walking behind.

Mingo and Brutus walked fast in order to stay warm. At first, Holland rode ahead and then stopped to wait behind thickets out of the wind until they caught up. After several stops, the gusts chilled him to the bone, so he left them.

When he rode away, Mingo said that if Molly were with them he'd light out for the swamps across the Suwannee River. Brutus reminded him that nobody knew for certain if any slaves had made it to safety and that they'd freeze to death if they tried.

The farther the two men walked, the more the wind chilled them. They made every effort to keep their legs and feet dry by walking in the sandy ruts, but when they came to puddles, they had to walk beside the track through dripping wet weeds or palmettos. Moisture soaked their pants and dampness steeped through their scruffy, thin soled shoes. Their feet became numb.

By sunset, the temperature dropped more and the sky cleared. A quarter-moon shimmered through the high pine boughs in the failing light. Both men began to shiver. "If we don't git to camp soon, we goin' to freeze whether we run away or not," Mingo mumbled. They began jogging to stay warm.

As they rounded a black jack oak thicket, they spotted a fire flickering far ahead. Mingo sped up. Before he had run a hundred yards, a wail echoed through the woods. He stopped and turned toward Brutus. "Was dat a panther?"

"Maybe. Sometimes dey sound like a person screamin'."

Mingo sprinted toward the fire and heard another shriek.

As he ran across the camp toward the flames, he saw a form suspended from a timber lashed between two pines. At first he thought it was an animal, but as his eyes adapted to the firelight, he realized it was a person. Mingo heard a bullwhip crack and saw its tip snap against the man's back. Another panther scream ripped the night.

"What you looking at?" Wall yelled from the darkness beyond the firelight.

Enraged, Mingo leapt toward him. At the same time, Wall snapped the whip. Before Mingo could react, he felt braided leather burn across his neck. Grasping the whip, he jerked it, pulling Wall off balance. Before he could recover, Mingo grabbed him around the neck with his left arm, pulled his head down and punched him with a right uppercut. Wall's knees buckled. As he slumped forward, Mingo kneed him in the face and felt his nose crack.

Mingo heard a thud behind him and pivoted with his hands raised to block an attack. The defensive motion was unnecessary. Holland collapsed at his feet. Brutus stood behind Holland rubbing the knuckles on his right hand. "How many times have I got to save you, boy? He was 'bout to lay you low wid dat pine knot."

Mingo shivered involuntarily. Holland stirred and moaned. Wall was so still he looked dead except for the blood pouring from his broken nose. "What we goin' do now?" Mingo asked.

"I reckon you didn't think about dat," Brutus snapped. "Fetch rope. Let's tie up dem Crackers and take de boy down."

Mingo ran toward the tack shed as Brutus stripped the holsters and the bowie knife sheaths off the white men's belts. Then he cut the rawhide thongs securing the man to the timber and lowered him to the ground.

Brutus hogtied his prisoners tighter than any pig had ever been bound. He forced their wrists together and tied them behind their backs. Then he rolled them on their stomachs, flipped a slipknot around their ankles and looped the bight around their necks. Pulling the line taut, he bowed their bodies until their feet jammed against their heads. Brutus tied off the lines with half hitches, checked the knots and turned to help the flogged man. Although other slaves consoled him as best they could, he continued to wail.

Across the fire, a slave yelled, "You niggers goin' git us all kilt."

Brutus bellowed, "Listen up! Listen up!" As everybody quieted, he said, "Me and Mingo done it. We're the ones the Crackers will come after. Ya'll ain't done nothin', but ya have a choice. You can stay, or you can come wid us. Dem dat want to come, step over here. Dem dat wants to stay, stand by de fire."

Holland, semi-conscious and terrified, watched as four slaves joined Brutus.

Brutus said, "Listen here, this ain't goin' be easy. You dat's goin', saddle de horses and hitch de ox to the cart. We'll take half the food and supplies. Gather up cots, bedding, a tent, shovels, axes, hand tools, and pots and pans. Take all de guns and ammunition. Mingo, search de tents. Make sure we have all de weapons."

The slaves had never moved with such vigor. In a few minutes, everything Brutus wanted was piled on the cart along with Holland and Wall. Brutus pulled aside a slave who was staying behind and said, "We're takin' de Crackers so de sheriff don't blame you for what we done. We'll dump dem beside de road somewhere. Wait till mornin', den walk to Bronson and report dat we kidnapped 'em."

Brutus climbed up on the cart. After checking the lines securing Holland and Wall, he clambered over the gear to the seat, grabbed the bull whip and snapped it over the ox's head. The wagon rolled west following the lumber camp track until it came to the Florida railroad where Brutus turned southwest along the grade that passed through flatwoods and across marshes.

The night stayed cold. By morning, frost glistened off the maiden cane, grasses and sedges. The grade squeezed so tight between ponds that Brutus worried he'd be forced to abandon the cart, but just before he had to he found a crossroad that veered to the south. He followed it until the ox clomped onto a wooden bridge where he stopped. Climbing down from the wagon, he walked to the back where his captives stared wild-eyed at him. Although blood still oozed from Wall's flattened nose, he threatened Brutus, "You better untie me right now or you're a dead man."

Brutus jerked the line around Wall's neck and told the others to unload the Crackers. The men dragged the prisoners off the cart, lugged them away from the bridge to a palmetto patch and heaved them into the brush. The bound men crashed through the fronds and thudded against the roots. Holland moaned and tried to wrestle free. Wall lost consciousness.

Brutus yelled, "Hurry up. I 'spects de sheriff will be on our trail 'fore long."

By mid-morning, the road curved back to the west toward the railroad tracks. When it reached them again, the ox strained to pull the cart up and across the grade. Once on the other side, Brutus continued straight across on a sandy road. At an intersection, he stopped. "Sarah said dis trail to the left goes south toward Cedar Key, but we have to go west to find de river. Mingo, ride ahead and scout for a route. Search for half an hour, den come back."

In an hour, or so, Mingo returned on a lathered horse. "In a few miles dis road joins another one and heads south. I didn't find a cross-road as far as I went. What we goin' to do, Brutus?"

"Ain't got no choice; keep movin'. By noon they'll have word 'bout us in Bronson. It'll take de sheriff a while to gather up a posse, but he'll be on our trail 'fore night fall. We have to find de Suwannee soon."

Midafternoon, as the group rounded a bend, they saw two riders approaching them. Brutus said, "No use hidin'. Dey seen us already. I'll do de talkin'. Dey don't know about us or dey wouldn't be comin' on so easy."

Brutus reached under the wagon bench into a box and felt the pistols though their presence gave him little comfort. Jake had shown him how to load his shotgun but never had let him shoot it.

Two scruffy riders wearing gray jackets and armed with pistols stopped by the wagon. One pulled a plug of tobacco from his pocket, bit off a wad, and muttered, "What you boys up to?"

Brutus looked down and rubbed his forehead. "Movin' camp for our Mas'rs Holland and Wall."

"You have a pass?"

"Nossuh. Mas'rs comin' on behind us."

"Looks like you've been pushin' your animals hard."

"Mas'r Wall told us to move along."

"Where you goin'?"

"Don't know. Boss just told us to follow dis road."

The second rider smirked and said, "Typical. Nigras don't know their arses from a hole in the ground."

"Looks fishy to me. They ain't got no pass and their owners ain't around, but I ain't heard 'bout none runnin' off."

"I know Holland and Wall. Ain't heard they're movin', but that ain't our worry. We've got to finish our patrol."

The first rider said to Brutus, "If you ain't bein' straight with me, I'll have your hide." He spat on a wagon wheel.

"Yassuh, boss," Brutus replied as he urged the tired ox forward.

Brutus kept the group moving as fast as he could make the ox walk until they came to a deeply rutted, sandy road that continued south. Fortunately, a less traveled crossroad veered west toward the river. Brutus turned onto it and ordered Mingo to scout it. He returned too soon to have gone far. "Bad news. Dis trail only circles back to de main road."

As Mingo walked his horse beside the wagon, Brutus jiggled the reins to keep the ox moving while he stared across its back without speaking for several minutes. Finally, he said, "We'll hide de gear we can't carry in de thickets along dis road. You lead de men west through de woods to de river. I'll drive on ahead with de horses and den turn off into de woods. I'll go as far as I can and den abandon de cart and de animals. I'll circle back and catch up with ya'll."

Brutus forced the worn-out ox to plod along the track for a few miles then turned it onto a vague, overgrown logging trail that snaked into the brush. After half a mile, the track dead-ended at an impassable bay head.

He gathered up the pistol, shotgun and ammunition that he'd kept hidden under the seat and then climbed down from the empty wagon. He untied the horses from the cart, unhitched the ox and slapped the exhausted beast on the haunch. It didn't move. He yelled at the horses and smacked the closest one. They trotted to a nearby clearing where they stopped to graze. Brutus set off at a run. When he stopped to catch his breath, he felt the wind gusting and noticed dark sky to the northwest.

As he trotted on, heavy, gray clouds rolled across the sky that blocked the setting sun. In the gloom, Brutus almost missed the place where Mingo and the others left the track. As he turned to follow the dim trail, raindrops plopped around him.

Soon the rain pounded hard. When he stopped for a breather at a black water creek, he realized with a start that he'd lost the trail and his sense of direction. Gasping, he forced himself to quiet down and think. In despair, he realized he needed to backtrack. Doubling back, he couldn't find the trail in the rain. Realizing that he was lost and worrying about the posse, he decided he had no choice but to return to the creek and follow it in hopes that it flowed to the Suwannee.

Although he sometimes had to crawl to make his way through briars and brambles, Brutus stayed on the bank as much as possible. When he couldn't force his way through the jungle, he waded the creek. The effort exhausted him, but he took satisfaction in knowing that only the most resolute posse would follow him in the heavy rain, through the tangled thickets and down the stream.

Brutus tramped forward late into the night. Where the brush was impenetrable, he slid down the creek bank and splashed into waist deep water. Afraid that he might fall into a deep hole, he clambered out of the water at every sandy bank or clearing. Finally, too exhausted to go on, he slumped down at a leaf-covered clearing. He tilted his slouch hat back to keep the rain off his neck and wrapped Loring's jacket around his head and shoulders for warmth and then crossed his arms under his head. Although wet and cold, Brutus rested until the rain stopped and the sun broke through the clouds after dawn.

As the day brightened, he noticed that the impenetrable tangles all around him left no choice except to slide back into the creek. To his relief the water didn't get deeper, so he kept slogging forward until he came upon sandy mounds with huge cypress trees growing around them. He grasped a cypress knee, pulled himself out of the stream and clambered up a hillock. From it, he could see through the trees to open water. He prayed that it was the Suwannee although he couldn't imagine how he could cross such a wide river.

He headed upstream. Around midday, he smelled smoke on a breeze blowing toward him. He crept forward in low crouch along the mounds that edged the water while being careful not to rattle any dead palm fronds that littered the ground. Before long he heard muffled conversation carried on the wind. He hid and listened until he recognized Mingo's voice. He ran forward, grabbing his friend in a bear hug.

Mingo exclaimed, "Man, are we glad to see you! We was worried de posse caught you."

"No posse goin' take Brutus without a fight." He patted his shotgun and smiled. "I smell dinner. What's in de pot?"

"Ain't nothin' left 'cept 'possum scrapens."

Brutus lifted the iron lid on a cast iron Dutch oven that rested atop a few smoldering sticks. The pot was empty except for a thin layer of grease, charred meat and bits of pone. A man handed him a spoon. He mixed the remaining cornmeal into the grease and wolfed down the concoction. After he had scraped the kettle clean, he asked if anyone had heard dogs. Nobody had. "Good, but we have to be more careful. A posse could sneak up like I did. I smelled smoke way back yonder. Put out de fire."

No one argued. As a man kicked sand over the coals, Brutus asked, "Have you found a place to ford de Suwannee?"

"No. It's wider and deeper than I expected and lest we find one soon, we're trapped." Mingo replied

The men shouldered their bundles and trudged upstream along the sandy ridges. After a few hours they heard a rhythmic rumble. Mingo held up an arm to stop the group as the clamor from a thudding engine reverberated louder. "Hide!"

The men jumped behind logs and palmettos as a steamboat belching black smoke rounded the nearest bend. Atop the cabin, two men dressed in gray shirts held long rifles.

As the engine's noise faded downstream, Brutus said, "We were lucky dem soldiers didn't see us. Mingo, why don't you scout upriver? We'll hide here. No use all of us goin' until we know where we're headed."

Brutus led the band a mile back from the river where he stopped at a clearing. "Make yourselves comfortable. We might have a long wait."

Everybody dozed off into a sound sleep. Barking dogs that he knew had to be leading the posse awoke Brutus late in the afternoon. He roused the others and scrambled for the river. The dogs sounded closer. Near the shore not far from him, he heard a scraping noise against the bank that caused him to check the percussion cap on the shotgun. A great blue heron squawked and flew away. As Brutus strained to see or hear what had spooked the bird, he heard Mingo's soft whistle.

"Good thing you signaled. I was so nervous I might have shot you. What did you find?"

"A rowboat."

"Well, I'll be. You make a mighty fine scout." A dog howled close by.

CHAPTER TWENTY-TWO

CHUNKY POND

Florida

The day after Mingo and Brutus left for the lumber camp, a deputy sheriff galloped up to the gate at Deer Hall. Loring heard the hoof beats and ran out onto the porch. Without dismounting, the deputy yelled across the yard, "Runaways have kidnapped Holland and Wall. They took all the weapons in the camp. Sheriff says you have to join a posse to hunt them down."

Loring had no desire to take part in a manhunt and doubted the sheriff had authority to force anyone to join the chase, but he also knew he had to sign on or become more of an outcast.

"You have any more details?"

"All I know is faithful slaves walked into Bronson. They told the sheriff six ran off. The ringleader was a big buck named Brutus who convinced the others to join him."

"Brutus? That's hard to believe. I rented him and he never gave me any trouble. Something must have set him off. He's not the type to lead an uprising."

"The story could be wrong. Like always, we had to pry the details out of the nincompoops who blew the whistle."

"Where can I find the sheriff?"

"He's already after 'em. You're supposed to pick up the trail at the lumber camp and catch up as fast as you can. The runaways headed out on an oxcart, so they can't be far."

By this time, everybody had gathered around. Molly blurted out, "Is Mingo with them?"

Sarah grabbed her arm.

With that, the deputy wheeled his horse to collect more men.

Loring turned to Blanche. "Sounds like serious trouble. You better pack several days' food."

Chad asked, "Loring, is there anything I can do?"

"No, just stay here till I return. I suspect they'll try to hotfoot it across the Suwannee, but you can never tell. They might head over here, so you and Jake need to stay alert. Billy, saddle up Ginger."

Loring walked inside to an armoire, unlocked a drawer and took out a well-oiled model 1851 Navy colt .44 caliber revolver and a box of ammunition. He flipped open the cylinder and loaded six cartridges. "Honey, I'm leaving the LeMat here for you. It's loaded. Keep the cabinet locked with the key in your pocket. If any runaways come around, keep the doors barred and stay inside. Send them on their way. If they don't leave, shoot them. If you have to fire the LeMat, use the shotgun barrel first. You're less likely to miss with buckshot."

Blanche looked stunned but didn't protest.

"I'll take my shotgun with me. Billy can use the .20 gauge. I'll talk to Jake."

Loring found Jake in the barn helping to saddle Ginger. "Jake, did Brutus say anything about running away?"

"Yassuh, like most darkies he did, but I didn't put no stock in it."

"Well, apparently, he was serious. Now, I have to join a posse to hunt him down. You'll have to help look after the place while I'm gone. If any runaways show up, and that includes Brutus, make them move on. If they won't, shoot them. They're dangerous. Jake, I'm depending on you to protect Deer Hall."

"Yassuh, Mas'r Loring."

Loring ran back to his house with Billy. After gathering his family around him, he hugged Little Buddy and said to Billy, "Son, you look after your Mama and help Jake around the place."

"Yes, Daddy, I will." Billy said and threw his arms around Loring's neck.

With Billy and Little Buddy clinging to him, Loring grabbed Blanche, hugged her and gave her a kiss. "Love you. I'll be OK. I'll be back as soon as this mess is sorted out."

As he rode away, Blanche sniffled and prayed to herself, *Dear God, keep him safe.*

At the lumber camp, Loring found it deserted and in disarray. He hallooed several times, but nobody responded. At the storage lean-to, barrel tops littered the ground. At the fire pit, he lifted the lid from a cold cast iron pot and saw that it was empty.

He sat down at the long table to take a drink from his canteen. As he lowered it to the table, he sensed a stirring behind him. Dropping the container, he jerked his pistol from its holster and whirled.

He felt foolish when all he saw were leaves vibrating on the breeze. Still, he continued to scan the brush. In a palmetto patch fifty feet away, he thought he could discern the outline of someone's head pressed to the ground. He leveled his pistol. "Get out here, right now." A black man stood up with his hands straight in the air. In a high- pitched, staccato voice he yelled, "I didn't do nothin' Mas'r. I told dem not to do it. I told dem---"

"Calm down! Walk over here real slow." Loring barked.

The black man walked to the table with his hands above his head while never taking his eyes off the pistol pointed at his chest. "Mas'r, I swears, I told dem niggers---"

"Quit jabbering. Sit down at the end of the table."

With infinite patience Loring questioned the black man about what had happened at the camp. Scared and upset, the slave often regressed into unintelligible ramblings, but Loring persisted until he sorted out the facts.

"You know where Brutus is headed?"

"Nossuh. Somewhere across the Suwannee River. "Who's goin' to look after us?"

The question stumped Loring. He wondered if Holland and Wall were even alive. He knew one thing for certain. Runaways had to be prevented from marauding. "You stay right here till your owners get back. Clean up the camp and take care of the place. Nobody will hurt those of you who stayed loyal. Those who ran off will be punished. If you stay here, you'll be OK. You understand?"

"Yassuh, Mas'r."

"Good. Which direction did the posse go?"

"Down dat trail over yonder."

CHAPTER TWENTY-THREE

Otter Creek Bridge

Florida

Loring didn't rush to catch the posse, but he made good time in the brisk weather. Ginger covered ground so fast that Loring decided to take a break at the Otter Creek Bridge.

He had always enjoyed spotting fish in the water by the bridge. Although stained a weak tea color by tannin from fallen leaves, it remained transparent unless riffled by the wind. He had seen many species swimming in the still stream: mullet, soap fish, bass, mudfish, perch, redfish, gar, and stump knockers. Once, on a gigging trip with Jake and the children, he'd seen a huge fish with hide like an alligator that must have been six feet long. Somebody said it was a sturgeon. He hoped to see one again.

Where workmen had cut trees along the creek for bridge timbers, alligators often basked in the sunny clearings. On occasion, Loring and Jake had hunted them for their skins and tail meat.

After he rode Ginger onto the bridge, he dismounted. Dropping the reins over the mare's neck, he turned her loose to drink and graze. The horse didn't go to the water but walked past the bridge embankment to nibble on the weeds growing along the creek. Loring didn't see any alligators on the banks and figured they were hiding in their caves in the cool weather. He looked for fish for a time, but gave up because the wind rippled the water too much to see below the surface. He decided to move on.

As he walked toward Ginger, he heard rustling in a palmetto patch. At first, he thought the sound was a squirrel jumping onto dried palm fronds and didn't pay much attention to it. When he heard the noise again, he guessed it was a hog rooting in the palmettos. Slowly, he walked to Ginger and pulled his shotgun from its scabbard, half-cocked the hammer, and eased toward the commotion.

Fronds crackled. Then he heard a thud. He figured the sound could only be made by a hog; a deer or a bear wouldn't be so clumsy. As he crept forward while being careful not to snap a twig underfoot or to catch his pants on briars, a muffled grunt came from beyond the palmettos.

His eye caught a tinge of blue that looked like dungaree material. He edged forward with his shotgun raised until he saw Holland struggling to free himself.

As soon as Loring cut the rope from around his neck, Holland tried to speak, but his voice cracked from the damage done by the tight constraint. After Loring sliced the ropes from Holland's wrists and ankles, he tried to stand, but his legs too were stiff from being tied in the awkward position for so long. As he sat rubbing his legs, Loring made out something about Wall being nearby.

At a clearing carpeted with wire grass, Loring found scuffed ground. He followed the trail which led him to Wall. He was semi-conscious, his nose was smashed, his face was bruised and his eyes were swollen shut. Loring bent down and cut the ropes binding him and shook him hard. Wall groaned.

Holland staggered up. Loring said, "He's in bad shape. Can you help me move him?"

"No, I'm about to pass out."

"Follow me. I'll drag him to the bridge."

The jostling revived Wall enough that he could speak, but Loring couldn't understand anything coherent except, "I'm goin' to kill the niggers."

At the bridge, Loring explained to them that the sheriff had ordered him to join the posse and that he had to move on. Holland protested and begged him to take them to Bronson. Loring refused. "I'll leave you a tin of crackers and a pistol. You'll be OK. I'll let the sheriff know where you are. Someone will come by before long anyway."

With that, he handed Holland his pistol, mounted Ginger and rode away. Later that day, he heard hounds barking ahead of him and knew the posse couldn't be far. Where the road skirted a depression pond, he overtook the sheriff who eyed him as if his arrival was a surprise.

Loring reported, "I found Holland and Wall. Their slaves dumped them by the Otter Creek Bridge. They're both busted up, but they'll live."

"They tell you what happened?"

"Not in detail. I was in a hurry to catch you. Several slaves jumped them, stole their supplies, horses and all their firearms and ammunition."

The sheriff knotted his brow and clenched his teeth. "They have a leader?"

"Wall said a slave named Mingo jumped him although a man named Brutus appears to be in control."

"You know anything about those two?"

"Yes, sir. I rented them from Holland and Wall. They were no trouble."

"Where you reckon they're headed?"

"I have no idea, but we've all heard the rumors about runaways living in the swamps across the Suwannee."

"Let's hope they're headed for the river. They can't cross. We'll catch 'em lickety split."

Before sunset, a heavy downpour soaked the posse, but the handler kept the hounds on the track. After dark, the dogs reached the Clay Landing Road and continued straight across on a rough track heading west. The handler's confidence built as the dirt lane curved back toward the main road. He released the hounds from their leashes, and they sped down the track. Somewhere ahead and out of sight, dogs howled several times. "Sounds like they bayed," the sheriff said as he grabbed his pistol and kicked his horse into a trot. When he arrived at the empty wagon, he found the curs circling and sniffing the ground instead of cowing blacks like he expected. "Which way you reckon they went?" he yelled at the dog handler.

"Don't know. The track won't be easy to find in this rain."

Even in the difficult conditions, the dogs managed to sniff out the route after the handler put them on it. Although the trail circled around and strayed off in random directions, he knew his hounds had the scent. The sheriff didn't believe it. "Dang dogs ain't followin' nothin' but animal tracks."

"No, they ain't. I've seen this before. Runaways sometimes wander around in circles when they don't know which way to go."

Soon the undergrowth became too thick for the horses to crash through. The sheriff left them behind with a man to guard them. Forced to walk and weighted down by their grub and weapons, the posse made slow progress through brambles and briars.

After plowing through the brush for several hours, the sheriff stopped. "Your dang mongrels ain't after men. They must be on a bear. Nobody could force his way through this jungle."

"They're on a man's track all right. I saw a footprint in the mud a few minutes ago."

The sheriff called for a break. The exhausted posse sprawled on the ground and gobbled crackers. One man peeled an orange and passed around plugs. After a short while, the dog handler said, "It's too dangerous to keep pushing ahead in this rough country in the dark and rain. If we come up on them, one of us could be shot. Let's rest till morning and then go on."

The sheriff had lost all enthusiasm for the chase and agreed.

After a wet and cold night, the posse moved out at first light down a creek that flowed to the river. Like Brutus, the posse had to wade in the water where thickets blocked the route. The handler found the spot where Brutus had rested and then continued pressing forward until he reached the sandy mounds where the trail became easy to follow. He ran ahead of the others with the dogs. Late in the afternoon, several successive barks sounded as if the hounds were closing on their prey.

The sheriff had always enjoyed chasing down runaways and considered it fine sport, but not this time. This chase wearied him. The fugitives had forced him to travel on foot during a rain storm, crawl through jungle and wade creeks. He ached all over and felt queasy. With darkness coming on for the second night, he wasn't eager to catch up with armed blacks or to spend another long night in the woods.

Ahead a shotgun blast reverberated through the forest and a dog yelped. The handler dove behind a cypress tree and screamed for his hounds. Another shot sounded and a yipping hound ran by him dragging its guts. He shot it to put it out of its misery. As he reloaded his shotgun, the sheriff joined him.

"Don't go no farther. They already shot two of my dogs."

"Where are they?"

From ground level atop a dirt mound about a hundred yards away, the sheriff saw a flash as buckshot tore into a cypress knee beside him. Rattled from the near miss, he had the shakes. As he scrunched tight against the tree, he called for men to circle around the shooter. Nobody moved. The sheriff berated the men until Loring and another man backed well beyond shotgun range then circled around.

As the light faded, no sound or detectable movement came from behind the sandy bank. As darkness closed in, the sheriff shrieked in frustration, "If you don't surrender, you're dead men." Nobody responded.

After an hour maneuvering behind cover to slip up on the escapees without being shot, Loring knew he had to be close, but he couldn't see or hear them. As he narrowed the gap, he realized the only place the runaways could be hunkered down was in a pit between two sandy embankments. "Cover me," he signaled to his companion and then crept forward to look into the depression. When his compatriot fired toward the hollow, Loring dashed behind a tree higher up the bank from where he could see into the hiding place.

"Sheriff, nobody's here!"

"They have to be."

"Well, they're not, Sheriff."

The man near Loring shouted, "They've given us the slip; a boat's been beached here."

CHAPTER TWENTY-FOUR

DEER HALL
Florida

After Brutus' band had eluded the posse at the Suwannee River, the sheriff hurried to the Otter Creek Bridge to collect Holland and Wall. When he found them, both looked peaked. Wall was delirious and unable to stand without help. His partner had washed his smashed face in the creek and tied a neckerchief around his nose, but blood had soaked through the cloth. Although he was coherent, Holland looked wobbly. His head throbbed and movement made him dizzy.

The sheriff looked them over and said, "All things considered, you're in better shape than I expected. In fact, I'm surprised those rapscallions didn't kill you. What do you want to do, go back to your camp?"

Wall couldn't even respond.

Holland said, "I think we best see a doctor."

The situation thoroughly disgusted the sheriff. Holland and Wall's inability to control their slaves had caused him to look ineffective. Never before, had he failed to capture runaways when he could find their track. In his experience, every one had been easy to catch with dogs. Usually, they only took a bundle with some food and clothing, if that. This time, they took supplies, armed themselves and had outsmarted him. The failure besmirched his reputation. Worse, when word got around, more slaves might head for the river.

The sheriff said to Loring, "I'll take these men to the doctor. You go to the lumber camp and take responsibility for those who stayed. Make sure no more run off. As soon as I can, I'll contact the sheriff of Lafayette County to help me hunt down those who crossed the river into his jurisdiction."

Loring wanted to decline the mission as he had his own family, farm and slaves to care for, but he didn't want to risk antagonizing the sheriff. "Yes, sir," Loring assented while wondering how the lawman expected him to manage the assignment.

When he rode into the lumber camp, he saw three slaves sitting at the communal table. He checked the caps on his pistol and rode Ginger straight to them. They stood up without looking at him.

"How many of you are still here?"

The same slave he had talked to earlier said, "Four of us Mas'r. What happened to de others?"

"Sheriff's on their tail. He sent me over here to look after you until your owners return. Until then, you're under my supervision. Keep felling trees on your normal schedule. You understand?"

"Yassuh, Mas'r."

"You have rations?"

"Nossuh, Brutus took most everythin'."

"Show me."

Loring noted to his astonishment that every barrel and sack under the lean-to had been ransacked and left unsealed. Corn meal and dried beans littered the ground. Animal tracks in the sand and droppings on the barrels confirmed varmints had been into the supplies.

"Clean up this mess. Coons and rats will ruin what's left. Seal the barrels that still have anything in them. Don't eat more than your normal ration each day. Understand?"

"Yassuh, Mas'r Loring."

The slave answered in the obsequious fashion that irritated Loring because the response meant nothing. He knew slaves bowed and scraped even if they didn't understand instructions or had no intention to comply in order to avoid showing any independence or resistance that could risk punishment.

As he mounted Ginger to leave, Loring said in an authoritarian voice, "I'll be back soon and the rations better be secured and your work done."

The slaves stared at the ground. One mumbled "Yassuh."

When he reached his farm, Loring saw Jake plowing in the new field. He trotted Ginger across the open ground and asked if there had been any trouble. "Some blacks came around, but de children saw dem across de way. I fired over their heads to scare dem off."

From the porch, Molly saw the two men talking and ran to them. "What happened to Mingo and Brutus?

"Hold on. I'll tell you everything later. First, I need to get cleaned up and eat. Run to the house and help Miss Blanche fix me something."

"Please, please, Mas'r Loring."

"Molly, didn't you hear me? Get to the house. I'll tell you everything as soon as I've eaten. Brutus and Mingo are OK."

While he ate, Loring sent everybody outside except Blanche. "Honey, I'm worried. Apparently, Mingo and Brutus jumped them. I don't know if Wall will recover. His face is smashed and he's incoherent. Holland's head is black and blue and his eyes are almost swollen shut. Now we have to worry about unsupervised slaves at the lumber camp. Jake says some came poking around already."

Blanche interrupted, "Here, Honey. Drink some coffee. We're down to the last beans."

He blew on the coffee to cool it, sipped the sugary liquid and continued, "The sheriff has a rebellion on his hands. Brutus and Mingo are ring leaders. They stole all the weapons at the camp. They killed two dogs, shot at the sheriff and managed to slip across the Suwannee in a rowboat. Once word gets out, I'm worried that there's not enough white men left in the area to keep the other slaves in line especially with smart men like Mingo and Brutus to lead them."

"Don't fret. We'll be OK. Jake and Sarah are like family. They won't join any rebellion. The troublemakers are across the river. They won't risk coming back. I'm worried about Molly though. She's not been herself since Mingo left. She's uppity. Chad has to talk to her."

Loring finished his coffee and picked up a slice of sweet cornbread which he slathered with molasses. "This cornbread is not the only reason I was so eager to get home," he said as he grabbed Blanche's arm to pull her close. "Give me a kiss, and I'll promise not to fret."

Blanche pecked him on the lips and pushed away. "You better get outside and tell everybody what happened."

"I'll be back directly."

When Loring talked to the others he didn't mention Holland and Wall's drubbing or the gunfight. He summarized the chase and reported that Mingo and Brutus slipped across the Suwannee by boat.

Molly pressed for more details.

"To tell you the truth, Molly, I don't know that much. I only saw tracks and scrapes in the sand where they shoved off."

CHAPTER TWENTY-FIVE

CALIFORNIA SWAMP

Florida

In the stolen rowboat, the slaves floated with the current around several bends until Brutus spotted a place where the willows grew to the water's edge on the far bank. He said to Mingo, "Let us out. You go on down river. Find a place to hide de boat, den circle back and catch up wid us."

The slaves unloaded the rowboat under the brushy limbs and headed cross country. Burdened with tools, food and weapons, the men waded through black water, squished over soggy ground and climbed through dead falls and tangles. On higher ground they walked through hammocks where ferns blanketed the ground. Brutus estimated they had traveled about ten miles when they reached a large, blackwater creek which they forded. By morning, they reached the shoreline. After verifying that no people or boats were in the area, Brutus led the group along the shore.

Tired and grumpy, the men whined about having no rest or sleep. Brutus refused to listen and proceeded on. When they came to another large creek that emptied into the bay, he followed it upstream with the tired men trudging and stumbling behind. After a mile, he stopped at a clearing. "We'll rest here."

The men threw themselves down on the ground and slept. Brutus woke with a start when he heard "K'raah Kah Kah" in the distance followed by a shot. He jumped up. "Get up! Get up! Posse comin'."

The men scurried to gather their bundles and disperse into the brush. In a short while, the woods returned to its normal bustle. An ivory-billed woodpecker drummed at a hollow cypress and a flock of robins scurried through the treetops. Without warning, Brutus heard a limb snap behind him. As he whirled, he cocked his shotgun and almost pulled the trigger until he recognized Mingo, who dove behind a tree.

"My Gawd, Mingo. I nearly shot you. Don't ever walk up on us without a warning!"

For an hour or more, everybody laid low until Brutus whispered, "Mingo, I believe de shot came from upstream. How 'bout checkin' it out?"

After Mingo crept away, another shot, much closer, echoed through the trees. "Whoever it is, is not after us, but who could it be in dis swamp?"

Time dragged by until a third shot that sounded not more than half a mile from them hushed the forest for a minute until several blue jays commenced their raucous shrieks. When they stopped squawking, Brutus heard voices and motioned for everybody to stay hidden. As the unidentified voices came closer, he could almost discern words and then he heard Mingo laugh. Brutus relaxed, but he didn't put down his shotgun. A shout echoed through the trees. "It's me, Mingo; I'm coming in wid somebody."

Mingo walked up with a gaunt, black man with a short, fuzzy, white beard. His clothes were in tatters. He wore pants that were ripped off below the knee. Rough deer hide covered the seat. His threadbare shirt had patches on the sleeves and on the front where a pocket should have been. He wore homemade moccasins. His straw hat was rotting and full of holes although it sported a hatband decorated with a bright coral snake skin. He carried a rusty shotgun over his shoulder. In his left hand he held three, large white birds by their long necks.

Mingo introduced him. "Dis here's Washington; call him Wash. Found him huntin'. He invited us to come with him to his village."

A man grabbed a bird's wing and stretched it out. "Sure are big birds. What you goin' do with 'em?"

Wash laughed, "Lordy, whoopers makes better purlieu dan swamp chicken."

Brutus said, "Hold on. We got a posse on our tail. If we go to your place, dey will find you."

"Naw, dey won't. No posse comin' back here."

"How can you be sure?"

"You seen anybody since you crossed the Suwannee?"

"Not a soul."

"I 'pects not. Since de war started, Crackers have more to worry 'bout dan comin' over here after us. We can defend ourselves too." Wash patted his rusty shotgun.

Brutus took off his hat, ran his fingers through his hair and continued his interrogation. "How long ya been out here?"

"Six months, others longer."

As the men walked upstream toward Wash's camp, they came upon dead palm fronds littering the ground where people had felled cabbage palms for their hearts. In a few miles, well-trodden footpaths snaked along the creek bank. Around a bend, they came to a village that made the lumber camp at Chunky Pond appear luxurious. A few motley chickees and rickety lean-tos dotted sandy mounds along the creek,

From all indications, the people lived like the Seminole Indians in the old days. The only items evidencing modernity were a few pots and pans and an axe by the fire circle. Crudely woven palm frond mats served as walls and windbreaks. An open-sided chickee with its beams lashed in place with leather straps and vines served as a community dining room. People wore clothing made from coonskins, rabbits, and deer hides. Over all, the place looked scruffier than the poorest slave quarters.

Folks gathered as Wash led Brutus' band into the camp. The villagers were mostly young men although a few women and children crowded around too. They all laughed and joked as they introduced themselves. Some related how they ran away and made their way to the village.

Wash handed the whoopers to a young woman. "Enough funnin'. Des men is hungry. Git des birds plucked and cooked."

People set to work with a purpose that reminded Mingo how slaves behaved on their Sunday free days at the plantation in Carolina. While the men chopped wood for the fire and small palm trees for the hearts, the women cleaned the birds. The children scurried to fetch water from the creek with wooden buckets and to collect wild plants to add to the pot. People moved with enthusiasm unlike their lethargic pace when they worked at their slave tasks.

Wash pulled out a pipe from a pocket in his worn pants. As he lit the pipe with his last tobacco that he had pilfered when he ran away, he said, "You're welcome to stay here wid us. Nobody knows de future, but for now, we're survivin' and safe. Hard as it is, it's better to be free in dis swamp dan bowin' and scrapin' to white devils."

Everybody in the village looked so scrawny, Mingo had his doubts.

"What you eat?"

"Wild animals, fish and swamp cabbage. Huntin' is pretty good most times although game's scarce close to de village. Sometimes we git lucky and bag a hog or deer. Fishin' is OK. If we had nets, we'd have more fish dan we could eat. Sometimes de creek is thick with mullet. We make stick fences across it, but dat don't always work."

"If we stay, there won't be enough food for everybody."

"More mouths to feed but more hands too. You've got guns and bullets so you can hunt. De way Mingo slipped up on me, he'll make a good hunter. We'll be stronger wid you here. War or no war, Crackers will come after us sooner or later. We'll have to fight 'em."

Brutus and Mingo gathered the men upstream from the settlement to decide whether to stay. Although they knew that staying meant scraping out a living in a harsh environment, they all agreed that they had no other viable option for the time being.

The whoopers simmered until the meat fell from the bone. Then the women mixed it with rice along with cubed swamp cabbage. As the concoction cooked, they baked cornbread from the meal brought by the new arrivals in a Dutch oven hanging by the fire on a metal hook.

As the sky turned sunset red, everybody crammed around the communal table. Only a few people had tin plates and metal spoons. Most used utensils carved from cedar and cypress wood.

The stringy whooper meat with swamp cabbage and rice tasted delicious and everybody enjoyed a rare treat-the coffee the new arrivals brought. The village supply had long since been exhausted. Although substitutes like parched acorns had been tried, nothing had tasted like the real brew.

As the new arrivals settled in, they built more shelters and helped repair the existing ones. They rebuilt and extended the communal chickee. The experienced woodcutters hewed logs into boards so that for the first time the camp had a flat table. The villagers lived a hard-scrabble existence. They felt hungry most of the time, but survived, persevered, and felt happy as free people for the first time in their lives.

1862

My own dear husband,

I think you may as well give up and come home as to try and keep the enemy back for they have a very large force...and came prepared to conquer all Florida and establish a territorial government. I suppose you heard that the Government has abandoned this State and Government has ordered all the regiments that are mustered into the Confederate service away from East Fla. What is to become of us? I think we will have to leave or be made Lincolns subjects...

From a letter by Octavia Stephens who lived at Rose Cottage near Welaka, Florida to Winston Stephens, a soldier serving with Dickison's 2nd Florida Cavalry, March 13, 1862

CHAPTER TWENTY-SIX

CEDAR KEY

Florida

When Chad arrived in Cedar Key on the morning of January 16, 1862, he wanted to speak with Parsons about finding a ship although the subject had to be approached with caution. He knew the storekeeper had taken a major's commission in the militia, so as a loyal Confederate he'd be reluctant to discuss anything about sailings for fear a Unionist might relay the intelligence to the Gulf Coast Blockading Squadron. And, of course, he had every reason to be leery. Underground Yankee sympathizers supplied intelligence to the blockaders at every opportunity.

Chad waited until he was alone in the store with the owner and then chitchatted a few minutes before he asked about the war.

Parsons said, "The Northern public is clamoring for Lincoln to quit fooling around with the Anaconda Plan and invade the South with overwhelming force. Lincoln doesn't want to risk another fiasco like Manassas, so he's building up the army. Sooner or later, he'll order an attack. In the meantime, the snake tightens its coils. *Harpers Weekly* reported that there are 150 vessels in the blockade fleet with more under construction. Yankee gunboats are patrolling the Mississippi, Ohio and Tennessee Rivers and General Grant has an army at Cairo, Illinois. He can swoop down the Mississippi, the Cumberland or the Tennessee Rivers any time he wants."

"What will that accomplish?"

"We have to hold Tennessee. If we can't, Grant can invade Mississippi, Alabama or even Georgia."

"How long do you think the buildup will continue?"

"Hard to say. The blockade is crushing us anyway. Cedar Key is closed tight. Captains can't sail from here. Those that are not bottled up in the harbor use some godforsaken creek along the coast which ain't patrolled yet. Business has died. The new railroad's hardly used. No use hauling freight down here when it can't be shipped out. We had two Confederate companies stationed in town, but they were ordered to reinforce troops in Tennessee and Virginia. It looks to me like the dog-gone politicians and generals have abandoned Florida to the Yankees."

"Why would they do that?"

"The government decided that Tennessee and Virginia are strategic. The generals believe Florida's coastline can't be defended with the available manpower. Our militia never took the Yankee forts at Pensacola and Key West. Now it's too late. We got licked at Santa Rosa Island up by Pensacola when we assaulted Fort Pickens. We don't have a navy. Our privateer, *Judah,* was captured and burned by the *Colorado.* We're helpless. There's only twenty-five home guard posted here with three old Spanish cannons that might explode if they fire them. They can't possibly repel an attack. Hell, they can barely keep the peace."

"No captains sail from Cedar Key anymore?"

"Didn't you see the sloops in the harbor? They're been loaded and ready to sail for weeks."

How can I get out?

"Your best bet is to ask one of your farmer friends for help. Some captains bring centerboard coastal schooners up shallow creeks where they load up for a run to Cuba or the Bahamas."

Parsons reached to rearrange a lemon that slipped from its display when the men heard an unfamiliar rumble from across Waccasassa Bay. Parsons said, "Let's walk down to the wharf and see what goin' on."

As the two men ambled toward the waterfront, Chad saw smoke beyond Seahorse Key that undoubtedly came from a steamship. In a few minutes, a huge, double-wheeled gunboat emerged from the mist. Under full steam, heavy, black smoke belched from its stacks that amplified its ominous appearance. As it approached Seahorse Key, Chad made out the Stars and Stripes flying from its stern.

"What are our troops doing? Aren't they at least going to fire at the damn gunboat?" Parsons grumbled.

Chad saw soldiers on Seahorse Key scrambling into a rowboat and onto a flatboat without making any effort to fight. The soldiers in the rowboat pulled for the Cedar Key wharf while the men on the flatboat attempted to pole behind them.

Parsons rolled his eyes. "Look at those incompetents. Their poles are too short to reach bottom. They're drifting on the current."

The soldiers onboard the flatboat pulled out white handkerchiefs and waved them as the tide carried it toward the Yankee gunboat. Chad almost snickered.

The gunboat ignored the flatboat and dropped anchor. Sailors lowered small boats from davits that marines filled as soon as the launches hit the water. A cannon fired a shell that exploded among the railroad cars on the wharf. As the marines pulled for shore, the gunboat continued the cannonade that shattered warehouses and set fires.

When the rebel rowboat reached shore, the soldiers scrambled up the bank. A Rebel lieutenant appeared dazed and uncertain. Chad heard a private say, "Let's kill some Yankees!"

The lieutenant yelled, "Hold your fire. There's too doggone many and the gunboat has us covered. It'll be suicide to fight. They'll blow up the whole town."

The private raised his weapon to aim at the marines pulling for shore. "God dammit, I ordered you to hold fire." The officer pushed the private's rifle barrel toward the ground. The soldier sulked away. The lieutenant ran up a side street as Loring and Parsons sprinted for the store.

As the marines reached shore, they jumped from their boats and charged up the streets. Chad heard several shots and a bullet zing over his head as he ducked inside. He glanced back to see marines fanning out along the streets as others torched a warehouse and the depot.

Red-faced, Parsons ran behind the counter. "I warned the lieutenant that he'd better get ready. Damn home guard is pathetic."

The militia's retreat demoralized Parsons, and like the Rebel lieutenant, he realized resistance was suicidal. He yanked off his militia cap and his pistol and hid them under bolts of fabric.

Chad unstrapped his holster placing it under flour bags. Both men ducked down behind a counter waiting for the marines to reach the store. Soon, a sergeant yelled, "Everybody out with your hands up."

Parsons yelled, "We're civilians. We're unarmed. Don't shoot."

A warehouse flared into an inferno as the cotton stored in it caught fire and blazed. As flames enveloped it, the building exploded with a deafening whoosh sending a shock wave reverberating across the town. Parsons shook his head. "There goes the turpentine; what a waste."

Efficiently, the marines battered in the hatches of the sloops anchored in the harbor, searched them and then torched them. Then they set fire to the telegraph office, any railroad cars not destroyed by the shelling, and all other public property. A smoky haze enveloped the entire town.

Chad stood in the street watching in silence with his hands clasped over his head. His eyes watered and his throat and lungs burned from the acrid smoke. After a while, a marine sergeant herded him, along with Parsons and a few others, into a detention area guarded by the marines on a grassy slope by the water where a sea breeze thinned the smoke.

Confusion reigned among the Floridians already in the pen. Home guard troops and civilians were mostly indistinguishable. Nobody wore a full uniform and some militiamen wore no military insignia whatsoever. A young man in a gray jacket with sergeant's stripes yelled for the soldiers to form up, but they ignored him and squatted on their haunches or sprawled on the grassy bank watching the marines and the fires. He kicked at one man to no effect and then sat down in frustration himself.

A U.S. marine sergeant yelled, "Prisoners, stand at ease," and said to a guard so that the captives could overhear, "Shoot anybody who tries to escape."

As the day progressed and the fires burned down, the marines captured a few stragglers and began questioning the prisoners. A Yankee officer informed the people that unless they swore allegiance to the Union they'd be transported from Cedar Key as prisoners of war. Upset and angry that the Confederate government had abandoned the town without a fight and in order to stay with their families and to protect their homes and businesses, many scratched their names to the oath of allegiance.

A U.S. Navy ensign questioned Chad who explained that he was English, a non-combatant, in Cedar Key to buy cotton. The officer demanded proof. A letter of introduction from his English syndicate sufficed. Once his status was established, Chad asked the officer for assistance to arrange safe passage for escaped slaves.

"Sir, we are at war to suppress a rebellion, not to aid and abet contrabands. We will return all slaves we capture to their owners."

"I don't understand. Isn't the North fighting to end slavery?"

"Listen here, I don't have time for this now, so you best get moving before I change my mind and arrest you."

Chad hurried away but stayed in town until he finagled an appointment with the gunboat commander. To Chad's chagrin, the officer confirmed the ensign's position on returning escaped slaves to their owners, but he invited Chad to have dinner with him on the gunboat.

The next day, Chad hurried back to Deer Hall. As he trotted his horse down the lane toward the house, the dogs raised the customary hullabaloo until he whistled. At the gate, Chad jerked his horse to a stop. Dismounting quickly, he made for the front door just as Loring stepped out on the porch. Chad blurted, "Cedar Key has been occupied by the U.S. Navy!"

"What happened?"

"A gunboat came into the harbor. The home guard surrendered without a fight. The Federals blew up the wharf and the warehouses. They burned the depot, telegraph office, several sloops, and all the railcars in town."

As everybody gathered around, Loring said, "Billy, take Mr. Waldock's horse. Chad, come inside. Jake, you and the others go on down to your place."

Molly protested, "We deserve to know what's happenin'."

Loring lashed out, "Young lady, don't get sassy. Remember, you're living at my place. Chad, get your wench under control!"

Molly almost said something, reconsidered and followed behind Jake. As Loring and Chad stepped into the house, Loring took a bottle from the armoire and said, "I need a drink."

"I could use one too. I came by the lumber camp and it looks abandoned. I saw a couple of blacks run off in the scrub when I rode up. I didn't bother with them because I wanted to tell you about the attack as soon as possible."

As Loring poured rum into two mugs, Chad related how easily the navy and marines had subdued and occupied Cedar Key. "At first I was scared, but once they confirmed I was English, they treated me quite well. I stayed there until I could speak with Commander Emmons. From what I gathered, he had good intelligence about Cedar Key's defenses. He knew that the two companies defending the town had shipped out and that the cannons defending the harbor were unsafe to fire. He didn't confirm, of course, but I gathered that Union men provided him with that information because he mentioned small boats had visited his ship several times."

"How many men does he have and what does he plan to do?"

"As far as I can tell, he intends to occupy Cedar Key permanently."

"You think he'll follow the railroad up here?"

"The Navy didn't capture an engine and they destroyed the railcars that were on the wharf, so they can't use them for transport. I don't believe Commander Emmons has enough men to risk leaving the protection of the gunboat. For now, you don't have to worry."

"You have any indication that more troops are on the way?"

"No."

"What did the residents do?"

"They surprised me. Most signed an oath of allegiance to the United States, but then, they were under threat of expulsion from Cedar Key if they didn't."

"I'm not surprised. Many Floridians believe the Confederate government betrayed us when it sent our troops north."

"Commander Emmons released most of the soldiers he captured. He said that several signed the oath of allegiance, and the others took parole. Several had the measles. He sent them away because he didn't want to risk exposing his sailors and marines to sickness."

Chad took a swig from the mug, set it down and continued, "It puzzles me that the navy refused to protect escaped slaves. When I asked him about that, he told me that they are private property belonging to civilians. He has no intention of freeing them unless they're used to support the rebellion. He pointed out that for all he knows, the runaways belong to Unionists."

"His position surprises me too."

"In fact, Commander Emmons intends to enforce the law by returning escaped slaves. I thought the South seceded to secure slavery, but it looks to me like the Federals are fighting to preserve the Union."

Loring sighed. "The slavery issue is complicated. Lincoln says he doesn't seek to end slavery, but most Southerners don't believe him. Northern abolitionists want it ended right now. They're a minority but passionate trouble makers. Here, we have to deal with Secesh fire-eaters who will only accept unrestricted slavery nationwide. They refuse to listen to reason or consider any compromise. They made me practically a persona non grata after I ran as a Unionist for the Secession Convention. The whole damn mess depresses me. Let's lift a glass to peace and better times."

The men clinked the mugs and took a swallow. Chad set down his tumbler and stood up. "The main thing is that your farm is safe for now. If you'll excuse me, I'm going to tell the others about the attack."

At the door, Chad turned and added, "Loring, I apologize for Molly's sassiness. I'll speak to her. She's lovesick; that's all. If she's disruptive, I'll take her away."

"No need for that. I overreacted. She'll settle down as things return to normal. What do you plan to do? How can you make a living here?"

"I don't know. Maybe I'll go back to England."

CHAPTER TWENTY-SEVEN

BRONSON

Florida

Although Yankees occupied Cedar Key, daily life at Deer Hall continued as if the attack had never happened. Loring and Jake continued to expand the acreage under cultivation by using hogs to help clear the land. They fenced the voracious animals in a plot until they either ate or rooted out the underbrush and small bushes. After moving the animals to another area, they cut the remaining trees and shrubs on the land where the hogs had thinned it. Then they burned the slash. Smoke floated over the farm most days. When an acre was cleared, they disk plowed the virgin ground for planting.

The women continued cooking and cleaning every day and boiled clothes in an iron wash pot weekly. In addition to the housework, Blanche volunteered with the Soldier's Aid Society to make bandages and socks for the troops, so the women and children scraped lint, knitted, and darned every evening after supper. The handwork bored the children. When they could, they tarried over their own chores or hid in the storehouse where they played house or army.

Molly resolved not to leave Deer Hall until Mingo returned for her. Chad quit trying to arrange her escape because he knew he couldn't force her to abandon her man. Yet, he hoped that he would never return. His guilt about that made him so uncomfortable that he often stayed away from Deer Hall with the excuse that he had to attend to business although he had no reasonable prospects.

Time was running out for Chad. He didn't have the resources to stay in Florida and the war had destroyed his ability to earn money. As the blockade tightened, communication with his backers in England ceased. To complicate matters, very few growers tried to ship cotton after the Confederate government made it illegal. Either they feared the penalty for violating the law or believed obeying the law was their patriotic duty. Scofflaws didn't care about the law or duty, but were afraid to risk their investment by running the blockade.

Loring also had serious concerns. He was keenly aware that some neighbors questioned his loyalty to Florida; he suspected some spread accusations that he was a Yankee Sympathizer since he wasn't in the army. A friend told Blanche that if weren't for her work with the Soldiers Aid Society, hotheads would have burned Deer Hall. He stayed alert for trouble by wearing his pistol and keeping his shotgun handy in case marauders, black or white, showed up.

The bloody battle at Shiloh on April 6-7, 1862, with more than 10,500 Confederate casualties, dashed all hope for a short war. The Rebel defeats the same month at Fort Henry on the Tennessee River in Kentucky and Fort Donelson on the Cumberland River in Tennessee opened major water transportation routes for the Union armies which threatened the South's heartland.

Volunteers with the Confederate army had signed up for one year. When their enlistments ended in April 1862, the Confederate

Congress passed the first conscription law in American history that required men between the ages of 18 and 35 to serve for the duration of the war unless exempt as a preacher or as a slave owner with twenty or more slaves. The law allowed a substitute to be hired. Loring had no intention of doing that.

He and Blanche spent frustrating evenings deciding what he should do. Blanche encouraged Loring to enlist before he got drafted. Although the adventure of military service had some appeal, he had little desire to fight to uphold secession. More importantly, he needed to stay home to protect Deer Hall and his family from the Federal troops stationed at Cedar Key, runaway slaves and outlaws. He also believed that it was unjust, undemocratic and dictatorial for the government to force him to leave his family. But as much as he dreaded it, he knew Blanche was correct. He had to join the army.

On a trip to Bronson to buy supplies, he arrived while Captain Dickison, who commanded the Confederate 2nd Florida Cavalry, was conferring with the sheriff about runaway slaves and Yankee patrols. The sheriff introduced the officer, a slight man dressed like a typical Cracker cow hunter with heavy leather chaps, slouch hat and high boots. The only clothing he wore that identified him as a soldier was a gray jacket with faded gold embroidery on the collar.

When the captain asked Loring what unit he was with, Loring replied, "I haven't enlisted yet because I don't want to be sent out of state."

"Why don't you sign up with my unit? Our mission is to protect Florida from invasion and marauders. As you know, most Florida troops were ordered north to Tennessee and Virginia, so we're left without enough men or weapons for the job, but we keep the Yankees at bay with maneuver and unpredictability. They've occupied some towns that their gunboats can cover, but so far we've managed to stop them from invading inland."

"I suspect the Yankees keep you hopping. I have a farm by Chunky Pond and I'm worried that they will march up from Cedar Key. I hear that over in East Florida they are burning out civilians and stealing their livestock and cotton."

The captain said, "When the war started, they only destroyed public property and left private property alone. Not any more. Now, they haul off everything they don't burn. They're encouraging slaves to run away and that gives us a devil of a time. When the Feds occupied Jacksonville in March, people had to move their slaves inland from the St. John's to keep them from running to the enemy. We don't have the manpower to fight blue bellies and chase runaways too."

Dickison looked Loring over. "Mr. Bell, if you join my regiment, I can guarantee that you'll stay in Florida. The Secretary of War and the governor personally committed to me that my men will not be sent out of state." The gaunt captain paused, then said, "Hey, aren't you the Bell who ran for the Secession Convention as a Unionist?"

"Yes, I am, Captain. I thought secession was a mistake and still do for that matter. That said, now that Florida has seceded, my loyalties are with my state. We have no choice except to fight now that we've been invaded."

The sheriff said, "Don't worry about Loring Bell, Captain. When the war started, I wondered about him too, but shouldn't have. When I needed men for a posse to catch armed and dangerous runaways, he didn't hesitate to volunteer. I asked him to oversee slaves at a lumber camp near his place that the owners couldn't supervise, and he's done as well as anybody could under the circumstances. This man is as loyal as any Floridian."

"If Sheriff Maxwell vouches for you, that's good enough for me. I admire your honesty and apologize for being presumptuous. We'll sign you up as a private. You have to supply your own mount, but you'll be reimbursed for that."

"Can I be posted here in Levy County?"

"I can't promise that. Right now, most of my men are in East Florida along the St. Johns to block the Yankees from raiding inland from Jacksonville."

"Don't you have units posted here in the Suwannee Valley?"

"The troops over here are mostly militia and home guard although we patrol to harass the enemy at Cedar Key. If you want to enlist, report to the first sergeant. He handles the paperwork. Any trooper can direct you to him. Please excuse me; I have to get back to the men."

After the captain shook hands and left the room, Loring said to the sheriff, "Thank you for speaking up for me."

"No need to thank me, I only told him the truth. Between us, I'm wondering if you weren't right. I'm havin' my own doubts about the Confederacy. How can a free and independent people condone conscription? We've enslaved ourselves to the government to preserve black slavery."

Loring switched subjects to enlist the sheriff's help. "Sheriff, I hate to pester you about the lumber camp, but something has to be done. I've kept Holland and Wall's slaves supplied with food, but I don't have the resources to do it any longer. They'll run off if they aren't fed. Aren't those two healthy yet?"

"I reckon Wall is about as good as he's goin' get. His nose is flattened and one eye is askew. It drips all the time like he's cryin', and he keeps whinin' about headaches and dizziness though that's probably 'cause he drinks all the time. Anyhow, he says he's through with the camp. He's anglin' for a political appointment."

"What about Holland?"

"He's healed up, but too scairt to go back by himself and can't find anyone to go with him. He's movin' to the coast to boil salt for quick money. We aren't gettin' enough through the blockade, so the price is skyrocketin'."

"Well, something has to be done. Anyway, I guess I better go talk to the sergeant."

CHAPTER TWENTY-EIGHT

CHUNKY POND

Florida

Holland didn't have the money to hire anybody to go with him to the lumber camp and since no one volunteered, he rode to Deer Hall to ask for Loring's help. At the property line he saw Jake and Loring plowing new land. When he rode toward them, Jake reined Mike, looped the reins over the plow handle and stepped behind the big mule. Loring dropped his hoe and picked up what appeared to be a shotgun then joined Jake.

Holland yelled, "It's me, your neighbor."

Loring hollered for him to come on up. As he approached, Loring said, "Sorry, we didn't recognize you from a distance. Can't be too careful these days."

"Believe me, I understand. I wanted to stop by and thank you for looking after my nigras. How much do I owe you?"

Jake eavesdropped while he fiddled with the trace chains.

"You don't owe me anything. I tried to make them clean up, not waste supplies and keep working, but they never paid me much mind. They need an overseer."

"Are they still there?"

"Last time I checked you still had four. Day before yesterday, I took over a deer's hindquarters that should hold them a few days."

"Will you ride over with me?"

"I suppose so. I can make it back home before dark if we leave now. Jake and I have done enough for one day anyway. Jake, go ahead and knock off."

When Loring and Holland arrived at the camp, they found the four slaves standing around the cook fire.

Holland said, "You're good boys and did the right thing by not running away. Those that ran off will be hung. Do you have food?"

The young slave who had warned Brutus and Mingo not to hurt the white men said, "Nothin', Mas'r. We et all the deer meat Mas'r Loring brought us."

"You'll have cornbread with fatback in the morning."

Holland walked away from the fire toward his moldy tent. When he pulled back the flap, rumpled, grimy blankets covered his cot. "What the hell is this mess? Get this crap outa my tent right now." A slave shuffled over and rolled the bedding into a wad. As he exited past the center pole, he inadvertently brushed the white man who gave him a shove. "You niggers are going to shape up now that I'm back."

The slave almost fell. He threw down the bundle, turning toward his tormentor with tight fists and set jaw. Holland slid his hand over his pistol handle. The slave lowered his eyes and picked up the blankets. The white man regretted pushing the slave and knew he was off to another bad start.

He walked to the fire and said, "Things are goin' be better now than I'm back. Get a good night's rest. We're leaving these piney woods in the morning for the coast."

The slaves said nothing.

He said to Loring, "Why don't you stay here tonight? I have some rum in my saddle bags. We can sit by the fire and enjoy the evening."

"I appreciate the offer, but I've got to get home. Blanche will be worried about me if I don't come back this evening, and I want to be home as much as possible before I have to report to the army. You'll be OK if you keep your pistol handy and sleep light."

CHAPTER TWENTY-NINE

CAMP FINNEGAN
Florida

Loring enlisted in Dickison's regiment with the arrangement to report by May 1, 1862, which gave him time to finish spring planting. On the appointed day, he posted for duty at Camp Finnegan several miles west of Jacksonville. Before the staff sergeant assigned him to quarters, he noticed Loring's LeMat. "Wish we had shotgun pistols like that for the entire company. No pistol's more lethal at close range. You know how to use it?"

"Yes."

"We'll see about that tomorrow when we test you."

Loring roused himself when he heard an off key bugle before dawn. His tent mates jumped from bed, dressed, and warned him, "Get a move on, friend. You'll be assigned extra duty if you're late to roll call." He followed them outside while still buttoning his shirt. He stood where he was told and mimicked the other men's posture.

After roll call, the men straightened up their tents then ate a hearty breakfast: ham, eggs, and corn bread. Loring took a gulp of what looked like coffee. Its pungent taste caused him to spit it out and exclaim. "What is this?" The men laughed. One said, "It ain't what you think, private. You're in the army now."

Back in their tents after breakfast, the men cleaned and checked their weapons. One said to Loring, "Inspection's at eight o'clock. Be as neat as you can. An officer will look us over. If he asks you anything, look him straight in the eye and answer in a loud voice, 'Yes, sir' or 'No, sir.' Don't say anything else unless you're asked."

Loring got through the inspection without difficulty although the lieutenant asked him if he was the Loring Bell that ran as a Unionist for the Secession Convention. "Yes, sir," Loring barked. The lieutenant looked him up and down, then asked, "Can you kill Yankees?"

"Yes, sir," Loring said and stared into the lieutenant eyes. The lieutenant held his gaze for several seconds then walked on down the line.

Before he dismissed the formation, the officer ordered a corporal in Loring's squad to take him aside and to teach him rifle loading. As the two men cleared the formation, Loring heard the command, 'Left, Face,' then watched the company pivot in unison. At the command, 'Forward, March,' every soldier stepped off with impressive military precision. The corporal commented, "We're been practicin' for a review by General Finnegan. If you think we march well, wait till you see us drill on horseback."

The two men walked to the corporal's tent where he retrieved an Enfield rifle musket. Handing it to Loring he asked, "You familiar with this weapon?"

"No, sir."

The corporal grunted, "Don't call me sir. I ain't no officer."

Loring almost replied, "Yes, sir," but checked himself. "OK."

The Enfield weighed almost ten pounds and was over five feet long. Loring didn't like it and pushed the weapon toward the corporal. "I'd rather use my shotgun than this."

"You have to learn to drill with this rifle like everybody else. At noon, you've got to show the sergeant that you can load in nine steps."

Loring listened patiently as the corporal explained the procedure: load, handle-cartridge, tear-cartridge, charge-cartridge, draw-rammer, ram-cartridge, return-rammer, cast-about, and prime. Loring thought it foolish to go through all those steps to load a rifle. He could do it much faster his own way. He didn't need to be told where to grab the barrel, where to put his thumb, or how to angle his feet and a dozen other petty particulars.

The corporal showed him the procedure several times then handed the rifle to him. After a pause he said, "Load." Loring reached for a cartridge. "What are doing? Start over. Get in position. Haven't you learned anything?"

"Look, Corporal, I know how to load a weapon. Why do I have to follow all these ridiculous steps?"

"You got to do it the army way; you have to be coordinated with the other men. Everybody can't be doin' somethin' different. I know it seems silly, but humor me. If we can't show the sergeant that you can load in nine steps, we'll both get reamed out and you'll git extra duty."

"OK, Corporal, I'll do it your way. Show me again."

Within an hour, Loring was exasperated. Loading a weapon was second nature to him. The army method slowed him down. Try as he might, he kept making mistakes like forgetting to brush his leg with the rifle, or turning his hand too much, or angling his feet wrong. The corporal reprimanded him. "You boys who know how to shoot are the hardest to teach. You don't pay attention, so you keep makin' the same mistakes."

Loring felt like throwing the rifle on the ground. "I've about had it with this picky stuff."

"Take it easy; do it at your own pace."

The corporal stepped back, lit his pipe and watched Loring struggle through the steps time after time as he corrected himself.

The corporal finished his smoke and said, "You've got it. Now, be crisp. When you get to the cast-about step think about your thumb on the S plate and touch your heels together. Let me show you again."

The corporal took the rifle and barked the order, "Load," and moved through the steps without a perceptible pause. He tossed the rifle to Loring.

"Load," the corporal ordered.

Loring stood in the load position and moved through the steps till he dropped the rammer removing it from the barrel. The corporal chuckled.

"Slow down. No need to hurry that much. Do it right, speed will come."

By late morning, Loring not only knew the drill; he found himself enjoying it. Now and then the corporal tweaked his fingers or nudged his foot with his boot. "You're doin' first class. The sergeant will be impressed."

After the noon formation, the sergeant pulled the corporal and Loring aside.

"Does this man know how to load an Enfield?" The NCO asked.

"Yes, sergeant." the corporal answered and handed the rifle to Loring. The sergeant barked, "Load."

Loring snapped to an alert posture. He held the rifle with his left hand at the middle band with its butt on the ground between his feet and placed his right hand by his cartridge belt. He ran through the nine loading steps and finished by forcing a percussion cap on the cone with his thumb, half cocked the hammer, and stood at the charge bayonet position. Loring looked straight ahead, waiting for the next order.

The sergeant said, "Good job, men. Let's see if he can shoot. Meet me at the range at 1:30."

The corporal and Loring arrived early at an open pasture a half-mile from the camp that was bordered by a bayhead. When the sergeant arrived, he pointed across the field at a square, red target tacked to a swamp maple tree at chest height. "See that spot? Let's see you hit it."

Loring loaded the rifle in the nine steps, raised it to the firing position and squinted down range. *Damn, this is a long shot.* He aligned the front and rear sights on the target for a split second, but the barrel wobbled so much that he couldn't keep the front sight on the target. He strained to hold the weapon steady.

The sergeant said, "You better not hold her up so long. It's heavy."

He was correct. Holding the rifle steady became more difficult by the second. Determined to prove himself, Loring took a deep breath. He lowered the rifle barrel a few inches then pointed it above the target. Lowering it until the front sight caught red, he squeezed the trigger. The big rifle kicked hard against his shoulder. The discharge deafened him for a second as powder smoke blocked his vision.

The sergeant, watching the target with an extendable telescope, exclaimed; "Lucky shot. You nicked the target high and to the right. Try again."

Loring loaded and lifted the rifle. He took a deep breath. He brought the sights in line with the target and squeezed the trigger.

The sergeant exclaimed, "You're dead on. Can you do it again?"

"I reckon I can. This rifle is damned heavy, but it shots straight."

Loring reloaded and fired again. The bullet ripped another hole in the target.

"Damn, you're a good shot. We might make you a sharpshooter. Can you ride as well as you shot?"

Loring shrugged.

"Saddle your horse. We have a squad practice this afternoon and I want to see how you ride."

As Loring and the corporal turned to walk toward the corral for their horses, the squad arrived in columns of two at a full gallop. At the open field, the man in front held his hat high. The columns separated to form a line. When the riders reined the horses, they stomped and jerked their heads, eager to keep running, so the cavalrymen had to hold the reins tight to keep their heads high.

"Takes good riders to be able to form up like that," Loring said to the corporal.

"We've been practicin' for the general's review so he can impress the ladies."

By the time Loring and the corporal returned on their horses, the exercise had begun. Each man, in turn, galloped his horse across the field to a small, orange flag that flapped in a light breeze. At that point, the rider turned toward the bayhead. As he came abreast of it, he fired his pistol at a bull's eye tacked to a tree trunk. A spotter in a hole in front of the targets poked up a green pennant when the shooter hit the mark, causing the men to cheer. If he missed, the spotter waved a red flag. Then, the squad booed and jeered as the rider circled for another try. Loring watched one soldier fire three times without hitting the target.

The sergeant waved the dejected man to the rear. As soon as he trotted his horse behind the squad, the sergeant signaled for Loring to move out.

As he trotted forward someone sneered, "Yankee sympathizer." Loring's face flushed. He jerked around in the saddle to see who insulted him. Unable to identify the trooper, he focused on proving that he could ride and shoot. After snapping open his LeMat pistol to check the shotgun cartridge in it, he nudged Ginger into a canter while holding the pistol along his leg with his right hand. As he turned toward the target, he kicked the mare into a full gallop while bracing with his knees. Approaching the targets, he glimpsed the spotter cowering in the hole. Sweeping his weapon forward off his leg, he fired. As he turned toward the squad, Loring glanced over his shoulder. The spotter wigwagged the green flag.

As Loring walked Ginger into line, the sergeant motioned out a wiry rider who pulled a Confederate Colt from its holster. He accelerated his pony around the field like Loring, but he didn't ride high in the saddle. He leaned over his mare to put it between him and the target. He brought his pistol over the animal's neck and fired. The spotter waved the green flag and the men cheered. One man threw his hat in the air. Loring had never seen such expert riding and shooting.

The corporal said to Loring, "That's how to do it. You're a good rider and a good shot, but you need to think like a soldier. Always stay low in a fight. Yankees will be shootin' at you. You'll git yourself kilt high in the saddle."

That evening the supper was pork, collard greens, black-eyed peas, and corn bread. The substitute coffee was as bad as before. Afterwards, the bugler blew formation again. After the men came to attention, the sergeant put them at ease and passed out mail.

When the sergeant dismissed them, Loring's tent mate said, "We now have free time until taps."

After Loring checked on Ginger, he strolled back to his quarters where he found two tent mates engrossed in a chess game set up on a barrel top. The other soldier sat beside them smoking his pipe as he watched each interminable move. Loring had no interest in the competition, so he retrieved a pen and writing paper from his saddlebag to write a letter home.

My Dearest Blanche,

I'm safe at Camp Finnegan. I reported yesterday and started soldiering today after being assigned to the third squad. I share a tent with three other fellows who seem friendly enough.

The tent's pitched over a rough floor so we're off the ground. There's an arbor in front with Spanish moss draped across it for shade. My tent mates said we'll thatch it before rainy season.

Only one company is in camp right now as the others are off on patrol. We're a motley bunch. Nobody has a full uniform and some men don't even have gray jackets. Although the company is supposed to have fifty Enfield rifles, I haven't seen them. I guess they're locked up somewhere. Most of the men have their own pistols, but some don't have any weapons at all.

So far, soldiering isn't so bad. Where else can you get paid to ride and shoot? My corporal taught me the army way to load an Enfield rifle. Believe me, it's a picky procedure. I had a hard time till I figured out that that I should do it their way even if I think mine's better.

This afternoon, the squad took target practice from horseback. Riding Ginger and firing my LeMat, I did better than some although one fellow made all of us all look like tyros.

The food is mostly pork and cornbread. The so-called coffee is not worth the name. A fellow told me they mix a little coffee with parched cottonseed. Rations are supplemented with game. Already, I miss the tasty food at Deer Hall.

I don't know when I'll see fighting. The Federals withdrew from Jacksonville before I arrived at camp. Rumor has it that they want to occupy Jacksonville again so that Unionists can form a new state government. Of course, the governor has to stop that. We'll have a battle on our hands if the Yankees come back to take the town.

My tent mates say the place is already a mess. Secessionists burned out Unionists when the Federal gunboats first reached the mouth of the river. If the Yankees come back, they'll probably burn what's left.

Don't worry about me. My squad leader taught me to stay low. While we wait for action, he says we'll drill and drill till we're sick of drill and then drill some more.

Needless to say, I worry about you every minute with the Yankees so close at Cedar Key. It looks like they're content to stay there, but that could change. Everybody knows we don't have enough troops to stop a concerted incursion. It's a crime that I'm forced to be off in the army with danger so near Deer Hall.

I miss you too much already. What husband could not miss your gentle manner and your ringing laugh. Some people say you are the "romps" or as the highfalutin' would say you have "joie de vivre." It's beyond me that anybody who knows you doesn't love you. So be careful, my love, while your faithful husband is away.

I'm not happy to be away from you and your affection. Yet, I must be patient for so long as this war drags on and learn to live without kissing your sweet lips and holding you in my arms

Give the children all my love. Give Little Buddy a big hug from me every night. Remind Billy that he needs to help Jake look after the place.

A hearty howdy to Molly, Chad, and to Jake and Sarah and their youngsters.

A thousand kisses, your affectionate Husband,
Loring.

CHAPTER THIRTY

DEER HALL

Florida

Before he had left for the army, Loring decided to plant food crops instead of cotton which he couldn't sell anyway. To further discourage thieves, he sowed potatoes rather than other comestibles in the belief that if marauders or soldiers came, they wouldn't steal a crop they had to dig, and the family could uproot them as needed.

After Loring left, Jake and the boys were in the field hoeing or plowing every day except Sunday. At midmorning when the sun broke through the morning haze, they quit for breakfast. After eating, they tended to the animals and completed the other chores like winching water from the well. They returned to the fields in the afternoon to fight the endless battle with weeds. They talked and joked as they worked. Sometimes they sang or chanted to break the tedium. Billy spent more time with Jake and Joe than with his own family which vexed Blanche. Once she overheard a conversation between Billy and Joe that sounded more like a foreign language than Standard English. She told Billy, "Young man, speak proper English." Billy paid her no mind.

The sweaty work hardened Billy's body and callused his hands. Boyish peach fuzz transformed to dark, course hair over his upper lip and along his jaw. Working shirtless in the sun as he preferred tanned him so deeply that Blanche complained that his dark skin made him look like a black man.

The women continued to work hard but with less efficiency due to shortages caused by the war and blockade. Cloth became too expensive for Blanche to buy. Although she couldn't weave fabric, she decided to produce knitting yarn from goat hair. She borrowed an antique spinning wheel from a neighbor, and an old slave woman taught her how to operate it. Once she learned, the machine clacked until the afternoon light became too dim for handwork.

Unable to buy manufactured candles or to obtain kerosene for the lamps, the women experimented with homemade substitutes. They crafted candles from beeswax or lard, and in the lamps they burned oil rendered from alligator fat. The homemade candles and gator oil burned with uneven, smoky flames that produced inadequate light for close work and stank with a sickening odor. Nevertheless, Blanche managed to spin enough yarn that Molly and Sarah could knit socks and small blankets. The minimal output at least gave Blanche the satisfaction of contributing to the war effort.

Molly fretted all the time that Mingo had been captured or killed. She whined so much about missing him that Sarah told her bluntly, "We've heard enough. You aren't de only one missin' your man. Imagine how much Missis Blanche and the children miss Mas'r Loring. We all have to keep goin' until dis war ends. Nobody else is carryin' on like you. Even de chil'luns do their best to keep smilin'. Little Buddy cries herself to sleep every night when she prays for her Daddy, but she doesn't mope around all the time."

Molly had no intention to quit worrying about the man she loved, but Sarah's comments stung. Sure, Blanche missed Loring, but he sent a letter once in a while. Why didn't Mingo, at least, send a message so she knew he was alive? In frustration, she almost lashed out at Sarah by reminding her that she had no right to talk since she still had Jake at home. Before she did, she remembered that she had no other place to live except Deer Hall and that if forced to leave, Mingo might never find her.

She decided not to say or do anything to give Blanche any reason to send her away. From then on, she determined to maintain a cheerful facade even as her heart ached. Moreover, she made herself indispensable.

Chad stayed at Deer Hall more but not only because he had no business elsewhere. He noticed Molly's change in attitude and hoped that she had finally given up on Mingo. To his surprise, he started to enjoy domestic life which he had never experienced as a traveling factor. More astonishing, he found himself growing fond of Blanche. He spent time with her, not only at meals, but on the porch in the evenings after everybody else had gone to bed. He found pleasure talking with her and that she relied on his advice to manage the farm. In time, he came to feel that a strong, self-reliant woman like Blanche who could still maintain good spirits in spite of hardship might make an ideal wife.

Developments on the war front foreshadowed catastrophe. When the Union Army occupied Jacksonville for three weeks during March and April of 1862, the Federal Command used the town as a base to raid into the interior. The forays liberated slaves, burned public and private property, and confiscated food and supplies. Captain Dickison and his Florida troops did their best to block Yankee incursions but couldn't stop them all. Often, the 2nd Florida Cavalry arrived after the Federals had moved on. Even when the Floridians could catch up to the invaders, the Rebel troops didn't have enough men or firepower to repulse them. The raids confirmed what everyone suspected; without reinforcements, Dickison's small force and local militia couldn't stop a concerted invasion.

Support for the Confederate Government deteriorated. From the beginning, hard core Unionists stayed loyal to the United States. Many who lived in the Federal occupied zones signed loyalty oaths in order to remain there. As the war continued, more Floridians shifted allegiance to the Union as they became disillusioned and disgusted with the Confederate government. Unionists in East Florida organized to form a new, loyal, state government when Jacksonville was occupied. Had the Northern command not withdrawn their troops, they could have succeeded. For that loyalty, Unionists had their property confiscated by Rebel officials in accord with the Confederate Sequestration Act of 1861 that classified them as enemy aliens which made them bitter and revengeful.

Rebel and Federal deserters, common criminals, escaped slaves, and armed gangs roamed the countryside looting and burning isolated farms and settlements. Neither civilian law enforcement nor the Confederate military had sufficient manpower to stop the depredations.

Blanche's neighbors told her about a raid on a plantation across the Suwannee River in Lafayette County where an armed band came in the night, surrounded the house and penned the family inside with gunfire. While several marauders peppered the house with bullets, others stole all the comestibles and animals. The outlaws never showed themselves enough for the victims to identify them other than that they were whites who disappeared into the swamps after the attack. The assault gave credence to the rumors that insurgent Unionists were forming guerilla bands

Blanche prayed for deliverance every day but prepared for the worst. Loring had instructed her to take no chances if marauders or Yankee troops came to the farm. He had told her, "If you have warning, bury the valuables, drive the livestock into the swamps, and hide out."

Jake suggested a rallying place in a dense hammock east of Bronson. He led everybody there to make sure it could be found in an emergency. Blanche hid rations in several places around the farm and at the hideout. The men, including Jake, kept weapons handy.

In normal times, Blanche would have asked Chad to leave. However, with danger all around, she thanked God that he stayed at Deer Hall to help manage the place and to fight raiders if necessary. As for Molly, Blanche appreciated her companionship as much as she valued her help with the chores.

One evening after the women had quit their knitting, Molly was jumping rope in the yard with the girls. As she twirled the line she glanced down the lane and saw three men approaching on horseback. She shouted an alarm, "Riders! Riders!"

"Jesus, help us," Blanche said under her breath while Molly hustled the girls inside and then clanged the bell to warn the men who were repairing a broken plow at the barn.

Blanche called for the dogs, but the excitement had alerted them already. They tore through the open gate for the approaching horses. As Chad, Jake and the boys ran from the barn to the house, the lead rider reached the yard. He could hardly control his mount as the hounds snarled and snapped at his horse's legs.

Chad ran behind a tree where he crouched for cover. Staying out of sight, Jake ran around the house, entered through the back door and ran up to a front window. Billy followed Jake and took a position by the window on the other side of the dogtrot. As the women wrestled to secure the heavy bar in its iron brackets, two shots startled everybody. A dog yelped. Blanche lifted the brace to run out, but Molly stopped her by grabbing her arm and pulling her back. "Don't go out there till we find out what's goin' on."

Blanche jerked away from Molly and dashed to the window by Jake. She spotted both dogs lying dead in the dirt. All three riders sat on their horses with their pistols drawn. Two wore gray uniforms. The other was dressed in civilian clothes with a slouch hat pulled low that couldn't hide his ugly, crushed nose even in the poor light. Blanche shouted, "Wall, why in the hell did you shoot my dogs?"

Wall ignored her and yelled, "Loring, is that you behind that tree? You better have furlough orders or you're under arrest."

"Chad Waldock here. What do you want?"

The Confederate government has commissioned me as the Suwannee Valley impressment agent. I'm surveying all the farms to determine the availability of military necessities."

Blanche hollered again, "You know we don't have military necessities here. Why aren't you fighting with the army?"

Wall laughed, "I'm exempt. Ain't you never heard of the twenty nigger rule?

"You never owned twenty slaves, and half of yours ran off."

"My, my, ain't we picky, Missis Bell. I've got the bill of sale, and that's good enough for Richmond. Anyhow, I ain't here to argue about conscription, I'm fixin' to inventory your property for the government."

"You aren't inventorying anything. Get off my land right now."

"I warn you, Missis Bell. As an official of the Confederate States of America, I have the obligation to survey this place in order to collect the government tithe and impress supplies as necessary. I am sure you have corn and cotton stored on this place and I intend to survey it. I have the authorization right here in my pocket."

"I don't care what paper you've got, get off my land!"

"Can't do that, Ma'am."

He pulled his foot from the stirrup and lifted his leg to dismount.

"You heard the lady. Stay on your horse and get off this property," Chad yelled.

Wall reached for his pistol, but he stopped when he saw shotguns poke out from both windows.

"You're resisting a government official. That's treason. You best reconsider."

"Get off my land!" Blanche shrilled.

"We've smoked out traitors, men. We'll be back with soldiers to round up all you Yankee lovers."

As the three men rode away, Blanche broke down sobbing as Sarah, Molly and the girls did their best to console her.

CHAPTER THIRTY-ONE

BIG BEND COASTAL WATERS
Florida

In a few months, Mingo and Wash had bagged nearly all the big game like hog, deer, bear, and gators within a day's walk from the village. By mid-summer, their take had become limited to small prey such as 'possums, coons, squirrels, and swamp rabbits and fowl like swamp chicken, limpkins and ducks. In time, even the small game became scarce and fewer fish were in the creeks. Food ran so low that Brutus called a council. He came straight to the point. "All of us can't survive here. There ain't enough to eat. Some of us have to leave."

Wash said, "Where can we find another safe place? We can't risk leavin'. We can make it here."

Mingo suggested fetching the vittles and supplies left hidden in the forest.

Brutus said, "It's too risky to cross the Suwannee. What we hid is likely spoiled by now anyhow."

"I can slip around without patters catching me. The cornmeal and dried peas was bagged and sealed in barrels. It might still be OK if de Crackers didn't find it."

"It's mighty dangerous, but what choice do we have? We need the tools we left over there even if de food is rotten."

Early the next morning, Mingo set out with two men.

At the Suwannee, Mingo searched every plausible creek to find the boat that he had hidden months before. The water in the river had dropped several feet since then and lush growth made the river look much different. Tired and frustrated after several hours, he sat down on the bank where high water had scoured out crisp, white sand that felt damp and cool through his pants. "I believe we are lookin' in de right place, but all de river bends look so similar, it's hard to know. I'm sure nobody found de skiff as well as I hid it. We've got to keep lookin'; unless we find it, we can't cross de river."

With dogged determination, he retraced his route. At a creek he had already searched, he found the boat under a broken limb that a windstorm had blown down from a live oak. Mingo and the two men with him slid the boat down the sandy bank to the water and rowed across the river. Far up a stream on the east bank, he hid the boat at a place where he could line up tall pines as markers.

He led the men cross-country through the thickets and swamp. For hours, the men sloshed through creeks and pushed through brush until they climbed a sand hill ridge where walking was easy between well-spaced rosemary shrubs and sand pines.

Once across the ridge, dense forest closed in again that forced the men to squirm through the brush or to follow vague animal trails. The tedious tussle through the tangles made Mingo anxious that he'd lost the way, but he persisted until he came to a sandy track that he believed to be Clay Landing Road. Although unsure about which direction to turn, he decided to go north. After a mile, he found the track that Brutus had followed with the cart.

A quarter mile from the dim road, he found the cache easier than he expected. The men tied the supplies into manageable bundles and then headed back for the village. When they reached the main road, they sprawled in the shade to rest. Before long, they heard a horse.

They grabbed their bundles, scurried into a gallberry thicket and scrunched down. Through the underbrush, they glimpsed a horse harnessed to a travois packed high with supplies and ridden by a lanky man wearing a brown slouch hat. Mingo eased back the hammer on his shotgun to half cock.

After the travois scraped by, he heard the familiar voice of the cook who had stayed behind at the lumber camp. As the slaves trudged by the hiding place, Mingo stood up and forced air between his teeth, "Pssst." The slaves turned toward the sound but couldn't see anybody behind the gallberry bushes until Mingo stepped around the thicket and said in a low voice. "It's me. Be quiet. One of you come over here. The rest of you, keep walkin'."

One man peeled away from the others and Mingo asked, "Where ya'll headed?"

"Holland's takin' us to the coast to make salt."

"Where's Wall?"

"Don't know nothin' 'bout him. What you doin'?"

"We live in a village in the swamps 'cross de Suwannee River. We've here to gather up supplies. Why don't you join us?"

"No way, Mingo. Holland said the sheriff is puttin' together a big posse to hunt you down."

"If he does, we'll fight. How's de war goin'?"

"Nobody tells us; I heard Holland talkin' to a white man 'bout a battle at a place called Shiloh. He said the Confederate general was no good and should have destroyed de Yankee army, but all he accomplished was gittin' thousands killed."

"Thousands, you say?"

"Dat's all I knows. I need to git. Holland is edgy. He threatened to lock us in chains least we keep together. How you doin'?"

"It's tough, but we're free. We'll be in contact," Mingo said as the man turned to rejoin the others.

As he picked up the unwieldy bundles, Mingo had an inspiration. "It'll be hard to slosh through de swamps all the way to the river with dis stuff. Let's find a place along de shoreline or up a creek where ya'll can hide. I'll bring de boat around to pick you up."

At first, the others argued that they shouldn't separate but finally agreed that traveling by boat had to be easier than walking to the river. Setting out, they followed animal trails toward the coast until they came to a small rise where a tall snag leaned over an inlet. "Ya'll wait here by dis dead tree. It's a landmark dat I can see from de water."

The trip to the boat turned out to be more difficult that Mingo anticipated. In many places, he couldn't follow the shoreline because heavy undergrowth grew to the water or merged with the needle rushes that he couldn't walk through. He had to backtrack often, but after a day's hard travel, he reached the skiff.

After sleeping under the boat for the night, he set out early the next morning. Returning with the rowboat wasn't easy either. In open water where the wind pushed it, he just managed to keep it on course by straining against the oars. In the channels that cut through the rush flats, he made good headway until shallow water made rowing impossible. Then he used an oar to push against the mucky bottom to force the boat forward. The blade often slipped, but he managed to make progress toward the snag until the boat ran hard aground on mud. As he sat breathing hard, he realized that the water was rising.

He waited a couple of hours until the tide floated the skiff enough that he could push it ahead.

As he rounded a turn in the salt creek near the snag, he stepped up on a seat so he could be seen above the needle rush bordering the creek. On alert, his men spotted him and ran to the shoreline. When Mingo poled the boat close enough that they could grab it without sinking into the mud, they snugged the bow against the bank.

After loading the boat with the supplies, the men jumped aboard. To move the heavily laden skiff, Mingo had to row with all his strength to make progress against the current and sea breeze. An hour passed before he reached open water and turned toward the mouth of the Suwannee.

Sweat poured off his forehead as he rowed. He concentrated so hard that he didn't notice anything other than the whorls made by the oars until the man riding in the bow yelled out that he saw smoke out on the Gulf. Mingo shipped the oars and twisted to look where the man pointed as the skiff drifted with the wind toward shore.

All three men stared into the glare off the Gulf which blended with the haze in the shimmering light so well that they could only see smoke, not a ship. It was so far away Mingo ignored it, but as he pushed with an oar to correct the skiff's drift, a sailboat tacking from behind a nearby island caught his eye.

Mingo redoubled his effort to pull for an inlet as the gray sloop bore down. Within minutes it came within hailing distance. A shout rang out, "Stop rowing or we'll shoot. Put your hands in the air!"

Mingo estimated the distance to the inlet. Unless the sailboat ran aground in the shallow water, he'd never make it before it closed. An insistent command resounded over the water, "Halt!"

He shipped oars. As the sloop glided close by the rowboat which was drifting with the breeze, a sailor called out through a megaphone, "Keep your hands up!"

As Mingo and the others sat waiting, they heard shouts that had no meaning for them, "Ready about," followed by a pause, "Hard alee."

"What dey mean by dat?" a man said as the sailboat tacked across the wind to sail toward the skiff from the opposite direction.

As it came along side the rowboat, the helmsman pointed the bow into the wind and luffed the sails. As sailors lowered and secured the canvass, marines kept rifles aimed at the men in the skiff.

A man on the sailboat asked, "Are you armed?"

Mingo noticed that his shotgun was in plain sight atop the gear. "A shotgun."

"Who are you and what's your business?"

"My name is Mingo and these are my friends. We're going home."

"Do you have any weapons except that shotgun?"

"Nossuh."

As sailors secured lines to the skiff and dropped anchor, a marine climbed into the rowboat. The man who had yelled through the megaphone wore a pistol and asked, "Where you headed?"

"Home dat's all. What you goin' do wid us?" Mingo said as he watched the marine rummage through the gear.

"I'm asking the questions. Where is home?"

The marine in the rowboat interrupted, "Nothing here, sir, except the rusty shotgun and some ammunition. No cotton or anything valuable; just tools and some moldy provisions."

The interrogation continued. "Where is home?"

"We lives in de swamps."

"Are you contraband?"

"What you mean, contraband?"

"Are you runaway slaves? Does that gear in the boat belong to you?"

Mingo looked down and scratched his forehead with his fingertips.

"Answer me!" the officer barked.

Without looking up, Mingo replied, "Yassuh, we ran away. Mas'r Wall beat us."

"You hungry?"

"Yassuh, dat's a fact."

"Good, we'll take you to the ship. We'll give you a hearty meal. Lower your rifles, men."

A sailor untied the skiff, payed out the painter to let the rowboat slip behind and then secured the line to a cleat on the sailboat's stern.

When the sloop reached its mother ship, the officer instructed the captives to clean up and throw their old clothes overboard. After a dowsing with sea water, they soaped up, rinsed with fresh water and then dried themselves with white towels. Mingo felt cleaner than he had in months. A sailor brought them new underwear, naval bell bottom trousers, cotton shirts, socks and brogans. As they admired each other's crisp appearance, the officer returned and said, "The captain has invited you to dinner."

Mingo and his men followed along a gangway and up a companionway to a large stateroom where several officers sat around a table covered by a white tablecloth set with silverware, white china and crystal glasses. The layout was not only a far cry from the wooden bowls and utensils at the village, it was fancier than any he had seen at White Oak Plantation.

While sailors in spotless uniforms talked among themselves, a black waiter edged around the table filling delicate glasses with what Mingo guessed was wine. The situation felt so fantastical to him that he almost didn't hear the sloop commander when he said, "Captain I'd like to introduce you to the men we picked up today. Men, meet Captain Howland."

The captain noticed Mingo's discomfiture and said, "Relax, men. You've had a rough day, but you're now among friends. As you can see, Master Weeks has been ordered to make sure that contraband, sorry, escaped slaves like you are treated well. How do you like your new clothes?"

The men nodded without speaking. The captain continued, "When the war started, government policy was to return runaway slaves to their owners. Now, that has changed. Congress has passed a law that our forces don't have to return slaves who come into our lines. Do you understand what I'm saying?"

When none of the slaves answered, Master Weeks said, "I explained this to them, but I'm not sure they believe it."

Mingo said, "Aren't we still property of de gov'ment? We want our freedom."

The Captain said, "Well, well. Who have we here?"

"Sir, this man appears to be their leader. His name is Mingo. He's clever. While sailing to the ship, I showed him some seamanship. He could handle a cutter with a little instruction. He claims to be a good hunter."

"I see. Well then, I want you men to understand that we will not hold you against your will. If you want to leave, just ask Master Weeks and he'll make arrangements. In the meantime you are my guests for dinner. As I said before, relax. Enjoy the food and wine. Tell us a little about yourselves. You can decide what you want to do later. Are you with me?"

Mingo looked into the captain's eyes and replied, "Yassuh."

"Good, then before we start dinner, I propose a toast."

As he stood up and lifted his glass, he motioned for everyone to do the same. Mingo, mimicking the officers, felt quite foolish.

The captain waited till everybody held their goblets high, then continued, "Here's to the men who have the guts to escape from insurrectionist slave owners. God willing, we shall soon subdue the Rebels so that no one suffers involuntary servitude in our great nation."

The other officers answered in unison, "Hear, hear."

Following the example of the captain and the other officers, Mingo took a swallow from his glass. The wine went down easy unlike the sharp moonshine that he had drunk at White Oak.

"Sit down, sit down," the captain said. "I want to hear about your escape."

Conditioned by years of slavery to keep their mouths shut around white men, Mingo and the other runaways didn't say anything.

"Don't be afraid. You're among friends."

Mingo asked, "Are we really free to go? What are you goin' to do wid us?"

Sensitive to the fear in his voice, the captain answered, "First, we'll give you a good dinner, which won't be as good as I'd like because we haven't been re-supplied with fresh food in some time. All we have is canned meat, flour and desiccated vegetables. Second, we'll give you a good night's rest and send you on your way tomorrow."

"You ain't goin' to turn us over to de sheriff?"

"No. I shall not return slaves to their owners unless ordered to do so. In fact, those of us in the East Gulf Blockading Squadron intend to do everything within our power to help slaves escape from Rebel bondage. Tell me about your escape."

For the first time, Mingo thought that perhaps the rumors were true that Yankees intended to free the slaves if they won the war.

"We ran away from Mas'r Wall's lumber camp. He beat my friend so bad it killed him. When he flogged another man, I couldn't take it no more. I grabbed the whip." Mingo stopped.

"Go ahead," the captain urged. "The more we know, the more likely we can help you."

As if a floodgate had opened, Mingo talked about everything that had happened from the time he was taken to the barracoon in Charleston to his escape from Wall. The only times he stopped talking was when the captain or another officer asked a question, which he used as an opportunity to scoop up huge bites of meat and potatoes.

Mingo ate plenty but nothing compared to his friends who gobbled the hearty fare without talking. The officers listened in fascination as he described the gory fight at the lumber camp, the escape from the posse at the Suwannee, and the slaves' sparse living conditions.

When he finished, the captain said; "How can we help your people?"

"Sir, we never have enough food. We hunt, fish, and cut swamp cabbage, but it's tougher every day. We ain't got much ammunition. Our clothes are so worn out some folks wear animal skins. We worry 'bout a posse coming after us all de time."

The captain said to his first officer, "Give these men as much flour, canned meat, and clothing as they can transport in their boat."

Then the captain turned to Mingo and said, "Mingo, are you willing to help us in turn?"

"Yassuh, but what can we do for you?"

"You are all excused except for Mr. Weeks and Mr. Mingo. I want to talk with them in private."

After the others left the room, the captain said, "Mingo, here's how you can help. You know the countryside. You can watch the Rebels and report their movements to us."

"Yassuh, we know de country, but how can we get information to you?"

"I'll send Master Weeks in his cutter to meet you. You provide intelligence and the navy will keep you supplied. We need to know the location of Rebel camps, troop movements, blockade runners, salt works and supply lines. Almost any information will be valuable. Encourage other slaves to run away. Every Rebel chasing escaped slaves is one less fighting us."

Mingo considered the risks. If he agreed to cooperate with the captain, he and his men would be at war with the Florida government and local white folks. So far, they had been left alone in the swamp, but he knew the Crackers would march through hell to destroy his band if they learned that they were helping other slaves to run away or assisting the U.S. Navy. He hesitated.

The captain continued, "Mingo, you don't have to get involved with us. I know what I'm asking is extremely dangerous. We're at war. If the Rebels know you are working with us, they'll kill you."

"De sheriff and patters are after me already. Dey's probably a death sentence on my head, but I have to think 'bout de others. I will help you, but I can only speak for myself. I believe my friends will join me, but each man has to decide for hisself."

"I understand Mingo, but the more men who help us, the more havoc we can wreak on the Rebels."

"What ya mean?"

The officer stared straight into Mingo eyes. "Your men can help us fight. We'll supply you with weapons. You can coordinate attacks with us."

Once Mingo grasped the captain's intention, he committed to help the Navy with enthusiasm. For more than an hour the three men discussed possibilities and tentative plans. Finally, the captain said, "Mingo, I have one last request. While you're harassing the enemy, can you liberate some fresh meat and vegetables for us? My sailors are sick and tired of canned food."

Mingo laughed, "Captain, am I to understand dat on top of askin' us to risk our lives to help you fight, you want us to bring you fresh food?" He paused for effect, "It's a tall order, but considerin' it's you who asked, we'll do it."

The captain smiled. "Mingo, together we're going to make the Rebels pay for their treason and for keeping you and your people enslaved. I'm assigning Master Weeks to coordinate our efforts."

CHAPTER THIRTY-TWO

BRONSON

Florida

After being chased off Bell's place, Wall hunted down the sheriff and found him a few days later at the Bronson Café eating breakfast with the Chairman of the County Commission who was complaining about the outlaws and runaways holed up across the Suwannee. The sheriff had heard it all before and was mumbling something between mouthfuls of grits when Wall barged up.

"Sheriff, I demand that you arrest Blanche Bell. When I went to her place on official business to inventory her property, she chased me off at gunpoint."

The sheriff looked up, sighed, and said, "What the hell are you talkin' about? You, of all people, want me to arrest Blanche Bell? She does more for the Soldier's Aid Society than anybody. Her husband is in the army. I seem to remember he joined the posse to hunt down your slaves after you let them escape. Have you forgotten that Loring Bell rescued you at the Otter Creek Bridge? Are you nuts?"

The sheriff grabbed a biscuit, pulling it apart to dab at the red-eye gravy spread across his plate.

Wall raised his voice, "Sheriff, as an agent of the Confederate government, I'm demandin' that woman's arrest."

The sheriff put down his biscuit, pushed back from the table and glared at Wall. "Boy, you best pull up a chair and calm down."

Everybody in the café stopped eating.

Wall yanked a chair from under the table and sat down between the sheriff and county commissioner. The lawman ate several more bites before asking what happened.

"Blanche Bell prevented me and my two assistants from inventoryin' her property for impressments."

"I heard that already. What happened?"

"She ordered me off her property at gunpoint."

"Are you tellin' me that a woman forced you and two soldiers off her property?"

Someone snickered across the room.

"Sheriff, she wasn't alone. That Englishman Chad Waldock and two others, Bell's son and perhaps his nigger to boot, had the drop on us."

In the back room, the black dishwasher dropped a plate with a clatter.

Glancing around, Wall continued, "Sheriff, we ought to discuss this in private."

The sheriff answered in his usual drawl, "You've interrupted me and made public accusations against an upstandin' citizen. Now, let's hear what you have to say."

Wall's face flushed which made his bad eye water more than usual. He longed for his whip so he could teach the sheriff respect.

After a few more bites the sheriff said, "What warnin' did you give when you rode up?"

"None. Why should I?"

"Did ya draw your weapon?"

Wall felt everybody's eyes in the whole cafe.

"My pistol."

"Why?"

"Bell's blasted hounds were nippin' at my horse's shanks. I yelled for somebody to call off the dogs. When they didn't, I shot them."

The sheriff nodded. "Let's see if I've got this right, you and two men rode up to the Bell place and shot their dogs?"

Wall seethed. "I had to shoot them before they bit my horse."

The sheriff locked eyes with Wall.

"You're damned lucky that Blanche didn't shoot you. You've got a lot to learn about the people who live in the Suwannee Valley, boy. You may have political connections to land a cushy government job, but don't think you can ride roughshod over the people around here. In South Carolina, or wherever you came from, people might bow and scrape to their so-called betters, but people who live in these woods ain't like that. They think they're just as good as anybody. You understand, boy?"

Wall opened his mouth to protest, but the sheriff cut him off.

"If you weren't a Confederate official, I'd charge you with killin' Blanche Bell's dogs, but I'll give you a break. You're going to ride over to Deer Hall with me and apologize and pay her fair compensation. Then, you can ask real polite if you can inventory her farm."

Several days later, Chad noticed two, well-dispersed riders coming down the lane. He ran inside and grabbed the shotgun over the fireplace while yelling to Billy to warn Jake.

When the lead rider came within hailing distance, he yelled, "It's Sheriff Maxwell. I'm comin' up."

Chad relaxed but didn't put down the shotgun as the riders approached the house. When he was certain the lead rider was, in fact, the sheriff, he leaned his weapon against the wall. "Welcome, Sheriff."

"Hello, Chad. I need to talk to Blanche."

As the other rider approached, Chad noticed that it was Wall. The sheriff said, "I thought I told you to stay back." Wall reined his horse.

Chad met the lawman on the steps where the two men shook hands as Billy, toting his 20 gauge shotgun, ran to the corner of the house where he stood watching Wall.

Blanche stepped out on the porch. "Sheriff, what a pleasant surprise, can I offer you a glass of lemonade?"

"No, thank you. I came on business. Somehow Wall got himself appointed impressment officer. His job requires him to inventory all the farms in around here, so I came along to make sure he doesn't cause you any more trouble. I understand he shot your dogs."

"Yes, sir, he did."

"He's goin' to apologize and pay you fair compensation."

"Sheriff, I don't want that man on my property."

"I know that, but you've got to let him do his work. If you run him off again, he'll come back with soldiers and arrest you. We've got enough trouble in the county already."

The sheriff yelled to Wall, "Come up here."

After Wall hitched his horse, he walked across the sandy yard, climbed the steps onto the porch and stopped. The sheriff asked, "Don't you have something to say to Mrs. Bell?"

Wall reached in his jacket for his billfold from which he pulled a five-dollar Confederate note that he held toward Blanche. "Missis Bell, I'm sorry I had to kill your dogs."

Blanche glared at him. "Keep your money, inventory my farm, then get off my property." She wheeled, slamming the door behind her.

Before Wall could put the money back in his billfold, the sheriff said, "I'll hold that for Mrs. Blanche. Get on with your job."

Wall scowled.

As he handed over the bill, he snarled at Chad, "Where's your wench?"

Chad drew back his fist, but the sheriff stepped between the men. Wall jumped back, drawing his pistol. The sheriff yelled, "Hold it! Put your damn weapon away. Ain't you learned nothin'?"

Wall stared icily at the sheriff as he eased down the hammer with his thumb. After jamming his pistol in its holster, he walked to his horse. As he lifted himself into the saddle, he muttered, "I ain't through with you yet, boy."

Chad wasn't sure if he was speaking to him or Sheriff Maxwell.

As Wall rode toward the barn, the sheriff said, "No wonder we're losing the war with assholes like that runnin' the government. While I wait, I might as well take up Blanche's offer for some lemonade."

Chad stepped inside and soon returned with two full glasses. "This is good lemonade made from Myers lemons I brought up from Homosassa. It'd be better if we had sugar. We only have honey for sweetening."

As the two men sipped their drinks, Wall rode around the farm jotting down in a leather bound book every valuable item. After inspecting the outbuildings, he rode away without returning to the house.

As he rode out of sight, the sheriff stood up and took the five-dollar Confederate bill from his pocket. "Mighty peaceful out here. I hate to leave. Give this to Blanche. She'll need it. Times are tight."

Chad answered, "She won't take Wall's money."

"Then you hold it for her. No telling when Loring can come home. Ya'll be careful; marauders burned a farm over by Clay Landing last week. I'll follow Wall back to Bronson. Thank Blanche for the lemonade."

Chad stuffed the bill in his pocket. "You be careful, keep your eye on Wall."

The sheriff mounted his horse, tipped his hat, and rode away.

CONFEDERATE CAVALRY CROSSING THE ST. JOHN'S RIVER

(Courtesy Florida State Archives)

CHAPTER THIRTY-THREE

St. John's River
Florida

Loring adapted well to the camp routine and found it easier than the tedious farm labor to which he was accustomed. His shooting and riding skills earned respect from the other men. Better yet, his knack for drill earned a recommendation from the first sergeant for drill instructor, a position that exempted him from onerous fatigue duties.

Most soldiers resisted drill at first figuring that it had no practical benefit to real fighting. They called it "make work." Unlike the other drill instructors, Loring made the lessons enjoyable challenges, not oppressive duty. He joked with his trainees while the other instructors demanded strict discipline at all times. To their relief, Loring put his charges on report less. The other instructors criticized him for his easy, non-military ways although the first lieutenant noticed that his trainees learned faster and performed better.

Squads rotated hunting trips to supplement the rations. After a while, the soldiers noticed that Loring and his men brought back more meat than the others. Others sometimes returned empty-handed or with miserly game like 'possum or coon while Loring's unit often bagged a hog or deer, and once, a two-hundred-pound bear.

One rainy day, the company's third lieutenant cut a deep gash across his palm when his knife slipped skinning a hog. He tied a cloth around his hand to stop the bleeding and kept butchering. That evening when he unwrapped the bandage, he noticed that the vein along his wrist was red. The next morning, a dark, crimson line extended to his elbow. He conferred with the company doctor who examined the cut and squeezed odiferous, yellow pus from the wound. "Looks like erysipelas," the surgeon said.

"What's that?" asked the lieutenant.

"Putrefaction. We may have to operate."

The lieutenant almost vomited because he knew that "operation" was the euphemistic word for "amputation." "I've gone through many a skirmish without suffering so much as a scratch. Now you're telling me you have to cut off my hand."

"I'm afraid so; there's nothing else to do. Wrap your hand with charpie. We'll check it after formation tomorrow."

The next morning, the lieutenant was delirious with fever.

The doctor examined the wound and said, "Tie him down on that table near the cook fire. Heat irons in the fire. Let's get this over with,"

Two privates grabbed the lieutenant dragging him to a table where they tied him on his back by his arms and legs. "Let him have a slug of rum, we ain't got no ether," the doctor said as he handed a trooper a bottle. The soldier helped the lieutenant drink several mouthfuls while the doctor stropped a long-bladed knife against a smooth leather strap.

As the surgeon sliced through muscle, the lieutenant fainted. Working fast, the physician cut and pulled aside flesh, staunched the bleeding with the hot irons, then sawed through the bones.

The doctor handed the severed hand and forearm to a private. "Bury this."

Gathering the skin folds, the doctor stitched them together and covered the stub with a bandage.

For several days the lieutenant passed in and out of consciousness, but every day his fever increased. A week later, he died.

That afternoon, a corporal ordered Loring to report to the captain. After the customary salutes, the commander came straight to the point. "We have to replace the third lieutenant. As you know, Confederate Army units elect their own officers. I want you to put your name up. The men respect you. You have leadership skills. Most of these Crackers are so hardheaded they won't listen to anybody, but you manage to cram something into their thick skulls."

Loring demurred, "Why don't you put your name in, Sarge? You have more experience and you've seen the elephant."

"I considered it, but I can't read and write. Paperwork is beyond me."

Loring didn't want to jump ahead of combat veterans, yet the promotion tempted him. A lieutenant made more pay. Plus, the job entailed more variety and responsibility than drill instructor. "Let me talk it over with my squad."

His tent mates and the other men in the company encouraged him, so he committed. His only opponent was the captain's first cousin who was unpopular with the troops. When the ballots were counted, the results were so lopsided in Loring's favor that the entire unit must have voted for him except for the few he had placed on report.

The next evening at a dress parade, the captain pinned a lieutenant's slim, gold pip on his collar. Afterward, at the officer's mess, the captain lifted his glass to Loring. "Here's to our new lieutenant. We've lost our best drill instructor but have found a good and brave officer."

"Hear, hear," everybody responded.

As they quieted, the captain tapped on his glass with a knife and said, "Listen up. A dispatch reported this afternoon that the gunboat *Isaac Smith* is steaming upriver on the St. Johns past the *Patroon*, which is anchored just above Black Creek. I think we should ambush the *Isaac Smith*."

The first lieutenant said, "An excellent idea, Captain. My new third lieutenant is tired of camp life. We need him to put his skills to better use than huntin' bear."

Well before dawn, the first lieutenant ordered a cavalry detachment to head out in columns of two. Loring rode beside him. As they settled their horses into a comfortable walk, the officer said, "This expedition will give you experience. The first rule is not to take anything for granted. We have no indication that any Yankees are in the area, but we always post scouts. They outnumber us and they're better armed. We have to think like guerillas, not a regular army. We can't afford to lose men or equipment by stumblin' into a fight. Remember, we ambush Yankees, not vice versa."

"Yes, sir."

The detachment traveled south and by late morning reached a dirt intersection a few miles above Middleburg where the first lieutenant halted the troopers. "Men, take a break. Lieutenant, come with me."

Loring walked with the first lieutenant into the shade under a live oak dripping with Spanish moss. The officer squatted on his haunches, pulled off his sweat-stained gauntlets and spread a ragged map on the ground. A light breezed lifted the edge. He grabbed a broken branch, pulled the moss off, and used it to weight down the windward side. "Loring, we have one advantage over the Yankees. We know the country; they don't. About the time they learn it, they rotate personnel. Where do you think we can ambush *Isaac Smith*?"

Loring studied the unfamiliar geography along the St. John's River for a minute before he answered, "Unless the gunboat steams close to shore, the river is too wide for an ambush until Pilatka."

"That's right; it'll stay out of sharpshooter range."

Loring traced the St. John's with his finger. "The river narrows considerably after Lake Dunn. Do you think her captain will take her that far south?"

"I suspect so. Yankees want to control the river, so he'll probe as far as he can. It's navigable past Lake George. You can bet they'd like to blockade the Oclawaha River which is our last supply line that's open to the coast."

Loring put his finger at the confluence of the Oclawaha and the St. Johns. "Right here by Welaka the river is narrow. What are the banks like?"

The first lieutenant smiled, pleased to see that Loring thought ahead. "Mostly swamp, but we might find a place to set an ambush."

The first lieutenant rolled up the map and walked with Loring back to the troopers. "Listen up, men. Once we're past Middleburg, a squad will shadow the *Isaac Smith* as she steams south. Corporal, take four men and keep tabs on the gunboat. Report to me every evening by courier. I'll take the column south via the Bellamy Road to Fort Holmes. We'll wait for the ship across the river from Horse Landing."

Two days later a courier reported that *Isaac Smith* still had not reached Pilatka. "Sir, the ship's makin' slow headway. It's sinkin' every boat on the river it finds and destroyin' or burnin' every dock and building on the waterfront. The crew's loadin' up all the slaves they come across. We've watched several runaway groups wave her down."

The lieutenant said, "We're found a good ambush site. Let me know when the gunboat reaches Pilatka."

When the report came, the commander dispersed the men a hundred yards along the river at the ambush site and ordered them to dig rifle pits. "Once we start shootin', the gunboat will return fire with cannon. Unless we are well dug in, we'll take casualties."

The men whined about digging holes through the roots and into mucky ground. Loring agreed because he felt the holes weren't necessary with so many trees and logs to hide behind. He asked the first lieutenant to walk out of hearing from the troopers to ask if the work was worth the effort. "Lieutenant, roots make it almost impossible to dig a hole and water seeps in as soon as the men dig down."

"No matter, deep holes will save lives. You'll see. The men will be sorry that they don't have deeper ones if the ambush comes off. You make sure every rifle pit is large enough so the troopers can scrunch down well below ground level. Confirm that nobody has disturbed vegetation or thrown up dirt that will give away our position."

The lieutenant ordered a wiry, young man to climb a majestic cypress tree that overhung the river to look out for the gunboat. While the man climbed from limb to limb, Loring examined the preparations for the ambush. Despite grousing, the men had dug their holes deep enough. The surroundings looked natural except for fresh dirt one trooper had spread across the ground. Loring ordered him to cover it with Spanish moss.

As he finished his inspection, he heard a shout from the treetop. "Gunboat's comin'!"

The lieutenant yelled, "Get your ass down from that tree." When the lookout reached the ground, he continued, "Men, shoot the sailors. Concentrate on the roundhouse; that's where the officers will be. Don't fire till I do. After you've taken a shot, stay down in your hole while you re-load because they're goin' open up with cannon."

As a few men made final adjustments to their firing lanes by snapping off a twig here or there, the gunboat's engines hammered full ahead to speed through the narrows causing a bow wave to crash over the muddy band and into the brush along the shore. As the ship glided into the lieutenant's firing lane, the gunboat loomed like a fortress with its high iron sides. Cotton bales filled all the gaps along the rail. The lieutenant waited for a target, but none appeared until he glimpsed an officer's cap through an open port.

He aimed, exhaled and squeezed the trigger. The hammer fell, but the discharge delayed a critical instant as the powder ignited. Lead pinged against steel. Shots poured from the rifle pits at the gunboat. The first lieutenant swore under his breath, "We ain't got no targets. We'll be lucky to hit one sailor."

Sporadic rifle fire continued along the line which was answered by a volley from the gunboat. Minie balls pzzzed through the brush and thudded into trees. For a few seconds everything was quiet except for the hammering gunboat engine. Then a blast thundered above the din.

The air above the rifle pits seemed alive with malevolent, iron insects. Grape shot flew through the vegetation shearing leaves and limbs which showered down on the troopers. A second cannon fired. A shell exploded overhead that spewed red-hot shrapnel into a cypress root by Loring's rifle pit. He hunkered down as far as he could in a vain effort to burrow into the mud.

"Stay down! Stay down!" the lieutenant yelled as some men poked their heads from their holes.

A half-mile beyond the ambush, the gunboat fired one last shot. Deafened from the earlier shell burst, Loring never heard the first lieutenant's warning and stood up just as the parting shot exploded.

For days after the battle with the gunboat, Loring suffered headaches. At times, he felt woozy when he stood up. On occasion, he had to grab a tree or tent pole to keep from falling. Now and then, his thinking seemed clouded although by the time the gash on his forehead healed into a ragged red scar, he felt almost like his old self.

1863

My Dear Husband,

I think if we fight much longer we will come down as low as slaves, and I think we had better give up, and have our husbands with us, slavery if such it will be, will be much harder when we are subdued after our husbands are killed. Oh, how I wish the war never had started…

From a letter by Octavia Stephens written at her farm, Rose Cottage, near Walaka in East Florida to her husband Winston Stephens serving with Dickison's 2nd Cavalry.

CHAPTER THIRTY-FOUR

CAMP FINNEGAN
Florida

As the war dragged on, army life and the conditions at Camp Finnegan wore out the soldiers; they became sickly and listless. Everybody awoke before reveille each morning to coughing fits. At first it was only a man here or there, but in short order, all the soldiers had the scourge. The malady persisted in every season and all weather, rain or shine, hot or cold. Perhaps breathing the smoke that always hovered over the camp explained the spasms or perhaps living cooped up in the drafty tents and dank shelters caused the contagion. Nobody knew, but they all had to endure it.

Another scourge was the rats that lived in the shelters with the soldiers. One private killed so many by throwing his bayonet like a javelin at them that his comrades nicknamed him "Spear Chucker."

The rats attracted snakes which lived under the tent flooring. Most, like the black snakes, rat snakes, and spreading adders were harmless. The men welcomed them because they ate the vermin. Others were dangerous. Once, a six-foot rattler slithered into a shelter and a lieutenant blasted it with his shotgun although standing orders prohibited discharging firearms in camp. Another time, as a private pulled his blanket off his cot to take them to the washerwoman to boil, he found a ground rattler nestled in the pine straw he used as a mattress. From then on, everybody called the squad "Rattlers."

Constant patrolling, poor food, and sickness transformed the soldiers into scrawny, worn-out imitations of their former selves. Without enough companies to properly rotate picket duty, Loring and his men never had enough rest. They patrolled day and night. When not scouting, they had to stand guard around the camp's perimeter as well as to look after the horses and supplies. In addition, they had to chase escaped slaves and guard Yankee prisoners.

As army rations became short, the camp barely managed to feed itself although the soldiers raised hogs, chickens, ducks, and geese. Details constantly foraged, hunted and fished to bring in such fare as game, oysters and mullet, which the cooks fried in hog grease.

Soldiers searched the countryside for feral cattle which they rounded up to ship to the Confederate armies in Virginia and Tennessee. The men groused that it wasn't fair that they had to ship beef north when they didn't have enough meat for themselves. However, as food supplies dwindled, beeves often injured themselves and had to be shot for the cook pots.

Loring managed to find free time to write letters home and to read newspapers when he could obtain them. After the skirmish with *USS Isaac Smith,* Captain Dickison instructed his officers to find a way to sink the gunboats. Loring become obsessed with the challenge. By chance, he found a solution in a *Harper's Weekly* newspaper article about the siege at Vicksburg. In it, he noticed a paragraph about a new weapon called the "torpedo" that CSA General Rains had developed. The weapon wasn't described in detail other than to report that it caused a powerful explosion that was triggered by an electrical deto-nator. Loring didn't know what that was, but he wanted to learn. He jumped up. "Sarge, here's an article describing a way to sink gunboats."

"Don't tell me you have another harebrained idea."

Loring smacked the rolled up paper against his palm. "Says right here in this Yankee paper that on December 12, 1862, Confederates used an electronically detonated torpedo to sink the *USS Cairo* in the Yazoo River near Vicksburg, Mississippi."

"Well, I'll be durned. This time you have somethin'. Let's talk to Captain Dickison."

The two men walked to the Commander's shelter and found him outside in the sun reading reports while a slave polished his boots. "Captain," Loring said, "Sorry to disturb you, sir, but have you seen this article that reports the Yankee gunboat *Cairo* was sunk in the Mississippi by a torpedo? I don't know what that is, but it may be the answer to our prayers."

The officer scanned the article and then read it a second time. He looked up at Loring and snapped, "I can't believe you interrupted my work to show me an article in a Yankee newspaper."

Loring and his sergeant gawked at the captain. Loring stam-mered, "Sir, I, I don't mean any disrespect. I just thought---"

The captain laughed. "Boy, my boots are shiny enough. Loring, come with me to the telegraph office. I'm cablin' General Finnegan to send torpedoes."

CHAPTER THIRTY-FIVE

DEEP CREEK

Florida

As Loring gained experience, the captain put him in command of patrols. He enjoyed the opportunity to be in the saddle away from the boring, dirty camp where the biggest fight was with the lice the men called gray backs. Usually, the missions were uneventful because the Yankee troops stayed close to the protection of their gunboats or in comfortable strongholds like St. Augustine. Dickison didn't have the manpower to dislodge them, so he left them alone except for harassing actions.

Primarily, Rebel patrols shadowed the enemy while always on the lookout for an advance in force. More often than not, the missions accomplished no more than verifying intelligence that citizens had already reported. Occasionally, they found a Yankee foraging party or stragglers. In those circumstances, sharpshooters picked off the careless troopers. Successful missions were sporadic at best as the Federal troops generally stayed in their safe occupation zones where they counted themselves lucky not to be posted farther north where titanic campaigns resulted in casualties by the thousands.

Rebel patrols always had to worry about running into larger Yankee units or an ambush. Usually, they avoided Federals by using unmapped, backcountry trails known only to natives. To counter the advantage, Union commanders hired locals as scouts, but they couldn't trust them. If not Rebels themselves, often their friends and relatives were, so they led Yankees soldiers away from Confederate forces whenever they could. Nevertheless, Rebel patrols stayed wary.

Once as Loring led his men down a dirt lane, the point guard reined his horse, drew his pistol and signaled danger. Ahead of him, the road squeezed through woods just wide enough for a wagon to pass, a perfect ambush site. Loring pulled his LeMat, checked the caps and walked his horse forward while constantly scanning the forest for Yankee sharpshooters. When he reached the sentinel, the soldier reported he'd seen black people duck under a wooden bridge.

Loring nudged Ginger behind a massive, longleaf pine to dismount. Watching and listening for movement around the bridge and in the forest, he signaled for the squad to form a skirmish line across the lane with flankers spread several hundred yards on each side. Once in position, he waved them forward to verify that the Yankees had not set an ambush by using the blacks as a diversion. The troopers edged forward with their weapons at half cock. When they reached the creek without incident, the sergeant waved them across to set a perimeter. Once they secured the area, he scampered down the creek bank to look under the bridge. He couldn't see well in the dim light filtering between the planking, but as his eyes adjusted, he made out a black woman standing waist deep in the water with three youngsters clinging to her.

"Come on out from under there before you catch a chill or a gator snatches your children."

As the woman clambered from under the bridge, the sergeant asked, "You have a pass?"

Trembling from the cool water and fear, the woman answered, "Nossuh."

"Any Yankee soldiers around?"

"I ain't seen none, Mas'r."

"Where you from?

The woman stood in silence with her head down. The sergeant barked at her to answer. As if transformed, the woman lifted her head and looked straight at him. "I done run away from Mas'r Levy, and I'm goin' to de Yankee lines for de freedom President Lincum promised."

The sergeant said, "You're makin' a mistake leavin' home. Even if you find the Yankees, they won't help you. You can't make it without Senator Levy to look after you. I ought to whip you for bein' on the road without a pass."

"Yassuh."

Standing orders required that runaway slaves be returned to their owners, but Loring didn't have the manpower to do that. He said to the woman, "Will you promise to go straight home if we don't arrest you?"

"Yassuh."

"Do you have any food?"

"Nossuh."

Loring handed the woman a few hardtack crackers.

"Thank you, thank you, suh. My chil'luns ain't had nothin' to eat for two days."

"That's why you better go on home where you belong," the sergeant said.

When Loring and the sergeant walked away from the woman toward their horses, the sergeant said, "Word gets out that you didn't arrest Senator Levy's runaways, you'll have hell to pay."

Loring looked around to make sure no troopers were close enough to eavesdrop. "I'll take my chances. Blacks know about the Emancipation Proclamation, and they can see we're losing the war. It's a new day and we best adapt. When Lee invaded Maryland last September, he took 12,000 casualties. Sure, the Yankees had more, but the General was forced to tuck his tail and hotfoot it back to Virginia. If McClellan had pursued him, he could have destroyed the whole army."

The sergeant retorted, "But the march into Maryland forced McClellan out of Virginia."

"You're right, but what happens now? Lincoln fired McClellan for not being aggressive. Sooner or later, Lincoln's going to find a fighting general. When he does, Lee's done for. Every day the South is weaker while the North is stronger."

"We didn't lose at Sharpsburg; General Lee held the field, then withdrew."

"He held the field, so what? Napoleonic rules are obsolete. This war will be won by death and destruction, not who holds the field in bloody battles. Modern warfare is total war. Lee invaded Maryland to avoid a defensive war that he knows he can't win. Now he has to fight a war of attrition. The North is strangling us. Yankees control Kentucky and Tennessee. Our largest city, New Orleans, is occupied. Our armies are stretched to the breaking point. Supplies are scarce and Grant's on the march toward Vicksburg."

"I see your point, but we can hold on. The North is stymied. The Yankees invaded Virginia. We whipped them. It's easier to defend than attack."

"Eventually something has to give unless we get help from France or England, and that's not likely. You can bet Lincoln will keep attacking. Sure, we'll still win fights, but it'll wear us out. Morale is terrible. Our men volunteered to defend their homeland, not invade the North. They're pissed off about conscription and now believe that the Confederacy exists to preserve slavery. The rank and file don't have a dog in that fight. Our government has failed to protect their families which is another reason they've lost their motivation. Men are deserting everyday to go home and look after their folks."

The sergeant didn't interrupt Loring's tirade.

"Lee ordered our Florida troops north to defend Tennessee and Virginia. At Sharpsburg he took more casualties than we sent. We can't withstand loses like that. Here at home, the enemy can overrun us anytime they decide to make the effort."

"So far we've held the interior."

"For how much longer? Sooner or later we're going to be hit in force. Yankees aren't just fighting to preserve the Union anymore. Once Lincoln issued the Emancipation Proclamation, our government has to win the war to preserve slavery. Yankee abolitionists will never tolerate enslaving the freedmen again, and the freedmen would rather die first. Now Lincoln has to force the Confederacy to surrender. Both sides are painted into a corner with no room for political compromise. We'll fight till one side is destroyed. Under Yankee law, that Mammy and her pickaninnies back there are free as birds."

CHAPTER THIRTY-SIX

CHUNKY POND
Florida

"Tell us 'bout de Yankee ship again," a child asked Mingo as youngsters huddled around the campfire with him one chilly evening. Another giggled, "Tell us 'bout de captain's big belly."

The small fry never tired of hearing about Mingo's scouting adventures for the U.S. Navy. Although they'd heard him talk about the trip to the gunboat so often they could describe everything that happened almost as well as he could, they begged to hear it again.

After Mingo described the fat captain in meticulous detail from his bald head to his polished shoes, he asked, "Ain't it strange how a man with a shiny head like dat could have such a bushy mustache?"

A woman interrupted, "You chil'luns let Uncle Mingo have some rest. It's time for bed."

"Please, please let Uncle Mingo tell us more about de Navy ship," a tot protested.

"You heard me. Git to bed. Uncle Mingo's got better things to do besides tellin' you chil'luns stories. Now kiss him good night."

They swarmed around him. Each gave him a peck on the cheek, which he returned with a hug. After the woman hustled them away, the men stayed seated around the fire. Mingo said, "We have to meet

Master Weeks at Pine Island on the new moon. We need to head out on our scouting mission soon, or we won't have time to finish it before we have to report. We've got to decide who's going with me tonight."

Without hesitation, Brutus said, "I am."

Mingo nodded. Another man said, "We ain't stayin' here while ya'll go off to eat high on de hog on de gunboat."

"We'll be lucky to see de gunboat dis trip. Wash, can you watch over de camp if I take three men which is all that'll fit in the skiff wid me?"

"Take what you need. The rest of us can defend our home. Just show dem Crackers they're in for a good whuppin' now dat we're in de fight."

The men laughed then continued squabbling about who should go on the patrol. Mingo cautioned, "There'll be many more opportunities. Everybody will have a chance. We have to leave men behind to guard our village. Crackers know we are hidin' out here. Sooner or later, dey'll come for us. Those who remain have to stay alert."

Wash said, "We'll be ready, Mingo. Now dat we've got rifles and ammo, it'll take a big posse to take us on."

In addition to Brutus, Mingo chose two more men who agreed to follow his orders without question.

As dawn broke, Mingo pushed off. Brutus braced against the stern using an oar like a rudder as the boat drifted downstream while Mingo sat in the bow watching yellow warblers flit through the canopy over the creek. Near the river's mouth, he noticed turkey buzzards perched still as statues on bare limbs at the top of bald cypress trees while they sunned their wings until the thermals warmed enough for easy flight.

As the skiff drifted from under the tree canopy into open water, dazzling light forced Mingo to squint and shield his eyes. The air sparkled. Wind gusts bent the cord grass causing it to change color from brown to rusty green and then back to brown. Overhead, black-beaked terns circled. Occasionally, one hovered, wings flapping in a blur until it folded them to streak head first toward the water. On most plunges, the small birds spread their wings to abort the dive before hitting the surface. On every fourth or fifth attempt, one splashed into a wavelet and flew up with a squirming minnow in its beak. Now and then, as one flapped away with its prize, a gull swooped at it to steal its catch. Then the fisher became an acrobat, diving and turning erratically to evade the thief.

"Beach de boat. I want to make sure der ain't no Crackers around," Mingo ordered.

The skiff crunched onto a sandy beach littered with oyster shells bleached white by sun and salt. Mingo took a Navy telescope from his military haversack. Jamming it in his shirt, he grabbed a branch on a tall oak tree, threw his heels around the limb, pulled up and rotated atop it. Then he climbed up from branch to branch. Near the treetop, he leaned against a bough so he could scan the Gulf. After bending back twigs for an unobstructed view, he scanned the area. He didn't see so much as a rowboat anywhere in the wide expanse from tidal marsh to the horizon.

After returning to the boat, the men took turns rowing. After a long day, they reached the snag. After concealing the rowboat with branches and palmetto fronds, he led the patrol east toward the Clay Landing Road. He didn't stop except to check his map. He pushed the men hard, but they didn't complain. No matter how much he made them sweat, they stayed eager to move forward although the same effort under the whip would have exhausted them.

When the group approached the main road between Cedar Key and Clay Landing, Mingo called a halt and gathered the men around him. "Like we planned, we'll split up here so we can scout all de roads and trails from Cedar Key to Clay Landing and east as far as Orange Lake. Remember, we'll rendezvous at de old lumber camp by sunset in five days."

Mingo scouted the roads east of Bronson and the villages of Wacahotee, Newton, and Flemington without finding any Rebels, but the circuit took longer than he anticipated. On the appointed day, he worried that he'd be late to the rendezvous, so he trotted through the woods with his heavy, unwieldy rifle. Late in the afternoon as he approached the camp, he heard Brutus and the other men jabbering. Mingo hallooed and then ran up to them. "What's all the excitement?"

Brutus pointed at a dead man crumpled on the trail. Another said, "I seen Wall kill him. I scouted my assignment and got here early dis afternoon. Nobody else had showed up. It was quiet, just a Lord God Woodpecker knockin' a hole in dat tall pine.

Mingo suppressed the urge to shake the man. "Git to de point!"

"I was sittin' at dis here table waitin' for ya'll when I heard a horse whinny down the trail. I jumped up and hid in dat palmetto patch over yonder. When the rider came close, I sees it was Wall. He rode up right here and dismounted. I wanted to shoot him, but remembered you told us not to fire unless we was attacked. De devil sat down, took out his pistol and put it on de bench by his leg. Before long, I sees a rider wearin' a badge comin' up. When he got close, Wall shot him."

Mingo asked, "Did dat scoundrel see you?"

The man looked down without answering.

"I asked you a question!"

"After he killed and robbed de man, he must have noticed my tracks 'cause he walked straight toward me. I ran away, but he shot at me just as I tore into dat thicket over yonder. He jumped on his horse and galloped away."

Mingo declared, "Now patters will be on our tail for certain."

CHAPTER THIRTY-SEVEN

LITTLE PINE ISLAND
Florida

Brutus wanted to bury the sheriff so that wild animals wouldn't eat him, but Mingo rejected the suggestion, "We don't have time. Wall will have a posse after us. We better hot foot it. Let's go."

Mingo trotted from the camp. The men scrambled after him. When he reached the railroad, he stopped and waited for the others to catch up. "We're too easy to track if we stay together. Split up. Meet at the snag in five days. Travel through swamps so you don't leave tracks. Make sure no one is followin' you. How ya'll doin'?"

The men all said they were fine although Mingo noticed one man was bare footed. His feet were filthy and crusted with dirt and blood from briar and bramble scratches. "How come you aren't wearing your new brogans?"

"Navy shoes hurt."

"Can you keep goin' with your feet chewed up like dat?"

"Sure nuff. It's better than scufflin' de white man's hoe."

"OK then. Good luck."

Five days later, Mingo was relieved when all the men showed up although the barefooted man limped.

The scouting missions had been successful. Everybody had some intelligence. Several men had found salt works, one of which was at Live Oak Key on Waccasassa Bay.

The U.S. Navy already knew that the rebels had a camp at Clay Landing, but Brutus had ferreted out important details. "At least fifty soldiers operate from there. Their job is to watch our troops at Cedar Key and to block any incursion up de Suwannee. Dey patrol from de Suwannee River all the way to de Oclawaha. Dat leaves only a few soldiers to guard de camp and de river. They've built earth works, a bombproof shelter to store ammunition and a warehouse. Dey have a twelve-pound mountain howitzer, seventy horses, several mules and oxen."

"How you know all dat?" one man scoffed.

Brutus smiled. "Figured those Crackers had brothers workin' for 'em, so I found de quarters and waited. After a while, an old man shows up. Turns out he is de commander's personal manservant. He knows everythin'. De officers plan patrols while he serves meals."

Mingo smacked Brutus on the shoulder, "Brutus, dis is exactly de intelligence Master Weeks wants!"

As Brutus poled the skiff up the creek at the sharp bend near the village where a picket always stood guard, no one challenged the group. Mingo groused, "Wash should have a lookout posted here."

As the boat progressed upstream, the men expected to hear manmade noises from the camp from woodchoppers or children yelling and laughing. Instead, they only heard red-tailed hawks squalling atop a tree, mullet jumping in the stream, squirrels chattering and an owl hooting far in the distance.

Crisp air blew through the trees without a hint of the usual haze or campfire smoke. Brutus poled the boat faster. At a tiny dock, Mingo jumped ashore, looped the painter in a clove hitch and dropped it around a cypress knee. Scanning the area, he saw that the village had been burned. He hallooed. Nobody answered.

"What happened?" he wondered aloud.

Brutus stepped beside him, "I can't believe it. Where is everybody?"

Mingo said, "I'm sure Wash wouldn't let patters over-run the place without a fight."

Despondent and uncertain, the men wandered toward the old fire ring where only charred earth remained as the raiders had scattered the limestone rock used to encircle the pit. Someone had even kicked leaves over the ashes in an effort to obliterate all evidence that the village ever existed.

Brutus said, "Ain't no sign of a struggle or killin'. Patters must have snuck up and captured everybody. What we goin' do?"

Mingo vowed, "We'll free our people if it's de last thing we ever do. We've goin' make de white devils who took our people pay. It's past time dey learn we ain't goin' put up wid bein' treated like cattle no more. If we have to kill some folks, we will. Search de area. We have to find their trail. Meet back here at noon."

As the men fanned out to search the surrounding hammocks and swamps, Mingo walked around the burned village bleary-eyed until something mostly covered by Spanish moss caught his eye. He kicked back the stringy plant to uncover a burlap bag. He picked up the soggy sack, shook it, and threw it down. Frustrated that he couldn't find any clues, he sat on a stump. A melodious birdsong *teacher, teacher, teacher* wafted through the forest. The bird stopped calling when Mingo heard someone running toward him.

"Come with me. I've found Wash," Brutus yelled. As Mingo jumped up, Brutus turned around racing away. Mingo caught up to him when his friend stopped at a thicket and pointed, "Look!"

Resting next to a palmetto trunk, Mingo saw, a skull with weather-wore skin still clinging around the eye sockets. Scattered under the fronds, he could see more bones, some still joined by sinew. He pushed the head away from the crusty root with his toe. The forehead had a small hole. The back was torn away. "Looks like he was shot in de head. You sure it's Wash?"

"It's Wash, sure nuff. Right over there is de remains of his straw hat with de coral snake hatband. He must have been coming home from a hunting trip when the Crackers killed him."

"Yup, and the bastards just left him here for de animals."

"I'm glad dey did. Otherwise, I'd never have found him. When I walked by dis palmetto patch a buzzard flew up, so I checked to see what he was after."

"You find anything else?"

"A couple miles up yonder on a hill I found a place where de patters tied horses to a hitch line so dey could slip up on de camp. Didn't find nothin' else. It's high ground up yonder where we could bury Wash in sugar sand."

Mingo said, "I found an old croker sack at de village. We can put de remains in it."

Mingo asked Brutus to fetch the others and to bring back the burlap bag while he searched for Wash's bones that the varmints had scattered around the palmetto thicket.

When the other men arrived, they joined the search. Once Mingo was confident that the entire skeleton had been found, he eased the bones into the bag and carried them to the sand hill.

Using a broken hoe one of the men found in the village, Brutus scraped out a short trench by cutting the roots that crisscrossed the hole with mighty blows. Those that he couldn't chop, he ripped apart. When he dug waist deep, Mingo said, "That's far enough." Brutus stopped, looking up with tears in his eyes.

Mingo handed him the bag. Brutus gently put it down, folded the top over and smoothed it. As he climbed out from the hole, he said, "It ain't right to bury Wash without proper words."

"Who wants to say something?" Mingo offered.

Nobody volunteered.

"All right, I will. Lord, here we lay Wash. Jesus said, 'Blessed are the poor.' On dat score, Wash was blessed, sure nuff. He owned nothin' 'cept his raggedy clothes, shotgun, and knife. He lived off de land like de birds of de field. He could have had it easier on de plantation with a daily ration and a roof over his head. Instead, he chose freedom. Nobody owned Wash. He was our friend. He took us in and shared what little he had. Wash, we will not forget you or your example. You rest easy now. We will hunt down de patters who murdered you and stole our people. Lord have mercy on your soul and on de patters' who killed you because dey are certain to face our wrath as soon as we catch de bastards. Amen."

The men mumbled, "Amen."

While Brutus scraped sand over the bag and backfilled the hole, a man lashed two heart pine sticks together with a leather strap. After Brutus formed a neat mound over the grave, the man pushed the cross into the soft sand.

"What we going to do now?" one man asked.

Mingo said, "I'll meet Master Weeks like we planned. Brutus, you take everybody else and free our people."

"What if I don't find dem?"

"If you can't catch up, find out who de devil stole dem so we can kill or capture dem later. When you've done all you can, go to Little Pine Island and wait. I'll ask Master Weeks to fetch you and take us all to Cedar Key where de Navy can protect us."

Brutus wrapped Mingo in bear hug. "Be careful. I won't be around to watch over you."

Mingo patted Brutus on the back, pushed him away and said, "Let me go, you big ox. You look after your own self; see you at Little Pine Island."

Mingo walked to the skiff, pushed it into the current and floated down stream. By the new moon, he was waiting at Little Pine Island for Weeks. When several days passed without any sign of him or a gunboat, Mingo rationed his food and water. Careful to stay hidden, he constructed an inconspicuous lean-to in the interior of the island which he thatched with palmetto fronds.

Three times a day Mingo climbed a tall pine near his shelter and scanned the Gulf with his telescope. As days slipped by, Mingo almost lost hope that Weeks would post as he had promised. After ten days, he had eaten all his food except for one tin of hardtack. He decided to leave the next morning.

That night, Mingo worried about his decision and couldn't sleep. As a quarter moon rose in the east, he decided to walk around the island. As he ambled below the high tide mark, he saw a ship outlined against the horizon cruising south. Even with his telescope, it was too far offshore to identify. When it sailed out of sight, he walked back to his shelter more discouraged than ever. Before dawn he walked the beach and to his relief, saw a gunboat. He convinced himself that it was the *Tahoma*. When a sailboat pulled away from it, he prayed Master Weeks had the tiller.

Mingo watched as the sloop tacked by the island a half mile from shore. When it came about and sailed by the island again, he waved a signal cloth as instructed. Near the beach, the cutter turned into the wind luffing the sails. Mingo waded into the chilly water toward the sloop with his rifle and gear held over his head. When he reached it, Weeks said, "Glad you didn't give up on us. We couldn't be here on time because we were chasing a blockade-runner. We finally ran it aground at Ochlocknoy Bay where the Rebels set it afire. Did you gather any intelligence?"

"Yes."

"Good, the captain is eager for a report."

When Mingo and Master Weeks joined the captain for dinner, the first thing he asked about was fresh food. When Mingo explained he hadn't brought any, the captain said, "I hope you did better with information."

"Captain, we confirmed dat de rebel camp closest to Cedar key is Clay Landing on de Suwannee River. As far as we can tell, only a few squads are present most of de time. Patrols go down to Cedar Key, up to de Santa Fe River and over to de Oklawaha. Rebel morale is not good. De soldiers are worried 'bout us slaves runnin' off. Some believe de South is losin' the war. Some have deserted."

The captain unrolled a map across the table. "Show me Clay Landing."

Mingo traced with his finger the road that paralleled the Suwannee River up to Clay Landing.

"Right here, Captain. Just follow dis road from Cedar Key. Wouldn't take many men to attack de camp. Dey only have a howitzer."

"How many men are there?"

"Patrols come and go, but unless one is in camp der are only twenty men at most. If de militia is training, there's more, but dey're only ragtag old men and boys. Most don't even have weapons."

"How did you get your information?"

"We scouted it. Talked to de Rebel commander's servant. He hears everything," Mingo said, smiling.

"Well done. You find anything else?"

"Yassuh, Captain, we did. Der are salt works right under your nose just across de bay from Cedar Key."

"If it's so close, how come we haven't found it?"

"Captain sir, I don't know nothin' 'bout dat, but I do know one of my men seen it with his own eyes."

"I'll be darned. Rebels are mighty bold to boil salt that close to Cedar Key. Let's put a stop to it."

DESTRUCTION OF A COASTAL SALT FACTORY

(Courtesy Florida State Archives)

Note gunboat on horizon and launches approaching shore.

CHAPTER THIRTY-EIGHT

BRONSON

Florida

After shooting the sheriff, Wall walked to the lawman's body, unsnapped his holster, grabbed his pistol and jammed it under his belt. He fumbled through the dead man's pockets, found his wallet and stuffed it in his jacket. Then he looked for the sheriff's horse that had bolted.

Grazing nearby, the horse lifted its head when Wall whistled. He walked to it, petted it on the neck and then pulled the sheriff's shotgun from its scabbard and lifted his saddle bags. As he walked toward his mare, he noticed fresh tracks where someone had run toward the undergrowth bordering the abandoned camp. He dropped the saddle bags to the ground, checked the load in the sheriff's single-barreled shotgun and followed the tracks.

To his chagrin, a black man holding a rifle jumped up from the palmettos bordering the old camp and dashed for a thicket. Wall raised the shotgun to his shoulder. A small pine blocked his sight line at the instant he pulled the trigger. He jerked his pistol from its holster to fire again. Before he could aim, the man disappeared in the brush.

Moving fast, Wall holstered his weapon, picked up the saddlebags and ran to his horse. He tossed them behind his saddle, tied down the shotgun with a leather strap, mounted his steed and loped away. After a mile or so, he slowed his horse to a walk to search the leather pouches. Under a rumpled jacket, he found pistol ammunition along with a box of percussion caps. Turning his attention to the sheriff's billfold, he rifled fifteen Confederate dollars. Behind an inset, he found a folded, five dollar greenback which made him smirk to see that the sheriff wasn't above breaking the law.

At a depression pond bordered by pickerel weed, Wall nudged his mare into the water up to her belly where he sank the lawman's pistol, shotgun, saddlebags, and wallet.

Kicking his heels into the horse's sides, he rode hard to Bronson. When he reached the sheriff's office, he yanked his frothing mount to halt beside the fire bell. He yanked its rope again and again clanging the alarm as loud as he could.

Two grizzled men, one who had a gray beard that reached his chest, doddered up. "What's the ruckus, Wall?"

"A nigger shot the sheriff. We need to put together a posse to run him down. Where is everybody?"

The graybeard said, "All the men 'cept us went to Clay Landing to train with the militia."

"Then, you'll have to do."

The graybeard suggested, "I reckon we could go if old lady Brasswell will let us use her cart and mule."

"Go ask her. I'll look for weapons."

Wall broke into the locked sheriff's office looking for weapons and money. Not finding either, he sat down to wait.

In an hour, the old-timers returned in a wobbly two-wheeled cart pulled by a decrepit mule that doddered worse than the old men. Graybeard clutched a flintlock double-barreled shotgun. The other man held one just as old although modified to use percussion caps.

Well after midnight under bright moonlight, the makeshift posse reached the sheriff's corpse. As they approached it, they could see that wild animals had already ripped open the body and pulled out the entrails. The oldsters climbed down from the cart while Wall sat on his horse watching. As graybeard examined the body, the other walked around studying the ground for tracks.

Wall said, "We'll bury him for now in a shallow grave so the animals can't eat him. We'll come back for him after we run down the murderer."

The graybeard kneeling by the body said, "Whoever shot the sheriff hit him square in the heart. How can we bury him? We don't have a shovel. Why didn't you bring the sheriff's body with you?"

"I wanted to get to town as fast as possible."

The one studying the ground asked Wall a keen-edged question, "How many men did you see?"

"I was riding behind the sheriff when I heard a shot. As I wheeled my horse, I saw a nigger with a rifle dash off through that thicket over yonder. I managed one quick shot but missed."

The old-timer said, "There's tracks all over the place. There must have been four or five of them."

"How do you know that?" Wall asked.

"I scouted for General Jackson in the first Seminole war. My eyes ain't much good no more, but in this moonlight I can still see enough to know there's too many men for us to take on, that's for sure. The militia will have to deal with them. Let's gather up the body and head to town."

The old men lifted the sheriff's body. As they slid it into the cart, Wall rode off. When he was out of sight, the old scout confided to his friend, "Something's fishy. Wall never ran his horse after nobody. Ain't no tracks like that atal."

"What you reckon happened?"

"I don't know, but that buzzard's lying."

CHAPTER THIRTY-NINE

DEER HALL
Florida

A gator's bellow, or some other night noise, woke Chad. Through the open window he saw Chunky Pond glistening through thin, low hanging fog in a bright, moonlit night. The scene looked so inviting that he decided to piss outside instead of using the chamber pot.

He slipped into dungarees, pulled on his Wellington boots and tiptoed across the porch. He stepped off onto the soft sand and walked across the back yard to a red cedar tree growing beside the fence where he squeezed behind a limb. As he admired Orion low on the western horizon, he heard a crash at the smokehouse.

Chad buttoned his pants, jogged back to the house, clomped across the porch, and dashed inside for a shotgun.

"Billy, get up! Sounds like a bear at the smokehouse," Chad called out as he checked to make sure his shotgun was loaded.

In long strides Chad headed toward the smokehouse. As he broke into the open beyond the scrub oaks, he saw four men running pell-mell across the pasture.

"Stop!" Chad yelled. No one hesitated. He aimed his shotgun at the last man, fired and missed. "Stop!" The men kept running.

Chad fired the second barrel. The men disappeared into the woods and mist.

As Chad reloaded, Jake and Billy ran up. "What is it, Mas'r Chad?"

"Some men broke into the smokehouse."

"Did you hit one?"

"I don't think so. In the morning, we'll see if we can track them. In the meantime, I don't think they'll be back tonight, but stay on guard. I'll let Blanche know what's happening."

When Chad reached the house, Blanche met him at the door, "We haven't had bears at the smokehouse since I don't know when."

"It wasn't a bear."

"Whites or blacks?"

"Whites."

"Who you reckon they were?"

"Don't know. Criminals-maybe deserters."

Blanche said, "Probably shirkers. With Yankees marauding everywhere, our men are comin' home to protect their families. The army has tacked up posters in the Bronson depot with long lists of names."

"I didn't see the first sign of a uniform, but I suppose they throw them away. I'm surprised they would come by here, but they could be on the way to Cedar Key where the U.S. Navy has established camps for them and their families. I heard some are even enlisting with the Federals."

"Who knows? Maybe they were draft dodgers. Some have hid out in the swamps since the conscription law passed. They must be desperate by now."

When Blanche and Chad had exhausted speculation about the marauders, Blanche excused herself and said she needed to write

Loring a note. She retrieved a letter from him written on a single sheet of paper covered with writing on both sides. She turned the sheet sideways to write across his words and thought, *It's going to be hard for Loring to read this cross-writing, but this is the only paper I have, so it'll have to do.*

Dearest Husband,

Please come home. Tell the captain you must have furlough. I don't know if I can continue to hold on without you.

Everybody is doing their best, but we just never seem to get caught up. At least the crops look like they'll be good this year. We've had rain just when we needed it. Unless something unexpected happens, we should have enough food for another year.

Our main fare this spring has been potatoes, collards and turnips with fatback. A while back, Chad scrounged twenty-five pounds of dried black-eyed peas. Did they ever taste good. He saved enough for Jake to plant a patch in the field by the pond.

Last week Billy found a bee tree at the bay head across the pond. Jake built a fire by the trunk, climbed the tree, and sawed off a hollow limb. It was so plumb full of honey that he strained two gallons into crocks. Good thing too. Nobody has sugar, or salt, for that matter.

You told me that the army was having trouble with desertions. I don't mean to worry you, but we had an incident. Thank the good Lord, Chad was here. He heard something out at the smokehouse. He figured it was a bear, but it was four men. They stole all but one ham before Chad ran them off.

The county is unsafe. Everything seems to have gone downhill since those blacks bushwhacked Sheriff Maxwell. There aren't enough men to put together a posse and the Commander at Clay Landing says the army has more important business than chasing marauders. I suppose he's right, but there's no law and order anymore. This dreadful war has to end soon. Thank the good Lord that you haven't been hurt seriously. Every day I pray for your safe return.

The children send their love. Little Buddy sure misses her Popi. Like you'd expect, Billy works like a man. As time goes by he seems more upset about the war. He even threatened to volunteer, but I won't hear of it. One soldier in the family is enough. He's becoming a man too fast and is hard for me to handle. He needs his Daddy here to control him.

Tell the General it's not fair that you don't get furlough.

Hugs and kisses,

Your Little Blanche

For once, the letter arrived at Camp Finnegan in just a few days. As soon as Loring completed his daily reports, he penned an answer:

Dearest Blanche,

I just received your letter and I'm worried sick.

Marauders scare me. Make sure that all of you have the weapons loaded and handy at all times. I'm so thankful Chad is there while I'm forced to be away.

Deserters can be dangerous. Don't take any chances with them whatsoever. Don't let anybody in the house, or offer them food or drink, even if you think they're honest soldiers traveling home. They might be scoundrels trying to trick you. It's not worth the risk. Soldiers on legitimate furlough have no reason to come to Deer Hall, so be suspicious of anybody that shows up unless you know them.

I'm in line for a furlough but probably won't get one. We don't have enough men, especially officers, to properly rotate details and patrols. Last month, I let another lieutenant jump ahead of me. I'm sure you'll understand why. He received an urgent telegram that his wife caught yellow fever. He owns a farm near Micanopy and has several children. The captain gave him instructions to come back as soon as arrangements could be made to take care of his family.

In the meantime, General Finnegan put all furloughs on hold. He believes that the Yankees are planning to invade Florida. No doubt, they want to cut our supply line to the armies in the field. Our "cow cavalry" is still rounding up beeves so we're still sending meat north. Without the cattle and the hogs we ship, they couldn't keep fighting.

Like us, many of the Yankee soldiers are sick of the war. They signed up to save the Union and now realize they're fighting to free blacks and don't care for that.

Intelligence says the Federals are planning to invade using escaped slaves they've trained as soldiers in South Carolina. A few deserters came in from their lines with the same report, so it's probably true. If black soldiers invade, it'll be hell to pay. It's a felony for a slave to enlist as a Yankee soldier. If they do, their white officers will be complicit in crime and will be hung if they're captured.

I'm sure blacks can make good soldiers if they have competent officers. This war better end soon or we'll we end up fighting our own slaves.

I believed for a while that England and France might recognize the Confederacy, but that looks doubtful after our defeats at Gettysburg and Vicksburg. Our best hope is that Lincoln won't be re-elected. If our armies can hang on, the voters will give up on a war president. I believe Lee can hold out in Virginia, but I'm worried about Bragg in Tennessee. If the Yankees break through at Chattanooga, Sherman and Sheridan will be on the way to Atlanta.

Enough about the war. I love you and miss you so much. Every night I fall asleep thinking about you and our dear ones.

Continue to be strong. God willing, peace will come soon so I can come home.

I'm convinced Jake and Sarah will stay loyal and that Chad will do everything he can to help you.

Love and kisses to you and children. Thank Chad for running off the thieves and say hello to everybody.

Your loving husband,
Loring

CHAPTER FORTY

LIVE OAK KEY
Florida

"Mingo, you ready for combat?" Weeks asked.

"I've waited too long already."

"Your wait's over. I finally have the captain's OK to destroy the salt works that your men found. Get a good night's rest. We'll cast off tomorrow at 5:00 AM."

By the time Mingo came out on the ship's deck the next morning before dawn, a front had cleared out the humidity so the stars and constellations sparkled. He noticed that the captain had moved during the night and had anchored between Cedar Key and Atsena Otie Key. From the new location, he could see the glow from refugee and contraband fires at the U.S. Navy camp on Seahorse Key.

He found Weeks supervising marines who were lowering launches from davits into the water and asked, "How come de Captain brought de ship so close to Cedar Key? He usually stands off more at night."

"I suggested that he bring her into the harbor so that we don't have to row so far to Live Oak Key. While the marines load up, let's check the location one more time."

On the chart for the Cedar Keys and Waccasassa Bay, Weeks had drawn an 'X' to mark the salt works' location on Live Oak Key. "Verify that I have the correct place. The men will be surly if they don't find anything but palmetto scrub."

After Mingo verified the spot, Weeks plotted a course from the ship, past Dog Islands, then north along Scale Island to Cedar Point across from Live Oak Key. When he finished, both men joined the marines waiting in the launches.

"Sergeant," Weeks asked, "Does each man have forty rounds of ammunition and a full canteen? Did you stow a water bladder?"

"Yes, sir," the sergeant snapped.

"Cast off. We've got boilers to bust."

The marines bent to their oars to pull away from the ship against an ebb tide. Before long, sweat soaked through their heavy blue shirts and dripped from under their caps. As the sun rose, they powered the boats with powerful, coordinated strokes past Scale Island.

When the boats passed Cedar Point, Weeks said, "Sergeant, let's take one launch ashore at the tip of Live Oak Key to reconnoiter. Stand off with the others in case there are sharpshooters."

As the launch ground onto a muddy shore scattered with oyster and clam shells, marines jumped from the boat and scrambled for cover. They spread out and worked their way along the shore. In an hour, a corporal reported to Weeks that his men had several buildings under observation that were clustered among live oaks about a mile away. Weeks and Mingo followed the corporal to the most forward position where Mingo could see light gray smoke drift up that dissipated among the tree limbs.

Weeks said, "Sergeant, what do you recommend? Rebs must have spotted us by now."

"Sir, no doubt. Bring up more men; a squad can advance along the shore while another circles through the woods."

"Get it done. Mingo, stay with me."

As they crept forward with the squad, they observed a white flag fluttering from the nearest house. Weeks relaxed and holstered his pistol. As he snapped the flap down, two reports in quick succession cracked from the building causing everybody to dive behind logs or trees.

"Son-of-a-bitch! Why do we even want cowards like those bastards in the Union?" Weeks said.

The sergeant yelled, "Anybody hit?"

"No, sir," a marine shouted.

"What are we facing?" Weeks asked the sergeant.

"It wasn't sharpshooters, or we'd have casualties. Let my marines take them out, sir?"

"It might be a trap. Wouldn't surprise me if they have a company hidden up there."

"Not likely, sir. If there were more, they'd have already opened up on us. I'll send scouts up."

"Sergeant, you're probably right, but I'm not going to risk men when we don't need to."

"Sir, we should teach those bushwhackers a lesson."

"While I have no doubt that your men can clean out this rat's nest, we've confirmed Mingo's report. We'll come back tomorrow."

"With all due respect, sir, my marines can finish the job today."

"You'll get your chance. At sunrise tomorrow morning we'll be back with a howitzer."

"Yes, sir," the sergeant said, smiling.

On the way back to the ship, Weeks pulled into Cedar Key and gave the marines two hours liberty while he scouted for a transport suitable to carry a cannon. Near the harbor, he found a weather-beaten flatboat that had been beached for months. "Mingo, this derelict is perfect. It must have been used to haul cotton down the black water creeks around here. We'll chain the howitzer on it. Tonight we'll tow it over to the island across from the settlement. The Rebs are goin' have an unpleasant wake up."

In two hours the marines reported back as ordered. The sergeant formed them up by squads. All men were present and accounted for although two men smelled of alcohol. Weeks ordered their squad to repair and float the flatboat.

It was in worse shape than it appeared. It leaked so much that the marines had to pound oakum in the cracks and seal them with tar. It was after midnight before Weeks felt the transport was seaworthy enough to winch the howitzer on board.

When Weeks suggested that the sergeant rotate squads, the NCO protested. "Sir, the men who were mousetrapped yesterday are pissed off. They want to finish the job."

By first light, the howitzer rested on the beach across the bay from the settlement. A private rammed home a shell. Another corporal adjusted the barrel's elevation. A sergeant standing to the side yelled, "Ready!" He paused for a quick safety check then yelled, "Fire!" A marine yanked the lanyard.

An explosive shell blew the corner from the house that had flown the white flag. Marines scrambled to reload the howitzer. When it was charged, the order rang out again, "Fire!"

The second shell hit the porch where it exploded. The roof disintegrated and the wood frame house caught fire. "Switch targets to the next house. "Ready! Fire!"

Before the sun had cleared the tree line, flames engulfed the buildings. Two collapsed. The third burned so hot that trees around it burst into flames. Thick, black smoke darkened the sun. Ashes and soot drifted over the marines. Weeks yelled, "Cease fire, cease fire," as the last shot from the cannon winged toward the inferno with little chance to cause more damage.

No one fired at the marines. Weeks assumed that everybody in the settlement had skedaddled when they saw the marines unloading the cannon.

"Sergeant, take two squads and confirm the place is clear. Destroy everything that hasn't burned. Mingo, go along. You found it, you deserve the honor."

When Mingo and the sergeant reached the settlement, they found a low-slung brick structure tucked behind trees that concealed it from view. Along one side, workers had stacked several cords of dried oak and hickory. Inside, the Rebs had constructed a rudimentary salt works using evaporating pans cut from old boilers with space underneath them for fire.

The sergeant said to a private, "Load the wood on the flat boat; the refugees on Sea Horse Key can use it. Then blow up the factory. Wreck everything. Don't leave anything in one piece around this Secesh cesspool."

1864

The military value of partisan's work is not measured by the amount of property destroyed or the number of men killed or captured, but by the number he keeps watching.

~ Col. John S. Mosby C.S.A.

CAPTAIN J. J. DICKISON

(Courtesy Florida State Archives)

CHAPTER FORTY-ONE

ST. MARY'S BRIDGE
Florida

"Breakfast is served, gentlemen," a gray-headed slave said as he dished out watery grits to Captain Dickison, Loring and several other officers. Dickison stared at the glob spreading across his tin plate and said to his servant, "Is this all we have for breakfast?"

"Yassuh, Mas'r, we done et everything else. Mealy bugs in de grits too. Sorry, sir. Couldn't strain dem all."

Dickison shook his head, picked up his spoon, and said to Loring, "I expect the Blue Bellies are about to make a move. They've been back in Jacksonville for only a day and they're already probing our lines. I've pulled in all the detachments. What do you figure the Yankees are up to?"

"Sir, I think they're preparing to attack. You did the right thing by concentrating our men. We'll need everybody to stop them."

Captain Dickison stirred the chow congealing on his plate. "Poor excuse for rations. Whatever is mixed in these grits, doesn't look like weevils to me."

He scratched his chin. "Now that we've abandoned Camp Cooper they might hit us from the north, but they'll probably come straight west down the tracks from Jacksonville. I'm sure the Yankees aim to control the railroad junction at Baldwin. I expect they'll try to knock out the quartermaster depots in Lake City and Gainesville too. General Bragg's chief commissary officer reported that beef and bacon supplies are exhausted in the other states, so our armies have to depend on what we can supply. I've wired General Finnegan for reinforcements from Georgia."

Dickison took another bite and made a terrible face. He stirred the grits, dabbed black specks out with his spoon and rubbed them off on his napkin. "We've got political problems too. Unionists are still stirring up to trouble in St. Augustine. The traitors passed a resolution affirming that the Secession Ordinance is null and void. They're organizing a new government in which Secessionists will be forbidden to vote or run for election. Damn Yankees already appointed tax commissioners inside the Federal lines to appropriate and auction off the land owned by Confederates."

Loring said, "I'll bet the Blue Bellies have occupied Jacksonville so Lincoln can argue that Florida should be readmitted to the Union. He hopes that a Unionist government would give him Florida's electoral votes."

A courier rode up at a full gallop and jerked his lathered horse to a stop. As he dismounted from the wheezing animal, he said, "Sir, sorry to disturb you, but Yanks are on the move."

Dickison asked, "Where and how many?"

"At least a mounted company. They're headed west from Jacksonville. Some Yankee sympathizer who knew the back trails led them around our pickets through the swamps. They've overrun Milton's light artillery on the Jacksonville Road. By luck, a picket heard their horses just before they attacked. Most of our soldiers got away, but the Blue Bellies captured eighteen men, cannons, and a bunch of horses and mules. By now, they're probably well on the way to Baldwin."

Dickison said, "No need to speculate about their intentions now. Mount up, let's ride."

In fifteen minutes, Loring had his company trotting east along the sandy road that paralleled the railroad tracks. Midmorning, he saw thick, black smoke in the eastern sky. "Yankees must be burning the warehouses at Baldwin. Their commander is darn bold to push so far from Jacksonville so fast. He may not stop. Have the point guards keep a sharp eye," Loring warned as he spurred his horse into a trot.

Within an hour, a vidette leading the detachment signaled riders ahead. Loring halted the troops as the picket braced in his stirrups, raised his rifle, and then held fire as several cavalrymen wearing tattered, gray jackets galloped by him. When they reached Loring, they reined their horses.

A sergeant saluted. "Sir, Yankee cavalry is hot on our tail."

"How many?"

"Don't know, but plenty. They overran our artillery battery at dawn. We've been snipin' at them when we could, but it ain't done much good. We dropped a few, but they keep on comin', mostly nigras."

"How far are they behind you?"

"Sir, we separated at Baldwin when they stopped to plunder. I suggest you fall back with us before they overrun you too."

"Isn't there a bridge at the South Fork of the St. Mary's?"

"Yes, sir. It's about two miles back."

"Stay with us, Sergeant," Loring ordered as he spurred Ginger into a gallop and waved the detachment forward to secure the bridge.

Loring pushed Ginger so fast that he overran his forward guard. As he approached the objective, he saw blue-jacketed troops riding hard toward him from the opposite direction. As the gap between them closed, several Yankees reined their horses and raised their rifles. Smoke puffed from them. The point guard tumbled off his horse. Loring pressed his head against Ginger's neck and pounded forward.

Pistols shots cracked around him. "Boys, hold your fire, they're out of pistol range," Loring screamed as he spurred Ginger harder. He felt her accelerate and wondered how the mare still had the energy to run as he kicked her again and smacked her with the reins.

A hundred yards from the bridge, Loring sensed Ginger could win the race. At fifty yards, smoke spurted from the blue-jacketed skirmish line again. A horse beside Loring stumbled that caused its rider to sprawl headlong into the road. Across the bridge, Loring saw yellow corporal's chevrons on the sleeve of the lead Yankee rider. He fired his LeMat at him.

The Yankee corporal's horse tumbled and threw its rider. The troopers behind him reined their horses. Loring dismounted. He fired the LeMat rifled barrel at another soldier, then snatched from its scabbard his Spencer carbine that he had found beside a dead Yankee soldier. He fired at a soldier wheeling his horse in the sandy road. The rider fell. Several Rebel soldiers rode up to the abutments. They opened fire on the enemy which knocked another Yankee from the saddle. The concentrated fire forced the enemy cavalrymen to fall back out of range.

As they milled about in the distance, two squads reinforced them. Their sergeants ordered the men to dismount and form a skirmish line and advance.

"Disciplined troops we're facing, Sergeant. Watch the flanks," Loring yelled as he aimed at a soldier darting in a crouch from tree to tree.

Loring fired and missed. He levered another shell into the chamber of his carbine. As he scanned for another target, blue jackets flashed in the open for an instant and then disappeared behind trees or bushes, but they always pressed forward.

Firing downstream from the bridge had become incessant when a man dashed up to Loring, "Sir, they've crossed the river. They're goin' to cut us off."

Loring looked down the line and saw his soldiers falling back while firing at Yankee skirmishers who whooped as they ran forward. A gray-jacketed soldier broke and ran.

"Mount-up, fall back."

A mile from the bridge, Loring halted the detachment. "How many men did we lose, Sergeant?"

"One dead for sure, sir. It's too hectic to know for certain."

"Post a rear guard. Let's hope Captain Dickison sent more men. We're heavily outnumbered."

Loring led his detachment west to Sanderson Station where the railroad maintained a depot and a water tower to fill locomotives at a siding. The only other buildings were a warehouse pressed up to the siding and a few dilapidated houses scattered along the main line. On the dogtrot of one shack, Loring spotted two spinsters. He rode over to them, "Mornin' ladies, How ya'll doin'?"

"Gittin' along."

"Any men folk around?"

"They're all away in the army, or dead," a woman sniffled. "Two of my sons were killed at Sharpsburg."

"Sorry to hear that, Ma'am. I hate to admit it, but Yankees are chasing us. You better hide your valuables and run away. They're marauding."

One old lady threw up her arms. "Oh, my God. Just when we thought things were as bad as can be, they're worse. You sure Blue Bellies are on the way?"

"Yes, Ma'am, and they're not far off. What's in the warehouse over there?"

"Turpentine and several carloads of comestibles. It's guarded twenty-four hours a day."

Loring tipped his hat. "Ya'll better hurry. Enemy troops will be here soon."

An old lady yelled something, but Loring had already wheeled Ginger. He trotted to the warehouse where he found a barefooted boy about the same age as his son standing guard at a sliding door with a rusty shotgun. "Son, you're relieved. Yankees are on the way. Head for the woods and hide. Don't let them see you with that shotgun."

"But---"

"Soldier, don't you know better than to argue with an officer. Clear out, now!"

Well after midnight, near Ocean Pond, Loring found Captain Dickison who asked for a report.

"There's at least a company, maybe more. They're aggressive. We've been in a running battle since we made contact. Pickets report that they are moving in a massed column now and not marauding anymore. They're more leery the farther west they come."

Dickison said, "Can't say that I blame them. If they only have a company, we'll outnumber them as more detachments report. I've telegraphed for reinforcements from Gainesville and Madison. Another train will leave from Tallahassee at noon. Half our men are militia. I don't know how effective they'll be, but we're going on the offensive. Have your men ready to counter-attack at dawn."

Loring had nothing to eat for supper except hardtack and found only a handful of cracked corn for Ginger. His men and their horses were worn-out, but he had to prepare them to fight, "Sergeant, keep the horses saddled. Let the men sleep until two-thirty. Feed them, then be ready to ride. Make sure their canteens are full. We'll head out at three-thirty."

When Loring's detachment moved out, a fresh cavalry company led by Dickison himself joined them. At daybreak, skirmishers made contact with the enemy near Newburg. The Yankee commander had no desire to tangle with fresh cavalry, so he retreated toward Jacksonville in good order with a rear guard that maintained harassing fire with enough lethality to wound several soldiers.

East of Baldwin, Dickison halted his troops, "No use runnin' them. They could be leadin' us into a trap. Press them with skirmishers so they don't know we're breakin' contact."

Loring could barely stay awake when he and several other officers made their after action reports. Dickison commented, "You look peaked, Loring. That Yankee outfit gave us a run for the money. A prisoner says the commander is Colonel Henry with the 40th Massachusetts Mounted Infantry. You have to admire his aggressiveness. He hit us a damn good lick. What's your tally?"

"Sir, they captured at least twenty prisoners, the cannons and at least thirty-five or forty horses and mules from Milton's artillery. They burned, or stole, a million dollars worth of property and a bunch of slaves ran off after them. We confirmed five Yankees killed. A skirmisher reported he saw a wagon loaded with wounded. We lost three men and five wounded."

"Gentlemen, I know you're all worn out. We've done the best we could with what we have. Looks like the enemy finally intends to fight. Rest your men and re-supply. They'll be back in force directly."

CHAPTER FORTY-TWO

DEER HALL

Florida

Wall stopped his detachment among the high, yellow timber on the hill overlooking Deer Hall near the place where Mingo had walked with Molly so many months before. Except for Wall, his men looked like well-armed desperados. The only thing to identify one man as a soldier was his rectangular brass belt buckle with C.S.A. stamped in bold letters. A barefooted soldier who drove a spavined mule pulling a four-wheeled flatbed cart wore a union blue kepi cap.

Wall, however, looked cavalier dressed in a full, gray uniform with a colonel's insignia embossed on the collar and gold piping on the cuffs. Soft leather boots came to his knees. His belt and buckle were like the soldier's driving the cart except the leather was shiny black with a pistol holster attached. He wore a gray Stetson low on his forehead at a jaunty angle. The only things he lacked to make a perfect soldier's daguerreotype portrait were a plume in his hat and a handsome face.

Lifting himself in the stirrups, Wall reached back and grabbed binoculars from his saddlebag. A raspy *stripp* high in the pines distracted him. He glanced up. "Damn woodpeckers ruin the pine timber by pecking holes in the trunk that drains the sap and rots the heart," he mumbled.

He loved to shoot the small, red-cockaded woodpeckers - not to protect the timber, but for the hell of it. He checked the impulse. Raising the binoculars to his eyes, he scanned the farm. Near the barn he saw Jake shoveling manure into a cart hitched to Loring's big mule. At the house he saw three women on the porch sewing. *Good, the saucy, mulatto bitch is still there.*

He pushed the binoculars back in his saddlebags. "Men, we'll make impressments here. The army needs that mule and wagon. Take all the meat and foodstuffs we can find. Be sharp. The man of the house is off with the army, but an Englishman hangs around. There's also a slave and a boy who might be armed. If any of them threaten you in the least, shoot 'em."

As Wall and the other riders walked their horses down the hill toward the farmstead, Jake spotted them. He yelled a warning as he dashed to unhitch Mike from the cart. Wall kicked his horse into a run. As he galloped toward the farmhouse, he spotted two young girls, one white and one black, running into the woods.

Wall galloped straight to the front gate while the other riders fanned out around the house and outbuildings. A curtain fluttered at an open window. "Sorry for the inconvenience, Missis Bell," Wall shouted. "I have orders from the Confederate Army to impress every-thing our troops need."

Wall then turned to watch a rider leading Mike, still hitched to the cart, toward the house. Jake trudged behind. Wall shouted at him, "Get away from here, boy, if you know what's good for you."

As Jake shuffled away, Chad ran into the yard. "What's all the commotion?"

Wall answered, "Stand where you are, Limey! Hands up! Private, cover him. Shoot him if he moves." Chad heard an unmistakable click as the soldier cocked his pistol.

"Let's get what we came for!" Wall shouted.

The rider holding Mike's lead looped it into a clove hitch and tossed it over a fence post. He wheeled his horse to join the others who were already ransacking the barn, storehouse and smoke house. Wall dismounted and walked through the gate onto the porch. He banged on the heavy oak door with his fist. When no one answered, he kicked it and then sat in a rocking chair watching his men.

In a short time, a soldier rode up. "Sir, ain't no hams in the smokehouse and nothin' in the barn, or that other building, except a peck of cracked corn. The only stock we found is a milk cow in the pasture. Didn't find no cotton."

"Fetch the cow."

Hey, Limey, don't you have a horse?" Wall yelled.

"I traded her for food."

Wall stood up and was about to bang on the door again when Blanche opened it. She stepped onto the porch. "Colonel Wall, I beg you. Don't take my cow and mule. We need milk for the children. We can't plow without a mule."

"Our soldiers can't fight the Yankee invaders without proper supplies. You have a patriotic duty to contribute to the war effort. What are you hidin' in the house?"

"I'm not hiding---" Wall pushed past her into the main room. The kerosene lamp centered on a doily atop a gueridon table caught his eye as he stomped to the kitchen where Molly and Sarah cowered in the corner. As Wall stepped toward the women, Sarah raised an iron skillet. Wall smashed her arm with his fist that sent the skillet crashing to the floor. "Don't you ever raise a hand to me!"

He grabbed Molly under the chin and twisted her face to his. "Army needs servants; I've a mind to impress you."

Molly stared straight into Wall's eyes. He squeezed hard and then shoved her against a counter.

Wall jerked open the cupboard doors and scraped out china, which clattered to the floor where it broke into a hundred pieces. Then he threw open the flour box lid.

"Where are the hams?"

Blanche replied through clinched teeth. "Marauders stole them all."

"What's in the crockery jug?"

"Honey."

Wall grabbed the jug and stomped outside as a soldier rode up holding a kerosene lamp and a flour sack draped behind his saddle. "I found this fancy lamp and a little cornmeal at the house over yonder," the soldier said as he put them on the wagon bed.

"There's some meal here too. Fetch it along with that lamp in the front room."

The soldier went inside. He returned with a half-full cloth bag and the kerosene lamp. He tied the bag closed with rawhide string and plopped it beside the one from Jake's house and then jammed the two lamps between them.

Blanche stood on the porch crying. Wall turned to her, unbuttoned his jacket pocket and pulled out crumpled Confederate bills and held them toward her. She made no effort to step off the porch to take the worthless paper. Wall opened his hand. The folding money fluttered to the ground. "Ma'am, on behalf of the Confederate States of America, I thank you for your contribution to the war effort."

"You thief!" Blanche seethed.

"You best hold your tongue or I'll charge you with sedition. Let's go, boys."

Blanche slumped to the floor.

When the cart pulled by Mike with the cow waddling behind was a quarter mile down the lane, the soldier guarding Chad eased down the hammer on his pistol and kicked his horse to join his compatriots.

CHAPTER FORTY-THREE

GAINESVILLE

Florida

When the after-action reports to Captain Dickison were completed, Loring went straight to his tent and collapsed on his cot without eating. Exhausted and overstimulated from the skirmish, he didn't sleep well. He dreamed about battles and burning homes interspersed with visions of Blanche and the children. Half-awake, he felt his cot shake.

"Sir, sir, wake up."

Loring sat straight up, disoriented. "Sir, Captain Dickison needs to see you."

"What?"

"Sorry, Captain Dickison ordered me to fetch you."

"Doesn't that man ever sleep?"

"Don't seem like it. He wants you and all the other officers at his headquarters right now."

"Thank you, private."

Loring guessed that the summons in the middle of the night meant that the Yankees were on the move again. Until now, Captain Dickison's tiny 2nd Florida Cavalry regiment had bamboozled the Yankee generals and kept them cowed along the coast under the cover of their gunboats, but Colonel Henry's raid exposed the vulnerability of "Dixie's" land as the Yankees called Middle Florida which they named in respect for Commander Dickison. Without reinforcements, the Florida troops had little hope to stop concerted raids.

At the commander's tent, the officers looked as sleepy and bedraggled as Loring. Dickison himself looked haggard although he still showed spunky determination to hold back the enemy. "Men, we stymied the last raid. Now we have to throw back another. Yankee troops are marauding as far south as Gainesville. A dispatch says the 4th Massachusetts has occupied the town. If we can catch them there, we can send them packing."

An officer standing next to Loring asked the critical question. "Sir, how many invaders hit Gainesville?"

"Dispatch says three companies."

A lieutenant gave a low whistle.

Dickison said, "I figure the raid on Gainesville is diversionary in preparation for an attack in force. Pickets report detachments are probing west from Jacksonville again. Intelligence reports 5,000 men are preparing to advance. Probably, the only reason they haven't already is that General Gillmore doesn't know how few men we have. If they move west from Jacksonville, General Finnegan has ordered us to stop them."

An officer said, "Sir, ain't no way we can block 5,000 men."

"I know."

Loring asked, "What'll we do, Captain?"

"We fight 'em. General Gillmore has given us an opening. We'll hit the 4ᵗʰ Massachusetts in Gainesville to put them on the run toward Jacksonville. When they retreat, we'll break contact and pursue with skirmishers while our main force will hightail it back to Lake City. We'll entrench across the pike by Ocean Pond. When Gillmore moves west, he'll have to come through us unless he goes around through the swamps. Wouldn't we like that?" Dickison smiled.

Loring wondered how Dickison could be so undaunted when faced by such overwhelming firepower. Loring admired his leader's guerilla tactics and had no doubt that he deserved the appellation "Swamp Fox." Still, in a stand up fight, the odds favored superior numbers and resources.

Dickison snapped orders, "Loring, take a ten-man detachment and find Lieutenant Colonel Pyles who's at his place near Newmansville. He has already called out the militia. Captain Chambers with Company "C" is camped near Hogtown west of Gainesville. I've telegraphed him to meet up with your detachment and Colonel Pyles at the intersection of the Newmansville and Fort Clarke Roads. Your combined force should be enough to attack the enemy at Gainesville. I've held a train at Trail Ridge for you. I've given orders to the railroad to transport you as far south as Hatchet Creek. We can't risk taking a locomotive closer to Gainesville. You understand?"

"Yes, sir."

As soon as Dickison dismissed the officers, Loring ran to his company area to confer with his first sergeant. "Do we have ten men ready to ride?"

"Sir, the men can buck-up, but the horses are tuckered out, and we don't have any reserves."

"Do the best you can. Have the squad ready to ride in a half-hour."

The sergeant pulled ten of the best men from their tents into formation. After putting them at ease, Loring explained the situation to the sleepy troopers, "The Captain has ordered us to Gainesville to attack Yankee raiders. As soon as we can eat, we'll move out."

At the mess tent, Loring watched the men gobble fat back and mealy grits between hacking coughs and wondered, *how much longer can they soldier on without proper shelter, food, and clothing?*

The detachment trotted south over a sandy road that ran beside the New River Swamp where bald cypress stood brown and bare against the overcast winter sky. A chilly wind fluttered the dead fronds on the sable palms. "Perfect weather to make time. If it was any hotter, the horses wouldn't hold out," Loring said to his sergeant.

As the detachment reached Trail Ridge, Loring saw pitch-black smoke pouring from a locomotive's stack as the engineer waited under full steam. A plank ramp led up to a flat car with wooden rail siding. "Hurry and load the horses, men. We've got to hustle to make Hog Town by this afternoon."

The lighter-wood flaming in the locomotive's firebox gave off an odor that caused Loring to yearn for the quotidian days burning stumps at Deer Hall with Jake.

The soldiers led the horses up the ramp and tied them to the wooden rail. As they pulled the heavy boards on the flatbed, Loring signaled the engineer to go. As he released the brakes, the train groaned and squealed from every coupling - jerking forward, then crawling down the track toward Hatchet Creek.

"Why doesn't the engineer push it?" Loring asked his sergeant.

"Don't know, sir. We could go faster on horseback."

In frustration, Loring worked his way between the horses to the front of the car and climbed over the wooden rail. He stepped across the coupling, climbed forward to the wood car and yelled to the engineer, "Can't you go any faster?"

The engineer shouted, "No, the tracks are in terrible shape. We'll derail if I do."

"Let's chance it."

The engineer tapped the accelerator lever up a notch. The train bounced and swayed so much that he dared not push it any more.

Loring scrambled back to the car with the horses, verified guards were on lookout and ordered the others to rest. "Get some sleep. The wood car has room enough for you to stretch out on a clean floor."

By the time the men unloaded the horses at Hatchet Creek, the sun had broken through scattered clouds. "We've still got twenty miles to ride. We'll be late," Loring grumbled to his sergeant.

The detachment made good time. When it reached the rendezvous, only Captain Chambers had arrived. As the two officers speculated about Lt. Colonel Pyles' whereabouts, he showed up with a few old men and boys. Some sported rusty shotguns; others didn't have weapons.

After the usual formalities, Lt. Colonel Pyles took charge. "My people report that the enemy has burned or destroyed all public property in Gainesville. They've barricaded the streets in the center of town with cotton bales. It looks like they aim to occupy the town unless we can force them out."

His tone became onerous. "Slaves are helping them. There's no indication that the Yankees have armed them yet, but we've got to run the enemy off quick or they might. If they do, we'll have hell to pay."

"What's the plan?" Captain Chambers asked.

"I'll work my way around Hogtown Creek with the militia and twenty men so we can charge down Main Street. Captain Chambers, put the rest of the men into position to advance down Liberty Street from the west. Everybody be in position by late afternoon. We'll make a coordinated attack at five PM sharp."

After Lt. Colonel Pyles moved out, Captain Chambers set off with the remaining soldiers. By four-thirty, he had them ready to go only one mile from the Yankee fortifications where civilians reported that the enemy was well-protected behind cotton bales and makeshift barricades. The Federals appeared unaware that Florida troops were in the vicinity. Captain Chambers ordered Lt. Reddick's detachment to lead the assault, followed in close order by Loring's.

The soldiers walked their horses through the trees in order to stay hidden from Yankee pickets as long as possible. By four-fifty they were a half-mile from the Yankee lines when a picket shouted, "Rebel cavalry! Rebel cavalry!" Lt. Reddick blew a long blast on a whistle. The cavalrymen spurred their horses into a run toward the Yankee barricade. When they were halfway to it, Loring and his men followed.

As he closed on the objective, Loring could see enemy soldiers scrambling for cover behind the fortifications. Loring spurred Ginger hard as a smoke puff appeared between two cotton bales. As the lead horses came within a hundred yards from the objective, dense smoke billowed up from behind the fortifications. Ginger stumbled. Loring's initial reaction was that at long last he had pushed her too hard. As she slid headfirst into the dirt, he realized she had been hit. Tumbling from the saddle, he landed with Ginger's body between him and the Yankees. His rifle was jammed under her.

More men and horses went down to Loring's right and left. He raised his head above Ginger's body, but all he could see through the smoke were cotton bales and no targets. The smoke cleared for an instant. He caught a glimpse of a blue jacket. He fired his LeMat just as a slug tore into Ginger's neck. He doubted he'd hit anybody but hoped the buckshot from his short-barreled shotgun made the Yankees stay down so that his compatriots could advance.

He watched two riders reach the barricade. One wheeled at the barrier and stood in his saddle to shoot over the cotton bales. His head exploded in a blur of red gore. He toppled from the saddle with his left boot snagged in the stirrup. His horse dragged him ten feet, reared and collapsed on him. The second cavalryman jumped his horse over a low spot and disappeared.

Another concentrated volley poured from the barricade which scattered the attackers down side streets and behind buildings. From cover, Loring's men fired sporadically at the enemy with no visible effect.

Only two men had reached the objective and one had been killed. Probably, both were dead. Like Loring, several men hunkered down behind their mounts waiting for a chance to scramble to safety. One man with a bloody leg crawled behind a building just as a slug slapped into the wall by him. Several horses lay dead in the street. Wounded ones kicked and whinnied while making futile efforts to stand.

Loring dashed from the cover of his dying horse. Slugs whined by him as he slid beside the wounded soldier with the leg wound. Nobody signaled retreat, yet those who had survived the attack quit fighting except for a few Rebel sharpshooters who kept up sporadic fire to keep the enemy pinned down.

Ginger groaned and lifted her head. Loring edged as close to the dying animal as he dared without exposing himself to fire. Aiming between her eyes with his LeMat, he hesitated, then squeezed the trigger.

Loring felt sick. The attack had been an uncoordinated fiasco. Nothing indicated Lt. Colonel Pyles had advanced. Knowing that their officers had let them down, the soldiers were sullen. Loring agreed that the attack had been brainless. He knew Dickison would have never ordered a frontal assault against a fortified position with so few men. The Yankees could simply concentrate too much firepower against the small force.

When Lt. Colonel Pyles rode into camp that evening, Lt. Reddick confronted him before he dismounted, "Why didn't you advance?"

Loring listened in disgust as the officer made a feeble excuse about sharpshooters stopping his men from getting into position. The explanation made Lt. Reddick so angry that he reached up to pull the Lt. Colonel off his horse.

Loring grabbed the lieutenant by the shoulder and spun him away from the confrontation. "Calm down! With all the firepower the Yankees had, it wouldn't have made any difference."

A sharpshooter walking toward the medical tent with a bloody cloth tied around his left hand overheard the officers, "We didn't have a chance. Some of them had repeating rifles."

Captain Chambers said, "What do we do now?"

Lt. Reddick spit tobacco juice into the sand, "We have to do what Capt. Dickison ordered - attack the bastards and drive them back to Jacksonville. We might just capture some repeating rifles in the process."

That evening, Lt. Colonel Pyles became hardnosed as he barked orders and demanded reports perhaps in the forlorn hope he could atone for his earlier failure. At an officer's conference, he commenced by blaming the day's defeat on the soldiers' timidity. "We had a good plan that would have worked had ya'll attacked aggressively."

Lt. Reddick said, "Sir, with all due respect, the Yanks have repeating rifles. A frontal assault was foolhardy. Now, if we had a howitzer---"

"Lieutenant, are you questioning my judgment?"

Lt. Reddick rolled his tongue around his cheek, looked away and spit his whole chaw into the dirt. He looked straight at the Lt. Colonel. "No, sir."

"Good, here's what we'll do." The colonel sketched out a plan similar to the afternoon's debacle.

Loring felt ill.

Lt. Reddick interjected, "Sir, may I suggest---"

"No, you may not. We have orders to drive the Yankees from Gainesville, and that's what I intend to do. If your men don't pussy-foot, we can overwhelm the Yankees."

Lt. Reddick's jaw tightened and he flushed red. The colonel knew that the only thing preventing the lieutenant from attacking him was his superior rank. Secure in that knowledge, he assigned squads for the attack as if shuffling toy soldiers around a game board. Lt. Reddick received the same assignment as before. The Lt. Colonel ordered Loring's detachment to attack from the east.

"Everybody be in position to attack at dawn. When the bugler sounds charge, do so without any hesitation. Any questions?"

Lt. Reddick kicked the dirt, wheeled and walked away. Loring jogged to catch up. The lieutenant snapped, "That bastard has some gall to blame my men for not being aggressive when he never even got to the line."

Loring nodded in agreement. "He's rattled, bullheaded and didn't learn a thing from his failure. An idiot can see our small force doesn't have a chance in hell to overrun those barricades without being butchered. They can pour continuous fire on us with repeating rifles. I guarantee Captain Dickison wouldn't be so foolish. He'd hold them down till he could bring up a howitzer."

As the two lieutenants continued walking toward their soldiers, Lt Reddick warned, "Loring, you almost got killed today. You need be more careful. You're lucky it was only your horse that was hit. When this war winds down, Florida will need good men like you."

"What do you mean?"

"All I'm saying is keep you head down, damn it. Don't let Pyles' stupidity get you killed."

To everyone's relief, Lt. Colonel Pyles' plan was never tested. When the Floridians divided their force during the night, the Yankees slipped away. Lt. Colonel Pyles secured Gainesville without another shot being fired.

The Yankee raiders had accomplished their mission by ransacking the military warehouses. They carted off or destroyed all the equipment, supplies and cotton. They wrecked the railroad tracks and carried away or killed all the horses, mules and cattle they could find. Some blacks had enlisted on the spot to help defend the barricades in Gainesville. Others ran away with the Union troops. As a result, surrounding plantations didn't have enough manpower or draft animals for spring planting.

Although the raid was a disaster for the local economy, the Yankee troops had maintained good military discipline. Captured food supplies were distributed to the civilian population and Gainesville wasn't burned. At least, when the food ran out, the population would still have shelter. Still, the destructive incursion so deep into the interior demoralized Confederate Floridians. It confirmed everybody's suspicions: interior Florida was defenseless from a concentrated Yankee attack.

As ordered, Loring raced north with his soldiers to Olustee to help meet the expected Yankee assault. When he arrived, he learned to his relief that the enemy advance had stalled. For some inexplicable reason, General Seymour had come as far as Sanderson and then backtracked to Baldwin. The delay was a godsend to the Floridians because during the night several Georgia regiments arrived from Savannah. With reinforcements on the line, General Finnegan and Captain Dickison believed they could not only match General Seymour's troops; they could whip them. Morale soared.

CHAPTER FORTY-FOUR

OLUSTEE

Florida

When Loring and his men arrived at Ocean Pond on February 19, 1864, from Gainesville, they were not fit for duty. General Finnegan himself saw the weary troops and said, "Lieutenant, rest your men tonight. We have our positions set. You accomplished your objective by chasing the Yankees out of Gainesville. Hold your men in reserve to support Colonel Smith's cavalry."

Under the tall trees where the army camped, Loring raked pine needles together with his hands, spread his coat over them, pulled up a thin blanket and collapsed into deep sleep.

An off-key bugle roused him awake to a crisp, calm day. Smoke from the campfires drifted through the pines and settled low over the palmettos. At morning formation and breakfast, the men acted as if the threat from 5000 troops marching west to kill them didn't exist. As a result, Loring guessed General Seymour had turned back to Jacksonville. He asked Lt. Reddick if that had been confirmed.

"No, but I hope he did. Today's too beautiful to spoil with killing."

As Loring's detachment made its way through the mess line, a courier rode into camp with news. At dawn, the Yankees had marched west from the south fork of the St. Mary's River in three, dispersed columns shadowed by a brigade of cavalry and horse artillery with Lt. Henry's unit in the lead.

"If Lt. Henry's in the advance, we're in for a fight," Loring said.

The mood in camp changed. Battle-hardened veterans looked for quiet places to write a note or read their Bibles. Others scurried about with worried expressions as sergeants inspected men and equipment. Soldiers filled their cartridge boxes and checked their rifles.

Two peach-fuzzed, Georgia privates sat on empty cartridge crates stropping heavy Bowie knives. A lanky, veteran said, "You boys ain't goin' need those pig stickers when you meet the elephant." They ignored him and kept honing their razor sharp knives.

Loring led a roan pony pulled from the reserves to a wagon loaded with cracked corn from which a supply sergeant distributed feed. As a noncom poured Loring a ration he said, "General ordered extra grain for the horses. We have to be at full speed. Yankees are only eighteen miles off."

"Wish I had a horse that could put these rations to use as well as my Ginger. This horse isn't half the animal she was."

The sergeant said, "Next."

Loring fed the horse, inspected her shoes and curry-combed the swaybacked animal. "Hang with me as best you can, girl," he whispered to the old mare.

Loring had just finished combing the horse when a corporal ran up with instructions for him to report to Colonel Smith. Loring jogged to the headquarters tent where he found the commander addressing cavalry officers huddled around a table with a map spread across it. Loring edged as close as possible without jostling any one. The Colonel nodded at Loring and proceeded.

"General Finnegan wants us to draw in the enemy. We have 4600 men supported by three batteries of artillery waiting for General Seymour here at Ocean Pond. He has to come west along the railroad grade or his army will get tangled up in the swamps. General Finnegan has ordered two infantry companies forward to meet the enemy. When they engage, they have orders to give ground and fall back to our breastworks. Our job is to provide cover so they're not overrun. Don't separate from them. We're goin' to fall back slowly so we tire out the Blue Bellies as much as possible before they get to our trenches. We'll divide our cavalry into three columns. The middle column will go down the railroad; the others a half mile on either flank. Double your outriders and keep skirmishers at least a mile ahead. Any questions?"

After two Georgia companies tramped east with cavalry flanking them, three regiments supported by artillery formed up. To Loring's surprise, they moved out. Hundreds of gray-clad men marched forward with their regimental colors flapping. Officers shouted orders; bugles sounded. The columns undulated forward like a huge, destructive organism. Either General Finnegan had changed the plan, or somebody had the orders confused for so many men to move forward.

Loring asked Lt. Reddick, "Why is the General ordering so much infantry forward? Wouldn't it be better to wait for the Yankees behind our fortifications?"

"You'd think so. Seymour has to force his way through our breast-works if he wants to make it to the Suwannee River or Tallahassee. We'll see. By tonight, Finnegan will be either a hero or a goat."

"Yeah, and this battle is not going to be like the Indian fights we're used to."

"Not by a long shot, but it'll be the same result for the men who bite the dirt."

After noon, Loring heard the first sputter of rifle fire far to the east. Word passed through the camp that the Yankees were forcing back the skirmishers.

Dull thuds rumbled through the trees as a battery opened fire. On the picket rope, the horses lifted their ears and turned their heads toward the noise. Another battery thundered. Rifle fire became continuous.

Loring estimated the distance. "They must be at least two miles out." The roar of volleys reverberated through the pines. "Whole regiments must be opening up," he speculated as answering salvos resounded across the woods.

The horses stamped. Some bucked and tugged against the hitch line. Loring and his men walked among the frightened animals petting and talking to them as much to calm themselves as the horses. The noise from the battle became incessant. Thin smoke smelling of burnt powder drifted through trees.

"Somebody is catching hell up there," Loring said.

"I wonder who?" Lt. Reddick answered.

Loring couldn't make out anything definitive from the jumbled thunder except that the cannons sounded closer which was not a good omen. Over the clamor, Loring heard horses approaching fast.

"Riders!" he shouted as he drew his LeMat in case the approaching cavalrymen were Yankees. Uncertain, he aimed at one as they pounded through the trees toward him. At the last instant before firing, he glimpsed gray.

Relieved at first, Loring then wondered if the enemy was hot in pursuit. He quickly unhitched the mare from the picket line and mounted, ready to fight. The lead rider pulled his lathered horse to a stop yelling, "I've come from the front. The infantry is out of ammunition. Follow me to bring them more." He wheeled his horse racing toward the railroad cars down the track.

The entire detachment sped after the cavalrymen who stopped at a boxcar and exchanged quick words with a guard. Then he jumped inside the open door to help the guard drag wooden cartridge crates to the entrance. The two men wrenched the tops open to snatch cartridge boxes and pass them on to the riders who stuffed them into their saddlebags and pockets.

Loring edged his mare next to the door and grabbed several boxes. "Where do we take them?"

"Follow me!" The cavalryman jumped from the car to his horse.

"Make time! Our men can't hold the line without ammo!"

Loring rode hard to keep up. To his relief, the mare ran faster than he expected although after a mile she flagged and several riders passed him. He spurred her harder to no effect.

Ahead, a shell exploded in the top of a pine tree just above the horseman ahead of Loring. The explosion blew limbs from the tree that knocked the cavalryman's horse off its feet. The soldier went airborne and smacked against a lighter stump. When Loring sped by, he noticed ammunition scattered all around the dead man whose bloody head was akimbo.

As Loring came up behind a line of soldiers, he saw an impetuous officer riding in front of them yelling, "Stand firm, stand firm. Make yourselves seen!"

A few gray-clad soldiers stood in the open, firing at will. Most cowered behind trees or logs. Across from them, a line of blue-clad troops lifted their rifles in unison. Behind the line, Loring crouched behind the mare like the lanky soldier at the practice range so many months before. Smoke burst from a hundred rifles with a deafening roar. Confederates who had stayed in the open fell all along the line. As if by a miracle, the officer in front had not been hit. He continued to yell like a banshee.

The Yankees prepared to charge the decimated Rebel line. Shells exploded in the trees above the blue-jackets that tossed some soldiers into the air while flattening others. Gaps opened in their line, which delayed their intention.

Along the Confederate line, men scrambled to get ammunition from the riders. Ripping open the paper boxes and grabbing cartridges, they loaded and fired as fast as possible. As Loring threw the last box of ammunition from his saddlebags, he raised his LeMat to join the melee.

Yankees soldiers crumbled although the line steadfastly held its position. By sheer will, the survivors lifted their rifles for another volley. As they flashed, Loring saw a Minie ball smack into a Rebel sergeant's forehead blasting bloody froth and brains from his skull.

Artillery shells continued to explode in the treetops above the attackers that suppressed their fire although some still managed sporadic shots. As the smoke enveloping their line floated upward,

Loring saw that the enemy verged on collapse. Blue-jacketed soldiers walked backward as they reloaded. Georgians cheered. A few dashed forward. An officer yelled at a bugler. His signal halted the Rebel line as shells whined over them into the attackers. Rebel soldiers who kept running forward were blown apart along with their foes.

As officers and sergeants reformed the Georgia line, a captain sent a courier scampering to tell the artillery to adjust fire. Soldiers dropped to one knee, reloaded, gulped water from their canteens and waited. The line held for a minute till the bugler sounded charge. With yelps, the men sprang forward as did Loring.

The line undulated onward. Soldiers stopped, fired, reloaded and then ran forward to catch up to the men in front. Targets were scarce as the Yankees kept falling back. Smoke, timber, and brush blocked the pursuers' view as the Confederate Battle Flag advanced steadily under the shells that whined overhead to explode among the retreating Federals. Still, the black troops maintained enough lethal fire to slow the Confederates by picking off men here and there. Rebel officers and NCOs urged their men to press harder to prevent the enemy lines from re-forming.

A Rebel guidon carrying a swallow-tail flag took a bullet to the stomach that caused him to drop it. As another private scrambled to lift it up, a wind gust cleared the smoke covering the field for an instant. Through the haze, Loring saw black soldiers standing in another long, blue line.

They lifted their rifles to their shoulders. The Confederate line thinned as soldiers jumped for cover. Still, the Yankee volley shredded the attacking Rebels. Minie balls thudded into soldiers who had not noticed the reserve line in time to react.

A confederate battery ranged in to decimate the supporting line as the Confederate soldiers continued to fire at will. "Keep the pressure on, boys. Run 'em," a sergeant yelled.

A shell shredded the Battle Flag. The counterattack wavered. Officers and sergeants kept exhorting the men to move forward. A soldier turned to run. A sergeant hit him in mouth with his pistol knocking him to the ground. "Get up! We'll not have shirkers on this line." Blood gushed from the private's mouth. He groveled and then turned around to fight. Slowly, the two lines separated as the Yankees fell back. A lieutenant ordered skirmishers to keep moving forward. "Keep poppin' 'em."

The Confederate infantry was spent although a 32-pound cannon mounted on a railroad car crept forward behind the skirmishers pouring explosive shells on the retreating Yankees.

Loring heard shouts and several shots nearby. His spurred his mount toward the commotion.

As he approached a stand of wax myrtle, someone screamed, "Don't shoot. I surrender," followed by a shot. Loring rode around the bushes to find a black soldier crawling on his elbows with his legs dragging in the dirt. A Union Colonel with only a bloody pulp for a face lay sprawled next to him. Another black soldier pleaded in wide-eyed desperation, "Jesus, have mercy, save us, sir!"

Two Confederate privates stood side by side. One loaded his shotgun as the other aimed at the soldier with hands above his head.

Loring yelled, "What the hell are you two doing?"

The one loading pulled his ramrod from the barrel and said with a sneer, "Don't you know about General Order 60? White officers commanding blacks are outlaws. The nigra lovers incited insurrection so they ain't prisoners of war. They're criminals along with the insurgents."

Loring yelled at the privates, "Damn it, you can't execute soldiers who have surrendered. General Order 60 doesn't permit cold-blooded murder."

One private said, "You best move on."

Before Loring could grab his pistol, he found himself staring down the muzzle of a double-barreled shotgun. The wounded black soldier trying to crawl away collapsed. The other private said, "I can't believe he's still alive."

"Finish him!" the other yelled.

A shotgun blast blew out his brains.

Loring gagged.

The one covering Loring waved his shotgun at him. "You damn sissy. Git the hell out of here. You're lucky you're wearin' gray."

Loring yanked hard on the mare's reins to turn her away. She stumbled but recovered her balance to leap away as a shotgun discharged behind him.

Loring ran the mare to a Confederate Colonel who had several junior grade officers huddled around him. "Sir, surrendering troops are being murdered. We have to stop it."

The colonel looked aggravated, but Loring couldn't tell if his irritation was from the interruption or something else.

"Sir, excuse me, I saw---"

The colonel cut him short, "Who are you, Lieutenant? What unit are you with?"

"Sir, my name is Loring Bell. I serve under Captain Dickison. We have to stop---"

"Captain Dickison, uh, isn't he the famous Florida guerilla fighter some call Dixie, the Swamp Fox?"

"Sir, surrendering Yankee soldiers are being---"

"Don't Captain Dickison's officers show respect for a superior officer by answering direct questions?"

"Sir, I don't know if Captain Dickison is famous or not. He does the best he can. Black troops are---"

"Yup, Dixie's kept the Yankees at bay down here although his luck would have run out today if we hadn't showed up."

The officers laughed.

Loring tried again, "Sir, I saw a black soldier---"

The Colonel growled, "Captain, Lieutenant Bell is in a tizzy. Go with him and investigate. Lieutenant, I'm quite sure that Confederate soldiers conduct themselves in accord with the rules of war. If there's a problem, it's only a few bad apples."

As Loring led the captain toward the scene of the executions, he observed for the first time the dross of war on a major battlefield. Muskets, rifles, cartridge boxes, haversacks, and canteens were strewn helter-skelter among the wiregrass and palmettos. Busted caissons lay on their side with dead mules still in harness. A cannon barrel, blasted off its carriage, rested on the ground. Mutilated, bloody bodies littered the woods all around. Wounded men with pallid, fearful eyes staggered about or sat wild-eyed.

Dead Rebel and Union soldiers lay interspersed with one another as if death had resolved their differences. Nearly all the dead Yankee soldiers left on the field were black, a circumstance that raised vexing questions. Had black troops been sent to the hottest spots? Had the

Yankees carried their white comrades from the field and left the others? Had Confederates allowed the whites to surrender but killed the blacks?

Loring couldn't find the dead Yankee colonel and his black soldiers. Too many wax myrtle stands and palmetto patches looked similar across the confused, torn-up, battlefield. In desperation, he rode from one cluster of bushes to the next.

After a time the captain complained, "I ain't got all day. I suggest you find your unit. Look over there. Black prisoners are under guard. Nobody's being executed. Don't you see our men loading wounded nigras into ambulances? If you don't find whatever you're looking for right quick, I'm leavin'."

In exasperation, Loring stammered, "I know- I know what I saw. The soldiers mentioned General Order 60."

The captain said, "Between us, it's despicable that our government declared white commanders of nigra troops outlaws. That foolishness was bound to bring out the worst in some men. Besides that, it makes the Yankees fight to the bitter end knowing they'll be executed if they surrender. In every battle with black troops, we pay with blood because of that order."

The captain's words were no consolation to Loring who continued, "Those who murder prisoners, black or white, ought to be---"

The captain cut him off, "Nothing we can do. I suggest you go back to your unit. Try to forget whatever you saw although I'll say this: if we lose the war, those responsible for General Order 60 will have to face the consequences."

The captain rode away.

Feeling ill, Loring walked his mare toward his detachment area. The battlefield looked even more gruesome to him now. The ground looked like hogs had rooted it bare where artillery shells had smashed into the dirt. Explosions had shattered trees and torn men apart in more terrible ways than mere bullets ever could. Where the lines had been, severed heads and limbs were strewn about. A brogan stitched together with twine held a severed foot. A jaw jutted from a wiregrass clump. The top of someone's fuzzy head lay on a haversack as if someone placed it there to rest. Near it, Loring spied the dead colonel whose face had been mangled by buckshot fired at close range. He dismounted to attempt to identify the colonel. With his head turned away from the gore, he rifled the officer's pockets and found that every one had already been stripped. On the ground by the dead man he saw a broken watch, a diary and an ambrotype with a pretty lady's picture etched in tin. Loring skimmed the diary's delicate writing. It identified the dead Colonel as C.W. Fribley of the 8th U.S. Colored Troops. Loring vowed to get the mementoes to the colonel's wife.

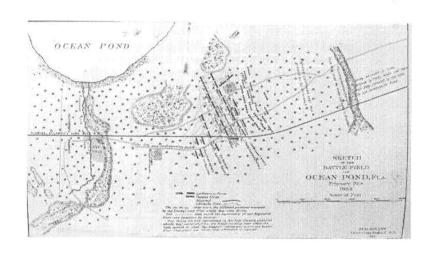

Ocean Pond Battlefield (Olustee)

(Courtesy Florida State Archives)

THE ESCAPED SLAVE IN THE UNION ARMY.—[SEE PAGE 12.]

Escaped Slave In The Union Army

(Courtesy Florida State Archives)

CHAPTER FORTY-FIVE

HOMOSASSA
Florida

Mingo's men reconnoitered the entire Suwannee Valley and the Big Bend from St. Marks to Bayport for the United States Army and Navy and kept the Confederate strong points such as Clay Landing and Columbus under surveillance. His scouts also pinpointed the location of salt works, warehouses, and public property so Yankee patrols could destroy them.

All the Confederate camps had slaves who worked as cooks or factotums who provided Mingo's men with valuable information about military movements, logistics and projects. In time, a Confederate trench couldn't be dug or Rebel supplies moved down an isolated creek without Mingo and Weeks knowing about it.

The U.S. Navy systematically destroyed all the salt works along the Gulf Coast and patrols operated inland burning bridges and wrecking public property. The raiders also razed private property if it could be used by Rebel forces or was owned by Confederate officials. Some undisciplined Yankee troops demolished or burned every structure they came across.

Federal operations wreaked havoc on Florida's economy while simultaneously strengthening Union forces. Incursions liberated slaves who then enlisted in the U.S. army. Civilian morale plummeted which stimulated whites to switch allegiance. So many Rebs changed sides that the U.S. Army organized the United States 2nd Florida Cavalry Regiment. Master Weeks transferred from the navy to the army with the rank of major to command the unit and coordinate operations.

No plantation, town or village was secure from attack. Resistance provoked destruction. So many slaves ran away that the productive capacity of plantations dependent on their labor crashed. Without slaves to do the plowing, hoeing and harvesting, weeds took over the fields and crops failed. Food became scarce and expensive.

Captain Dickison didn't have the men or resources to protect the countryside. After the battle of Olustee, Union General Gillmore kept his troops concentrated at Jacksonville. This required Dickison to maintain a blocking force in East Florida at Camp Finnegan which left him with too few men to scurry around the Big Bend to counter Yankee patrols. At best, he managed occasional, undermanned counter-patrols.

As Mingo's men learned the back trails and roads, their knowledge neutralized the Rebels' tactical advantage earlier in the war. The United States 2nd Florida Cavalry copied Dickison's guerilla tactics. It hit fast and hard to capture or destroy as much as possible and then raced to safety before Rebs could react.

Mingo particularly enjoyed one operation that dealt a severe psychological blow to the Secesh population. He led a combined US Naval and US Army detachment up the Homosassa River to attack Margarita Plantation owned by Senator Levy, one of Florida's first

United States Senators, one of the wealthiest men in Florida, the namesake of Levy County, a Confederate senator and the "Father of Florida's Railroads."

Before dawn, boats carrying the troops eased past the tidal marsh at the river's mouth. They traveled upriver on crystal clear, spring water toward Tiger Tail Island where Levy maintained one of his several mansions. Sailors rowed up river in absolute silence except for an occasional splash when one mistimed a stroke which sounded almost indistinguishable from that of the mullet jumping near the boats. Nevertheless, as cautious as the raiders were, an alert guard spotted them and clanged a brass bell as a warning.

"Forget goin' to de dock, head to de shore," Mingo ordered the helmsman in the lead boat. As the boat turned, someone upriver fired a rifle at it. A spent slug ricocheted off the water to thud into the hull without enough force to penetrate the wood. Near shore Mingo jumped overboard into the clear water that looked only knee deep. He sank to his chest before he touched bottom. When his foot hit a rock, he slipped on mossy slime. His head went under water. Somehow he managed to keep his rifle dry, flail to the surface, grab a tree root and pull himself up onto a rough, limestone bank.

"Throw me a line," he shouted. "I'll pull de boat closer. Hurry, we'll soon have riflemen on us."

A marine threw a coiled rope to Mingo who tugged the launch against the bank. As he snugged the line around a cypress knee, a rifle cracked. A Minie ball whizzed by. "Hurry! Spread out! Form a skirmish line. Don't let them pin us down."

Marines jumped to the bank. They splashed through ankle deep water, dodging behind cypress trees as they ran. "Go! Faster! Go!"

Mingo yelled as smoke puffed from behind trees up river. He braced his rifle across a limb waiting for a clear shot. When he glimpsed a straw hat, he fired. The shooter ran away in a low crouch. A marine to his right fired at another running man with no better luck. Mingo yelled, "Move! Press them!"

As Mingo ran forward through the trees and brush along the river, the firing stopped. He lost sight of the enemy. Along with marines, he kept pressing forward until he reached a clearing where he saw a warehouse built upon a wharf. A bent, black man with his hands up stepped from behind a wagon. "De whites done run off."

"You sure?"

"Yassuh, de whites skeddadled when dey seen de soldiers."

Up a tree-lined lane that led to a plantation house, Mingo heard someone yell, "Kill him!"

Mingo jogged toward the ruckus where he found several black men, some holding ropes, surrounding a muscular man as big as Brutus. Against impossible odds, he punched and kicked to break away from his tormentors who closed in around him. Twisting and dodging, he knocked down two attackers with quick jabs. Somehow, he held his own until a man hit him from behind with a club that dropped him.

Before he could get up, several men jumped him. They forced his hands behind his back to tie them together while another slipped a noose over his neck. "What's going on?" Mingo yelled.

"Dis man is de meanest driver in de world. We're goin' to hang him while we got de chance."

"No, you ain't," Mingo yelled.

The muscular man groaned. Blood poured from a gash over his right eye, gushing over his face, down his neck and onto his chest. As he struggled to his knees, the man holding the rope around his neck yanked it pulling the big man to the ground.

"Drop that rope! We're taking this man into military custody," a sergeant with a drawn pistol yelled.

The man holding the line jerked it once more then let it drop. Another tossed a club-shaped lighter knot into the weeds.

The sergeant picked up the rope and handed it to a private. "Keep this man under guard. Shot him if tries to escape." More people gathered around. The sergeant said, "Ya'll get back. This man is in military custody. If you interfere, we'll arrest you too. Stand back!"

Although one man muttered something under his breath, they obeyed the order. Several others bolted toward Senator Levy's mansion. Mingo followed them toward the two-storied, white-columned house at the end of the lane where a crowd milled around in the yard and on the porches yelling, squabbling and shoving one another.

Tall, double doors stood wide open and askew. Someone smashed a chair through an upstairs window. What people couldn't carry, they tossed into the yard. Mingo saw bedding, clothing, pots, pans, furniture, and pictures sail over the porch rails. When the items hit the ground, people fought over the spoils. At the edge of the yard, a scrawny girl wearing only a grass skirt struggled to pull on a pretty white dress with a red sash. A smaller girl clutched a rag doll to her chest.

Two old women grabbed a mahogany table varnished to a high sheen. Too heavy for them to carry, they dropped it. A leg snapped off.

As Mingo reached the piazza, someone threw a corner table from the second story porch. The marble top shattered to pieces.

Someone yelled, "Burn de white devil's house."

Mingo forced his way through the crowd and inside where he found every room on the first floor stripped. As he climbed the stairway to the second floor, he smelled smoke. At the first room by the landing, someone had piled papers, some with gilt edges, in a corner and set them afire. Already, flames burned hot enough to curl the wallpaper far up the wall. Two men battered a roll-top writing desk to pieces. As it fell apart, they threw remnants on the fire. The thin, wooden dividers ignited the instant they hit the blaze.

A gossamer curtain burst into flame. Fire leaped from the second story window. A crone yelled something about being free at last. Down the lane near the water, Mingo saw more smoke billow above the trees which meant that the warehouse must be afire too. He ran back to salvage everything he could. When he arrived, flames licked an outer wall, but had not yet enveloped the building. Looking through the open door, he saw wooden casks stacked against the far wall. He grabbed a man who was leaving the warehouse with a full croker bag thrown over his shoulder. "What's in those casks?" The man jerked away, "Molasses."

Mingo yelled at marines by the dock "Help me roll de casks out before dey burn."

The marines rolled a few barrels out of the warehouse before the flames made the building too hot and dangerous. As Mingo stood back to watch it burn, the marines assigned to search the plantation reported that not a single white person had been found. Also, the slaves had set fire to most everything. Whatever wouldn't burn, they smashed except for their slave quarters and the stone sugar mill. One squad reported that some blacks celebrated their liberation by expropriating rum from a warehouse and drinking the spoils.

Major Weeks said to Mingo, "There must be hundreds of people here. What are we going to do?"

"We have to be careful. If we use force, dey'll turn against us. Tell dem to be here at noon to claim freedom. When you explain de options, I'll bet we enlist more soldiers than on any other raid."

Mingo sent runners to all the slave quarters scattered around the huge plantation to make sure that everybody had the word about the "freedom assembly." Before long, people streamed toward the landing including some drunken men.

As the new freedmen gathered around, they bombarded Mingo and the marines with questions about the war, treatment of runaway slaves, and President Lincoln's Emancipation Proclamation. Soon, more than three hundred slaves crowded around the landing, dancing and singing.

A line of soldiers holding rifles affixed with shiny bayonets stood at ease in a semi-circle guarding the wharf, the wagon, and the few molasses casks salvaged from the warehouse. Slaves sauntered up to them to admire their uniformed saviors.

At noon, Major Weeks climbed upon the wagon, "Listen up. Listen up!" he yelled as loud as he could as everybody squeezed closer to hear. "Ladies and gentlemen of Margarita Plantation---" Pandemonium erupted. The slaves whooped, clapped, hugged, and called out hallelujahs. A young woman said, "Ladies and gentlemen? White folks never called us nothin' but niggers."

"Quiet, please! Quiet! Yes, ladies and gentlemen. You are no longer slaves. You are free men and women." The slaves whooped louder than before. People jumped up and down. They clapped in rhythmic unison and begin to sing the "Battle Hymn of the Republic." Major Weeks wondered how they had possibly learned the song in the Florida backwoods as he joined in on the chorus. After two verses, he raised his hands above his head and brought them down again and again to silence the crowd.

After a time, the singing tapered off. A few people in the crowd yelled, "Hush up, listen to de man!" As the crowd quieted, Major Weeks lifted a paper above his head, "This is President Lincoln's Emancipation Proclamation setting you free." Another joyous outburst exploded from the crowd. When it calmed, the major read the portions of the Emancipation Proclamation that liberated the slaves. The new freedmen concentrated on every word.

When Major Weeks finished reading, he added, "By the power invested in me by the President of the United States, and as an officer of the United States Army, you are hereby declared free, American citizens." Whoops rang out and people clapped although not with as much vigor as before.

Major Weeks continued, "With freedom comes responsibility. We will do what we can to help you, but you have to take care of yourselves. We are limited in what we can do because the United States is at war with traitorous secessionists who want to keep you enslaved." A few angry shouts rang out.

"We need your help to subdue the traitors. I'm asking you men to enlist in the army to help us fight your oppressors. Help us whip the Rebels so that all your people can be free. Those who enlist will be issued a new uniform and will receive full pay and allowances. Talk to that sergeant over there with chevrons on his sleeves if you want to join with us."

Men edged toward the sergeant. "Those who don't enlist in the army also have a choice. You can stay here, or you can come with us. I suggest you leave. We can place you under the Navy's protection in camps at either Cedar Key or Egmont Key down at Tampa Bay. At either camp, you'll have food and shelter. Your children can go to school. In return, you have to obey the rules and work to keep the camp in order. If you want to go with us, speak to the corporal over there, the soldier with two stripes on his sleeve. You're free; the choice is yours."

With those parting words, Major Weeks climbed down from the wagon. A few people clapped although the exuberance had drained from the crowd as people thought about their own future. The prospect left many perplexed. Most had never been off the Levy plantation.

Enough men enlisted to form a company. Most of the others accepted the offer to go the navy refugee camps which caused a logistical and tactical nightmare for Major Weeks. Now, he had the responsibility to protect hundreds of civilians in enemy territory. He decided to ferry the people to Shell Island at the mouth of the Homosassa River where a gunboat could cover the island to keep Dickison from capturing the freedmen. From there, the people could be loaded on ships for transport to the camps.

As the last boat pulled away from the wharf at Margarita Plantation, Mingo jumped on board with a bag filled with fruit that a wizened slave had given him. He set the bag down, pulled out an orange and ripped apart the soft skin with his index finger. The peel came off in big swatches. Juice squirted on his hand as he pulled a plug free and popped into his mouth. "Mmm, Major Weeks, dis is delicious. Try a slice."

Major Weeks tasted one. "It's excellent. I think it's called a Homosassa after this river. Someone gave me one for Christmas last year."

"De old man said oranges, grapefruit and lemon trees are planted in blocks on sandy ground away from the river. After the war, I'd like to come down here, buy some land, and go into de citrus business."

"Mingo, my friend, how'd you like a partner?"

CHAPTER FORTY-SIX

DEER HALL
Florida

Blanche never rested. Managing the household and the farm took all her energy, and then to make matters worse, Sarah caught ague. Without medicine, Blanche had no effective way to treat her. Every day Sarah wasted away, either burning with fever or shivering with chill. The strain to care for her changed Blanche from an attractive, vivacious woman to a careworn matron. She no longer faced the world with a smile. One, hot, summer day after washing clothes in the iron wash pot all morning, she confided to Molly, "We've adapted to deprivation, hard work and constant fear. But now, with Sarah sick, I wonder if we can hold on?"

"We don't have a choice. Everything will be fine if Mas'r Loring could come home. He'll get a furlough before long."

"No, he won't. His last letter says the army cancelled them because there aren't enough men. He is in the saddle all the time. My only hope is that a patrol brings him to the Suwannee Valley so he can stop by."

The girls, both barefoot and wearing home-made, palm frond hats, walked up. Little Buddy carried a bucket with a few black-eyed peas in it. "These are the last ones, Mama."

Blanche stirred the mottled pods with her hand, "Is this all?"

"Yes, Ma'am, we picked every one. We went up and down every row three times."

"You girls go find Billy and Joe and tell them I need them."

As the girls trudged away Molly looked into the bucket and said, "There's not enough for a serving."

"I know it. I'll have the boys chop some swamp cabbage so we can add the hearts to the peas. Maybe Jake snared another rabbit or squirrel that we can throw in the pot too. Billy's probably off hunting again. Maybe he'll shoot a hog although I'd rather have him home. He seems to be gone all the time."

"I have to tell you sumpthin'. Last week, Joe told me dat when he was gator huntin' with Billy, dey ran across a patrol wid a string of horses. Billy rode off with de soldiers who was checkin' the railroad tracks. He still meets up wid dem sometimes."

"My God, he'll get himself killed! Why didn't you tell me sooner?"

"I didn't know until Joe let de cat out of de bag yesterday. Billy threatened to beat him if he told anybody."

"That devil. Without Loring around, he's gone wild. When I told him he couldn't enlist in the army, he had the audacity to sass me. I tried to give him a switching, but he grabbed my arm. I asked Chad to talk to him, but Billy told him he didn't have to listen to any man but his Daddy."

The girls looked for the boys in the fields where they spent most of their time hoeing or pushing a home-made hand plow in the constant battle against sandspurs, broom grass, and other weeds. The girls found Joe working alone while singing a chantey. When they asked about Billy, he said, "I reckon he's off huntin'.

The war had entangled the once inseparable boys in conflict. Billy supported secession. Joe supported the Union, so they squabbled all the time. When Joe threatened to run away to join the U.S. Navy, Billy threatened to kill him.

The relationship between Little Buddy and Annie had changed too. They still played together, but without their lighthearted, childhood innocence. Annie now understood that she could never be equal to her playmate.

Little Buddy pined for her father all the time. Every night when Blanche kissed her goodnight, tears welled in her eyes as she prayed for his return. "Mama, why does Daddy have to be away fighting?"

Although Molly maintained a cheerful façade, she ached for Mingo's return. To pass the time, she spent many evenings chatting with Chad. She loved hearing about his travel tales and his business deals. Best of all, she liked the fact that he treated her as an equal. In spite of herself, she felt guilty for enjoying the time spent with Chad. To compensate, she mentioned Mingo at every opportunity.

During the first years of the war, the blockade inconvenienced Chad, but as the war dragged on, it ruined him. No one had collateral for loans. So many slaves had run away that most farmers didn't have enough hands to plant and harvest food crops, much less labor-intensive cotton. Even those who managed to hold on to their workers didn't plant it for fear of attracting Yankee raiders. In any event, collateral for loans became moot as his partners refused to risk financing a commodity subject to destruction or confiscation by blockaders.

Without any business prospects, Chad exhausted his money and would have felt like a failure except that he found fulfillment helping to keep the Bell farm viable. Of course, productivity plummeted without draft animals, yet by planting crops that were easier to raise like collards and black-eyed peas, he achieved subsistence output as long as everybody worked hard. Bogged down managing the household and nursing Sarah, Blanche deferred to his decisions to make the farm as fruitful as possible. The responsibility gave him purpose.

Jake worked side by side with Chad on all the menial tasks without complaint although Chad noticed he asked more questions about the war as time passed.

Chad's attraction for Molly increased. He loved that she stayed vivacious and strong-willed in spite of the daily hardships that wore everybody else down and as she matured, she looked more beautiful too. He yearned for the North to win the war to destroy a social system that denied him the right to express his feelings. In spite of himself, he fantasized that a Rebel bullet might kill Mingo.

Although war weary and haggard from toil, Blanche remained a strong, attractive woman in Chad's eyes as well. Nevertheless, he managed to maintain coolness towards her even while living in close proximity. Although he sensed that Blanche was vulnerable and starved for affection, he had resolved never to betray his friend's trust and remained steadfast.

1865

"And if we are true to ourselves, and worthy of freedom, let us trust that the blessing of God will yet crown with success our efforts in a cause so noble. Only the skulkers and extortioners, the timid and craven, tremble and forget their manhood in the hour and presence of danger and adversity. ...There are now the strongest reasons for standing firm and true to our colors, maintaining discipline and gathering and concentrating our strength."

~MAJOR GENERAL SAM JONES

From a circular issued a Headquarters District of Florida, Tallahassee,

APRIL 28, 1865, FOLLOWING THE NEWS OF LEE'S SURRENDER IN VIRGINIA.

(Courtesy Florida State Archives)

STATION FOUR SKIRMISH, CEDAR KEY

(Courtesy Florida State Archives)

CHAPTER FORTY-SEVEN

LEVYVILLE
Florida

After the successful raid on Levy's plantation, incursions along the coast accelerated. Mingo and his men scouted for opportunities to exploit any Rebel weakness so that the U.S. Navy and the U.S. 2nd Florida Cavalry under Major Weeks could attack at the most opportune times.

The U.S. Navy destroyed all the major salt works along the Big Bend. Only temporary, inefficient operations with small fires under tiny kettles avoided detection and destruction. For all practical purposes, production ceased along with all other trade. No longer could sailboats slip up hidden creeks or into isolated bays without Mingo's network finding out about them and reporting their location.

On a freezing day in January, Brutus returned to Cedar Key from a scouting mission to Clay Landing. After slipping around the Rebel pickets posted outside the town, he hurried to tell Mingo about unusual intelligence that his informant had given him. "It's mighty strange what Governor Milton's doin'."

"What's dat, Brutus?"

"To force out de dissenters across the Suwannee in Lafayette and Taylor Counties once and for all, he's ordered de families along Warrior Creek and de Econfina River to move to a compound by Tallahassee. The army plans sweeps through both counties."

"Why?"

"De governor can't tell de dissidents from de loyal folks, so he's forcin' everybody out. Whites are mad as hell. We can raid Clay Landing while de troops conduct de operation. We can compound de damage because several wagons filled with supplies just arrived there from Tallahassee."

"Brutus, dis is important information. Let's find Major Weeks."

They found him inspecting a sailboat that a gunboat had captured on the Withlacoochee River. "Look at the condition of this sloop. It's not seaworthy without a major refitting. The sails are rotten, the running rigging is ragged and the hull is worm-eaten. This boat's condition confirms that the enemy is on the ropes."

Mingo said, "And now we have an opportunity to strike a major blow at de Rebels. Brutus, tell Major Weeks what you found."

When Brutus finished his report Mingo said, "Give me a company and we can capture the wagons at Clay Landing and raid Levyville at de same time."

"I don't know Mingo. It's ten miles or more from Cedar Key to Clay Landing. If Dickison shows up, you'll need more than a company."

"The army will have their hands full rounding up people across de Suwannee. If we move fast, we'll be back to Cedar Key before he can respond."

"Mounted squads guard the roads. When they report that we've marched out with more than a patrol Captain 'Dixie' will rush over here with a 2nd Florida Cavalry detachment."

Brutus added, "His pickets are spread thin around Cedar Key. With any luck we can slip by dem, or we could take a boat up de Suwannee like we did last summer when we snatched dat cotton stored upriver."

Major Weeks replied, "We can't risk going by river. That worked once, but now they guard the Suwannee more carefully. If they caught us on the river, the whole detachment could get wiped out.

"Let's use de abandoned trail dat goes to de salt works we destroyed at Live Oak Key," Mingo suggested. "The Rebs rarely patrol it and won't expect us to use dat trail to raid Clay Landing."

"I'd want to use at least two companies, and it'd be cumbersome to transport that many men and their horses across the bay. Besides, the Live Oak Key route is too long. A patrol or informants will spot us and give away the operation. Let's take out the picket posts on the main road and disable the telegraph so our movements can't be reported. We'll head straight up the railroad then use the Devil's Hammock cutoff to the Waccasassa Road. Dixie won't know where we're headed until we commit. The Swamp Fox can't be everywhere."

Mingo laughed and said, "You bet he can't. We know Levy County as well as he does now."

"I'm convinced. Let's do it. One thing is certain, my new recruits are eager for action. They'll help us liberate slaves from the farms all along the march."

By dawn, Major Weeks had his men on the move north past Station Four with cavalry squads racing forward to wipe out the

Rebel picket posts. At Yearty's farm, they encountered the first one. Although the lead squad surprised it, the cavalrymen only captured three men; four others escaped.

When informed that not all the Rebel lookouts had been killed or captured, Major Weeks reconsidered, "Even though we cut the telegraph, those four pickets who escaped will still spread the alarm. Dickison will react."

Mingo argued, "Yes, but he'll be too late. By de time he mobilizes and finds us, we'll be back to Cedar Key. Why don't we divide de force? Take de cavalry to Levyville and de infantry to Clay Landing."

Major Weeks said, "I'd pull the infantry back now if the men weren't so eager. Let's chance it. Mingo, you and I will take the cavalry to Levyville. Brutus, you go with Major Lincoln and his infantry to Clay Landing."

Mingo rode hard to scout the route. He checked every side road as well as potential ambush sites. He found nothing to indicate that Dickison had reacted to the raid. Still, scouting used precious time. Two days slipped by before the detachment reached Levyville. The village awoke to find black troops posted at every intersection with orders to burn everything useful to the Rebels, roundup all the livestock, and liberate slaves.

In a few hours the soldiers assembled a small herd of cattle, a few horses, a wagon and fifty slaves. All public property was set aflame.

Major Weeks said, "We have to hustle or we risk being cut off. We've accomplished enough. You keep scouting. Take a squad. Check the surrounding farms. I'll wait at Station Four for the infantry."

Mingo led his squad southeast from Levyville. Mostly, he found burned and abandoned farms. The houses and barns still standing were ramshackle. At one isolated farm, a wan woman in a ragged, threadbare dress, stood on the porch when the squad rode up. "Please don't burn me out," she begged. "I'm Union. My husband enlisted with Major Weeks."

"What's his name?" Mingo demanded.

"Rily Wright."

"Any of you know Rily Wright?" Mingo yelled to his men.

"Nobody answered. A staff sergeant said, "I don't remember seein' his name on any rolls, but we have so many new recruits I couldn't say for sure."

The woman blubbered, "He enlisted a month ago with the U.S. after servin' in the Confederate 6th Florida Infantry Regiment in Tennessee. He was wounded at Chickamauga. He deserted when my babies got sick, and the army wouldn't give him a furlough to come home. My babies died before he got here which made him so mad he joined up with the Union."

Mingo said, "We won't burn your place, but we have to take your cow." The woman fell to her knees, "Please, don't take her. I'll starve without milk."

"Ma'am, I hate to, but I have orders. My advice is for you to come wid us to Cedar Key where de army will give you food and shelter. Private, fetch de cow."

At most farms, Mingo didn't find any livestock or anything else worth confiscating for that matter; Confederate impressment officers, marauders, deserters, contrabands, or refugees had stripped the farms already. In total, he only found three slaves, a wagon and ten head of cattle. Driving the cattle slowed his pace to a walk. In order to search more farms, he ordered his sergeant to escort the booty back to the main force while he continued scouting with a corporal.

At dusk as the two men trotted their horses into an abandoned farmyard, a shot rang out. The bullet smashed into the eye of Mingo's horse. The corporal's horse shied and bolted.

As his horse fell, Mingo jumped clear and sprinted for cover as his assailant fired at him. Dashing through a gallberry thicket, he kept moving to distance himself from his attacker. When he came to a swamp, he pushed through the thick underbrush around the edge and waded into the water that was warmer than the air.

Once across the swamp, he kept heading east. He skirted Devil's Hammock and circled around Blue Springs. At the railroad, he knew that he was only three or four miles from Deer Hall and Molly. He decided the detour was worth the risk.

As he approached Deer Hall, he smelled an odor that reminded him of the burnt salt works. When he got closer, he realized the stench came from piles of gray ashes where Jake's house and the barn should have been.

As he stood gawking at the remains of the buildings, someone yelled, "Hands up." Mingo couldn't see anybody. "Throw your pistol to the ground with your left hand, now!" The voice sounded familiar.

"Jake, dat you? It's me, Mingo."

He heard the hammer ratchet down and Jake exclaim, "Mingo, my God, it's good to see you! Dressed like dat, I thought you was a Yankee deserter comin' to steal. How you doin'?"

"I'm fine. Cold and wet, dat's all. What de hell happened here?"

"Outlaws burned my house and de barn."

"Who was it?"

"Don't know. Mas'r Chad, me and Billy opened up on dem. We suspects it was either de Coker or Strickland band dats been terrorizin' folks 'round here."

"Waldock's still here, huh?"

"Thank goodness! We couldn't git along without him. Look at you. Good clothes and totin' a pistol. Are you a soldier?"

"I scout for Major Weeks."

"Missis Blanche ain't goin' be happy to hear dat."

"How's Molly?"

"She's well. To tell you de truth, she runs de house. Missis Blanche is plumb worn out."

"Has Waldock mistreated Molly?"

"No, he looks after her like she was a white gal."

"What ya mean?"

"I reckon Mas'r Chad is sweet on her, but he don't take advantage like some white men who own a pretty woman."

"He better not."

"What you talkin' 'bout, boy?"

"The war has changed everythin', Jake. Now that we're free, we can stand up for ourselves. We can't allow white devils to take advantage of our women folk no more."

"Mingo, don't cause trouble with Mas'r Chad. Nossuh, he treats Miss Molly like a lady. Let's git to de house and warm you up."

Annie saw Mingo first and ran to him, squealing with joy. As he bent to pick her up, he stopped. "My, look at you. How you've grown, sister." Annie grabbed his hand and pulled him toward the house.

"Molly, Molly, look who I found!" Annie yelled as she pulled Mingo onto the porch. Molly smothered him with hugs and kisses as everybody gathered around.

After Mingo gave Molly a long kiss, Chad offered his hand. Mingo hesitated, then shook it.

Blanche stood by the door wiping her hands on a stringy, gray apron.

"Hello, Missis Bell," Mingo said.

"Mingo, what's going on? Why are you carrying a pistol? In those blue pants and pea coat, you look like a soldier."

"Ma'am, I ain't enlisted. I scout for the United States Army and Navy. A mission brought me nearby, so I figured to stop by and see 'bout ya'll."

Blanche's eyes watered. "Are you bringing Yankees here to burn us out or to steal what little we have left?"

"No, Ma'am, I'm here on a social visit."

Just then Billy stepped around the corner of the house with his shotgun pointed at Mingo.

Chad snapped, "Billy, hold it! Mingo's our friend!"

Molly jumped between Billy and Mingo.

Blanche shrieked, "Billy! Put down that gun! Billy, Billy, come back here!"

She watched in tearful resignation as her son ran away clutching his weapon.

"The boy's incorrigible. He stays away from home half the time."

Chad said, "Come inside by the stove to dry your brogans and pants while the women fix something to eat."

When she served him, Blanche said, "Hoecakes and gravy is the best we can do. We don't have any eggs, meat or coffee."

Mingo looked at the unappetizing, blackened hoecakes. He guessed they were fried in gator fat. He ate it anyway. Little Buddy and Annie sat by him pestering him with questions about the army and the navy. Blanche hushed them, "Mind your manners, girls. Let's not talk about de war."

Mingo asked, "How ya'll gettin' along?"

Jake answered, "All de stock is gone and we can't tend de fields like we should without draft animals. I even miss dat ol' rascal, Mike. We ain't starvin' 'cause we can still find varmints like coons and 'possums. Trap 'em not to waste ammunition. Deer and hogs are hunted out. Ain't no scrub cattle left in de woods. Gators are scarce too. People kill dem for oil."

Annie added, "We catch stump knockers and cooters in de pond. We ate up all de gophers."

Molly laughed and said, "You can't say we don't have variety. We've learned to cook everything from swamp chicken to turtle eggs. Poke greens in spring ain't so bad once you get used to dem. Of course, everythin' would be better wid salt."

Blanche added, "We survive, that's about it. Salt isn't all we need. Don't know when we last saw wheat flour, sugar, coffee or tea. Of course, we couldn't afford them if anybody had them to sell. Confederate money is next to worthless. We can't even get lemons or molasses after Senator Levy's plantation was raided by the navy." She glanced at Mingo.

Mingo started to say something but reconsidered. He sopped his hoecake in the dark gravy that tasted fishy. "I've got to excuse myself and head back to my outfit." Molly clutched his arm.

"Don't go," Annie begged, grabbing him by the hand.

"I've got to, honey. I'll come back to visit when I can. Thank you, Missis Blanche, for de breakfast and hospitality. Goodness knows de war is hard on everybody. I hope dat Mas'r Loring makes it home safe and sound. I consider him a friend and understand dat he's only doing his duty."

"Yes, we all have our duty, Mingo," Blanche replied.

Molly and Mingo walked hand in hand from the house to the path through the scrub oaks. When they were out of sight, Molly grabbed him and hugged him. After a long kiss, she said, "I'm so proud of you, but Missis Blanche don't know what to think."

"Free black men like me are her worst nightmare. White folks like her need to learn dat we're just as good as dey are, but some of dem is sure being hardheaded. Come with me to Cedar Key."

"I would, honey, but where would I live, in a tent? You'll be off scoutin' and I'd be left alone without knowin' nobody. Besides, I need to look after Sarah and de children. When the war's over, I'll go with you anywhere you want. It can't last much longer, can it?"

"I don't think so. De Rebels are whipped but won't admit it. Sherman has marched clear across Georgia and Lee's army is starvin'. Dickison can't stop our forays anymore."

"I'm worried sick that you'll get yourself killed in some piddlin' fight dat doesn't amount to a hill of beans."

"I can take of myself. I'm more worried about you. Deserters from both armies are hidin' in de swamps. Refugees from Georgia and South Carolina are fleein' down here in droves. Some are desperate and dangerous."

"Honey, I'll be OK. Jake and Chad look after us here."

"Chad Waldock worries me too."

"You hush up about him; he's a good man."

Mingo reached into his pocket and pulled out a crisp American five-dollar greenback and five ones. "Here, take dis money. Things will get worse before de war ends. I'll do what I can to keep an eye on dis place. I love you."

Molly's eyes watered. "Please be careful."

They held each other in silence for a long time; then Mingo brushed his hands along her hips. Taking her chin in his hands and lifting her face to his, he kissed her, held her tight, then said, "I've got to go."

In tears, Molly ran back to the house.

Mingo couldn't get his mind off her as he walked in a daze down the trail that led to the railroad. Beyond Chunky Pond, a rifle shot in the distance startled him from his reverie. He stopped to listen. Several blasts followed in short order. He knew the pattern - return fire. He drew his pistol and trotted through the forest toward the firefight.

As he worked his way through the trees, he glimpsed several blue-jackets a quarter mile away advancing toward him. Several stopped and fired. A staccato of bullets ripped through the trees that made him worry about being hit by friendly fire. Then he saw their objective; between him and the advancing troops someone fired a few sporadic shots from a bayhead. He figured that with luck he could come up behind the sharpshooters and pick off one or two. He crept forward in a crouch to stay hidden in the undergrowth.

Not far ahead through the trees Mingo heard sharp voices. "We got to move. Don't you see all those nigger soldiers?"

"I see 'em all right. I'm goin' git one."

"Come on, boy. You goin' git us both kilt. We can't fight the entire Yankee army. Run!"

"Just a damn second. Give me one last shot."

Mingo crept toward the voices until he saw two men, one wearing a gray jacket and the other dressed in tattered civilian clothes who aimed a shotgun that he had braced against a limb. From a crouch, Mingo raised his pistol in one smooth motion and squeezed off a round. The bullet's impact spun the enemy to the ground. Even from a distance, Mingo saw blood soak his shirt under the armpit. The other soldier dove into a palmetto patch. Mingo fired at him and missed.

He dropped to one knee scanning for more targets. Dead palmetto fronds crackled as the Rebel soldier ran away from the approaching Yankee skirmish line.

Mingo threw his hands up and yelled. "Don't shoot!"

Someone ordered, "Ceasefire! Hold your fire!"

A black soldier with master sergeant's chevrons on his sleeves and soaked in sweat walked up. With his pistol pointed at Mingo's chest, he demanded, "Who are you, and what the hell are you doin'?"

"My name's Mingo. I'm a scout for Major Weeks."

The sergeant's pistol didn't waver. "What are you doin' here?"

"I got bushwhacked on a patrol. I was workin' my way back to de railroad when I stumbled upon dis firefight. I thought I could help. You can see I ain't no Rebel."

"You're a deserter."

"I work with Brutus, a big black man. You must know him. He can vouch for me. He's a scout on de Clay Landing raid."

The sergeant instructed a soldier to take Mingo's pistol. After the man had secured the weapon, the top kick pointed his toward the sky and eased the hammer down with his thumb. "Keep him under guard. His story is easy to check. Brutus just happens to be with the company right now."

In ten minutes, the sergeant returned with Brutus who ran to Mingo and wrapped him in a bear hug that squeezed the air from his lungs.

Brutus said, "The corporal with your patrol reported you were shot."

"My horse was shot from under me. Comin' back to find Major Weeks, I stumbled upon dis skirmish. I shot dat dead Rebel over yonder."

"Major Weeks and de main force is down de road headin' to Cedar Key. We're a rear guard coverin' de detachment. Rebs keep pesterin' us."

As they talked, two of the soldiers walked to the dead man. As they rolled him over to rifle his pockets, his hat fell away exposing his blond hair that Mingo recognized. He ran to the body, stopped, and turned away, bending over with his hands on his knees. "Little bastard ain't old enough to shave," a soldier said.

Brutus put an arm around Mingo and whispered, "It ain't your fault. Boy ought not to have been out here."

The sergeant asked, "You know the whippersnapper?"

Brutus said, "We worked on his daddy's farm. He was a good boy."

The sergeant said, "I don't care if you knew the little bastard or not. He was tryin' to kill my men and got what he deserved. Damned Rebels will sacrifice their own chil'luns to keep us down."

Brutus protested, "De boy's folks is good people. Treated us better than any white folks ever did."

In a choked voice, Mingo added, "We're takin' his body to his Mama."

The sergeant barked, "No you ain't. We've got a job to do and you're subject to military discipline. We ain't got time for sentiment."

Brutus stepped toward the sergeant. "You heard us. We're takin' dis boy home. We ain't enlisted in no army. We're free men."

The sergeant yanked his pistol and pointed it at Brutus, "Drop your weapons! You're both under arrest. Corporal, take them under guard to Major Weeks so he can deal with their insubordination."

All day the U.S. 2nd Florida Cavalry played cat and mouse with the C.S.A. 2nd Florida Cavalry. The Rebel cavalrymen, out-numbered and outgunned, took pots shots now and then, but mostly stayed out of rifle range or fell back as soon as the Yankee rear guard advanced toward them. At Station Four, Major Weeks stopped the column. After posting pickets, he said to Captain Pease, "Take charge. We'll bivouac here for the night. I'll take the prisoners on to Cedar Key and bring back transportation for the wounded and contrabands. I have to deal with an issue that's come up with two of my scouts."

The major found Mingo and Brutus guarded by a corporal who he dismissed.

As soon as the guard was out of hearing, the major said, "What the hell happened?"

Mingo summarized the afternoon's events.

When he finished the major shook his head and said, "This damn war has brought us so low that we're killing our own children! The sergeant was in his rights, but I can't blame you two for being upset. If anybody asks, tell them you got latrine duty as punishment. Stay away from that sergeant. Now, get some rest. I have to take the prisoners to Cedar Key."

Mingo said, "What about Billy?"

"I'll send a soldier under white flag to the Rebel lines to report the casualty and determine if the Rebs found the body. They'll have to worry about him. That's the best I can do."

Drained from his eventful day, Mingo collapsed into a fitful sleep. Dreams of blood and death haunted him as a white boy's contorted and ghoulish face startled him awake again and again. At dawn, still exhausted, he washed in the ditch water by the railroad track and then lined up beside the mess tent for coffee.

Before he made it into the shelter, rifle fire sputtered beyond the picket line. Mingo ignored the commotion in the belief the Rebels were only harassing the detachment like the day before. Then pandemonium broke out among the troops as the sound of continuous musketry rolled across the camp. A bugle sounded.

Mingo climbed up the railroad grade. From the high ground, he saw a horde wearing washed-out gray and faded butternut shirts rushing toward the camp. Flashes from their rifles cut through the morning mist and the gray smoke that boiled around the Rebels. Bullets whined through the camp dropping several soldiers. Captain Pease yelled for the sergeants to put out skirmishers on the right and left and to counterattack.

Soldiers dropped their breakfasts, grabbed their rifles and ran for cover. A deep boom drowned out the rifle fire for an instant. A shell screeched overhead and then exploded at the mess tent killing several soldiers.

Mingo picked himself up from the ground. After checking himself for wounds, he pulled an injured, unconscious soldier into the ditch. A twisted, steel peg protruded through the soldier's bloody pants. Mingo yanked it free from his thigh. Blood gushed from the wound as Mingo snugged a bandana around it. As blood soaked the cloth, Rebel fire increased.

Wounded and stunned soldiers staggered around disoriented or else huddled behind cover. Most hotfooted it into the ditches or the woods beside the railroad grade. Some retreated along the tracks toward Cedar Key.

Every few minutes the Rebel cannon fired. After the soldiers dispersed, the shells caused few casualties, but the ear shattering noise and the explosions demoralized the troops. Captain Pease howled for a counterattack. The Rebs shot down those who rushed forward causing their comrades to stay hunkered down.

The Rebels poured steady fire into the Yankee position. Mingo could see muzzle flashes through the smoke. He fired toward them without knowing if he hit anyone. The Rebel cannon ranged in on the troops who cowered below the railroad embankment. A shell ripped into it that blew up several soldiers. "Fall back, men! Fall back!" the captain ordered above the din.

From behind the Confederate line a bugle sounded. The Rebel fire diminished. As the smoke from their guns drifted up, Mingo saw the enemy soldiers pulling back and then he heard galloping horses.

He turned to see Major Weeks riding hard from Cedar Key toward the camp with scores of troopers. The reinforcements swept up Captain Pease and his men, pulling them forward. The Rebels mounted their horses and rode away before the Yankee troops could overwhelm them. Union cavalry chased them for two miles but stopped when Rebel fire limited pursuit on the narrow road.

Major Weeks ordered Lt. Poole to maintain contact with the Rebs with a small detachment while the Major returned to Station Four to consolidate his force.

Near sunset, a courier sent by Lt. Poole galloped into Station Four on a lathered horse. The report he delivered required action. "Lt. Poole says the Rebels have been reinforced at Yearty's farm. He estimates they have 500 men and four cannons. He's fighting a rear guard action."

As the courier finished his report, musketry rumbled in the distance. Major Weeks shouted to his officers, "March the men back to Cedar Key on the double. We can't stop a night attack by such a large force."

In good order, the troops marched across the trestle to the town. An hour later, Dickison's men stormed into the abandoned camp to recapture the wagons, supplies, and cattle that Major Weeks had confiscated on the foray.

In his after-action report, Dickison reported that his force of 145 men had killed, wounded, or captured seventy Union troops. Major Weeks reported his losses as five killed, seventeen wounded, and three captured.

CHAPTER FORTY-EIGHT

KEY WEST

Florida

After a hearty meal prepared and served by former slaves who had enlisted in the navy, General Newton, Rear Admiral Stribling and several officers sat smoking Cuban cigars in the officers' mess at Fort Taylor in Key West. General Newton lifted his glass of Madeira. "Here's to Lincoln and another Union victory at Fort Fisher in Wilmington."

"Hear, hear," the officers chorused with glasses raised.

The general took a swallow and continued, "Gentlemen, now that Wilmington is closed, what port will the Rebs use?"

A navy captain said, "We have ships on station at all their major ports and their navy is destroyed. The chance of sailing through the blockade is low, say one in ten, and then with only tiny boats."

General Newton smiled, "I agree. Still, they're compelled to try, and I believe the most logical place is the West Coast of Florida."

Admiral Stirbling said, "Why? No decent ports are open. Fort Pickens commands the harbor at Pensacola. Our station at Egmont Key has closed Tampa Bay. It's the same at Charlotte

Harbor. We even control the blackwater streams up and down the coast. They're hard pressed to bring a stinking mullet skiff into the Gulf."

The general leaned back in his chair. "Admiral, you're one hundred per cent correct, but the enemy is desperate. Dixie risked having his force cut off in South Florida when he attacked Fort Myers last week. The only thing that made him withdraw was the 110 New York's stiff resistance. His aggressive response to Major Weeks' Clay Landing Raid leads me to believe he's probing our defenses for a weak spot."

The general stood up and walked over to a framed chart of the Gulf Coast from Mobile Bay to Key West. He stabbed his finger at it. "Right here, gentlemen. St. Marks is their last hope. Although you have a gunboat stationed off shore to choke off all the passes, one ship can't do it up there like you've done at Tampa Bay and Charlotte Harbor. We can beat the traitors to the punch by securing the St. Marks River.

The general's aide said, "It's mostly swamp and marsh up there. There are damn few roads, so it's hard to maneuver with any sizable force. The terrain works in the Rebs' favor. They can easily mobilize up there too. A railroad runs straight from St. Marks to Tallahassee. Dickison can respond faster to a raid at St. Marks than he did to the one against Clay Landing. Our troops could bog down and be cut off up there."

"It's tough for us, as well. Unless the coast is secure, it's dangerous to send a gunboat up river where it could get trapped. Remember how Dixie's cavalry captured the *Columbine* on the St. Johns River last summer," Admiral Stribling added.

The general changed the subject. "What do you all think about Lincoln's idea of amnesty for the traitors who encouraged secession and started the war?"

An aide answered, "Sir, with all due respect to the President, I think it's preposterous. Every secessionist office holder and every staff officer ought to be hanged. The rest should be stripped of their civil rights. This war has cost us too much to forgive and forget."

Several officers lifted their glasses and clinked them together, "Hear, hear!" When no one came to the defense of Lincoln, the general said, "Perhaps we should call it a night. We have another busy day tomorrow training the new recruits flooding into our lines."

As the officers said their goodnights and filed from the room, General Newton motioned for Admiral Stribling to hang back.

After a black orderly closed the door, he said, "Admiral, I've got a proposition that you should find appealing."

The admiral smiled and said, "Last time somebody said that I had to grab my billfold to keep it from walking off."

"Seriously," the general continued, "The war's all but over. Lee can't hang on and Johnston's on the run toward North Carolina with Sherman on his ass. How long you figure it can last - a month, six weeks?"

"I'd say six weeks. For all practical purposes, Lee's whipped. I don't believe he'll let his men be slaughtered."

"Exactly, the rebellion's finished. Have you thought about where that leaves us?"

"Not really."

"I have. Once the Rebels surrender, there'll be demobilization. Most of us will be discharged. The rest will be stuck commanding occupation troops in some shabby, Southern, backwater town doing our best to keep whites from killing uppity freedmen. I don't know about you, but that prospect doesn't sound appealing."

"What are you saying?"

"Hear me out. We need to make a name for ourselves before Lee surrenders. Unless we do something bold that the public and Congress will notice, we're nothing but surplus officers destined for oblivion."

"What can we do here? Nobody cares what happens in Florida. Nobody knows about the tough, nasty work that we do here day in and day out that allows the glory hounds to win battles."

"My point exactly. Do you realize that Tallahassee is the only capital east of the Mississippi that hasn't fallen?"

"Hadn't thought about it."

"It's true, and you know what?" The general slammed his hand on the table. "We can liberate Tallahassee! The press and Congress will notice the downfall of the last Confederate capital."

"Dramatic, yes, but easier said than done. Remember Olustee and Major Weeks' skirmish at Station Four. If he hadn't scurried back to Cedar Key when Dickison came with reinforcements from General Miller, he'd have been overrun. In fact, we're lucky Dixie didn't take Cedar Key. It's a long march from the Gulf to Tallahassee. The Floridians will rally with everything they have to defend their capital."

"Major Weeks is a good officer, but timorous. Speed, Admiral. That's the key to the whole operation. Shock them. March to Tallahassee before General Miller knows what hit him. If we occupy the capital, Governor Milton's Secesh government will collapse. With Tallahassee under federal control, there are enough Union men in Florida to organize a loyal government. They'd have done so long ago if the Secessionists didn't intimidate them."

"From a strategic standpoint, it'll put pressure on Lee and Johnston to surrender, but..."

The admiral hesitated which worried General Newton. Unless he convinced Admiral Stribling to support his plan, he had no way to capture Tallahassee. He needed navy transports to get his troops to St. Marks and navy gunboats to secure his supply line while he marched to the capital.

Then the admiral continued, "What do you consider an overwhelming force?"

"I'd say everything we can spare; a thousand army troops. You could provide five hundred sailors and marines."

The admiral gave a low whistle. "I don't know if we have the transports."

General Newton pressed ahead. "The logistics we can solve. The question is, are you with me? We'll surprise the Rebs and capture St. Marks. I will take personal command. My troops will move up the railroad to Tallahassee so fast, Miller won't know whether he's coming or going."

The admiral extended his hand. "John, I'm with you all the way."

At a joint staff conference the next morning, General Newton took the lead, "Gentlemen, Admiral Stribling and I have decided to embark on an operation that will shorten the war and bring Florida back into the Union. Its success depends on absolute surprise. What you hear in this room is top secret and restricted to a need-to-know basis. Is that understood?"

The officers assented without hesitation. "Good. Our objective is to close the last port on the Gulf Coast and capture Tallahassee starting with an amphibious assault at St. Marks. When it's captured, we'll thrust straight up the railroad to Tallahassee. Any questions?"

An army major said, "Sir, can troops be ferried up river to St. Marks? If not, we have a problem. The terrain is mostly marsh and swamp between the coast and St. Marks. If the navy can't get transports up river, we'll have to disembark the troops at the lighthouse on the coast and fight our way to the town along one narrow road."

The General dismissed the observation. "Our landing will be a surprise. Their pickets can't slow down the force we'll use. Major Weeks can put his black scouts to work. They'll find alternative routes to St. Marks."

"Sir---"

The general interrupted, "This will be a joint operation. We'll use every resource at our disposal including Major Weeks' 2nd Florida Cavalry at Cedar Key."

One morning in late February, 1865, before reveille, Major Weeks pulled back the canvas flap on Brutus and Mingo's tent on Sea Horse Key. "Get up! We have work to do. A launch is waiting to take us to the *Alliance* to meet General Newton. Hurry up."

Major Weeks held the tent flap open to let the cold wind that whipped off the bay blast through the shelter to rouse the men as fast as possible. As the scouts rolled out from under their wool navy blankets, they jumped into their clothes, buttoned their pea coats and pulled wool watch caps over their ears as fast as possible. As he stepped outside, Brutus said, ""It's cold as a witch's tit. Look at the scud flyin' off de whitecaps in de bay."

Mingo asked, "What's up, Major? I thought we was takin' new recruits to de firin' range today."

"Change of plans, I'll tell you about it when we're on board *Alliance*."

At the beach, sailors pushed the launch into the chop, scrambled aboard and then bent to the oars with all their strength to make headway against the wind and spray that covered the boat with a salty mist.

Once on board *Alliance*, Major Weeks walked his scouts straight to the officers' wardroom. "Grab some breakfast. Warm up. I'll be back shortly."

Brutus mumbled, "Somethin' big is in de works."

"You reckon Dixie has concentrated for an attack and we missed it?"

"Naw, not likely. Nobody has reported anything unusual."

Neither man had finished their scrambled eggs with bacon when the Major returned. He led them down the gangway to a conference room where an ensign and an army captain were bent over a large chart.

When Major Weeks and the two black men dressed much like ordinary sailors entered the room, the captain and the other officer looked up in surprise. Before either could say anything, Major Weeks cut them short. "I'm pleased to introduce the men who lead a guerilla group that scouts for us, Mingo and Brutus. Their reports have allowed us to make many successful raids. With their help, we've destroyed all the salt works around the Big Bend. They'll be invaluable to us to plan the assault."

Noticing the officers' misgivings, Major Weeks continued, "Let there be no misunderstanding; these men know what they're doing. You will cooperate with them one hundred per cent as if they were fellow officers. Do I make myself clear?"

"Yes, sir," both officers shot back.

After the introductions were completed, Major Weeks said, "Here's the situation. Admiral Stribling and General Newton have decided that a joint naval and army force will assault St. Marks. Once the navy controls the river and the town, the army will advance up the railroad and occupy Tallahassee."

Mingo interrupted, "Tallahassee? That's at least twenty-five miles from the coast. Dickison will come lickety-split like he did when we raided Clay Landing."

"That's why I've included you to help plan the operation. Your assignment is to find routes from the coast to St. Marks and figure out a way to stop Dixie from reinforcing General Miller at Tallahassee. Without reinforcements, the enemy's home guard doesn't have a prayer to stop us."

The ensign interjected. "I see a major problem already. The only charts we have are coastal charts that are out of date. The most current is 1858. Look here," he leaned over the table and pointed. "The coast is well-demarcated, but inland there's no detail. Only the main roads and streams are mapped. It shows only one road from Lighthouse Point to St. Marks."

The captain said, "We have to have local knowledge. We have a Post Office Department map that's more detailed inland. Unfortunately, it is also from 1858. At least it aligns with the coastal chart as far as I can tell."

Mingo said, "I'm familiar with de Post Office map. It's accurate as far as I know. Nobody has reported any new roads in the St. Marks area after raids or scoutin' missions. I'm not surprised either. It'd be hard to build a new road up there 'cause it's mostly salt marsh dat transitions into swamp. When is de go date? Do we have time to scout?"

Major Weeks said, "No, General Newton wants troops embarked today. He's bringing everybody from Cedar Key except a guard detail. We have six companies to load on transports. I've got to supervise that. We're to be prepared to sail tonight. Have a plan ready for my review by noon."

When Major Weeks left the room, the four men stood looking at one another. The white officers had no confidence in the black irregulars. The black men felt ill at ease and unwelcome. After a few seconds, the navy ensign said, "We better get started. We can't afford to waste time. First, let's verify that the map and the charts align."

A cursory examination showed that they matched, but with so little detail on each, there had to be gaps. Mingo said, "I've scouted up de St. Marks River by canoe. Dey look consistent wid what I saw. I can tell you one thing sure nuff; it'll be hard to take gunboats up river. De channel's narrow and twisty. The Rebs have a battery at Port Leon dat de ships will have to pass. They've also placed torpedoes and obstructions in de river."

The ensign concurred, "Expect torpedoes. After the Rebels sank the *Cairo* at Vicksburg, they've used them all over. Dixie sank four ships in the St. John's last year. In December, the infernal machines sank a tug in Mobile Bay."

Mingo said, "Wid so much marsh along de coast, I don't know where to land troops except at de light house or Port Leon. Can we take transports upriver dat far?"

The ensign traced the river with his finger. "It'll be tough but doable. The river has enough depth according to the chart."

The army captain said, "If the navy can disembark troops at Port Leon, we could have a two-pronged attack. We'll bring a column up the road from Lighthouse Point. The other column can proceed directly from Port Leon to Newport. The Newport Bridge is the key. If we can secure it and take the town, St. Marks will be isolated."

The captain asked, "Is there any other way across the St. Marks River?"

Mingo said, "De only bridge is at Newport, but several miles up river, there's a place called Rockhaven where troops could ford. A little farther north, de river goes underground at a natural bridge. An old road parallels de River along de east bank that we considered using to bring out contrabands from plantations farther north. We never did because de Rebels kept guards posted at de East River Bridge. I don't know how passable de old road is. I've never scouted it myself. Have you, Brutus?"

"No. If de road hasn't been used, it'll be slow going. It's rough country."

The captain said, "Taking that into account, securing the Newport Bridge is even more important. We'll have to move fast. Let's assign a company of cavalry for that objective."

The ensign offered, "How does this sound? We'll land troops at both Port Leon and the Lighthouse. Cavalry will race to secure the East River Bridge and Newport Bridge. Once Newport is secure, the main force will swing south to assault St. Marks. Meanwhile, gunboats will push upriver and bombard the town. Any Rebel troops still there will be trapped at the confluence of the St. Marks and the Wakulla Rivers."

The captain said, "Should work. An infantry company can keep the Rebels bottled up while the main force marches to Tallahassee."

Mingo said, "We're forgetting one thing. Major Weeks ordered us to prevent the Rebs from bringing reinforcements. As soon as dey find out we've landed, dey'll bring troops from all over North Florida and South Georgia. At Olustee, rebels brought reinforcements by train which was a force multiplier for Dixie."

The four men studied the postal map to find the best places to block reinforcements. The captain sighed, "Even if we control the railroad between St. Marks and Tallahassee, the Rebs can still bring reinforcements to the capital by train from the east and west. I don't see how we can block those routes."

While the others talked, Brutus kept studying the map then interjected, "Here's how. Tallahassee is between de Aucilla River on de east and de Ochlocknoy on de west. Raiders could take out de trestles over both rivers."

The captain said, "Why didn't I see that sooner? We have a plan. Let's put it in writing for Major Weeks. We'll keep it simple since General Newton will change it anyway."

After more discussion on each point, the men reached a consensus which the captain transcribed.

Recommended Order of Battle

Combined Naval/Army Operation against St. Marks and Tallahassee, Florida

1. Raiding parties shall proceed to the Aucilla River and Ochlockony River railroad trestles and destroy them in order to prevent Rebel reinforcements from reaching Tallahassee by rail.

2. Land cavalry and infantry at Lighthouse Point. Cavalry shall proceed up the road to secure the East River Bridge.

3. Once East River Bridge is secure, cavalry shall proceed to Newport and secure the bridge over the St. Marks River.

4. Infantry shall proceed double-quick to Newport then swing south to attack St. Marks.

5. Block the Rebel troops at St. Marks from leaving. Once that is accomplished, the main force shall swing north via the railroad to attack Tallahassee.

6. The navy shall land a force at Port Leon and secure it.

7. Sailors and marines shall proceed via the road to the Newport Bridge where they shall combine forces with the army. The navy shall run gunboats up river to support the expedition from the rear by preventing the enemy from crossing the St. Marks River.

8. Navy gunboats shall destroy the batteries at Port Leon and St. Marks.

9. Speed is essential to secure the East River and Newport bridges before they can be defended or destroyed.

When the captain finished the last sentence he said, "Looks good, but we need a map. I'll sketch it out and attach it. A weak point is protecting the expedition's rear. If the navy can't secure Port Leon, the advance should be reconsidered."

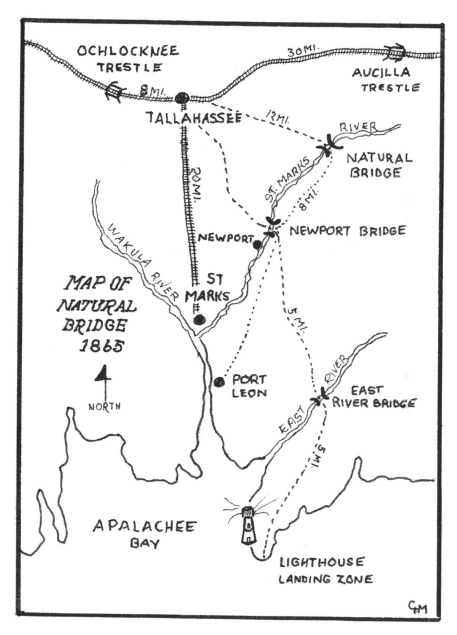

The ensign said, "I concur. We need to stress that to Major Weeks. Another problem is uncertainty about the force the cavalry will encounter. If there's concentrated resistance, the entire operation will bog down."

"Do you know what we can expect?" the captain asked Mingo.

"Our missions up dat way were to find salt works and liberate slaves. We only encountered pickets. Only home guards were posted at East River Bridge. A good squad can take 'em out."

The ensign asked, "How about Port Leon?"

"Hard to know. We always slipped by at night in canoes. An alarm was raised once. Nothing came of it except a few wild shots. Pickets probably weren't sure what they saw in de dark. We confirmed batteries cover de river."

At noon, Major Weeks returned. When the captain handed him the battle plan, he read it and then studied the map for several minutes. "Good job, men. What are the weaknesses?"

The captain said, "The railroad bridges over the Aucilla and Ochlockony have to be destroyed to prevent Rebel reinforcements and Port Leon has to be secured so the general wouldn't have to worry about being cut off as he moves inland."

"Men, I like your plan. I think the general and admiral should too."

Mingo suggested, "Me and Brutus can raid de railroad bridges."

"I rather you stay with the expedition. We can use Strickland's guerilla band to take out the Aucilla Bridge. He knows the area and can avoid Rebel patrols. We can send that fellow, Green, who helped us raid salt works at Apalachee Bay to take out the Ochlockony trestle."

Mingo asked, "Can we trust dem for such important assignments?"

"I think so. They work with us fairly well. They know the land and Union sympathizers will help them. You two could do it with an army patrol, but if anybody spotted you, the alarm would be raised.

Strickland and Green can slip around without anybody reporting them to the home guard."

"Strickland hasn't always cooperated with us."

"I know Strickland is obstreperous. I'll send written orders to him and Green so that there is no possible misunderstanding."

"What you mean obstrep---?"

"Hard to control. Anyway, the admiral trusts them enough to supply them with arms and ammunition. They've raised hell behind Rebel lines."

Brutus added, "Yup, and terrorized civilians all around Big Bend too. Dey burn out people who won't help dem. Dey'll do de job all right, but der own way."

"Good point, Brutus. They better follow my orders to a 'T.' Warn them that if they mess up, the navy will cut off their supplies. That will get their attention. I'll write the orders right now."

February 27, 1865
To: William Strickland
From: Major Weeks, United States Army

You are to proceed immediately upon receipt of this order with the men you deem necessary and in the manner you deem most expeditious to the railroad trestle across the Aucilla River. You shall destroy the tracks and burn the trestle.

Signed: Major Weeks, US Army

After Weeks prepared a similar order for Green to destroy the Ochlockony trestle, he excused himself in order to brief the plan to

General Newton and to Lt. Commander Gibson, the ranking naval officer in the fleet. The officers liked the plan but rejected the recommendation that the cavalry secure the bridges.

Lt. Commander Gibson said, "I agree the advance has to move fast, but we don't have the transports to take horses. We hardly have enough for the men. Plus, disembarking horses at sea will probably slow the operation more than the time gained later."

Major Weeks argued that the first squad should be mounted, but General Newton sided with Lt. Commander Gibson. "It will be too hard to offload horses, particularly if this damn wind holds. A few mounted infantry won't make a difference anyway. I'll put a company in the lead so any resistance can be overwhelmed without bogging down the advance."

Lt. Commander Gibson said, "When we informed Commander Shufeldt, who commands the West Gulf Blockading Squadron, he promised to send every ship that he could spare to help us. We'll rendezvous at the Ochlockony Buoy after dark. A pilot will take the transports across the bar to land your infantry at the lighthouse. We'll take gunboats and transports with marines up the St. Marks River to Port Leon."

"I need the navy's commitment that my army can be re-supplied, and I can't risk Rebel troops crossing the St. Marks River behind me."

"Don't fret. I have no doubt that my marines can take Port Leon. My gunboats will blast any Rebels who attempt to cross the river. "

"You better. If you fail, I'll have a thousand men cut off without supplies."

CHAPTER FORTY-NINE

SNYDER ISLAND

Florida

As soon as the conference ended, Major Weeks rushed to tell his scouts that the plan as modified was a go. To make sure the guerillas destroyed the trestles as soon as possible, his scouts had to deliver orders right away to Strickland and Green at their hide outs on Snyder Island and Shell Island where the US Navy supplied them.

Mingo held a cutter so close-hauled in the heavy air that the rigging hummed as the boat sped across the gulf at hull speed toward Snyder Island. As the sun set in an orange blaze, Mingo could still differentiate it from the low-lying coastline. A half mile from shore, Mingo brought the cutter into the wind, dropped the sails and ordered the signalman to wig-wag the recognition sign.

As the sailor waggled the flag and sailors secured the flapping sails, Mingo slipped his telescope from its case and scanned the shoreline. Not so much as wisp of smoke hinted that anybody lived on the island. In the fading light, he couldn't see anything but forest.

Usually pickets responded to the signal flag right away. When they didn't, Mingo worried that Rebels might have attacked the camp. As he scanned the tree line for the last time before the light completely failed, he detected a man high in a tall bay pine waving the counter-sign using a signal flag that was solid red with a white square in the middle.

"Hoist the jib, pull the hook. We'll run her up to the beach."

As the bow swung with the wind, Mingo caught a breaker. As it passed under the boat, the cutter wallowed until he pulled the tiller to catch a gust and regain momentum. Pushed by the waves and the breeze, the sloop surfed toward shore until it scraped bottom as white water swirled around it. The next swell lifted the boat again plunging it farther onto the beach. Marines jumped over the side sprinting for the vegetation line to secure a perimeter.

As two marines tied the launch to a tree with a heavy line, Mingo drew his pistol, jumped overboard and ran across a narrow, sandy beach where he took cover behind stubby palmettos burnt by salt spray. From the woods farther inland he heard a muffled shout against the wind that sounded like, "Who are you?"

Mingo cupped his hands around his mouth and yelled, "Mingo, with orders from Major Weeks."

In the dusk a hundred yards from the beach, he could make out a man flanked on each side by guards with rifles. "Is that you, Strickland?" he yelled.

"Yes, relax."

Mingo holstered his pistol.

The men flanking Strickland stopped. He walked up to Mingo without extending his hand or saying hello.

Mingo reached inside his pea coat, pulled out a folded paper, and handed it to Strickland who stuffed it in his pants pocket. "I can't read it in this light. What is it?"

Mingo recited the order almost verbatim. Strickland asked, "Why the hell does he want to do that?

"I don't know. My assignment is to deliver de order. Major Weeks said to tell you dat your mission is important. If you don't follow orders, he won't supply your band wid anymore supplies, arms and ammunition."

"Weeks must be plannin' a big raid. Where?"

"Don't know. I follow orders and don't ask questions."

"That's why you nigras make good slaves."

"Strickland, you've got orders. I suggest you move."

CHAPTER FIFTY

OCHLOCKONY BUOY
Florida

Well after midnight, Mingo sailed the cutter near enough to the beach at Shell Point to allow Brutus to wade ashore. "How are you goin' to git to Green without bein' shot? You can't just mosey into his camp in the middle of de night."

"I'm familiar with his place from de raids we made on salt works together. I know de trails. I can git in."

With that, Brutus disappeared into the blackness. Mingo expected a shot any second and jumped when an owl hooted nearby. He took a deep breath and then said to the marine by him, "Feels like de wind is dyin' down and moisture in de air is buildin'. It feels warmer too. Is de cold front finally passin' through?"

"Looks like it, but if the wind drops, fog will roll in."

"Dat worries me. We got to drop Green at the Ochlockony River and get back to the ship real quick, or we'll have a hell of a time finding it."

An owl hooted again which was followed by a sharp, three-note bobwhite whistle. "Hold fire. Brutus is coming in," Mingo told the squad leader who passed the word to the marine pickets.

Brutus walked forward with Green and introduced him to Mingo. "Dis here is Mr. Green. He led us to several salt factories. I never had so much fun bustin' stuff."

"Glad to meet you, sir. Did Brutus tell you why we're here?"

"No."

"Mr. Green, we need your help again. I have orders for you to destroy de railroad trestle at de Ochlocknoy River. How soon can you move out?"

"Right away."

Do you have enough men?"

"I've got all I need. The Rebs don't post guards up there."

"How will you go?"

"Up the river is quickest. I have a canoe hidden near the mouth."

"Gather up your gear. Let's sail."

By the time Green returned to the boat, the wind had backed off making the waves sound louder and more powerful. As each whitecap reached the cutter, the marines shoved it over the breaker toward deep water until it floated enough for them scramble aboard.

After men hoisted the sails, Mingo brought the sloop to a beam reach although the wind barely filled the canvass. After an hour, the breeze died. "Let's row, men," the marine sergeant said. "We need to make the mouth of the Ochlockony before dawn."

The marines rowed all the way past Piney Island before a puff filled the sail from across the stern. As the boat picked up speed before the wind, Mingo ordered the oars shipped. In the erratic puffs, the cutter wallowed in the troughs that kept Mingo shifting the tiller from side to side to avoid jibing.

"Keep your heads low, men," the sergeant warned. "If the boom comes across and conks you, it'll crack your skull."

The sailboat made such slow headway in the light air that Mingo didn't tack into Ochlocknoy Bay until dawn. On the lee of Ochlocknoy Point, the wind completely died, forcing the marines to row.

"Where do you want us to drop you, Mr. Green?" Mingo asked.

"They patrol the mouth of the river. Land at Shell Hammock. From there, I can slip around them."

Mingo held the cutter in the middle of Ochlockony Bay. "Sure wish we had made it before daylight. Thank goodness de fog is thick enough to hide us from pickets."

As the marines rowed farther up the bay, the fog thinned. "It's so bright now, we better land. Pickets will spot us if we go to Shell Hammock," Mingo said as he pushed the tiller to turn the cutter toward shore.

"Keep a sharp eye," the sergeant ordered.

The launch slid over wavelets as the marines powered it toward shore with rhythmic strokes. A quarter mile from shore a shot cracked. The lookout at the bow fell backward among the rowers. Oars clashed together and the tiller flexed as the cutter veered.

A bullet whined by Mingo's head. As more lead ripped into the boat's hull, the sergeant yelled, "They're aiming at you. Get down!"

Smoke puffs drifted above the scrub oaks along the beach, but no enemy could be seen. "Let's give them a volley. On my count, fire," the sergeant said.

"One, two, three!" The marines lifted their rifles above the gunwales firing toward the smoke. Everything stayed quiet for a few seconds, then more bullets whacked into the boat.

"Pull, men, pull. We've got to get out of range," the sergeant yelled. As the marines rowed away, a corporal cut off the sleeve of the wounded man's shirt so that he could examine the wound where the bullet had slashed across his bicep. "You ain't hit bad. Flesh wound," the corporal said as he tied a bandage around the man's upper arm.

Mingo said, "Mr. Green, now dat we've been spotted, what do you suggest?"

"No choice but to head back around Ochlockony Point to Dickerson Bay. Drop me off at Stokley Landing which is around Piney Island. We'll have to go overland."

In the early afternoon, Green disembarked. As soon as he did so, Mingo plotted a course to the Ochlocknoy Buoy to rendezvous with the *Alliance*. "Sarge, here's de plot. We'll stay near shore as long as possible. We'll slip by Smith Island, Shell Point and den to Live Oak Island. After dat we'll be in open water and will have to dead reckon. With luck, we'll find de buoy."

As Mingo expected, the fog thickened beyond Live Oak Island. Farther from shore, it cut visibility to less than fifty feet. The only sound was the oars biting into the water until several porpoises rose near the bow exhaling with sharp blows. They swam for several minutes beside the cutter, dove, and disappeared.

"Get some sleep, Mingo," the sergeant suggested. "There's nothing you can do till we reach the ship."

Mingo lay down atop the lazarette with a sail bundled around him. He closed his eyes, visualized Molly's face and slept until crashing thunder startled him awake. He jumped up and banged his head on the boom. The blow staggered him, but the bump on the head worried him less than the racket.

"What is it, Sarge?" Mingo yelled.

"A ship!" the sergeant shouted above the clamor. "Sounds like it's closing."

The marines shipped their oars. Everybody in the boat concentrated to determine the direction from which the reverberations came or to glimpse the ship through the fog. Mingo snatched open the lazarette hatch and grabbed a two-foot, tin horn. He pressed his lips against the mouthpiece, took a deep breath and blew as hard as could. The toot sounded unimpressive compared to the roar echoing all around him.

The cutter shuddered from a pressure wave as a huge steel bow broke through the fog. The roar intensified, gears clashed, but the ship didn't slow. The small boat lifted and spun sideways.

The lettering on the ship's stern read *USS Alliance*. "Keep it in sight. Row!" Mingo jammed the tiller over as far as possible to swing his craft behind the ship.

The cutter pivoted in a slow arc to follow in the gunboat's wake. In a half mile, the ship stopped dead in the water. As the sloop came along side, sailors dropped a rope ladder to it so that the men could scurry up. When Mingo reached the deck, Major Weeks stood at the rail. "Are the raids against the bridges underway?"

"Yes, sir. Strickland and Green have your orders and warning. We couldn't land Green at de Ochlocknoy River. Rebel pickets spotted us and drove us off, so we dropped him off at Oyster Bay so he could go overland."

"Did you explain how important their assignments are to the success of the operation?"

"Yes, sir."

"Excellent, I'll pass your report to General Newton. He and Lt. Commander Gibson plan to cross the bar as soon as the fog lifts and all the ships are assembled. Only thirteen ships are present and accounted for. The transports got separated in the fog. In the meantime, let's get you fed and rested."

As soon as they had eaten, Mingo and Brutus walked on deck. As the sun rose higher and the fog lifted, they watched a remarkable armada assemble. By afternoon, thirteen steam vessels and three schooners, all flying the stars and stripes, had rendezvoused near the St. Marks' bar.

Mingo said, "Brutus, have you ever seen so many ships?"

"No, I ain't, and you can bet de Rebs ain't either. Wid so many gunboats and transports gathered here, Secesh know dat we are comin' sure nuff."

Mingo and Brutus watched the ship *Proteus* winch a launch over the side. Several officers embarked and marines rowed it to the *Alliance*. As the officers came aboard, Mingo noticed the senior naval officer wore the insignia of a commander.

"Who's dat?" Mingo asked Major Weeks.

"Commander R.W. Shufeldt. As the ranking naval officer in the fleet, he will take command from Lt. Commander Gibson. He's coming aboard to confer with General Newton."

At the joint conference, General Newton discussed the fact that the Rebels had undoubtedly seen the fleet assemble and were mobilizing to meet the assault. He concluded with a suggestion, "Let them think we assembled here because of the fog and that we're headed somewhere else. We'll sail out of sight into the Gulf and come back after dark."

Commander Shufeldt demurred, "Lt. Commander Gibson stressed that we need to surprise the Rebels in order to have the best chance for success. Sailing away and returning after dark delays the operation. The Rebels aren't likely to fall for the ruse. Besides, it'll be tough to cross the bar after dark. Weather is perfect right now. Let's commence the operation before the enemy can mobilize."

The General responded, "They'll drop their guard when they see us sail away. We can take them by surprise after dark."

Commander Shufeldt rubbed his chin. "General, you've planned the operation from the beginning. I'll defer to your judgment."

CHAPTER FIFTY-ONE

AUCILLA RIVER TRESTLE
Florida`

As Strickland watched the cutter catch the breeze to sail away close-hauled to windward, he muttered to his henchmen, "Never thought I'd see nigras order white men around. When this war's over, we're goin' have a time keepin' them in their place."

He turned to walk up the sandy trail toward his headquarters with his guards ambling behind. At the camp, Strickland stopped under a palm frond-thatched chickee where an iron Dutch oven hung over a smoldering hickory fire that didn't make enough smoke to reach the roof. Strickland lifted the globe from a kerosene light, lit the wick and replaced the glass. He twisted a tiny wheel until a yellow flame flickered bright enough for him to read the order.

"Damn Yankees are up to something. Why you reckon they want us to destroy the Aucilla Railroad Trestle?"

"Like you say, Boss, Yankees got a big raid up their sleeve."

"Where? Everyplace along the coast between Tampa Bay and Pensacola is either occupied or accessible by gunboats. Wait a minute. What about St. Marks? Yankee gunboats have never made it up river to Port Leon as far as I know. *Spray* is still in action too. If the

Yankees can take St. Marks and Newport, what stops them from taking Tallahassee? I'll bet you my last Confederate dollar they plan to attack the capital."

"Boss, you must not be too damn certain to bet Rebel money. It ain't worth horse piss."

"Shut up! That's their plan all right. I was hopin' this war would end before Tallahassee fell. If it does, Florida will be smashed like Sherman wrecked Georgia."

"What are we goin' to do?"

"You're goin' to hightail it to the Camp Island outpost. Have them telegraph Weeks' order to General Jones. Tell them it's urgent to mobilize the home guard and bring Dickison from East Florida."

"What you goin' do 'bout those orders from Weeks?"

"You let me worry about that. Move your ass right now."

As the man ran to saddle his horse, Strickland said to the others, "We ain't got no choice but to burn the trestle. Weeks will come down on us hard if we don't, but we'll take our time goin' over there. It's goin' be a dangerous mission. The roads and the railroad are under close watch up there. We've got to slip around the patrols. If the bridge is guarded, that complicates matters. Let's wear Yankee uniforms so if we're captured, we'll be treated as prisoners of war and less likely to be shot."

"What's your plan?" a man asked.

"We'll take canoes up the Wacissa Slave Canal to Goose Pasture tonight. We'll lay low for the day. After dark, we'll head upriver as far as we can, then walk to the trestle. As soon as it's burning, we'll clear out before patrols come after us."

Within an hour, Strickland set out with five men in two, hefty canoes hewn from cypress trunks. After midnight, they reached the entrance to the Slave Canal which had been dug by slaves through the swamp separating the Wacissa River from the Aucilla River to give plantations in the hill country to the north direct access to the Gulf.

Strickland had not anticipated such a difficult passage. The route had not been maintained after the Florida Atlantic and Gulf Central Railroad connected the northern tier of Middle Florida to Tallahassee and Fernandina. In the narrow, meandering Slave Canal, they had to paddle with all their strength to propel the bulky canoes against the current. In many places, overhanging brush and trees blocked the route that required the men to hack their way through. On occasion they came to deadfalls too big to chop which forced them to drag the boats over or around limbs. Near daybreak, the tired squad paddled into an open expanse by Goose Pasture where they could see open sky for the first time since they had entered the canal.

Strickland whispered, "Stay in the wild rice near the west bank. There's a farm on the east side. I don't want some peckerwood to see us and raise the alarm."

The men eased the canoes forward through the river weeds to a clearing by the water's edge that bordered a forested hillside. "Let's hide here for the day, boys."

After the men gnawed hardtack, Strickland posted a guard and said, "Turn in. We've got another hard night comin'."

After dark, the men paddled up the wide Aucilla River until they reached Welaunee Creek. Strickland led his team upstream to a tributary with almost as much flow as the main channel. He followed the narrow branch until the canoes grounded on rocks where he ordered the men out. "We'll hide the boats and walk from here." A hound bayed in the distance.

For the rest of the night, the raiders tramped northeast, staying away from farms and roads by sticking to cow trails or tracks through the forests.

At daylight, Strickland stopped. "Listen up, men. The railroad is close. From here we'll stay in the woods till we reach the tracks. The trestle should be down the grade a mile or so. With luck, there'll be no guards so we can set it afire and skedaddle."

Strickland's dead reckoning was right on target. At the tracks he ordered a scrawny youngster, nicknamed Gato by the Cuban fishermen who traded along the coast, to climb a tall tree to check for guards or patrols.

Two men lifted him on their shoulders so he could grab a limb and pull himself up into the tree. In a minute, he was at the top where he shouted to Strickland, "I can see the bridge. Nobody's around."

"You see any smoke, a handcar, a train?"

"Nothin', Boss."

"Hurry up, and git down."

The men gasped as the lad plunged toward the ground in a controlled fall by grabbing limbs or bracing at the last instant. When he reached the lowest limb, he jumped and landed on his feet laughing. Strickland admonished him, "Damn, Gato, don't scare us like that."

To stay out of sight, Strickland walked through the woods parallel to the railroad tracks until he reached the trestle where he crept up the embankment to check for guards. When he verified that no one was around, he called the men to him and said, "We'll start fires by the pillars where the cross beams are near the ground. While we're doing that, Gato, you climb a few telegraph poles, cut the wires and smash the insulators."

As soon as the men piled kindling against several pillars, Strickland pulled a pint of turpentine from his pocket. He sloshed the flammable liquid on the wood, struck a match and threw it on the tinder. Flames leaped up the support posts as the men scrambled to add wood to the fires.

One man dragged a shattered crosstie to a blaze. Others laid limbs over the kindling. Fire crackled around the pillars and along the cross beams. "Pile on the wood, boys. Them big timbers won't burn through unless there's plenty of fuel."

As the blazes roared higher, the pillars, cross braces and stringers all caught fire. Black smoke billowed above the trestle.

From atop a telegraph pole, Gato yelled, "Train, train comin' fast."

"Let's get the hell out of here," Strickland hollered. "Soldiers will be on the train."

The engineer saw the smoke from around a turn but did not realize it came from the bridge. As the train rounded the curve on a downhill grade, the fireman yelled, "Jesus Christ! The trestle's burnin'! "

The engineer realized he couldn't stop before rolling into the inferno. "Got to take her through. Pray the tracks ain't wrecked."

He smacked the throttle lever hard against the full-throttle peg.

The fireman considered jumping until he looked down at the cross ties zipping past. As the engine entered the inferno, flames boiled around the cab and smoke filled it, blocking the engineer's vision. The train swayed on the buckled tracks but didn't derail.

Once across the bridge, the engineer braked. As he wiped sweat from his brow with an oily rag, he saw the wires hanging from telegraph poles that confirmed sabotage. Troops poured from the train.

As they scattered along the grade, the bridge collapsed behind them leaving one rail cantilevered over open space.

A captain ran to the cab and shouted to the engineer, "Let's go. At the next station I'll telegraph headquarters in Tallahassee to send a detail with dogs to run down the saboteurs."

By luck, the station master at the next depot knew a nearby farmer who raised catch dogs. The commander raced to the man's house and sent him along with a mounted squad after the saboteurs.

At the bridge the hounds circled in confusion without finding a scent until a private found the tracks where Strickland's men left the area. When the farmer set the dogs on the scent, they barked with excitement, racing down the trail with the horse soldiers trotting behind.

When Strickland heard hounds barking in the distance, he stopped to listen. "Damn, how'd they get dogs on us so fast?"

With hounds on their trail, the saboteurs started running. Gato took the lead and soon pulled away from the others. Unable to maintain the pace, Strickland and another man straggled behind. When they stopped for a breather, the hounds sounded close.

"We ain't goin' to make the canoes. Split up. Hide in a swamp."

Strickland sprinted across an open field as fast as his burning lungs allowed. Gasping for breath, he stopped and yanked off his jacket. As he tossed it down, he heard excited yaps close behind.

He raced for a bayhead. At its edge, he turned to check on the hounds. To his chagrin, he saw them break into the field at a full run. He plunged through the undergrowth until he reached water. Thrashing forward he tripped on a cypress knee and fell face down in the cool liquid. He stood up, yanked his pistol from its holster and aimed at the lead dog. Click, the wet pistol misfired. From habit, he jammed the now useless weapon back into its holster.

Desperate, he looked for a way to escape. Several yards ahead, the top of a cypress tree that had blown down in a storm provided a ramp out of the water. Strickland waded to the log. Grabbing a limb, he pulled himself upon the tree trunk. As he clawed his way up, the lead hound, with slobber-covered jowls and bared teeth, jumped at him.

As the dog scratched at the log to climb up, Strickland kicked it. He grazed its head causing the hound to tumble into the water as more dogs reached the log and clawed at it in a frenzy.

Climbing higher, he didn't realize soldiers had arrived until he heard a shout, "Hands up, Yankee." In response, Strickland crouched behind a limb. A pistol fired. A bullet gouged wood by his hand. Terrified that he'd lose his balance and fall among the enraged dogs, he held onto a branch with one hand but raised the other over his head.

As Strickland balanced on the log, the farmer waded up yelling and smacking at his hounds with a stick until he forced them back. One frenzied dog lunged at him. He thumped it hard across the ribs. It splashed away yelping. The rest then cowered.

"Climb down from there," a soldier ordered.

Strickland inched down the log into the water. A private said, "Hands behind your back."

One captor snatched Strickland's pistol while another tied his arms together with a rawhide strip. Once the soldier had Strickland bound, he knocked him down. As the prisoner lifted his head out of the dark water, the private shoved it under. Bracing his legs against a root, Strickland pushed hard to propel himself far enough from his tormentor to gulp air. The enlisted man, laughing, forced him under again. Strickland gagged. Using all his strength, he forced his head up. As his torturer pushed him under water again, a NCO yelled, "Stop! He's a prisoner, for Christ's sake. Don't drown the bastard."

Two soldiers led Strickland from the swamp while the others followed the catch dogs already on another man's trail. Strickland could hear their hot barks as they closed in.

Navy Map Of Scene Of Operation Against St. Marks,

(Courtesy Florida State Archives)

THE U.S. GUNBOAT MOHAWK CHASING THE REBEL STEAMER
SPRAY INTO THE ST. MARKS RIVER

(Courtesy Florida State Archives)

CHAPTER FIFTY-TWO

As Mingo, Brutus and Major Weeks surveyed the armada, they watched *Proteus* weigh anchor and steam toward the open Gulf. One by one, all the ships fell in line like biddies following their mother hen.

"We're not crossing the bar," Mingo observed. "Officers must have decided to land somewhere else."

Major Weeks explained the change, "We're going to come back after dark. The general thought that by sailing away we could trick the Rebels into believing that the objective is somewhere else. Of course, by now the whole Rebel army may well be at the East River Bridge."

As the afternoon progressed, the wind increased. By the time the ships turned back, a fresh gale blew from the northwest that whipped up breaking chop that slapped against the ships. When *Proteus* reached the bar three hours later, continuous whitecaps stretched along it. The pilot told Commander Shufeldt, "Sir, I can't make out the channel. We have to standby until we have a lull."

"Isn't there enough water to slide the ships over the bar?"

"I can't see the channel. Can't risk it."

"First fog, now wind, what's next?" General Newton groused.

The delay frustrated the major too. "Everything is working against us," he said to Mingo. "Damn pilot is probably a Rebel. I'm asking the general for authority to land an advance party to secure the East River Bridge. Ensign Whitman can take marines in launches up the river to support us."

After the general gave Major Weeks the authority to proceed, he struggled to load sixty men with the 2nd Florida Cavalry into launches. Once lowered into the water by davits, the small boats bucked in the chop and slapped into the ship when waves crashed against them. One man crushed his hand between the ship and the launch's gunwale. A boat sank when a swell broke over it. Two men in a floundering launch fell overboard.

Despite the difficulties, Major Weeks had his men loaded and underway by midnight. Mingo and Brutus rode in the lead launch. Near shore they jumped out, wading to the beach. To their relief, no one had fired a shot at the approaching boats, but the reprieve didn't last. As the third vessel slid onto the sand, scattered shots cracked from near the lighthouse. A bullet smacked into a soldier's stomach.

Troopers jumped behind the launches or fell prone on the salt grass to return fire. Others sprinted in zigzags toward the lighthouse. On the far side of the structure, more launches landed along the beach. With the ability to fire on the building from both sides, the Yankees gained a tactical advantage. The Rebel pickets mounted their horses and galloped away.

"Mingo, you and Brutus press those riders as much as you can while I supervise the landing," the major ordered.

After gathering a squad, the two scouts trailed the rebels down a faint, double-tracked wagon road that meandered over narrow causeways and through scrub forest that squeezed the pursuers together.

At the bottlenecks, Mingo had no choice except to halt the detachment until men could scout the road for an ambush. He didn't reach the East River Bridge until just before dawn. To his surprise, he found Ensign Whitman's men guarding the bridge. "Where are the Rebs?" Mingo asked.

"They didn't have the heart to fight. Didn't fire one shot before they skeddadled. They pulled out so quick they left a horse and a few rifles."

"We haven't taken fire since the lighthouse. I don't understand it. Maybe the general's trick worked and they didn't mobilize."

"They'll show. I suggest you post sharpshooters along the river with pickets across the bridge."

When Major Weeks arrived at the bridge after daylight, he examined the position and said to Mingo and Whitman, "Well done. We should be able to hold off a Rebel attack if the damn pilot quits lollygagging and takes the transports across the bar so we'll have more men. He said he would after dawn, but I don't trust him."

He had no more than finished speaking when the sound of galloping horses rolled through the pine thickets from across the bridge. The Yankee pickets posted there opened sporadic fire. In response, continuous gunshots resonated through the brush.

"Looks like the Rebs are here in force. Mingo, take that captured horse. Ride back to the lighthouse and tell General Newton we need support on the double. Brutus, take a squad across the bridge to support the pickets."

Musketry rattled along the river for half a mile on both sides. Brutus dashed across the bridge. Union pickets fell back under withering fire that forced them to jump behind a dirt embankment as Brutus crashed down beside them.

In the woods across from the bridge, advancing Rebel soldiers dashed from tree to tree. From behind cover, they fired, reloaded and ran forward again while concentrating their fire on the men behind the embankment. Bullets slammed into the dirt so often that the soldiers hugged the ground without lifting their heads to return fire.

Major Weeks yelled, "Men, give them cover fire! Brutus, retreat! They're about to enfilade you."

Brutus and those penned down behind the embankment needed no encouragement as they were dead men unless they moved. As they sprinted for safety across the bridge, Rebel soldiers dashed forward to take positions on the far side of the embankment.

As the day brightened, the skirmish settled into a pattern. Sharpshooters across river from one another fired occasional potshots at any man foolish enough to show himself. Otherwise, the battlefield became so quiet that the soldiers could hear the breeze rustling through the pine trees. In the lulls, a casual observer might never believe that men determined to kill each other lurked all along the river.

An hour into the skirmish, the major said to Brutus, "Move ten more men into position to help cover the bridge. Looks like they're concentrating for a charge."

As Brutus waved the men closer to the bridge, the Rebels discharged a volley from across the river followed by a yell that rolled through the pines like men calling up the dead.

"Here they come!" Major Weeks shouted. "Hold fire until my order."

Rebel soldiers flashed in and out of sight as they dashed forward through the smoke from their volley that floated near the ground in the humid air. When the lead runners sprinted within fifty yards of the bridge, another yell reverberated from the rebel line. More rushed from the trees in a wild fury toward their objective.

"Fire!"

Converging fire tore down several Rebels. One soldier reached the bridge but took a bullet that tumbled him into the water. The Rebels dove for cover and sprawled in the ditches and depressions beside the road as lead splattered into the dirt around them.

"They'll not try another bungled charge like that," Major Weeks said to Brutus as the skirmish settled into the same sluggish pattern as before.

During a long lull, Mingo rode up on a blown and lathered horse. "Bad news, Major. The general can't land. The lead transport *Spirea* ran hard aground crossing the bar. It jammed the channel. Nobody can say when the force can disembark."

"I knew it. That damn pilot is a traitor."

Mingo asked, "Can we hold the bridge?"

"We can if they don't bring up more men or get aggressive."

A breathless private rushed up. "Sir, enemy soldiers have crossed the river. There must be a ford up there somewhere."

"How many?"

"Several squads."

Firing erupted from upstream. "Brutus, move two squads to support the flank."

All along the Rebel line, firing intensified to support their compatriots attempting to flank the Yankees. Brutus and a sergeant hustled troops into position to repulse the attack. Their efforts were too late. Already, Weeks could see blue clad soldiers retreating along the river bank as the enemy pressed them with coordinated fire.

The next half-hour bordered on chaos as Major Weeks, Brutus and Mingo scurried from squad to squad to maintain discipline to assure that retreating men had covering fire. As the hindmost men fell back, Rebel skirmishers surged forward to maintain contact. The bridge was lost.

The terrain now worked to the Yankees' advantage as they retreated toward the lighthouse. At the narrows and causeways, a few men could hold back the advancing Rebels. Although outnumbered, the Yankee troops retreated in good order. Nobody panicked and casualties were light.

Late in the afternoon, transports finally came across the bar to disembark troops at the lighthouse. Soon, enough reinforcements had arrived to turn the fight back on the Rebels. Yankees now outnumbered their enemy giving them the capability to counterattack. By dark, Federals pushed the Rebs halfway back to the bridge. At a rise no more than a foot above the surrounding wetlands, Major Weeks ordered a halt to wait until supplies and artillery could be brought forward from the beachhead.

Near dawn, after all the troops were disembarked and equipped, General Newton renewed the attack. As the soldiers in the last Rebel squad retreated across the East River Bridge, they stripped away the planking. Across the river, a Rebel artillery unit wheeled up two, twelve pound howitzers to cover the remaining framework.

General Newton ordered Major Weeks to form up Companies G and H, Second Colored Infantry into a skirmish line to take the bridge. Major Weeks mumbled a protest, "Sir, do you see the cannons? The men will be charging straight into them."

"Weeks, that's an order. Take that bridge. Let's see what your black troops are made of."

"Yes, sir!"

Weeks conveyed the order to the sergeants who shouted instructions above the gunfire. As the two companies worked their way into position to rush the bridge, bullets zinged around them. Men fell, but they moved forward in a ragged line on their own initiative before the bugler sounded charge.

What might have been a suicide assault worked to perfection. Heavy fire from the advancing troops panicked the Rebel officer manning the cannons to fire before the Yankee troops concentrated at the bridge. The bursts caused few casualties while the uproar from the cannons bolted the Rebel horses. Still harnessed to their limbers and caissons, they twisted their traces. The artillerymen couldn't untangle them while under fire, and they couldn't reload before black troops streamed across the bridge on the bare stringers. In disarray, the Rebels ran, abandoning a howitzer and four dead soldiers.

Mingo heard General Newton mumble as he lifted himself in his stirrups, "I'll be damned." Then he shouted, "Now, we've got to secure the Newport Bridge before they wreck it. Weeks, move your men forward double-quick. Have a squad replace the planking so we can push the artillery across."

A few mounted skirmishers tried to slow the Yankee momentum without effect. Understanding the urgency, the troops ran forward to capture the second bridge. A mile from it, they saw black smoke billow above the trees.

When Mingo broke into the clear ground at the approach to the Newport Bridge, he found it engulfed in flames with Rebels entrenched on the opposite bank. Without orders, the veterans with the 2nd Florida Cavalry formed a skirmish line. Led by Mingo and Brutus, they dashed for the bridge.

When they reached it, flames and smoke slowed them as they looked for a route through the inferno. Mingo saw a path and yelled, "Over here, follow me."

Ahead of Mingo, burning planks fell into the river, opening a wide gap. As he stepped back in order to gain momentum to leap across, Brutus slammed him to the deck an instant before rifle fire erupted all along the enemy entrenchment. Minie balls whizzed into the smoke killing and wounding the soldiers still on their feet.

"Run, we'll burn up," Brutus yelled as he grabbed Mingo by the collar to pull him to his feet. Through the smoke, Mingo glimpsed rifles snap into firing position along the entrenchment. Brutus grabbed a wounded soldier, smacked out the flames on his sleeve and threw him over his back. In a crouch, he sprinted toward safety. Mingo cringed to hear the terrifying order "Fire!"

Blood, meat, and bone erupted from the back of the soldier Brutus carried. The bullet's impact knocked Brutus face down on the bridge. He jumped to his feet and, dragging the dead man, ran with Mingo to safety.

As they reached cover, they heard General Newton reprimanding Major Weeks for not securing the bridge. Their friend replied that his men had moved forward faster than could have been expected. The general blamed him for jeopardizing the entire operation. Nevertheless, the commander decided to execute his back-up plan. "I'll Advance with the 2nd Colored Infantry up the St. Marks via the road that parallels the river using your scouts as guides. My troops will cross the river at the ford to flank the Rebels. You hold this position with the 2nd Florida Cavalry. Don't let Crackers cross the river and get behind me. You understand, Major?"

"Yes, sir."

As soon as the 2nd Colored Infantry formed columns, Mingo and Brutus led them to the old road. The soldiers hurried as best they could along the overgrown, abandoned route. Without horses, they pulled and pushed the two navy howitzers and the captured Rebel cannon. General Newton trailed behind on horseback harrying his officers and NCOs to push the men faster.

At midnight, he sent an officer to the head of the column to find Mingo. When the officer galloped back with Mingo riding double behind him, General Newton carped, "Where's the damned ford? You said it was about five miles upstream from the bridge? We've come farther than that."

"Sir, it can't be far. I never scouted dis route myself. My men reported dis road goes to de ford."

"We're taking too much time. No rest till we're across the river."

The farther the column moved from Newport the more the road became overgrown which required the troops to scramble through head-tall bushes and chop small trees so that they could roll the unwieldy howitzers forward.

Just before dawn, Rebel snipers hidden in the surrounding jungle wounded several soldiers leading the column. The advance stopped. General Newton rode forward. "Damn it, move! Don't let a few skirmishers stall us."

Sergeants urged squads forward. In response, men crashed through brambles and briars to dislodge the sharpshooters. At daybreak, Mingo reported to General Newton, "Sir, we must have passed the ford. We've come upon a well-used road that must cross the river at Natural Bridge."

The General barked, "Major Lincoln, get the column across right now. Move it."

As the lead squads pressed forward along the road, Rebel sharpshooters opened fire again.

General Newton rode forward to find the column hunkered down. "Major Lincoln, why are you not advancing as ordered?"

"Sir, skirmishers are thick as hornets. There's only one, narrow, wagon road that is bordered by swamp and jungle on both sides. We can't see the sharpshooters. They're picking us off right and left."

"Then use two companies. Attack. Drive those skirmishers back."

Major Lincoln ordered his sergeants to send companies B and G, 2nd Colored Infantry, forward. As they moved up, the entire column trudged behind them along the wagon road. Flanking squads waded through swamp and fought their way through brush to keep pace. "Move, men. Faster," Major Lincoln kept yelling.

The ragged blue lines surged through the thickets as unseen Rebels continued to whittle away at them. Even after morning sun filtered through the towering trees, it didn't have enough intensity to brighten the dark shadows in the thick forest. At last, the column reached a clearing. As Major Lincoln moved forward through swamp mist and smoke, he glimpsed breastworks straddling the wagon road. Somewhere to his right, a cannon boomed. A shell tore through limbs, slammed into an ancient tupelo tree near the major and exploded. The hollow tree fell with a trunk-splitting crash.

Soldiers fell all around as Rebel riflemen behind breastworks picked them off. Intermittently, grape shot from the cannons whined through the brush as rifle fire continued to pour into the flanks from the dense swamp and jungle.

"Forward, men," Major Lincoln yelled again and again. Suddenly, he realized he was leading his men into a death trap of converging fire. "Fall back! Fall back!"

Exposed to fire from three sides, the black soldiers retreated while tripping and stumbling through undergrowth and vines.

Major Lincoln retreated down the road until he came to a field where he found troops constructing a log breastwork in the trees under the supervision of General Newton himself. He ran to the general and reported, "Sir, the Natural Bridge crossing is guarded by breastworks and cannons. The woods are so thick on each side of the road that you can't see the Rebel sharpshooters hidden there. We need more men."

General Newton replied, "As I expected, we didn't move fast enough. Our black scouts finally found the ford a mile back. I've ordered Colonel Townsend to use it to flank the enemy while you attack again. I'm taking this bridge."

Occasional rifle shots still reverberated through the jungle as Rebel sharpshooters spotted soldiers penned down in the kill zone.

Major Lincoln scurried to organize his men for another charge while Colonel Townsend formed up Companies A, B, and H for the assault on the ford. Brutus ran up to General Newton with unwelcome news. "Sir, the Rebels are getting reinforcements. They've extended their lines along the river from Natural Bridge past the ford. They're digging entrenchments across the river."

The intelligence didn't dampen General Newton's resolve. "I'm taking this bridge. Move out."

Major Lincoln spread his men across the narrow road. Despite their losses in the first charge, they didn't hesitate when he ordered them forward. At first, the Rebels only fired sporadic shots as if warming to the attack. When the lead soldiers came within a hundred yards of the Rebel breastworks, the fire increased to a barrage of whirling shot and shell. Major Lincoln bounded forward. As he reached the first embankment's crest, he confronted two, towheaded boys, twelve or thirteen years old, dressed in uniforms with their rifles leveled on him. He hesitated to shoot for a critical instant. Their rifles puffed smoke, drilling bullets into his stomach. He swirled and fell into the dirt as his weapon discharged a slug into the treetops.

With the commander down, the Yankee charge lost momentum while a steady roar continued from the Rebel lines. Major Lincoln felt someone grab his leg and pull him backward. Writhing in pain from the gut shots, he said, "Save yourself, soldier. Leave me. We never should have made this charge." Grapeshot ripped over their heads and into the growth along the road, shredding it to bits.

"Nahsuh, Major. I ain't leavin' ya," Brutus growled.

At the ford, Colonel Townsend's attack showed promise. Soldiers in blue were knocked down by intense fire, but the mass kept moving forward. Enough stayed on their feet that a few Rebels abandoned their positions. A squad manning a howitzer turned tail leaving the gun unmanned.

"Press them, men, press them. We've got them on the run," Colonel Townsend urged as he sprinted forward to the edge of a wide slough. Several soldiers jumped into the water to cross. They sank up to their chins. Bullets splattered into the water around them. In panic, they dropped their rifles, scratching the bank to climb out. Some slipped into water over their heads. One soldier stayed under water for several seconds. When he burst up to grab a branch to climb up, lead slammed into his neck.

"It's too deep to cross here; find someplace else," Colonel Townsend yelled.

A cannon spewed grapeshot among the bewildered troops.

Colonel Townsend worked his way along the bank looking for another place to ford the slough. Everywhere the black, sluggish water looked deep and dangerous. Rebels sniped at his men all along the line.

At Natural Bridge, the Yankees realized they couldn't overrun the Rebel breastworks, but kept fighting in the vain hope for a breakthrough. For several hours they exchanged fire from covered positions. When they ran low on ammunition, they fell back through the hammock, then across the field to General Newton's defensive breastwork.

When the Rebels realized the Yankee fire had tapered off, Captain H.K. Simmons asked for volunteers to go forward into the hammock to ascertain if the Yankees had retreated. "Come on, ya'll. Let's kill some more."

No one volunteered. The officer pressed them, "I'll lead the detail." Still, no one volunteered. "OK then, I'll order ya out. Loring, bring up a squad." Simmons led the men over the entrenchments into the shadow-filled hammock. As they crept forward, a few Yankees hidden in the jungle sniped at them.

Dodging from tree to tree, Loring pressed forward between Captain Simmons and Sergeant Stephens in a swamp fight with enemy sharpshooters. When he found good cover, he waited for a clear shot. Pressed by the Rebels, the Yankees fell back. When they did, Loring dashed forward while staying hidden as much as possible.

As Loring stood behind a tree reloading his LeMat, he sensed the Yankee fire increase. He yelled to Sergeant Stephens, "Willie, what can you see?"

"They're stopped behind stumps in that open field. Bring up more men. We can take them."

Loring ran back to the Rebel line. "Send up a company. We've chased the skirmishers from the hammock. They're holed up in a field. With cover fire, we can drive them back."

When the company reached the edge of the field, Captain Simmons formed them into a fighting line, waved his hat and yelled

"Charge!" Only a few men burst into the clearing where the Yankee skirmishers lay hidden. After the enemy troops fired a few ineffective shots, they jumped up and ran across the open space until they disappeared in the trees.

As Loring ran after them, he noticed a line of logs stacked waist high that snaked through the trees across the field. Sunlight glinted off rifles resting across the top logs. He kept sprinting forward although he sensed the few men who had followed Captain Simmons into the field were diving for cover.

"Take 'em, boys!" Simmons yelled.

Fifty feet into the clearing, Loring's mind flashed to the trooper at drill who kept his galloping horse between himself and the targets. He recalled his sergeant's specific words from that day. *A soldier rides low. Kill the enemy, don't let them kill you. Never unnecessarily expose yourself in a fight.*

He also remembered Lt. Reddick's warning after the brainless assault against the barricades in Gainesville. As he lunged to hide behind a massive stump that the woodcutters had chopped off waist high, the enemy laid down a volley along with canister and grape. Loring's body shuddered from the impacts. In crystal detail, he envisioned Deer Hall and his beautiful, tall wife standing resolute on the porch with her hands on her hips. He heard Little Buddy's exuberant laugh and felt her light kiss on his cheek. He struggled to picture his son's face but died before he hit the ground.

After four years of war the officers had still not learned that a frontal assault against fortified breastworks portended disaster. Every man who had run into the field was down. Only Sergeant Willie Stephens and a private were still alive, cowering in stump holes as Minie balls kicked up dirt around them.

General Newton retreated from the breastworks before the Rebels could organize an attack. "We're low on ammunition. Pull the troops back. Maintain a rear guard. Move double-quick to the East River Bridge. Drop trees in the road to impede Rebel cavalry."

The Rebels made no further effort to counterattack, a fact which surprised General Newton although he had no way of knowing that Rebel officers used the very excuse he had used to stop fighting. In actuality, nobody had the desire to continue the fight or take more casualties. The few Rebel cavalrymen that shadowed the Yankee retreat avoided contact.

General Newton rode stiff-backed in the saddle beside his retreating troops. When he arrived at Major Weeks' position at the Newport Bridge, the officers exchanged salutes. The General said, "We had the Crackers whipped until reinforcements showed up." The major said nothing. The general continued, "When all the troops have passed, maintain a rear guard. Send Whitman's sailors back to their ships," then he rode into a shady spot where he sat on his horse watching his demoralized troops straggle by.

Mingo arrived at the bridge sopped with sweat from chopping trees to block the road. With an axe on his shoulder, he walked up to Major Weeks. "Have you seen Brutus?"

"No, I haven't."

General Newton overheard the exchange and interjected, "Last time I saw him he was headed into the assault at Natural Bridge along with Major Lincoln. I haven't seen him since. Major Lincoln may know his whereabouts."

Weeks said, "Stretcher-bearers carried the major by not more than ten minutes ago."

Without a word, Mingo dropped the axe and ran to search for Major Lincoln. Within a mile Mingo found him lying under the shade of pine trees where the stretcher-bearers had stopped to rest. His face was ashen and contorted into a permanent grimace. Dirty stains coated his face where he had wiped it with bloody hands.

"Major Lincoln, where are you hit?"

The major groaned.

Mingo asked louder, "Major, where are you hit?"

"Gut shot," Mingo thought he heard him mumble.

"Where's Brutus?"

The major whimpered something Mingo couldn't make out.

A stretcher-bearer nodded his head from side to side as if to say, "You're wasting your time."

Mingo persisted, "Where's Brutus?"

The major mumbled, "Saved my life."

"Where is he?"

Putting his ear to the Major's mouth, Mingo thought he heard a faint "He was hit at Natural Bridge too," as the Major lost consciousness.

In a frenzy, Mingo ran up the abandoned road toward Natural Bridge. After wrestling his way through the brush barricade that he had dropped across the road on the retreat, he sprinted toward the next road-block when a bullet smacked him above the ear. Everything went black.

Regaining consciousness, he placed a hand against the wound. When he looked at his fingers, blood covered them. He shook his head in an effort to clear it. Taking a bandana from his pocket, he doubled it over on itself three times and tied it over the gash.

Ahead in the brush, he heard rustling and voices. "Why you reckon that moak was runnin' toward us? I'm sure I hit him. He has to be close by."

Terrified, Mingo worried that his pursuers meant to murder him like the black soldiers were slaughtered at Olustee. He crawled on his hands and knees under the brush to distance himself from the Crackers and then sprinted for the bridge.

When he reached the Newport Bridge, he found the last Yankee troops leaving. Loping past them, he didn't stop till he reached the lighthouse where he found troops embarking on launches for the return to the transports.

He ran from launch to launch looking in vain for Brutus. He found Major Weeks supervising sailors who were pushing the howitzer captured at the East River Bridge onto a barge. When Mingo ran up, Major Weeks said, "You hit?"

"Winged. I'm OK. Have you seen Brutus?"

"You have a surgeon look at the wound right now. I've seen men die who thought they were only grazed. I haven't seen Brutus. Didn't you find him?"

"No, I couldn't get past the Rebel skirmishers up the road."

"He'll turn up. You report to the surgeons. They're operating at the lighthouse."

That evening aboard the *Alliance,* General Newton commended the officers for their fine leadership that resulted in victory by driving the Confederates from the field and capturing the howitzer. The officers glanced around the room at each other. Major Weeks reported the causalities.

As he handed a list to the general, he said, "Sir, the preliminary reports are not good. Two officers are confirmed killed. At least ten others are wounded. Some of those will not live. Nineteen men are confirmed killed and eighty are wounded; again, many of those will not survive. One officer and thirty-seven men are missing. We took at least 148 casualties."

Weeks continued, "Both the 2nd U.S. Colored and 99th U.S. colored took heavy casualties. Both regiments were in contact with enemy from the time they disembarked until they returned to transports. Both regiments performed with valor. Every soldier did his best. The officers and men exhibited consummate bravery."

General Newton said, "Major, the bravery of the officers and men cannot be questioned. That being said, they never moved with the alacrity I expected. Had we reached Newport sooner---"

Major Weeks interjected, "General, the men moved as fast as possible on foot. If we had had horses---"

"Don't interrupt me." The general glared at Major Weeks. "We won the field and captured a howitzer at the East River Bridge. We destroyed a saw mill, gristmill, and factories at Newport. The enemy gunship, *Spray*, is bottled up in the river and out of action. The blockade is more effective than ever because ships can't move down river to the bay anymore. Had the navy accomplished its mission, we'd have had complete victory. Lt. Commander Gibson knew the navy had to bombard St. Marks and occupy Port Leon to keep me re-supplied during the advance. When Shufeldt took command, he dawdled. The navy never occupied Port Leon."

"Sir, Ensign Whitman and his men took the East River Bridge according to plan. It's true, the ships never made it up the St. Marks River to Port Leon. *Honduras* ran aground in the river, which blocked the other ships. According to Ensign Whitman, Commander Shufeldt continued to make every effort to move the ships upriver until he got word that the army was returning from Natural Bridge."

"The Navy failed in its mission. That was the critical factor. Dismissed."

The officers saluted. The general raised his hand in a dismissive gesture.

Major Weeks pivoted with military precision and followed the other officers from the room. Shutting the door behind him, he stepped into the companionway where he slammed his fist against the bulkhead. He gasped for air and dashed for an outside rail.

Mingo, with a clean, white bandage tied around his head, ran up to him. "Major Weeks, Major Weeks, what's wrong?"

Composing himself, the major said, "Mingo, glad to see you. How bad is the wound?"

"Like I said, winged, dat's all. Are you sick?"

Major Weeks glanced around to see if anybody else was within hearing. "What I'm about to say is between us. You understand?"

Mingo mumbled assent.

"Thank God, this war will be over in few weeks before officers like Newton get more brave men killed. He wanted to make a name for himself by capturing Tallahassee to compensate for his demotion from Major General. This battle was his chance for glory before the war ended. Instead, he got his ass whipped."

Mingo nodded.

"We gave him a good battle plan and it should have worked if he had listened. The lowest private knew speed was critical to the mission. What did he do? Every decision he made slowed the advance. He ordered the transports into the Gulf when the Rebs must have seen the invasion fleet. That was inexcusable. His refusal to bring horses was plain stupid."

"No doubt about dat. A cavalry detachment could have secured Newport Bridge before the Rebels brought up reinforcements."

"The general blames everybody but himself - the troops, the navy. In fact, his poor decisions caused the fiasco. He has the audacity to say he drove the Confederates from the field. Sickening. The casualty ratio from the battle is almost as high as Antietam Creek or Gettysburg. His hunt for glory and plain bullheadedness caused brave men to die for next to nothing--- a twelve pound howitzer."

Major Weeks spat over the rail.

"What about the Rebels? Their losses must have been high too."

"I doubt it. Less than ten men were confirmed killed. In the main, their soldiers stayed behind entrenchments or in the woods except for bungled charges at the East River Bridge and at Natural Bridge. Colonel Townsend reported that after we withdrew to our breastwork there, a Rebel officer led an assault. Only a few brave men sprang forward with him. When they saw our line, they dove for cover. Our volley killed the officer and maybe a few others.

"Is there any word about Brutus?"

"Nothing. He's missing in action."

CHAPTER FIFTY-THREE

TALLAHASSEE
Florida

The fact that General Grant had the Army of Northern Virginia bottled up demoralized loyal Floridians, but Sherman's march across Georgia to the sea and into South Carolina terrified them. If his army turned south, nothing stopped it from razing and plundering Florida too.

Destitute and shell-shocked refugees flooded into Florida from Georgia and South Carolina with harrowing stories about the destruction caused by the Union advance. Their reports about ineffective Confederate resistance ended all hope that the South could win the war. Southern armies were so near collapse that only God's intervention, could save them. Some people prayed for a miracle; others prayed for quick defeat to end the suffering.

However, despite all the losses after the fall of Atlanta in September 1864, the victory at Natural Bridge raised Floridians' morale. When reports arrived at Tallahassee that the retreating Federal troops had embarked on their ships, the capital erupted in jubilation. Perhaps all was not lost. For a day, confidence soared.

Loyal Floridians lauded themselves on their fighting spirit to repel a Yankee invasion while the Confederate armies in Virginia and North Carolina were in forced retreat. Men and boys all over West Florida, even those who had given up on the Confederacy, had steeled themselves to fight. They had flocked to join the home guard to repel the Yankee invasion in a desperate effort to protect their homes and families from devastation. Some had ridden sixty miles in a day and others had walked thirty or forty miles to reach the fray. The cadets from the West Florida Seminary, some as young as twelve with permission notes from their mothers, had enlisted. Mere lads had anchored the line at Natural Bridge. As the fighters arrived back at Tallahassee from the battle, womenfolk draped the heroes with garlands when they stepped from the train.

With the Confederacy so near collapse, General Newton had expected little resistance from Florida's decimated military and demoralized populace. Instead, brave troops with support from plucky citizens had crushed his invasion. People celebrated with dances and parties. Governor Milton honored the victors with ceremonies at the capitol.

Jubilation trailed off quickly. In truth, Florida had won an important victory, but the more citizens learned about the battle, the more they realized circumstances didn't bode well for the future. Intelligence from prisoners confirmed that many of the black soldiers were former slaves. Worse, several hundred, white Floridians had joined with the United States 2nd Florida cavalry after deserting from the Confederate army. Florida troops had summarily executed several who were taken prisoner at Newport. Bitter fault lines between Floridians couldn't be ignored.

The battle at Natural Bridge had won a reprieve, nothing more. Ultimate victory was chimerical. Every available resource had been used to repel General Newton. No more reserves existed. No Confederate army in the field could defend Florida. Another Yankee invasion was inevitable and unstoppable. Everybody knew the old order was in extremis - soon to be replaced.

An execution at Tallahassee foreshadowed dark days.

The men who captured Strickland and his comrade brought them in slave irons to Tallahassee. As Strickland stood hangdog with his hands tied behind his back, Wall grabbed him by the chin and lifted his head. "Don't I know you, soldier? What's your name?"

"Strickland."

"Weren't you assigned to the 6th Florida infantry?"

Strickland didn't answer. He met Wall's gaze with a defiant stare.

Wall slammed him in the solar plexus with a body punch. "Answer me, you sum-bitch. Were you discharged?"

Strickland doubled up, gagging from the blow. Wall slapped him. Strickland spit blood then said, "I volunteered then left the army to take care of my family after I served my term. The gov'ment had no right to make me stay longer. Go to hell! I fought while you --- you never left the bombproof department."

Wall smashed him in the mouth with his fist.

General Jones convened a court martial that afternoon. Strickland and another deserter by the name of John Brannon were convicted and sentenced to execution by firing squad the morning of March 18th. At formation on the 17th, the company's major selected ten men for the firing squad. Two men begged to be relieved from the detail because they had done business with Strickland before the war. The major refused. "You men will do your duty."

That evening soldiers considered mutiny. "By God, I ain't goin' to murder them men. I don't blame them for comin' home to their families. They faced the elephant at Shiloh and Chickamauga while shirkers like Wall never fought. I'll go over the hill myself before I do the shameful business."

A staff sergeant overheard the conversation and reported to the major. "Sir, the men are in an uproar about servin' on the firin' squad."

"Orders are orders. They'll damn well obey them."

"Sir, may I make a suggestion? Let men volunteer."

"Here's what I'll do. If the men assigned to the firing squad can find someone to substitute in their place, I'll allow it. But nobody, and I mean nobody, in this company will be excused from formation in the morning. We will have discipline."

The sergeant found volunteer substitutes.

In a clearing atop a high hill near the army camp, a detail dug two, deep holes ten feet apart in the ochre dirt. Nearby in the woods, soldiers chopped two, small, pine trees. After trimming off the limbs, they cut them in twelve-foot lengths, carried the timbers to the execution site, and stood each one in a deep post hole. They held them straight, backfilled the dirt, and tamped it down.

At sunrise, the major marched the company up the hill. He formed them in single file U formation around the two poles. As the company stood at attention, guards walked the prisoners dressed in Yankee uniforms to the tree trunks.

The major read the verdict and the sentence. "Privates Strickland and Brannon, a duly convened court martial of the Army of the

Confederate States of America has found you guilty of desertion and aiding and abetting the enemy. You are hereby condemned to die by firing squad at 8:00 A.M., March 18, 1865, by Order of General Samuel Jones."

"Bind and blindfold the prisoners."

Both prisoners stood straight while being tied to the poles. A guard pulled black bandanas from his pocket. He blindfolded Brannon and then stepped to Strickland who turned his swollen face to the sun just breaking through the morning mist. Light turned to darkness as the guard tied the cloth across his eyes and then stepped aside.

"Lieutenant Blackwell, do your duty," the major said.

The officers saluted. To the side, a snare drum commenced a soft rattle.

"Firing Squad, forward, march!" the lieutenant commanded.

Six paces from the condemned he shouted, "Squad, halt!" "Dress right, Dress!" Pausing, he then bawled, "Ready! Aim! Fire!"

Ten rifles cracked in unison. Bullets cut the line holding Strickland. He fell and rolled on his back. A soldier hollered, "Oh Lord," as acrid smoke drifted through the ranks. Brannan stood still for several seconds as if his life continued, then his knees buckled. A guard slashed the rope with his knife and the dead man fell in a heap. A soldier grabbed his arms to stretch the body flat across the ground.

"Lieutenant, march the company by the deserters," the major barked.

A muffled drumbeat continued until the last soldier passed by the dead men. Then the burial detail stepped forward to do its duty.

CHAPTER FIFTY-FOUR

CEDAR KEY

Florida

General Newton, fretting that General Jones might go on the offensive, hurried down the coast to secure his positions. He landed troops at Cedar Key and Egmont Key in Tampa Bay. He abandoned Fort Myers and sailed for the safety of Key West.

He continued to blame the navy for the defeat at Natural Bridge. His official report written on March 7 stated, "The navy was unable to cooperate in any manner; the ammunition was nearly expended and our communications broken owing to the failure of the navy to land a force of seaman at Port Leon as agreed."

The skeleton force left behind to guard Cedar Key had struggled to maintain order. When news of the Yankee defeat at Natural Bridge reached the town, festering animosities flared among the citizens. Some had only sworn allegiance to the Union under duress to avoid expulsion. Without enough troops in town to provide security, bitter secessionists burned Union homes and shelters. Some bushwhacked Unionists.

Compounding the town's insecurity, Rebel pickets probed the undermanned, Yankee, guard posts. For their safety, the U.S. Army evacuated all civilians, black and white, to Sea Horse Key.

People crowded into the camp with inadequate food supplies and limited water. A few lucky citizens had tents for shelter; however, most had to throw together palmetto frond huts to protect themselves from the sun and rain. Blacks and whites segregated themselves into compounds. People lived in fear not knowing if their neighbors were friend or foe.

When the *Alliance* disembarked the U.S. 2nd Florida cavalry, Major Weeks clamped down. "Any armed civilians will be arrested. Curfew is in effect from sunset to sunrise. Violators will be shot."

He also resolved to push the Confederates away from Cedar Key once and for all. "Mingo, scout the Rebel picket posts. We'll extend our perimeter at least to Station Four before Dixie can redeploy from Natural Bridge."

Twenty-four hours later, Mingo reported to Major Weeks. "Sir, the Rebels only have two posts near town that we can find - at Station Four and Live Oak Key where we burnt the salt works. There are less than ten men at either one."

"You sure?"

"Can't be absolutely certain, but we saw only one tent at Station Four. Only a few old mules and horses were at either place. The camps are shabby."

Major Weeks said to his lieutenants, "Let's drive them out. We'll place guard posts at Live Oak Key, Station Four, and Black Point. I don't want to take any chance that Rebels can slip around our pickets. Mingo, scout the entire coast from Raleigh Islands to Tripod Key. Make sure there are no camps hidden back in the swamps that they can use as a base."

The post at Station Four was dislodged first. Although war weary, the Rebel pickets had stayed alert. They warned their camp of the Yankee advance which allowed their compatriots to flee before the Federal skirmishers could overrun them.

A patrol found the Rebel outpost on Live Oak Key abandoned. Buoyed by these operations, Major Weeks extended the perimeter by sending patrols farther up the railroad. Still, he didn't find the enemy. He surmised that the Rebels had either abandoned the area or retreated into the nearly impregnable Gulf Hammock Swamp or across the Suwannee.

Cedar Key swelled with refugees fleeing from Georgia and South Carolina. Most walked into Cedar Key with nothing more than a carpetbag stuffed with clothing and perhaps a cook pot. A few came in wagons with their slaves. The impoverished civilians begged soldiers for employment who obliged by hiring them to do their fatigue duties: chopping wood, washing uniforms, digging latrines, and other menial chores.

Somehow the Confederate armies still held out in Virginia and North Carolina although cut off by enveloping Yankee armies. Without any way to resupply, Lee's army faced starvation. Most Floridians resigned themselves to Southern defeat. Many became despondent while others resolved to adapt to a new topsy-turvy world. A few, former, slave owners found themselves employed by black soldiers and were grateful for the opportunity.

Major Weeks had difficulty making his men mind their military tasks. No one wanted to be the last man killed in the war. No one volunteered for patrols. Mingo requested a leave to visit Molly. "Major Weeks, we've scouted de coast north to Horseshoe Point and south to de Withlacoochee River. We've checked every road and trail within a ten miles radius lookin' for Rebels. They're gone. Let me check on Molly. With so many refugees roamin' de countryside, Deer Hall's in danger."

"Mingo, we can't lower our guard. The Rebels haven't surrendered. Let's patrol up to Clay Landing. If we don't find the enemy there, you can take a detail over to Chunky Pond. Is Waldock still there?"

"He promised to stay."

When Major Weeks' patrol arrived at Clay Landing, it was abandoned. Refugees and escaped slaves making their way to Cedar Key reported that they hadn't seen any Confederate troops along their route. Mingo speculated that they had abandoned the entire Suwannee Valley, but Major Weeks doubted that so long as Dickison was still in the fight.

He said to Mingo, "I'll take a detachment up river to the railroad bridge across the Suwannee by Columbus where the Rebels have maintained a permanent camp since the war started. If they're still there, I'm going to send a squad under a white flag to ask for their surrender. You go ahead and take a squad to Chunky Pond. If everything is OK there, come up to the Suwannee Bridge. If you run into any enemy troops, maintain contact and trail them to their base."

Mingo with his ten man patrol galloped toward Chunky Pond. When he exited the woods to cross the field to the farmstead, he saw Jake and Joe sprint for cover. "Thank goodness, they haven't been killed or run off," he said to his sergeant.

He spurred his horse at a canter to the front gate where he jerked his brindle pony to a stop while the soldiers scattered to set a perimeter. "Molly, Chad, it's me, Mingo!" he shouted.

From behind the front door, a heavy bar squeaked as someone lifted it from its cradle. The door burst open. Molly dashed to him. He dismounted to meet her with open arms. He clasped her with his hands at her waist and lifted her over his head. She laughed and kicked, "Let me down! Let me down!" she squealed. As he eased her to the ground, they grasped one another, whirling in circles, then hugged and kissed in a long embrace.

When he looked up after the kiss, Mingo saw Chad and Blanche standing on the porch. He hardly recognized Blanche. Barefooted, she wore a threadbare, washed-out dress. She was gaunt with dark splotches around her eyes. "Molly, what's de matter wid Missis Blanche?" he whispered.

"Mas'r Loring was killed at Natural Bridge. Dey never brought him home. Billy's death almost did her in. Now, she's worse, about to break."

Mingo released Molly then climbed up the steps to the porch, "Missis Blanche, I'm sorry to hear 'bout Mas'r Loring, he was a good man."

Blanche fled into the house.

He turned to Chad, "What can I say?"

"Nothing. She blames herself."

Mingo shook his head. "Do ya'll have enough to eat?"

"What marauders haven't cleaned out, Wall has. We'd starve if Jake wasn't such a good hunter and fisherman. The war has worn out everybody and everything. Look around. What's not burned is ramshackle. Luckily, I stashed some seed that Wall didn't find, so with luck, we can at least make a garden and raise a few cotton plants."

"How's everybody else gettin' by?"

"Jake has rheumatism, but he can still outwork most men. Sarah's sickly. Blanche is so confounded that Molly has been doing everything. The girls are fine."

"How can I help ya'll?"

"We need food."

"We're travelin' light. My men only have rations for two days, but I'll scrape together what I can. When I get back to Cedar Key, I'll send some up."

Chad said, "Stay on guard. A Rebel patrol came through here yesterday and they might still be in the area."

Mingo jogged over to his sergeant who sat astride his horse with a Spencer rifle across his thighs. "Sergeant, keep the men alert. Post two pickets along the lane. A Rebel patrol may be around. Ask the men if they can spare some food for these people."

The sergeant said, "Why should we feed these damn Rebels? We ought to burn the place."

"Sergeant, women and children live here. Dat man on the porch I was talkin' to ain't no Rebel. He's English. He's helped us before and just warned me about a Rebel patrol. For your information, we killed de head of de house at Natural Bridge and we killed his son too." Mingo swallowed hard and shook his head. "We'll have no difficulty with des people, and by God, we'll help dem. De war is 'bout over. Let's think about de future and reconciliation."

The sergeant frowned.

Embarrassed by his hot-blooded harangue, Mingo said, "I didn't mean to be so preachy. Just ask de men to share what food dey can spare. Stay alert for enemy troops."

Mingo walked back to the porch, "Where's Molly?"

"She went in the house to check on Blanche. Have a seat. All I can offer you is water. Do you have any idea how Loring was killed?"

"If he was killed at Natural Bridge, he was mighty unlucky. We only killed a few Rebels. He must have been hit at de East River Bridge or at a stupid charge against our breastwork near Natural Bridge. Most times, enemy troops stayed behind cover or hidden in de trees."

"Makes sense. I'd bet Loring led a charge. He never wanted to go to war, but I'm sure he fought like a wildcat once he got into a scrape. How are you getting along?"

"Still scoutin' for the Union." Tears welled in Mingo's eyes. "I think Brutus was killed at Natural Bridge too."

"I'm sorry, Mingo."

"How's Molly holdin' up?"

"Better than anybody. She's always talking about you."

The door creaked open as Molly stepped out on the porch. "Blanche is lyin' down."

Mingo reached for her hand. They all watched the sergeant ride the perimeter for a minute until Molly asked, "How long can you stay?"

"I have to go. Major Weeks let me come over here to check on you. He's takin' a patrol up to Columbus on de Suwannee. I'm supposed to join him."

She sat in Mingo's lap and put her arms around him. "Honey, please don't leave me. You're not a soldier. You don't have to work for de army."

Chad interrupted, "You two want to be alone?"

Mingo said, "No. We ain't got no secrets from you. I mean to see de war through. You know what I'm goin' to do afterward?"

"What?" Chad asked.

"Marry dis beautiful woman if she'll have me."

"I'll have you all right," Molly said and kissed him.

Holding her around the waist he continued. "Me and my friend Major Weeks plans to go into de citrus business. We've been savin' our pay to buy land. You think you could be a farmer's wife?"

She kissed him again.

Shots reverberated across the field. "Get in de house, Molly!"

Mingo dashed for his horse.

Chad followed Molly through the door, slammed it behind him, and dropped the heavy bar in place with a clunk.

From the window, Chad and Molly watched Mingo and the sergeant race their mounts toward the woods where gun smoke floated through the trees. Several hundred yards from the woods, they reined their horses. Chad heard somebody yell although from such a long distance he couldn't make out what was said. The sergeant made a hand signal as two soldiers galloped across the field to join them.

Chad stayed at the window with his loaded shotgun ready for trouble, but it never came. In twenty minutes, Mingo trotted back to the house.

"What in the hell was that?" Chad asked.

"Just what you warned us about. One of our pickets spotted Rebels. He thinks he hit one. Dey fired back and circled through de woods, where dey ran straight into another picket. When he fired, dey hightailed."

"What are you going to do?" Chad asked.

"Major Weeks ordered us to maintain contact with any enemy patrols we came across. Dat's what we'll do. Let's hope dey'll lead us to a camp. Pickets thought der was only four or five; one is wearing a fancy uniform."

Chad said, "That's probably Wall."

Mingo reached behind his saddle and untied a leather cord securing a flour sack which he handed to Molly. "Dis is from de men. I'll come back as soon as I can."

"Mingo, let soldiers chase dem. It's not your job," Molly pleaded.

"Give me a kiss. I have to ride."

Molly handed the sack to Chad, then clutched Mingo's leg. He leaned down and kissed her on the lips then said, "I'm goin' keep fightin' till our freedom's guaranteed."

As she stepped back, he wheeled his horse, riding after his squad. Tears welled in Molly's eyes as she waved good-bye. Now she understood how Blanche felt when Loring left home the last time.

CHAPTER FIFTY-FIVE

LEVYVILLE
Florida

Blood splotches on palmetto fronds beside the lane confirmed that a Rebel soldier had been hit.

"Maintain intervals. Look out for a bushwhack," Mingo reminded the squad. He walked his horse along the lane following the hoof prints of five running horses and an occasional blood splatter. As he circled around a bayhead, a horse whinnied somewhere ahead.

"Sergeant, I think they've holed up. Let's dismount and slip through de trees."

The sergeant ordered a soldier to guard the horses. The others spread out and crept forward. A quarter mile ahead, a crow cawed and landed in a treetop. As Mingo crept closer, it took off, flew a hundred yards ahead and landed again. After another flight, he watched it glide for a landing at a tall pine. At the last moment before settling on a limb, it flapped its wings and then flew away in raucous protest.

Figuring that the Rebels had scared the bird, he signaled the location to his men with hand gestures. As the men neared the tree, they heard a yawp. Mingo halted and motioned the sergeant to him. "What you reckon dat ungodly sound was?"

"Sounds like a hurt animal."

"Watch for a trap. Circle around. I'll check it."

At the sergeant's signal, the soldiers moved out again. Mingo slipped from tree to tree until he reached a clearing. On the other side, he saw a Rebel soldier in a butternut jacket and slouch hat slumped against a cat-faced pine. The soldier gripped his blood-soaked side with his left hand. His head rested on his shoulder.

After his men passed around the clearing, Mingo edged forward while covering the wounded soldier with his pistol. He couldn't see a weapon and noticed that his holster was empty. The Rebel didn't move until Mingo kicked his foot. The soldier looked up, tried to stand, but collapsed against the tree. "Water, water. Mama, Mama, help me."

"What's your unit, soldier?"

"Water, water."

Mingo pulled his canteen strap over his head. Unscrewing the cap, he held the container to the soldier's lips. As the man sipped it as best he could, he stared at Mingo with glazed eyes. "What unit?" Mingo said as he shook the soldier's shoulder.

Water dribbled from the dying man's mouth. "Wall's impressment..."

He gagged. His lifeless eyes focused on nothing.

"Damn," Mingo said, closing the vacant eyes with two fingers.

He pulled the soldier's arm aside in order to reach inside the bloody jacket for identification. He found nothing.

Far away, the crow cawed. Mingo stood, screwed the cap on his canteen, pulled the strap over his head, and signaled the sergeant. As he did, he noticed a red ant crawling across the soldier's shoe. Before the sergeant reached him, more ants crawled onto the dead man faster than Mingo could brush them away. "Jesus, what are we going to do with him?" the sergeant asked.

"He was left to die without water or his pistol. We ain't leavin' him. He said he was with Wall's outfit. Both sides will be happy if we can take out dat bastard."

The sergeant told a soldier to wrap the body in a blanket and tie it behind his saddle.

The squad tracked Wall to Levyville, or what was once the town. Fire had destroyed almost all the buildings. The few remaining ones were open to the weather with their windows broken and doors smashed. The owners, or looters, had removed all the furnishings.

As far as Mingo could tell, Wall's squad had passed through the ravished village without stopping. "Let's take a break. We'll bury de Rebel in de boneyard."

The sergeant posted pickets and then assigned two men to dig the grave.

Mingo and a few soldiers lazed in the shade under a mansion's portico while others explored the abandoned houses. A private who stayed on the porch felt around the inside of his haversack. He said, "I ain't got nothin' left but one hardtack cracker."

Mingo said, "None of us do. Thanks for helpin' those people."

A corporal stomped down from upstairs, "House is empty. Not so much as a curtain left."

"Why you reckon nobody is around?" another asked.

"Can't say..." Mingo jumped behind a column as he jerked his pistol from its holster.

"What is it?" the sergeant asked as everybody snatched rifles and scrambled for cover.

"Saw somebody by that well over yonder."

The sergeant pointed at a soldier on the porch. With hand signals, he ordered him to investigate. He sent another to warn the gravediggers.

When the trooper approached the well, he found a stooped, gray-headed, black man drawing water. The soldier walked up behind him and barked, "Hands up!" Startled, the old codger dropped the winch handle. The rope whirred as it unwound from the spool until the bucket splashed into the water several feet below.

"What are you doing here?" the soldier asked.

"I lives up yonder in de woods behind dat big house. Fetch my water from dis well."

"Anybody else around? Soldiers?"

"Nossuh, nobody livin' around here no more. Dis mornin' four soldiers stopped for water den kept on ridin'."

"Relax, old man. We ain't goin' to hurt you. Come with me. My sergeant will want to talk to you."

At the porch, the sergeant asked why the settlement had been abandoned.

"Peoples got run off by de Suwannee River Liberators, Union men. Dey sent a letter tellin' everybody to leave or be killed."

"Why couldn't the home guard protect ya'll?" Mingo asked.

"White folks demanded dat de state do something at a meetin' with de commander at Clay Landing. He said de people got to do it demselves 'cause dey ain't enough soldiers to spread around to settlements like Levyville. Next day, folks up and left. Mas'r told me to stay to look after his place. Said he'd come back when things settle down."

"Who burned de houses?" Mingo asked.

"Weren't no Suwannee Liberators, dat's for sure. Few days after everybody left, soldiers came. Dey broke into all de houses. Dat's when de fires started. De leader was the same one who came through dis mornin'."

"How so?"

"I'd know dat man anywhere. He wears a fancy uniform with gold on de collars. Pulls his hat real low."

"How're you gettin' by?"

"I lives in a hidy place back yonder." The old man pointed. "Ain't comfortable like when Mas'r was here, but I reckon I can make it till he come back."

"You take care of yourself, old man." Mingo handed him his last hardtack cracker. "Sergeant, let's mount up. We've got Rebels to track."

Wall disguised his destination by avoiding roads and changing directions often. First, he headed east, then cut north across sand hills toward Newnansville, then northwest toward the Santa Fe River swamps.

"Wall will try to lose us in that rough country up there or ambush us, but I'll bet he'll take the Old Bellamy Road across the Santa Fe," the sergeant said.

By evening, the route confirmed the sergeant's supposition. Across the sand hills the trail entered flat, bottom land where palmetto, gallberry, and oak thickets pressed in on both sides. Mingo called a halt. "Sergeant, we're goin' be ambushed if we trail them through here. Let's cross de river at Santa Fe Rises and circle around Wall if we can."

"It's risky to travel the roads. If we run into a Rebel patrol, the horses are too tired to outrun them."

"Let's take de chance. If we can't find Wall, we can still meet up with de Major's expedition."

The men took a well-deserved break while the sergeant and Mingo studied a map. The sergeant said, "If we push it, we can make it to the Ichetucknee cutoff by morning. That should put us ahead of Wall so we can ambush him."

The patrol pushed the horses as fast as the tired animals could tolerate. Nevertheless, by daylight, they reached the cutoff. A sprinkle during the night had erased the tracks in the sandy road which confirmed that Wall had not used it since the rain. Mingo found an excellent ambush site beyond a sharp curve. The squad dismounted so that a private could take the horses at least a mile back from the road where they'd be out of sight and couldn't be heard should they whinny.

The sergeant set the ambush by posting a private at the curve as a lookout and spreading the others in hiding places among the pines and palmettos about seventy-five feet from the road. "We'll operate 50/50 with half of us resting while the others stand guard. We'll switch watch every two hours. Mingo, get some rest, I'll take first watch."

Mingo found a flat place between palmetto patches, piled pine straw several inches thick, and then threw his blanket over them for a makeshift bed. He felt like he had no more than closed his eyes when the sergeant yanked his foot.

"Wake up. It's your time to stand watch."

Mingo rose to his knees, stretched, brushed pine catkins from his shoulders and looked across the yellow-green palmettos and scrubby pines enveloped in a light mist. A ground dove cooed across the sandy lane.

He picked up his Spencer rifle, buckled his pistol in place, and pulled on his knee-high cavalry boots. Then he walked to the lookout post along an animal trail to avoid leaving footprints on the sandy road.

As he reached the post, a screech from up the road like wood rubbing against metal startled him. "What the hell is that?" the lookout asked.

"It has to be a wagon." Mingo whispered. "Let it pass. We'll decide what to do when it gets to the ambush zone."

Mingo sprinted in a half crouch back to the sergeant, and whispered, "A wagon is coming."

The sergeant aroused everybody and had them chamber rounds.

In a few minutes, a dilapidated wagon pulled by a feeble mule rolled into view. As it came forward at a crawl, a wheel made a rasping, periodic squeal. A black woman holding a bundle sat beside a white lady who drove the cart. With relentless resolve, she snapped the reins to keep the worn-out beast moving. As the dray pulled beside Mingo and the sergeant, they jumped up from their hiding places with their rifles pointed at the women and yelled, "Stop!"

The sudden noise caused the old mule to shy. It staggered sideways almost collapsing. In a flash, the driver reached under the seat. "Hands up," Mingo yelled. The black woman clutching the bundle bawled. Sweat beaded on Mingo's neck as he decided whether to pull the trigger on his Spencer. A heavy object clanked to the wagon floor. The woman raised her hands.

Keeping his rifle trained on the driver, the sergeant asked, "Where ya'll headed?"

"South," the white woman said.

"Where you from?"

"Near Macon. Drummers with Sherman's army drove me off. Ya'll goin' rob us?"

"No, ma'am. You have any food you could sell us?"

Through sniffles the driver said, "Wish I did. Soldiers stopped us last evening. They stole what little we had."

"Yanks or Rebs?"

The woman didn't answer.

The black woman interjected, "Dey was Rebels. One was a Colonel with gold braid on his collar. Nasty man. Got fresh with Missis Caroline. When a soldier seen de baby, he told de Commander to let us be."

The white woman glared at her.

The sergeant asked, "Soldiers say where they were headed?"

The black woman nodded. "While dey was shufflin' through our stuff, I heard one say our cornmeal should hold 'em till Columbus. Dey rode north toward Lake City."

Mingo slapped the old mule on the rump. As it stumbled forward, the sergeant yelled, "Private, get the horses. We're ridin' to Columbus."

The squad traveled northwest. The next day, on the road that ran north toward Little River, the man on point guard signaled for Mingo to come up. When he reached the soldier, the private pointed to horse tracks and said, "Riders came out on the road here. Looks like our bunch."

Mingo examined the prints in the sandy road, "Can you beat de luck? We've ridden at least twenty-five miles and almost bumped right into dem again. No doubt dey're headed for Columbus."

Far to the north, muffled gunfire popped in quick succession followed by heavier, louder reports.

The sergeant said, "Pistol fire and rifle fire. Sounds like a running skirmish that's coming this way."

"Off de road! Mingo yelled.

The squad crashed their horses into the brush and drew their rifles from their scabbards. Before long, horses pounded down the road toward the squad.

Quail burst into flight near Mingo's horse spooking the animal. It reared and bolted. Mingo clamped his thighs to his McClellan saddle to keep from being thrown while jerking the reins taut to quiet his bucking horse before it gave away the squad's position. Although he pulled on the reins with all his strength, the horse clamped down on the bit. Mingo couldn't control the animal. The approaching riders saw him and veered onto a side trail.

The squad opened fire. An enemy soldier slumped in his saddle. As he fought for balance, his horse reacted to the pressure on the reins, swerving into the brush. A limb snagged the soldier's jacket that pulled him to the ground with a thud as Yankee pursuers rode up at full gallop. Their lieutenant reined his horse when he saw soldiers in blue. Mingo asked him, "Who are you chasin'?"

"Don't know. We were coming back from Columbus when a vidette ran into them. They skedaddled, so we're running them down."

"What happened at Columbus?"

"Ask Major Weeks. He's behind us. Got to catch those Rebs"

The lieutenant wheeled his horse, kicking him hard.

A twenty-man detachment galloped up led by Major Weeks. When he saw Mingo, he waved the men ahead and trotted his horse over, "How's your gal?"

"She's fine. Rebels still at Columbus?"

"Sure are. I sent a lieutenant to the camp under a white flag to ask for their surrender. He found a young brevet captain named Dozier in command, who said that surrender was not an option without orders from Governor Milton or the commander of the North Florida Military District, General Jones, no matter what happens to the Confederate armies in Virginia and North Carolina."

"Corn Cracker diehards," Mingo said.

"They're hanging on to a lost cause. I'm still hoping they'll wise up so we don't have to kill more of them. To our surprise, their camp is in good shape. It has several cannons with enough men to service them. I considered attacking but decided against it without a bigger force. No use assaulting fortified positions and getting our men slaughtered like at Natural Bridge. I'll request General Newton to authorize an expedition if Dozier doesn't change his mind. You find any Rebels?"

"At Chunky Pond we ran across the same bunch you're chasin'. We've been playin' cat and mouse since. The dead one over there by the road is the second one we got. I believe Wall's leadin' them."

"We have to catch that scoundrel. Let's go."

Major Weeks nudged his horse into a fast walk. "No use tiring out our horses. Wall can't keep running his animals like he is. Let the others wear him down, and then we'll finish him off."

Around a sharp bend Major Weeks found his cavalrymen milling around. The major asked, "Why did you stop?"

"They gave us the slip. They must have left the trail when they went out of sight around a curve. We've looking for their tracks."

"Stay on his tail, Mingo. I need to report back to Cedar Key," Major Weeks said.

CHAPTER FIFTY-SIX

CEDAR KEY

Florida

Wall couldn't lose Mingo. Mingo couldn't catch Wall.

The trail led to Clay Landing where Mingo found the place deserted except for the old black man who had helped Brutus so many times. "Where did de riders go dat came in dis morning? Mingo asked.

"Dey loaded up on de ferry like dey was goin' to cross but didn't. Cut it loose and floated downriver."

All day, Mingo and his men searched downstream for Wall without finding any trace.

"He could have left the river anywhere or drifted all the way to the Gulf. We might as well head back to Cedar Key," Mingo said in exasperation.

When Mingo arrived, Major Weeks had good news. "Lee abandoned Richmond after his offensive at Petersburg failed. Joe Johnston made a desperate attack on Sherman's flank at Bentonville, North Carolina, but General Slocum stopped him cold. Lee and Johnston are both on the run."

"Hallelujah. How long you reckon dey can hold on?"

"Not long. Lee has no way to resupply. He's almost surrounded. Johnston is in steady retreat."

"Did you get authority to attack de fort at Columbus?"

"Sent the request to General Newton along with a tentative plan. Haven't heard a thing. After the fiasco at Natural Bridge, he's not eager to jump back into the fray. To tell you the truth, I'm not either. I expect the Florida troops will surrender as soon as Lee and Johnston quit. The Florida Military District, commanded by General Jones, is under Johnston's command."

"Do you need me for a mission? I want to check on Molly."

"Sorry, you'll have to wait. I need you to coordinate patrols until I hear from General Newton. And there's a report that salt works are back in operation at Alligator Point. I need you to check on that too."

What Mingo found at Alligator Point characterized a downtrodden Confederacy. On the site where the U.S. Navy had destroyed a substantial brick building along with its large evaporating pans two years before, he found a few men boiling seawater over open fires in shards left from the old boilers or in tin cook pots. He guessed they couldn't produce more than a few pounds of salt a day.

After burning all the firewood, Mingo and his men gathered the iron in a rowboat and dumped it into the bay. When he reported to Major Weeks, he said, "I've destroyed what was left of de salt works at Alligator Point. Have you heard from General Newton?"

"No, go ahead to Deer Hall. I'll send a courier for you if I need you."

Mingo rode out the next morning. Although he doubted any Rebels were still in the area, he proceeded as if on a scouting mission so as not to be bushwhacked. The only people he met were miserable and dejected refugees. He ignored them all until he came upon a two-wheeled logging wagon pulled by a woman and two children. The woman wore a Cracker bonnet woven from palmetto fronds and a threadbare gingham dress. The children wore skirts woven from broom grass and palm thatch hats. As Mingo approached, the children ran off into the woods. The woman dropped the traces in resignation.

With his pistol in hand, Mingo walked his horse toward the woman. "In the name of Jesus, we ain't got nothin' left to rob," the woman whimpered.

"I'm not going to rob you."

Tears rolled down the woman's cheek, "My sick husband is in the wagon. He was wounded at Atlanta, but he made it home. I've done the best I could, but he's got the gangrene and we're starving. Sherman burned everything on the place and killed our livestock. I can't take no more."

"Your husband armed?"

"No, he's so weak he couldn't shoot anyhow."

Alert for any threatening movement, Mingo pointed his pistol at the blanketed form as he walked his horse beside the wagon. He looked over the high wheel where a middle-aged man with matted, gray hair and a mottled face stared at him with vacant eyes. Mingo snatched back the dirty blanket. The man's shirt was torn off at the sleeve. The remnant, brown from dried blood, had been put to use as a bandage around his elbow and forearm. His upper arm was red and swollen; his hand and fingers black.

"Ma'am, your husband needs a doctor."

"That's why I'm on the way to Cedar Key. How far is it?"

"I'd say ten miles."

"I can't pull this cart that far. Help us. Please, help us."

"You look after your husband. I'll harness my horse to your wagon."

Since his horse had never pulled a wagon before, he left it saddled so he could ride it in the traces. As soon as he had the horse hitched, he nudged it forward at an easy walk.

After sunset, Federal pickets stopped him near Station Four. After a soldier with a lantern inspected the wagon's contents, he muttered, "You know you're haulin' a dead man?"

Mingo took the corpse to the hospital tent and then delivered the woman and children to the refugee camp. Worn out, he decided to wait until the next morning to leave for Deer Hall again. When he stopped by the cookhouse for a bite to eat, Major Weeks spotted him.

"Mingo, what are you doing here? I thought you left yesterday."

After explaining how he got waylaid, Mingo added, "Reckon I'll leave after breakfast. I'm not going to stop for refugees again."

"You can't help them all anyway. They're swamping us. So many have poured into Cedar Key that we have to ration food. Come over to my quarters; I've got something I want to show you."

Major Weeks escorted Mingo into his room on the second floor of Parsons' store that had been appropriated for officers' quarters.

"I've drawn a layout for our citrus farms on the Homosassa."

The major unrolled a large, hand-drawn sketch. "To make profitable groves, I figure we'll each need a half section. The land near the river is too wet for citrus, so we'll plant more in the sandy blocks on high ground. Our farms will straddle the old Yulee Plantation. One of us can build our house where Levy's mansion was and the other at the overseer's old place. We can use Levy's old fields near the river to raise food crops and sugar cane. We can build a packinghouse at Levy's dock to ship the fruit to Cedar Key by boat. From there it can go to Fernandina by the cars and from there to New York by ship."

Mingo studied the sketch. "It looks perfect. How much you reckon de land will cost?"

"It'll be cheap, but we have a problem."

"What?"

"Senator Levy is still the legal owner. I've filed an application with the Federal Direct Tax Commission to foreclose the traitor's land to get clear title. Commissioner Stickney wrote me that our application should be approved soon."

The two men discussed their plans late into the night until Mingo called a stop. "I need some rest; I want to leave early in de mornin'."

That night Mingo tossed and turned, dreaming about Molly in a beautiful dress at their splendid house on the Homosassa River, until the first notes of reveille shocked him wide-awake. Before the bugler finished, a much louder commotion drowned it out. Men shouted, rifles fired, a battery boomed.

Mingo reached for his pistol. But in some inexplicable way, the tumult didn't convey the exigency of a fight. He stepped from his tent as a man ran by yelling, "Lee's surrendered! Lee's surrendered!"

Military order collapsed as people shouted, screamed, danced, and embraced. Soldiers fired into the air. Artillerymen shot blank charges. Cedar Key had not seen so much gunfire since the Union navy attacked the town in 1862.

Mingo dressed quickly then raced to find Major Weeks. Two upset refugees glared at him as he hurried by them. He noticed one kick the dirt in evident disgust. He found the Major at headquarters talking to several officers, "I don't blame the men for being excited. I am too, but we have to have discipline. Cut the men some slack, excuse all non-critical fatigue duty today, but keep the guards on post and alert. I don't want any unpleasant surprises."

As the officers left for their companies, Mingo asked, "So it's really true? Lee surrendered?"

"That he has. Rumors have been filtering in from refugees for several days, but a packet boat came in this morning with official word. Lee surrendered at Appomattox, Virginia, on April 9th."

"Is the war over?"

"Not yet. That's why I've got to keep the post alert. General Johnston's army is still in the field. Neither the Confederate nor Florida governments have surrendered. With Lee out of the way, Grant can turn south. Johnston will be squeezed between him and Sherman. There's no way his worn-out army can hold off their combined armies. He'll either surrender or be wiped out.

And, Lee's surrender is not the only news. The courier also delivered orders from General Newton approving my plan to attack the Columbus Camp and to proceed on to Tallahassee if possible. I intend to advance until it's countermanded."

"Can't you delay de operation until we know what Johnston does in North Carolina?"

"Who knows what General Jones or the state government will do? Governor Milton decided suicide was preferable to reunion. Apparently, a lot of Crackers would rather die than live under Old Glory. I intend to press forward. Sorry, I can't let you go to Deer Hall now. We'll move out as soon as we have the logistics in order."

As more refugees and Confederate deserters poured into Cedar Key, Major Weeks' logistical and tactical problems multiplied. Every day, more turncoats volunteered to serve in the Union army with the U.S. 2nd Florida Cavalry regiment. Major Weeks figured most did so for the money. Some, undoubtedly, were infiltrators. To complicate matters, rumors spread that General Johnston had taken the offensive.

Major Weeks decided to advance to Columbus with the 2nd Florida Cavalry supported by U.S. Colored Troops. Three days after Lee's surrender, the horse regiment, at full complement along with five infantry companies supported by artillery, supply, and ambulance wagons, proceeded north up the railroad grade toward Bronson. Without question, Major Weeks intended the expedition to be a full-scale advance deep into Florida's heartland. He had two goals: link up with Sherman's troops in Georgia and, if practical, march all the way to Tallahassee.

In spite of the large force, Major Weeks still worried about Dickison. He ordered scouts to search for the enemy at least twenty miles from the main column.

On the second day out, a courier rode up from Cedar Key on a winded pony with the shocking news that President Lincoln had been shot at Ford's Theater on April 14th. Vice President Andrew Johnson had been sworn in as President.

Major Weeks conferred with staff to decide how to break the news to the troops. That evening he ordered the column into formation so that he could announce the assassination to everybody at once. When he spoke, he praised the President's memory. A captain read Lincoln's Gettysburg Address. Some white troops cried. The black troops bawled. After Major Weeks dismissed the formation, the black troops built huge bonfires, gathered around them and sang soulful hymns late into the night.

Several days later, a courier reported that Generals Sherman and Johnston had signed a "Memorandum as the Basis of an Agreement" and enclosed a copy. When Weeks read it, the contents were so unsettling that he read it aloud to Mingo. Sherman had apparently negotiated a surrender allowing state governments to be recognized upon taking an Oath of Allegiance. When that happened, the Southern people were to be restored to all rights, privileges and property. In return, the Confederate armies were to deposit their arms in state arsenals and disband.

When Weeks finished reading, Mingo asked, "What does it mean?"

"It means Sherman has given away everything we've fought for. If the traitorous states are to have all their rights restored, that could be read to mean the Emancipation Proclamation has been nullified. If so, we can forget our plans for Homosassa, and it leaves your status uncertain."

"Can Sherman do that? I'll die before I'll be made a slave again!"

"I don't know if Sherman even thought about the implications. He's a general, not a statesman. Like everybody else, he's sick of killing. I suppose the respective governments will have to approve the damn agreement. I'm not sure."

"What will we do?"

"Proceed with the expedition until we get orders. I've received nothing official about an armistice, no countermanding orders."

Near Columbus another courier arrived with a dispatch from General Newton. The courier said that the cabinet had rejected Sherman's armistice. President Johnson had dispatched General Grant to obtain General Johnston's unconditional surrender.

"What are my orders?" Major Weeks asked.

The courier handed the major an envelope that he ripped open with his forefinger, unfolded a page, and read, "You are to proceed forthwith to destroy the Confederate Fort and trestle where the Florida Atlantic and Gulf Central Railroad crosses the Suwannee River. If possible, proceed on to capture Tallahassee. No surrender except unconditional."

"Hot damn!" Major Weeks gesticulated with the order over his head. "Let's keep moving, men."

After crossing the Suwannee above Fort Fanning, the column proceeded toward Columbus without finding any Rebel troops even though Major Weeks doubled his patrols and scouted even farther afield. Frustrated that he couldn't find the enemy, he ordered Mingo to take a patrol all the way to Columbus.

After recrossing the Suwannee at McIntosh, Mingo came across several black families trudging south near New Boston.

"Where ya'll headed?"

Their leader answered, "Cedar Key, I reckon. We heard de Union army will feed us. White folks run us off from de Oakland place up by Madison. Made us leave wid nothin'. Told us Yankee soldiers was on de way to burn us out."

Mingo wondered how the frazzled, displaced people could survive as he interrogated them about enemy troops.

"We seen some Secesh soldiers preparin' to leave de Fort where de railroad crosses the Suwannee. Folks say dey was headin' for Tallahassee."

"How do you know dey was leavin'?"

"We walked over de trestle yesterday. Saw dem loadin' cannons on de cars."

As his patrol neared Columbus, Mingo couldn't assume the contrabands' information was accurate. He still expected to be challenged by pickets, yet he encountered none. When he reached the trestle, it was unguarded, the Rebel fort abandoned and ransacked.

He galloped back to report to Major Weeks. After a hard ride, he found the column halted with the officers in conference. After he related what he had found at Columbus, Major Weeks gave him welcome news. "Jeff Davis ordered Johnston to surrender his infantry and keep fighting a guerilla war with cavalry. Johnston disobeyed Davis' order. He surrendered on April 26th near Durham, North Carolina, upon the same terms as Lee."

"Is the war over now?" Mingo asked.

"You'd think. Rebels don't have any more armies in the field east of the Mississippi. Florida is the holdout, but we don't know what the Crackers intend to do yet. None of the patrols have made contact. The enemy has abandoned the Suwannee Valley."

A captain said, "Could be they're consolidating their forces at Tallahassee for a last ditch defense. Some may choose to die fighting rather than stick a pistol in their mouth and blow their brains out like Governor Milton."

Major Weeks said, "Here's what we'll do. We'll occupy the Columbus Fort, so that we control the railroad and the river. We'll send the 2nd Cavalry west toward Tallahassee until contact is made and then ask for surrender. If they don't surrender, we'll attack and finish this war once and for all."

As the federal cavalry rode west, they were not challenged by Florida troops until they were within thirty miles of Tallahassee where scouts spotted a few rag-tag Rebel cavalrymen in the distance. They stayed so far away, pursuit wasn't worth the effort.

Major Weeks hoped the Floridians weren't eager to die for a lost cause, yet he worried that they might attack his extended lines. He told Mingo, "I don't like the looks of this. We could run into a hornet's nest like Olustee. If General Jones intended to surrender, he'd have made contact by now. I'll bet he has fortified the hills east of Tallahassee. Find out."

Mingo's patrol crossed the St. Mark's River and then rode past the Lafayette swamp into the open country near Tallahassee. From the top of a high hill close enough to see the capitol dome, he stopped to scan the countryside with his telescope. The sight confirmed Major Weeks' fears.

Breastworks snaking across the hills blocked the St. Augustine Road. Mingo said to a sergeant, "Where did dey possibly get so many cannons?"

"Johnston must have sent them down here before he surrendered, but I can't imagine how they slipped them past Sherman."

"I'm goin' find out," Mingo said as he reached in his jacket pocket and yanked out a white handkerchief.

"What are you doing?"

"I'm going to ride up to their lines under a white flag to find out their intentions."

"Don't do that. Crackers will shoot you, white flag or no white flag. Remember what happened at those salt works by Cedar Key. They'll shoot white soldiers, let alone black ones---"

"I'll take my chances. I don't believe dey'll keep fightin' now dat Lee and Johnston have both surrendered. Anyway, I want a closer look at their lines."

Mingo tied the handkerchief to his rifle barrel that he held high. The sergeant fell in beside him as they walked their horses toward the

Florida lines with Mingo waving the white flag from side to side over his head. Near the breastworks, Mingo saw rifle barrels aimed at him. A sentry ordered, "Halt!" Mingo reined his horse and lifted the tiny pennant as high as possible. "Who are you? What's your business?"

"We're scouts wid de 2nd United States Florida Cavalry under General Newton's command. We have orders to speak with your commander," Mingo yelled.

"Wait there."

Mingo saw a rider whip his horse and gallop west toward Tallahassee. In half an hour, three riders came into view. They rode toward the breastwork, disappeared behind it and then appeared at the top a few minutes later.

A young officer in his twenties with close-cropped, blond hair wearing a gray Kepi cap yelled to Mingo, "What's your purpose?"

"I'm a scout for the United States 2nd Florida Cavalry. I have instructions from my commander, Major Weeks, to ask for de surrender of all hostile forces we encounter. Who are you?"

"Captain Dozier, Company F 2nd Florida Cavalry. What makes you think we'll surrender?"

"Don't know if you will or not, but my instructions are to ask. Major Weeks figured Florida's forces might have orders to surrender. Our understandin' is dat de troops in Florida and Georgia are under General Johnston's command. His army stacked arms on de 26th. You are aware, aren't you, that he surrendered?"

"Yes, General Jones and General Miller are conferring with Governor Allison later today. We intend to defend our homeland."

"My commander understands dat although he'd like to avoid killin' ya'll if he can. You Floridians can't hold out by yourselves no matter how determined you are. Major Weeks has instructed me to advise you dat ya'll get de same terms General Grant gave Lee in Virginia. My commander seeks peace, not retribution. Our expeditionary force is consolidatin' to attack, but our lines are open to you under a white flag."

"I will convey your message to my command."

As Mingo turned their horses to ride away, his sergeant chuckled.

"What are you laughin' at? Crackers still might shoot us in de back," Mingo snapped.

"Not with their cannons."

"What ya mean?"

"They ain't nothin' but painted logs."

CHAPTER FIFTY-SEVEN

TALLAHASSEE
Florida

Major Weeks, in order to observe the Rebel fortifications himself, rode out to the same hill where Mingo first saw the Confederate breastworks. After looking them over, he said, "We'll settle on a battle plan tonight. I'll not make a frontal assault after the experience at Natural Bridge. Although most of those cannons are fakes, enough are real that we'll take heavy casualties. Notify the company commanders that we'll make that farmhouse over there our headquarters. I want ideas to flank the fortifications. I'm sending a dispatch to ask for reinforcements."

That evening, as Major Weeks and his officers planned a cavalry sweep to attack Tallahassee from the north, a sergeant rushed up with news that Rebels had ridden into the lines under a white flag.

"Escort them here," Major Weeks ordered.

Mingo watched from the porch of the farmhouse headquarters as a Union cavalry squad rode up with two Confederate officers. One was the same boyish Confederate captain he'd talked to at the breastworks, the other, a lieutenant. Mingo followed as a Union captain ushered the Confederate officers inside. The Union escort said, "Sir,

I have the honor to present, Captain Dozier, 2nd Florida Confederate Cavalry." The officers exchanged salutes.

Captain Dozier said, "Sir, I have the duty to relay a dispatch from General Jones. May I confer with you in private?"

"Yes, except for our aides. Everybody except Mingo step outside."

Mingo and the Confederate lieutenant stood by as the others stepped out to the porch. As the last man to leave the room shut the door, Mingo stepped beside Major Weeks.

Captain Dozier protested, "Sir, a nigra shouldn't hear our discussions."

"Sir, this man is my aide-de-camp. You shall show him respect or this conference is over."

The officer flushed, but answered in a disciplined, military tone, "Yes, sir."

"What is the message from General Jones?"

"Sir, by leave of General Jones, General McCook, under General Sherman's command, rode into Tallahassee this afternoon along with several Union officers to discuss surrender. Five hundred Union cavalrymen are encamped north of Tallahassee. General Jones suggested an armistice until surrender negotiations are concluded. I have a dispatch to you from General McCook."

Captain Dozier handed Major Weeks a sealed envelope who tore it open and read:

April 30, 1865

All units operating in Florida shall suspend offensive operations until further instruction. Surrender negotiations are underway with General Samuel Jones, Commander Military District of Florida, C.S.A.

Edward McCook

Brig. General United States Army.

Major Weeks realized that General Newton's chance to redeem the defeat at Natural Bridge by capturing Tallahassee had passed. He looked up from the order and said, "Captain Dozier, why should I believe that an order delivered to me by a Confederate officer is legitimate? Why didn't a Federal officer bring it?

"Sir, the officers General McCook brought with him to Tallahassee are all involved with the negotiations, planning the demobilization and a new government. General McCook personally handed me the dispatch. It has been in my possession until I delivered it to you. Do you question my integrity, sir?"

"Of course not, I'm merely shocked by the turn of events. My command expected to accept Tallahassee's surrender."

"May I remind you, sir, General Jones has not surrendered. He is conferring with General McCook while he awaits instructions from Governor Allison. We may yet meet on the field of battle."

"I pray that will not be necessary. Advise General McCook that his order has been received."

Captain Dozier saluted. Major Weeks snapped one in return. The lieutenant executed a crisp about face and left the room.

In order to be prepared in the event surrender negotiations came to an impasse, Major Weeks continued to plan an attack although with scant progress. The officers couldn't agree on an overarching strategy and squabbled over minutiae. No one had his heart in the operation. After midnight, Major Weeks dismissed his officers. "Men, keep the troops on alert. We'll reconvene at seven A.M."

The scheduled conference was unnecessary. As the sky brightened that morning, two Federal cavalrymen rode into camp escorting Captain Dozier and his aide as before. As they passed through camp toward Major Weeks' headquarters, black soldiers dropped their breakfast to run behind them yelling, "Crackers surrender? De war over?"

By the time the squad reached the farmhouse, soldiers squeezed around the headquarters in hopes they could hear good news first hand. Major Weeks stepped out on the farmhouse porch as Captain Dozier dismounted. He climbed up the steps onto the porch, saluted and said, "Sir, it's my duty to report that General Jones has surrendered."

Pandemonium drowned him out before he could proceed. Soldiers yelled in jubilation while tossing their hats into the air. As the news spread through the camp, soldiers banged on pots and discharged their weapons in celebration. Somewhere across camp, a battery fired. Military order collapsed as it had at Cedar Key when news of Lee's surrender came.

As lieutenants and sergeants barked orders to assert control, Major Weeks motioned the Confederate officers and their Yankee escorts inside. As he shut the door, he asked, "What are the terms?"

"Same as Lee and Johnston's. Unconditional surrender. The officers can keep their horses and side arms."

"What are my orders?"

A Yankee major said, "You are to stay in the field. General McCook and General Jones fear civil disorder. Tallahassee itself is unscathed, but the countryside is in shambles. Contrabands, refugees, and deserters are roaming the roads. People are pouring south from the devastation in Georgia and South Carolina. You are to keep the peace and provide citizens with food and shelter."

"We have a problem. There's no civil law across the whole state. We never established a successful occupation and we hardly have enough food for the army. Will General McCook declare martial law?"

"The General understands the difficulties. He is conferring with Governor Allison to re-establish civil law and order. The general wants to avoid declaring martial law if he can. The first order of business is to get a provisional government in place. Rebel troops will obey the surrender order except for a few diehards. Most are exhausted and glad the war's over. A few firebrands have threatened to flee to the swamps to continue fighting as guerillas. General Jones has sent officers to convey the message that if they don't surrender, they'll be given no quarter."

Major Weeks said, "We know how to deal with rabble rousers. My scouts can track them down before they gather a following."

"Your orders are to hold tight by guarding the roads and railroad. You are to arrest any Rebel soldiers found with arms. A formal surrender ceremony is scheduled in Tallahassee for May 20. We expect that all Florida troops will be demobilized beforehand."

By the afternoon, Major Weeks had his expeditionary force reoriented from an offensive military operation to an occupying force. After Union soldiers took charge of the railroad stations and major intersections, they built aid stations to distribute food and medical care. Signalmen established telegraph communication with General McCook in Tallahassee.

As soon as Rebel soldiers stacked arms, most headed home without waiting for a formal ceremony. A few refused to accept defeat. When a courier attempted to deliver surrender orders to at unit at Goose Pasture west of Natural Bridge, he failed. The only soldier he found at the outpost was a corporal with a leg wound so severe that he couldn't ride. The injured trooper told the courier that the renegades had headed for the California swamp north of the Suwannee at the Big Bend.

On the second day after the surrender, Mingo and Major Weeks watched a decrepit engine chug toward Madison. It was the once proud *Governor Broome,* which was now pockmarked with rust where the Aucilla Trestle fire had scorched it. Overall, it looked like moving scrap. Major Weeks commented that the rattletrap needed a clever engineer to keep it running, particularly over the rotten ties and eroded embankments of the Florida Atlantic and Gulf Central Railroad.

Demobilized Confederate soldiers filled the cars. Nothing about their dress or bearing suggested their former military prowess. Most wore shabby civilian clothes. Only a few wore threadbare and tattered uniforms. Their shirts and jackets flapped in the breeze as if hanging on scarecrows. Many were barefoot. Some were wrapped in bandages. Some had missing limbs. Mingo wondered how such downtrodden men had ever fought so well.

In contrast to the demobilized Southern soldiers, jaunty Union troops riding guard in the cab, the wood car, and the caboose wore new uniforms with shiny buttons. Their brogans and leather accoutrements were polished to a high sheen. Their bayonets sparkled.

Later in the day as Major Weeks read dispatches from General McCook in Tallahassee, he yelled, "Mingo, listen up!"

"Patrol ambushed. Stop. Rocky Creek. Stop. Four Union and Florida liaison KIA. Stop. Three wounded. Stop, Attackers led by an unidentified man in Colonel's tunic. Stop. Be on lookout. Stop. Kill or capture. Stop."

"Dime to dollar, it's Wall and this dispatch gives us an excuse to take out the son-a-bitch. What you think he's up to?"

"He'll hole up in de swamps between de Steinhatchee River and de Suwannee. From there he can raid anywhere in de Suwannee basin. If it's Wall, he'll head to Deer Hall before long."

The major said, "Isn't there a beautiful woman who lives there?"

"You bet. Dat's exactly why he'll head over der."

"Well, mosey over and surprise him, why don't you?"

Mingo led a fifty-man, cavalry detachment to the abandoned Chunky Pond lumber mill where he found tracks and sign that guerillas had camped there. They had slipped away via a rough country track below Chunky Pond after posting a sharpshooter high in a tree to snipe at pursuers.

The sharpshooter lost his nerve. He fired from much too far. Although a spent bullet hit a trooper, it didn't have enough momentum to penetrate his skin. As cavalrymen chased the sharpshooter, Mingo diverted with a squad to check on Deer Hall.

From the lane, Mingo noticed the house was shut tight. A gun barrel glinted at a window. He halted the squad to survey the situation when the door burst open. Molly ran out hollering, "Mingo! It's Mingo!"

He dismounted. The couple hugged tightly and then kissed. Mingo brushed tears from her cheeks.

She babbled. "We were so scared. We've heard shooting off in the distance. Why did you bring soldiers here? Didn't the Rebels surrender?"

"Army did surrender, but a few scoundrels didn't. We're after a bunch dat may be led by Wall. We spooked them at his old lumber camp."

Molly snuggled against Mingo. "Thank de Lord you caught up to dem before dey came over here."

Standing on the porch, Blanche said, "Wall is an insult to the Southern cause. He's nothing but a common criminal."

Chad added, "He should to be hung for all the turmoil he's caused. Are we under martial law?"

"I'm not sure, but our orders are to kill or capture any armed Rebels we find. General McCook is conferring with Governor Allison to organize a government. A formal surrender ceremony is scheduled for May 20 in Tallahassee."

Blanche said, "We've all been through so much because of this war. It's past time that it's over, one way or the other. I was in Tallahassee the day Florida seceded. When the Stars and Stripes came down the flagstaff, I never dreamed that I'd see it flying over the capitol again."

Molly interjected, "When it goes back up, dat will be de most beautiful sight imaginable. It means freedom."

Jake shook his head. "We still ain't got nothin'."

"Don't worry, Jake," Blanche said. "You're free to go where you want and work where you want, but you're welcome to stay here. People are working out sharecrop agreements. We can too."

"I reckon so. You and Mas'r Loring always treated us better than most whites treated black folks."

Blanche changed the subject, "Did I hear you right, Mingo? The formal surrender ceremony is May 20? I'd like to see it. Chad, let's go. It seems like forever since I got away from this place."

Chad replied, "We can't afford train tickets."

"I have one Confederate bond hidden away."

"Ma'am, it's worthless. Nobody will take Confederate money," Mingo said.

Tears welled in Blanche's eyes. She sniffled and wiped her face with her hand. "Guess I better get used to living in poverty."

"Missis Blanche, de navy pays me in United States dollars. I've saved everything I could to buy a farm after de war. I'll loan you ten greenback dollars to go to Tallahassee on one condition."

"What's that?"

"Take Molly wid you. De surrender will be de biggest day for our people in Florida history. I'd like Molly to see it."

"God bless you, Mingo. Of course, we'll take Molly."

Mingo pulled a crisp United States ten-dollar bill from his leather wallet and handed it to Blanche. "Pay me back when you can. Right now, I have to chase down fire-eaters."

Molly grabbed Mingo's hand. She led him down the path toward the barn. Once out of sight of the others, they kissed.

"Mingo, I love you. The war is over. Stay with me. Let de army do the dirty work."

"Molly, I can't quit till dey all surrender. We'll run the scoundrels down in no time. Nobody will help dem now dat de war is over. Once I finish wid dis business, we can be together forever."

CHAPTER FIFTY-EIGHT

TALLAHASSEE
Florida

Before dawn, Molly, Chad and Blanche headed out to catch the train at Bronson. Despite the darkness, the sandy, white trail reflected enough light that they could see except in deep shadows. They walked in silence until Blanche mentioned the incessant songs the whip-poor-wills made as they called to one another across the woods. "You ever wonder why those birds sing the same monotonous call hour after hour?"

"When I first hear dem, dey sound pretty, but after a while dey get on my nerves. De song must be some territorial claim or maybe to attract a mate," Molly said.

"Have you ever seen one?"

"One evenin' I saw one fly up from a palmetto patch to catch an insect. I reckon dey is active at night and sleep all day. Some people say dey suck goats' teats."

"What are you talking about, Molly? That's ridiculous."

"I don't believe it, but dat's what people say. Nobody I know ever saw such a thing. I suppose some people believe most everythin' dey is told without botherin' to look for themselves."

When they reached the abandoned lumber camp, they rested at the weather-worn table. Blanche unrolled a gingham cloth wrapped around three, hardtack crackers. "It's not much of a breakfast, but it ought to hold us till Bronson."

"Did you notice dat as de sun came up, de whip-poor-wills stopped callin'?"

"No, I didn't. At dawn the wrens' voices were so bold and melodious, I didn't notice that the whip-poor-wills had stopped."

"Why are you two carrying on about bird songs?" Chad asked.

"Maybe they make us feel like the world will keep spinning after everything we've been through," Blanche replied.

Chad nibbled on his hardtack.

She continued, "Both of you should know, I couldn't have made it without your help."

Chad swallowed the remnants of his cracker. "War's been hard on everybody. Some like Governor Milton couldn't accept the change, but most people will adapt and carry on. I know we will."

Blanche reached across the table to grasp Chad's hand.

He eased his other hand atop hers. After a minute, he said, "I suppose we've dillydallied long enough. We'll never make Bronson if we don't get moving."

Two, black, Union privates stood guard at a charred loading dock, which was all that remained of the depot in Bronson. Chad asked one of them about the train schedule. The soldier pointed toward a white, canvas, army tent with U.S.A. stenciled across the canopy with the sides lashed up to allow the breeze through. Like the army camps, a ramada covered with Spanish moss shaded the entrance.

The shelter served as both a ticket and a telegraph office. Inside, a black man dressed in new denim pants and a white cotton shirt studied a booklet. On a table, a telegraph key clacked. "Excuse me, sir. Is there a train today?" Chad asked.

The black man did not look up.

"Excuse me. Do I buy tickets from you?"

"You can if you have American money."

"Three tickets to Tallahassee, please."

"I can only sell you tickets to Baldwin. It's another line from der to Tallahassee, and crews are still workin' on de torn up tracks between Baldwin and Ocean Pond. I don't know how much is finished."

"When does the train arrive?"

"When it gets here. Train ain't runnin' on no schedule, if it runs atal."

"What do you mean?"

"You may have a long wait. It didn't make a run yesterday 'cause de engine broke down. If it comes, you may not be allowed to board anyway. Army has priority."

"We'll take our chances."

Blanche reached into her bodice to find the folded ten-dollar bill she had tucked away. She handed it to Chad. He passed it to the clerk who examined it closely. Once satisfied that it was genuine, he handed Chad three tickets and change with an assiduous count.

Under the shade of a live oak by the station agent's tent, the travelers sat down at a makeshift table someone had constructed from scavenged lumber. They passed the time by chatting about the destruction around them and speculating how soon the region might recover. They soon exhausted the subject and conversation trailed off. As the day dragged on, the only sounds breaking the silence were the guards' hob nailed boots striking the platform, buzzing cicadas, and the clacking telegraph key. After a while, Molly fell asleep with her head on her arms. Blanche dozed leaning against Chad's shoulder. An hour later, a train whistle far in the distance roused them.

In a short time, the engine wobbled up to the station in reverse. Curious, Chad asked the station agent why it came up backwards.

"De turnaround at Cedar Key was blown up. It ain't fixed yet. De engine can't go no other way."

The locomotive pushed a passenger car and two flatcars. One flatcar contained several head of cattle and a few hogs; the other hauled cedar and pine logs, a hint of renewed economic activity.

After the uncomfortable train ride over the rough tracks which the car's worn out springs compounded, Chad hired a wagon at Baldwin to cross the gap where the rails had been torn up by the retreating Yankee troops after the battle of Olustee. Repair crews had replaced them west of Newburg where the travelers boarded another train to Tallahassee. Repair work at the Aucilla River trestle delayed the trip again.

The three weary travelers arrived in Tallahassee in mid-afternoon the next day. As they walked from the depot toward the capitol, Molly pointed out the Stars and Stripes atop the building. Chad and Blanche studied the flag drooping from the flagstaff to make sure Molly had not confused the American Flag with the Confederate Stars and Bars. "You're right, Molly. It's Old Glory although I didn't expect to see it flying over the capitol until the surrender ceremony," Chad said.

Blanche asked, "Do we still have a government?"

"I assume so although I'm not sure. We're probably under martial law."

Although the buildings in Tallahassee were not wrecked or burned, most needed maintenance and paint. The capitol looked grand on the crest of a high hill, but up close, even the huge live oaks lining Monroe Street couldn't screen its run-down condition.

A block past the capitol, Chad stopped a man to ask about accommodations.

"Mister, there ain't no vacant hotel rooms in this town. They're all being used for hospitals or soldiers' rest."

"Where can we stay?"

"People are renting rooms to earn U.S. dollars. Just this morning, I noticed a 'rooms for rent' sign a few blocks down East Park Avenue. Park is a cross street just a few blocks straight ahead."

When the threesome turned on Park, they spotted a large American flag hanging from a flagstaff centered over the porch of a large house. Shorter poles on each side of Old Glory flew a regimental flag and a headquarters flag. Two black soldiers clad in blue and holding rifles with fixed bayonets stood guard on the piazza.

As they walked by the house, a blond Confederate captain with a dispatch in hand hurried across the porch to his mount tied at the street. As he unhitched his horse, Chad intercepted him. "Pardon me, sir. What is this building?"

"General McCook's Headquarters. Please excuse me. I have orders to deliver."

As they walked past the house, the black guards standing still as statues followed them with their eyes.

Blanche commented, "Now I can see why the North whipped us. Everything those Yankee soldiers have is new and polished. Compared to them, our captain looks like a ragamuffin in his homespun pants, patched jacket and worn-out boots."

Chad said, "Southerners should have known that the industrialized North could wear down their agricultural economy."

"We believed our men could win and they darn near did, but Yankee invaders kept coming with more soldiers and new equipment all the time. Now, we're a conquered people that Negroes will control. Everything's disordered. It'll take a hundred years for Florida to recover."

Molly stiffened. "Miss Blanche, we don't want to rule nobody. We just want to be equal, dat's all. De American flag over de capitol means we ain't got to bow and scrape no more."

Chad, eager to change the subject, pointed. "Look, there's the place with rooms for rent."

At the house with a tiny, hand-lettered sign, Chad knocked on the door. He heard light footsteps and then a dead bolt slide back. A young woman dressed in an ankle-length dress "turned out" from a ball gown cracked open the door. Around her upper arm, she wore a black crepe band. "May I help you?"

"Yes, we need rooms for each of us."

"I can rent you two rooms, but she has to stay over in Black Bottom where she belongs."

All three spoke at once. Chad argued, "Look here, she is with us and you---"

Molly snapped, "I've got just as much---"

Blanche drowned out the others as she clasped Molly's arm, "Ma'am, she is my servant. As a lady, and a war widow like me, I'm sure you understand that I need her assistance. Please make some accommodation."

The lady glanced up and down the street and then at the U.S. dollars in Chad's hand.

"All right, but the servant has to stay out back in the carriage house."

Molly spun to walk away. Blanche held her. "It's OK, Molly. Be patient."

"Your servant is uppity. Lincoln may have freed the nigras, but they still have to stay in their place."

The next day, as Chad and the two women walked to the capitol, Blanche reflected on the jubilant crowd that had gathered around it for the Secession Convention. Now, everything was different. Very few Floridians bothered to attend the ceremony and those who did looked downtrodden and dispirited. The Yankee soldiers standing guard looked smug. Others, off duty, joked and laughed.

At the bottom of the capitol steps, a cluster of defeated warriors stood talking and smoking. Two leaned on crutches, wearing pants with a leg penned up. Another lacked an arm. Yet another soldier had a bandage across his eyes. They all looked exhausted and broken-down. The disabled veterans apparently wanted to petition the state for help although Chad suspected that until a new government was organized their chances were hopeless.

Union cavalrymen sat astride their mounts at regular intervals all around the block. They kept their horses' heads reined high and maintained an alert posture as if some threat might still materialize.

Inside the building the trio had no trouble finding seats in the House of Representatives Chamber. A few Confederate soldiers occupied the galleries on one side; Union soldiers nearly filled the others. In the center section several ladies in black dresses sat in silence. Blanche thought she recognized one to be Governor Milton's widow.

Confederate officers milled around one side of the dais while Federal officers stood at ease across the way. In the middle of the platform rested a highly polished, maple table bordered by two matching side chairs. Two officers, a Union major and the same Confederate Officer to whom Chad had spoken to the day before at General McCook's Headquarters, arranged a leather binder in the center of the table along with ink wells and quill pens. After everything was laid out, the Confederate officer picked up each pen in turn. After examining the nibs, he set the sharpened feathers beside the ink wells.

The three observers had no more than seated themselves when a lieutenant in blue standing beside a side door called out "Attention" in a sonorous voice that reverberated around the chamber. All the soldiers snapped to their feet as everybody else stood up. General Jones stepped into the chamber followed by General McCook. They walked to the table and took places across from one another.

After they exchanged salutes, General Jones said, "Sir, as commanding General of the Army of the Confederate States of America, the Department of Lower Georgia and Florida, I submit the surrender of those forces under my command upon the terms granted General Lee and General Johnston."

"Sir, on behalf of General Sherman, I accept the unconditional surrender of the troops under your command. As soon as your units have stacked arms, they shall stand demobilized. The troops may return to their homes. Officers may retain their personal side arms and their mounts."

The generals exchanged salutes again and then reached across the table to shake hands. The lieutenant called out, "Stand at ease."

The generals sat down at the table as the Union major slid the binder to General Jones. He scanned the document, wet his pen and then scratched his name. The Confederate officer standing beside the table passed the binder to General McCook who signed the paper with a flourish.

The generals stood up. Again the lieutenant called "Attention" as the generals filed from the room followed by their aides with the Union major clutching the leather binder. As soon as General McCook stepped through the door, the lieutenant called out, "As you were."

For a few seconds the officers across the platform from each other looked uncertain how to proceed until a Union captain stepped over to a Confederate officer and extended his hand. After they introduced themselves, the other officers followed their lead.

Chad thought that the ceremony less elaborate than he expected for such a momentous occasion. Blanche felt tears well in her eyes. Molly felt disappointed that nobody mentioned her newly won freedom. She said to Chad, "How come de General didn't say somethin' about freein' de slaves? What rights do we have now?"

Chad said, "I don't know. I'm wondering the same thing."

A well-dressed man in the next row of seats turned and said, "Excuse me for interrupting; I understand the General decided not to bring up the slavery issue at the surrender ceremony. He intends to read the Emancipation Proclamation and clarify the army's position at a ceremony this afternoon at his headquarters."

"Thank you very much for informing us. We'll not miss that," Chad said.

That afternoon, when they arrived for the ceremony; they found an audience comprised mostly of barefooted, black people dressed in threadbare, patched clothing. They filled the front yard and spilled into Park Avenue. A Union cavalry company stood in formation a block down Calhoun Street. Union and Confederate officers stood at-ease on the porch talking. As soon as Molly, Chad, and Blanche settled into a place by the street where they could see and hear, the same Union aide who had called the assembly to order in the morning yelled out, "Attention!" as General Jones stepped from the house onto the porch followed by General McCook.

General Jones moved to the side. General McCook stepped up on a small platform behind a lectern and said, "Stand at ease. Thank you for coming to the ceremony this afternoon that confirms slavery is forever abolished in Florida. As you know, I accepted the formal surrender of all Confederate troops under the command of General Jones this morning. Florida is no longer subject to Confederate law. The United States Army will maintain an occupation in Florida until a new government loyal to the United States of America can be formed. We have commenced work on that project and shall proceed with all deliberate speed to establish civilian government.

"Today is a joyous day. The long and painful war is now over. We as a people are once again united under the Stars and Stripes as fellow citizens." After pausing for applause and a few whoops, General McCook continued. "The surrender terms this morning signed by myself and General Jones are the same as those accepted by General Lee at Appomattox and General Johnston in North Carolina. We do not seek retribution from those who rebelled. As President Lincoln said, we go forward 'with malice towards none; with charity for all.' We seek to bind up the nations' wounds and will do all we can to achieve a just, and a lasting peace.

"I beseech you to discharge your duties as good and peaceful citizens in order to restore tranquility and prosperity to Florida. You have nothing to fear from the Union Army if you obey the law, but on one issue hear me plain. Slavery is abolished in accord with the Emancipation Proclamation. I'm going to read to you the pertinent portions so that there is no misunderstanding that Negroes formerly in servitude are now, and forever, free."

The blacks clapped and shouted approval with hallelujahs and whoops. The few whites around the perimeter of the crowd stood silently with their arms folded. After allowing the audience to calm down, General McCook then read from the Proclamation.

When he finished reading, he said, "My men will enforce the rights of former slaves, but the army does not have the resources to feed, clothe or shelter them. President Lincoln said that all freedmen are urged to labor for an honest wage. All people, both black and white, must now work together for a better and more prosperous Florida. Godspeed."

With that, General McCook stepped from the riser. He shook hands with General Jones and the other Confederate officers. As the officers, North and South, milled about, Chad noticed a dandy, dressed in a new, white-linen suit with a Panama hat pulled low on his forehead, squeeze next to General Jones who introduced him to General McCook. As the man shook hands, he whispered something to the general. The officer smiled and the man laughed. That's when Chad recognized Wall.

Chad attempted to push through the crowd to General McCook, but the people pressing around the porch made that impossible. The new freedmen, destitute and uncertain about their next meal, had expected help from the army. When none was promised, they pushed forward as close as they dared to the soldiers guarding the porch in a 'charge bayonet' position. The freedmen clamored for General McCook's attention shouting out,

"General, you supposed to help us."

"Where can we work?"

"Mas'r chased me off de place."

"Nobody got money to pay a wage."

"We're free to starve."

"President Lincoln wouldn't treat us like dis."

Chad yelled as loud as he could to make himself heard above the hubbub. "General McCook, I must speak to you," but the din from the crowd drowned him out.

Orders yelled out by the cavalry captain added to the commotion, "The ceremony is over. Clear the area! Clear the area!"

When the crowd made no effort to disperse, the captain ordered his troopers to draw sabers. As they had been drilled, the cavalry-men walked their horses toward the throng. It held its ground until a soldier slapped a freedman on the shoulder with the flat of his sword. When he turned and ran, the multitude fled from the horses.

Chad grabbed Molly and Blanche by the hands to lead them to safety. A block down the street, he yanked them onto a porch and exclaimed, "Can you believe that Wall has already ingratiated himself to General McCook?"

Molly looked at Chad in horror. "You saw Wall!"

Blanche interjected, "Are you sure?"

"Yes, who else dresses in expensive clothes and cocks his hat that low over his forehead?"

Molly shrieked, "My God, if it's Wall, where's Mingo?"

Blanche wrapped an arm around her, "Don't you worry about him. He knows how to take care of himself. He's probably on the way to find you right now."

"I believed things would be better when de war ended, but I still have to worry 'bout my man."

Chad said, "I'm sure he's fine. Wall and Mingo have been after each other since Mingo ran away. Mingo's always outsmarted him and always will."

Somewhat reassured by Chad's comment, Molly breathed easier.

Blanche gave her a squeeze, released her, then grasped Chad's hand, nestled against him and asked, "Why wasn't Governor Allison at the ceremony?"

A white man who had jumped on the porch with them said, "He hid for fear that McCook might arrest him. We ain't got a government. You can see what military occupation will be like."

Chad felt confident that he could adapt to the new circumstances and rebuild his life. He resolved to protect the women he loved. He slid his arm around Blanche and pulled her close while glancing worriedly at Molly.

She stood to the side with tears in her eyes as she watched the dispirited and angry freedmen scramble away from the cavalrymen. The bright future she had envisioned now looked gray. Despite the chaos swirling around her, she vowed not to give up hope for Mingo's return and their future together.

Blanche leaned into Chad and trembled with regrets for the past and foreboding for the future. From the high porch she could see the hills undulating toward the east. So unlike the wretchedness close by, the distant landscape looked green, lush, and productive. The urge to be across the Suwannee Divide at Deer Hall engulfed her. There she knew a fresh start and redemption awaited.

Glossary:

Barracoon: A holding pen for slaves.

Coffle: A group of slaves chained together for travel.

Moaks: A slang term for African Americans possibly deriving from Mocha, Yemen a city in Africa and the source of Mocha coffee.

Painter: A line attached to the bow of a boat.

Patters: A term used by slaves for patrols.

Peaked: (Accent on the last syllable) adj. Sick, ill, or worn-out. Often used by Crackers and slaves.

Scuffle hoe: A flat hoe used by pushing and pulling.

AUTHOR'S NOTES:

Historical Fiction:

The main characters in this work are fictional. Their stories reflect how people may have reacted to the dramatic political, military, and societal changes swirling around them during the Civil War era in Florida.

Actual historical figures are portrayed as characterizations, not biographical descriptions. Historical events are dramatizations, not historiography. Nevertheless, my hope is that *Suwannee Divide* conveys a realistic and engrossing portrayal of the Civil War era in Florida.

Dialect:

An issue for writers of historical fiction is how to treat dialect. Many people living in Florida during the Civil War era spoke non-standard English. The transliteration used in *Suwannee Divide* is not intended as a literal translation, but only to reflect the speech of various characters.

Historical Individuals:
Broome, James E.

He was one of the largest plantation owners in Florida and was elected as the third governor and the first Democratic governor of Florida from 1853 to 1857. He advocated for secession.

Call, Richard K.

He served as Aide de Camp to Andrew Jackson during the Creek Wars. He later served as Brigadier General, Florida Militia, during the Seminole Wars. He was Florida's Territorial Governor from 1835-1844. He opposed secession and wrote a pamphlet in which he called disunion, "High treason against our constitutional government."

When Florida withdrew from the Union, he told secessionists, "You have opened the gates of Hell, from which shall flow the curses of the damned which shall sink you to perdition."

Dickison, J.J.

The owner of "Sunnyside" plantation near Ocala, he commanded the 2nd Florida Cavalry C.S.A and was nicknamed the "Swamp Fox." His ingenious hit and run guerilla tactics kept superior Federal forces at bay until the end. Interior Florida where his troops operated was called "Dixie's Land" by the Yankees.

Known for daring exploits, his cavalry captured the Union Gunboat *USS Columbine* on the St. Johns River in May 1864. His troops fought numerous skirmishes and participated in both of the major engagements in Florida, Olustee and Natural Bridge. At Natural Bridge, his men arrived in time to turn the tide.

His son Charles, who served under him as a sergeant, was killed in August 1864 by enemy fire during a skirmish.

Dozier, Captain

He was the Commander, Company F, 5th Florida Cavalry C.S.A. and fought at Natural Bridge.

Ellison, William

He was a wealthy African American freedman in South Carolina who owned numerous slaves, a cotton gin machine shop, and over 900 acres of land.

Finegan, Joseph

Before the war, he was a large land owner and business partner with David Levy building railroads. Commanding Florida troops, he won the largest battle in Florida, Olustee (Ocean Pond). Unlike most fights in Florida, it was not a skirmish but a major battle with approximately 10,000 men engaged. It was one of the bloodiest of the war by percentage of casualties.

Gillmore, Quincy Adams

He graduated first in his class from the United States Military Academy and became an instructor of Practical Military Engineering there. He advocated the use of the rifled, naval cannons and was the first officer to effectively use them by pounding Fort Pulaski, a stone fort near Savannah, until it surrendered.

He was overall commander of the Union Florida Expedition that occupied Jacksonville for the fourth and last time in February 1864. His forces marched inland until defeated at Olustee. He delayed the Union advance which may have cost him victory. Most likely, his army could have overrun General Finegan's outnumbered Florida troops unless reinforcements had arrived from Georgia.

Green

Identified to history only as Mr. Green, he was a guerilla assigned by the Federals to destroy the Ochlocknoy trestle west of Tallahassee in preparation for the Union amphibious invasion at St. Marks to capture Tallahassee in March 1865.

Henry, Guy.
Colonel Henry commanded the 40th Massachusetts Mounted Infantry at the Battle of Olustee. His regiment, with the assistance of Unionist scouts, raided inland fifty miles from Jacksonville and southwest to Gainesville prior to the Battle of Olustee. His troopers overran Confederate units, liberated slaves and destroyed or seized property valued at more than one million dollars. His mounted infantry located the main Rebel army blocking the route to Tallahassee. Dickison met his match in Henry for aggressive hit-and-run tactics.

Jones, Samuel
After graduating from The United States Military Academy, he became an assistant professor of mathematics and tactics there. Prior to the war, he served on the Judge Advocate's staff in Washington D.C. A Virginian, he sided with the South. As Commanding General of the District of Florida, he signed William Strickland's death sentence for desertion. He surrendered Tallahassee on May 10, 1865.

Levy (Yulee), David
Floridians elected him to the United States Senate in 1845 when Florida was admitted to the Union. He was the first Jewish member of that body. He founded the Florida Railroad Company and was known as "Father of Florida Railroads." He owned plantations in Florida and was one of the state's largest slave owners.

He advocated for secession. After Florida withdrew from the Union, he served in the Confederate Congress.

The past is not dead. He was recognized in 2000 as that year's "Great Floridian," by The Florida Department of State and the Florida League of Cities. Levy County is named for him.

McCook, Edward M.

General McCook accepted the surrender of Tallahassee on May 10, 1865, followed by a formal ceremony on May 20, 1865. In a separate ceremony, he read the Emancipation Proclamation freeing the slaves.

Although not a professional soldier, General McCook joined the army as a cavalry lieutenant in 1862. By the end of the war, he was a capable and experienced cavalry commander and achieved the rank of major general. He fought against the best. He defeated General Nathan Bedford Forrest at Selma, Alabama, and was beaten in turn during the Atlanta campaign by General Joseph Wheeler at Brown's Mill, Georgia.

In May 1865, his division was assigned to secure Florida. He rode into Tallahassee with only a few officers by his side although he had posted five hundred cavalrymen nearby.

Miller, William

Although born in New York, he fought for the South. As Field Commander, he defeated General Newton at the Battle of Natural Bridge in March 1865. One of the last Southern victories, it saved Tallahassee which capitulated long after General Lee's army surrendered on April 9, 1865. It was the last capital east of the Mississippi to fall.

Milton, John

He owned the plantation "Sylvania" near Marianna. He was Florida's Civil War Governor from 1861 to April 1865 and a "fire-eating" secessionist. In his final speech to the Florida Legislature he said, "Yankees have developed a character so odious that death would be preferable to reunion." He committed suicide on April 1, 1865, before Tallahassee surrendered.

Newton, John

Unlike most of the Southern West Point graduates, he chose to retain his commission in the U.S. Army when his native state, Virginia, seceded. He fought in titanic battles such as Antietam, Chancellorsville, Gettysburg, and Fredericksburg. He served under General Sherman as the commander of IV Corps in the Atlanta campaign. After the fall of Atlanta, he commanded the District of Key West and Tortugas of the Department of the Gulf from 1864 to 1866.

After the Battle of Fredericksburg in December 1862 in which the Union suffered twice the number of Rebel casualties, Newton complained to President Lincoln that Major General Burnside, the commander of the Army of the Potomac, did not have the confidence of his generals. As a likely consequence, Newton had his appointment to Major General withdrawn.

The failed assault against St. Marks and Natural Bridge that he initiated can be fairly described as a Civil War blunder although he characterized it as a victory. In his defense, the port was closed and the Rebel gunboat *Spray* was bottled up in the St. Mark's river.

Perry, Madison Starke

He came to Florida from South Carolina in 1845 and owned a plantation in Alachua County. Representing the planter class, he served in both the Florida House of Representatives and the Senate and then was elected Governor of Florida (1857-1861). A firebrand secessionist, he reestablished the Florida militia in anticipation of Florida's withdrawal from the Union.

He wrote a letter to the South Carolina Secession Convention practically guaranteeing Florida would secede if South Carolina did so. He said, "Permit me to assure you, gentlemen, that gallant little Florida will be the next to follow your wise and patriotic lead. Upon the meeting of the Convention, Florida will, as certainly as anything, in the future can be certain, wheel immediately into line with the gallant old Palmetto. We are identified with your interest, in feeling, in determination not to submit to Black Republican rule, and a common destiny must be ours."

During the war he served as Colonel in the 7th Florida Infantry C.S.A. until his resignation due to illness in 1863.

The town of Perry, Florida is named for him.

Reddick, Lt. Samuel

After Federal troops occupied Gainesville on February 15, 1864, he led volunteers who charged Yankee barricades manned by troops with Spencer repeating rifles. His superiors failed to support him by moving their soldiers into position for a coordinated attack as planned.

Seymour, Truman

A United States Military Academy graduate, he was in the same class as George McClellan, Thomas "Stonewall" Jackson, and George Pickett. He fought in the Mexican-American War and in the Seminole Wars in Florida.

He commanded United States 54th Massachusetts at the attack on Fort Wagner on July 14, 1863, where he was seriously wounded by grapeshot which took him out of action for several months.

Placed in charge of the District of Florida by General Gillmore, he was the tactical commander of the Florida Expedition at the Battle of Olustee in February 1864. Later, he was assigned to Virginia and was present at Lee's Surrender at Appomattox on April 9, 1865.

Strickland, William

While serving in the 2nd Florida Cavalry C.S.A in December 1862, his captain refused permission for him to visit his gravely ill wife who lived about twenty miles from his post. He went anyway and then deserted to avoid the punishment ordered by his captain. He formed a guerilla band to fight the Rebels with much success. He and his men worked with Union Major Edmund Weeks to raid and destroy Confederate property, including salt works, along the Florida West Coast.

He served with the U.S. 2nd Florida Cavalry and was assigned to destroy the Aucilla trestle during the St. Marks Expedition to capture Tallahassee in early March 1865. Rebels ran him down with bloodhounds and took him prisoner. Confederates shot him by firing squad for desertion on March 18, 1865.

Weeks, Edmund C.

As acting Master with the United States East Gulf Blockading Squadron, he led many operations against Rebel facilities along the coast and the interior. He transferred to the U.S. Army as a major to command the United States 2nd Florida Cavalry in order to coordinate operations with the navy and guerilla bands fighting the Rebels. He commanded 2nd United States Colored Troops at the battle of Station Four near Cedar Key in February 1865 and led the U.S. 2nd Florida Cavalry at the assault on St. Marks and Natural Bridge in March 1865.

Ordered to Tallahassee for occupation duty after Florida's surrender, he stayed in Florida to become the third Lt. Governor during reconstruction and later served in the Florida House of Representatives.

Background Reading:

The story set forth in *Suwannee Divide* revolves around actual Civil War events.

Although there are innumerable Civil War sources, listed here are several that contributed facts for the story.

1. Buker, George E. Blockaders, *Refugees, & Contrabands: Civil War on Florida's Gulf Coast, 1861-1865* University of Alabama Press, 1993.
2. J.J. Dickison, *Confederate Military History Florida,* eBooksOn Disk.com, 2003.
3. Taylor, Paul, *Discovering the Civil War in Florida, A Reader and Guide,* Pineapple Press, Sarasota, Florida, 2001.

4. Blakey, Arch Fredric, Ann Smith Lainhart, and Winston Bryant Jr. Stephens, *Rose Cottage Chronicles*, University of Florida Press, 1998.

5. Rivers, Larry Eugene, *Slavery in Florida, Territorial Days to Emancipation*, Board of Regents of the State of Florida, 2000.

6. *Florida Memory*, http://www.floridamemory.com/ Institute of Museum and Library Services, Florida Department of State.

7. Cornish, Dudley Taylor, *The Sable Arm, Black Troops in the Union Army, 1861-1865*, University Press of Kansas, 1987.

8. Johnson, Clint, *Civil War Blunders*, John F. Blair Publisher, 1997.

9. Higginson, Thomas Wentworth, *Army Life in a Black Regiment*, W.W. Norton and Company, 1984.

10. Coulter, E. Merton, *Travels in the Confederate States*, Louisiana State University Press, 1948.

ACKNOWLEDGEMENTS

Numerous people inspired and helped me bring *Suwannee Divide* to fruition. My wife, Judy, and daughter, Erika, needed Job's patience to deal with my obsession, especially when the project floundered. My dad, Charlie, passed along oral history. My father-in-law, Charles Meyers, drew maps.

Special thanks to Susan Jewett for her patient editing and to Chris Driggs for designing an excellent cover. Several friends and my sister, Sharon Allworth, read the manuscript with a critical eye. Many others encouraged me, provided information and offered suggestions to make the book better.

The Florida State Archives provided historical images with efficiency, courtesy and good humor.

My heartfelt thanks to all.

Final Words

I hope you enjoyed reading *Suwannee Divide*. Feedback is welcome. You can contact me at GeneFLCW@aol.com and visit the website at: http://flcivilwarSuwanneeDivide.com/

Best regards,

Gene Jones
Sarasota, Florida
September 2012.

Made in the USA
Charleston, SC
05 January 2015